How to Kill a Man

Kristin DeVille

How to Kill a Man

Copyright © 2019 by Walking on Hot Waffles Publishers
in conjunction with Kenny Casanova & WOHW.com

© All rights reserved. No part of this book may be reproduced or transmitted in any form or by any means whatsoever without express written permission from the author, except in the case of brief quotations embodied in critical articles and reviews. Please refer all pertinent questions to the author.

ISBN: 9781794537705

Printed in the USA

CREDITS:

Written by Kristin DeVille
Edited & Formatted by Kenny Casanova
Published by Amazon and WOHW Publishing
Blurb by Kristin DeVille and Kenny Casanova
Image free for commercial use @ pixabay.com
Cover art by Kristin DeVille

WARNING:

This book is intended for a mature audience at least 18 years of age or older. Contains large amounts of graphic sexual content. It also includes forced sexual acts, incest, suicide, substance abuse and profanity. If you find any of the above easily offensive, then don't read.

This is a work of fiction. Names, characters, businesses, places, events and incidents are either the products of the author's imagination or used in a fictitious manner. Any resemblance to actual persons, living or dead, or actual events is purely coincidental.

SCORE

This book would be nothing without music.

Read with the music on? This is a suggested playlist; the very one that inspired me and kept me company while I wrote *How to Kill a Man*.

"Afraid" The Neighbourhood
"Winter Bird" Aurora
"Stronger" Kanye West
"Timberwolves at New Jersey" Taking Back Sunday
"Kingdom of Rust" By Doves
"Car Radio" Twenty One Pilots
"Let the Drummer Kick" Citizen Cope
"How to Fight the Loneliness" Wilco
"I'm Afraid of Everyone" The National
"Hey" The Pixies
"My eyes are Still Bright" Scars on 45
"Waiting for an Invitation" Benji Hughes
"You Kill Me" Paper Route
"Down on Love" Cannons
"Who We Want To Be" Tom Day
"Glad to See You" America
"Monster" Colours
"Terrible Love" Birdy
"Deep End" Ruelle

TABLE OF CONTENTS

CHAPTER ONE	3
CHAPTER TWO	11
CHAPTER THREE	21
CHAPTER FOUR	43
CHAPTER FIVE	57
CHAPTER SIX	74
CHAPTER SEVEN	94
CHAPTER EIGHT	108
CHAPTER NINE	116
CHAPTER TEN	125
CHAPTER ELEVEN	139
CHAPTER TWELVE	147
CHAPTER THIRTEEN	160
CHAPTER FOURTEEN	168
CHAPTER FIFTEEN	176
CHAPTER SIXTEEN	185
CHAPTER SEVENTEEN	196
CHAPTER EIGHTEEN	210
CHAPTER NINETEEN	242
CHAPTER TWENTY	256
CHAPTER TWENTY-ONE	267
CHAPTER TWENTY-TWO	282
CHAPTER TWENTY-THREE	287
CHAPTER TWENTY-FOUR	297
CHAPTER TWENTY-FIVE	306
CHAPTER TWENTY-SIX	319

*I still can't believe you're gone.
I'll say it now and another ten years from now,
Getting dressed up for your funeral was
One of the hardest things I've ever had to do.
I'll never forget the first day I saw you,
I'll never forget the last day I saw you.
Here's to one of the best men
That has ever walked into my life.
This book is my accomplishment,
And it's dedicated to you,* **Andrew Sherman.**

CHAPTER ONE

...SEVEN YEARS AGO

The electricity is sizzling in the air tonight. Everyone is jumping in an uproar of celebration and I am one of the many participants.

I stumble over my feet as I reach for the bottle of vodka. After hijacking the booze from Jesse, I look at him in my drunken stupor as I take a swig of the foul liquid. I feel the unpleasant liquid travel down my throat, reviving my insides. I let out an unrecognizable gargling sound and stick my tongue out. Jesse laughs at my sour face, which earns him a playful shove on the arm.

My body begins to feel warm and I can't seem to wipe this smile off my face.

We graduated today.

Jesse puts his weight on my stumbling frame to keep me in place, but I think it's only an excuse to touch me more. I lift my wobbly head to his gaze and I think I might be drooling. He wipes the corner of my mouth and mutters, "That's cute. Niagara Falls."

I let out a drunken giggle and slur, "What would I do without you?"

He smiles knowingly and casually lowers his lips to my ear. "You'll never have to worry about that."

I lean into his embrace and enjoy this while I can. In a couple months, I'll be moving to the big city. Come September, I'll be a freshman at NYU, majoring in Art.

My days left with Jesse were numbered. Being with him secretly was becoming very difficult, especially with us both living under the same roof.

I feel myself shift back and forth, wondering what Jesse is doing behind me. I then realize it's me who's shifting and that I'm having trouble keeping my balance.

"Genevieve, we need to get you home. You're bombed."

"I'm fine!" I shout louder than I should.

I let out an unceremonious scream, attracting the other partying seniors as they hold up their cups and scream back.

I break away from Jesse to explore the crowd a little more. I feel like mingling tonight. The air is thick and hot due to everyone compacted in this small house, shoulder to shoulder. I glance at the football team, realizing that I never paid attention to them in High School. Or maybe they didn't pay attention to me. I walk up to them in the hopes of striking up a conversation, when all of a sudden I fall into someone's arms.

It's Jesse, of course, who's inevitably behind me making sure I'm okay.

"You're everywhere!" I shout and take a swig of the bottle then hand it to Jesse. He gives me a disapproving look with his big brown eyes.

Those eyes.

Did I mention that Jesse is my step-brother?

Yep, that definitely puts a damper on things.

Step siblings. That means we're kind of related, but not biologically. Which is good, right? Because that would be incest and incest is fucking gross.

Some would argue that what Jesse and I are doing is disgusting, too. But they don't know us like we know each other. They haven't been through what we've been through together. This is something I constantly need to remind myself.

The truth is that I lost my virginity to Jesse. It all started a few months after his mother Pam died. Jesse's mom and my dad met at a baseball game about ten years ago. Both Jesse and I tagged along to this game but never spoke a word to each other.

I remember being so scared until he took off his jacket that revealed his Harry Potter tee shirt. Sprawled across his scrawny chest, it read '5 points for Gryffindor'. I knew I was going to like him a lot after that. Long story short, we all had dinner after the game and they immediately fell in love. Pam and Jesse moved in one month later with us. This gave me the family that I never had and always hoped for.

CHAPTER ONE

These days, my father Dale is all that we have. Thanks to cancer, Jesse's mom died a few years ago. She had a brain tumor, which took her life slowly and miserably for two long years. I really did love her like my own mother. At the time, Jesse and I were completely platonic.

It's hard to imagine where it all went wrong.

After Pam died, Jesse lost himself in various high school activities. He was going through a lot of natural changes. He also worked out a lot, and a lot of girls started to notice him. I was one of those girls. It wasn't long before we turned to each other for comfort. That comfort turned into affection, and eventually, that affection turned into something entirely too deep for us to handle.

When things turned too intense, I had to distance myself from him which gave the illusion that I didn't care for him anymore. That I didn't want him or crave him anymore. I found this is easier than dealing with all of the guilt. I know my step brother wants me more than he needs air. In fact, I'm pretty sure I feel the same way; however, my dad would not be too keen on that idea. There would always be a bridge between us. Something to always keep us apart. We were doomed from the start. I saw it coming, but you don't see with your heart.

I've always been the type of girl that wants to shout my love for someone on a roof top. I want to have the perfect husband and create the world's most perfect family. I wanted to own a little house with maybe a dog and send Christmas cards with our happy faces on it once a year. With Jesse, I was unable to do that.

I figured it was easier to be stone cold to him, but it wasn't. Not only was I hurting from the withdrawal of Jesse in my life, but we were fighting constantly now.

Keeping it a secret from my father has been a miracle. Extremely difficult. One in a million. A diamond in the rough... but somehow it worked.

Dale has a lot of demons of his own to deal with, let alone ours.

I jump as if I've been shocked, disregarding the past memories that I know I shouldn't be thinking of. I lean closely against Jesse and nuzzle against his chest. If I'm not in his arms, then all I do is think about him or gawk at him like a moron. So what's the point of being away from him? I jerk my head back to take a good look at his beautiful olive complexion. Flawless is the only word to describe it.

I can tell that he can't get enough of me. I can't get enough of him, either.

Even though he is my sabotage, he is also my salvation. I grab a handful of his shirt and I whisper, "I have something to tell you."

"I love you," he says, turning his inquisitive eyes to mine. He's so close that they're all I can see. Big brown eyes with long lashes fluttering at me like an eager summer butterfly.

I smile, satisfied, and murmur to him. Not quite sure what I say, but I'm only capable of one worded responses such as 'yes and now'. Maybe bigger words such as 'faster or harder' would suffice. We'll see.

As if Lacey and Julia haven't been annoying enough, now they're hanging off me like a couple of monkeys. A song startles me as I jump to attention and stand up straight like a soldier. Blasting through the speaker system at full volume is "Stronger" by Kanye West. I tilt my head back and let the song vibrate through my body.

"Home," I whisper into the shell of Jesse's ear. "I need you now."

He waves Lacey and Julia over eagerly and I have to laugh at that. They comply by skipping over like valley girls at a Starbucks convention.

We walk down the brightly lit street, littered with red plastic cups and used condoms, to where I parked my car. I look down the street one more time and take in the scenery that could easily be mistaken for the apocalypse. It's four years of homework, keg parties, best friends backstabbing you, and being in love with your step brother. A lot of people complain that it's four years of your life you will never get back. People say that school is like being in prison, but those are people that have never stepped foot into a prison. Funny how that works out.

CHAPTER ONE

They say that during high school, we're still not considered adults. At the age of eighteen, our frontal lobe is still not fully formed, which causes us to not think as rational as adults with a fully established frontal lobe. We're in high school. We make poor choices. We learn from our mistakes. We're kept a close eye on. This party tonight, and everything about it is the reason why school feels like a prison. This is freedom at its finest.

It seems like everyone is throwing a party tonight. After all, it's a Saturday night. Music is blaring from all directions and people are screaming out of their windows and minds as cars pass by.

Jesse volunteers to drive, but I refuse to let anyone drive my new ride. I saved up for years to drive my little Toyota. It's not the best looking ride, but it's mine.

"No one touches this car but me!" I scowl at Jesse. He puts his hands up in defeat, not giving me much of an argument. The two girls could care less. They are talking about a hot boy they just saw inside.

"And he gave me his home number and his cell number!" Julia brags to Lacey.

I catch a glimpse of Jesse rolling his eyes at Julia's comment as he slides into the passenger seat.

"Are you sure you're okay to drive?" Jesse asks.

I look at him as if he's ridiculous. He shrugs and huffs and throws his hands up in the air, adding, "I'm just sayin'. You were pretty drunk earlier."

I get in the car, straighten my body frame, and tell everyone to put on their seatbelts. Then I turn to Jesse; give him my best sober face and say, "I'm fine. Everyone's house is within a five mile radius."

We'll be fine.

Preparing for take-off, I adjust my mirror and seat, then I turn my stereo up as loud as it will go. Taking Back Sunday blares through the speaker system, the bass chugging in rhythm to the song. The girls stick their heads out the windows as Jesse sits back in the passenger seat with heavy eyelids.

I've never seen him look more beautiful than he does when he's resting his eyes. Call me creepy, but I've always loved watching Jesse sleep. His eyes are closed, showcasing his long, dark eye lashes. His full lips are parted as he breathes evenly and maybe even snores a little. My eyes leave the road for a moment, admiring his dark features. He has an olive skin tone with jet black hair and even darker eyes. His no good father's Brazilian roots surely paid off for him. At least he received something good out of that man.

We scream and sing in unison as I drive us down a narrow, curvy and bleak road. This, unfortunately, wakes Jesse up and he doesn't look happy about it. Then his eyes shift over to me and they melt like butter.

"Hell yeah," shouts Julia, as she takes another swig of the bottle she stole from the party.

"We're free!" Lacey adds.

I take my eyes off the road again to look at Jesse one more time. This time he is looking at me right back, hazel eyes blazing into mine. He smiles softly as he reaches over to stroke my hot pink, short hair. I heat up all over as soon as he touches my face. His hand slides down my cheek to my chin, then over to my lips, caressing them and quickly brushing a finger over my snake bites.

I cannot wait until we get home.

The road is dimly lit and difficult to see ahead. Between the girls yelling, Jesse using his magic touch, and the lights dancing in the road, I am having a hard time seeing and thinking clearly. I turn around to tell the girls to shut up, but when I turn back to the road all I see are blinding lights, which are attached to the car coming head on with me.

I swerve out of the road I don't belong in and suddenly slam into something violently. I can tell it's not a car we hit because the impact isn't as bad as it could be and we are all still restrained in our seats. We are all jolted out of our seats, but saved by the seatbelts we have on. I stare in horror ahead, knowing that I hit something…or someone.

Then unexpectedly, the airbags pop out violently, smacking me in the face and back into reality.

I feel a stinging sensation coming from my leg and realize that I'm bleeding like a pig from my knee. A huge gash is engraved across my knee cap, blood spilling onto my pants and the car floor. I go to lift it up and then scream in agony. I'm almost positive that my knee cap is in smithereens.

I look over to Jesse, who has a bloody lip. I hurt him too.

I'm afraid to look behind me. The girls have never been so silent.

"Did you get hurt anywhere else? Are you okay?" I ask Jesse, my voice shaky.

"I'm fine, but you're not," he says, breathing heavily as he takes a look at my knee. He is wearing the same facial expression that I am. Bewilderment, terror, and complete and utter shock.

I can hear the girls crying in the backseat, which in my book is a good sign. I shift my eyes to the road and discover something I wish I hadn't. I hit someone. A bloody hand peaks out from under the hood of my car, motionless. It is a small and slender hand, covered in crimson that drips off like syrup. I'm assuming a female, but I can't be sure. My breath halters as I shift in my seat uncomfortably. Jesse notices my terror and looks out the window with me. I know it when everyone sees what I'm seeing. Jesse hits the dashboard so hard it that it cracks, and the girls scream at the top of their lungs.

"What the fuck?" Lacey shouts. "Is everyone okay?" She starts sobbing as Julia goes to get out of the car.

"NO!" Jesse yells. "Stay right here," he orders.

I start sobbing uncontrollably when he looks at me and sighs. His face softens up and his eyes become full of worry. "Is your knee okay?"

"I think it's broken, but go check what I hit please," I beg. I cry. I do everything but look at that damn bloody hand again.

He takes a deep breath and nods. He sits there for a moment. He's still as a summer night lake, not a limb of his moving. I can tell that he is internally talking himself up to the challenge. I feel bad that he's the one that is doing it. It should be me. I should look at the mess I made.

"What are we going to do?" I cry. I cry until my tear ducts are dried out.

"Calm down, Gin," he whispers. Then he faces the girls. "Everyone stay in the car. I'm going to go check if she's okay," he tells them. He is out of the car faster than a bolt of lightning. I hold onto the steering wheel, gripping it so much that it hurts. My eyes are stinging from all of the tears that keep making their selfish way out. My stomach and chest feel like an ocean of acid, and there is absolutely nothing I can do about it.

I am screwed.

I see Jesse on one knee, assessing the damage and making sure not to touch her hand. His face looks horrified, his chest expanding with too much air.

Then his eyes lock with mine and that's when I see it. He then lifts what I assume is the woman's arm, carefully. He shakes her arm as her golden charm bracelet dangles around. She doesn't respond or move.

I knew my life is completely over when he lifts his gaze to me and shakes his head from side to side. He then gestures to his stomach, and mouths the word "baby".

I grab my phone and immediately dial the numbers 9-1-1, knowing that my life is very well over.

CHAPTER TWO

The judge sent me to prison for involuntary vehicular man slaughter. I received a seven year sentence without bail in state prison. Believe it or not, my lawyer claims that was "taking it easy on me" since everything that I did was unintentional to the woman and her baby in the womb. In the end, it was the whole being obliterated thing that got me in trouble.

I saw the woman's obituary when it was published. I wanted to know what she looked like, what color her hair or eyes were. What she did for a living. Her name was Angelina Daniels. I cut her life short at the tender age of twenty-seven.

Looking at her obituary made me feel worse than I hoped. She was incredibly good looking. With the most piercing blue eyes and black polished hair, it was no wonder she had *the perfect life*. She was one of those women that women like me envied. I couldn't help it.

She was fluent in five different languages and had studied abroad most of her college years. When she graduated, she became an educator at a very prestigious High School where she taught French and Spanish. She also planned on teaching abroad with her husband after their child was born.

The baby.

She was delivered into this cruel world prematurely at thirty weeks, where her mom would inevitably not make it. I could have driven myself crazy knowing that I took a woman's life and nearly killed her baby too. I could have ended the constant agony and negative thoughts that I was subject to after the accident. I could have ended it all and made it easier on myself.

The heart ache, the pain, the aftermath.

However, I didn't have many resources. Again, I was in a prison cell with not much to call my own. I was kept a close eye on, my freedom stripped from me the second I walked through their threshold. I was a healthy eighteen year old woman, so not many people were cutting me any slack. I didn't believe in God, so praying didn't do anything for me.

Anywhere I turned, comfort was not present. Solace was not an option. I was stuck. I was trapped with the pain and the torture of knowing I made a huge mistake that I could never make right again. All I could hope for is that she made a full recovery, and I really did hope for that.

Not only did the baby's fate depend on it, but mine did too. If the baby died, I would be sentenced more years in prison.

A few months after the accident, I received breathtaking news from a social worker that she made it. It was the first feeling of optimism that I had since I was locked up.

Court was no picnic. The judge didn't seem too fond of me, and at times I considered if she treated all of her defendants this way. Words that I kept hearing repeatedly were 'Reckless', 'Careless', and 'Negligence'.

All I kept thinking was that this little girl would grow into a woman without knowing her mother or having a conventional family. I am to blame for that. At times, the guilt felt so overwhelming that I couldn't breathe. So overbearing that I thought the life I had now wasn't a life worth living. I contemplated suicide many times, but one thing kept me out of harm's way.

One person.

Jesse and my friends were not present in the court room but were punished accordingly. They were all mandated community service for being involved, but didn't get the ultimate punishment like me; the person who drove the car.

My lawyer made me plead guilty for vehicular manslaughter even though I'd be sent to prison for a lengthy time at the tender age of 18. He believed that it would minimize my sentence if I owned up to everything that I did. I complied; hoping prison wasn't as bad as I'd seen on TV.

It was.

I was grouped with a lot of women my age and a little bit older. When I turned twenty, they moved me to a larger prison out west with more adults.

I loathed it with every fiber of my being.

CHAPTER TWO

In fact, I stayed away from human interaction as much as I could. My loneliness consumed me at best. It was in prison where I learned that I was an amazing artist. I had a hidden talent. I also read countless books in prison and learned that I loved to read.

The new prison had a lot of older women. More experienced woman. Hell, I'll just say it: crazier women. I wasn't ready for a place like that at all. Aside from the occasional teenage obliteration session, I was typically an innocent kid. Furthermore, a place like that was quite intimidating for me. I tried to weed out the 'good eggs' and 'bad eggs', but that was nearly impossible to do in a place with a bunch of felons running wild.

I did my time. It was slow and painful, just like my step mother's death. Like a band aid ripped off a hairy limb, hair by hair. But I did my time; every single second of it.

So this is it; the day that I'll be released from prison. I'm picked up by my assigned parole officer. I'd been grateful enough to know Officer Mitchell over the last few weeks that I was in prison. He's a middle aged man; about fifty years old or so. He has a head full of grey hair and wears thick rimmed black square glasses. He's quite handsome for an old guy. He kind of reminds me of Dr. Drew.

He pushes his glasses up his nose as he focuses on a paper he shuffles through. He sits there patiently, with perfect posture, encased in perfectly ironed clothes, waiting for me in the dingy waiting room. A manila folder sits on his lap, which I'm guessing are my things. The guards escort me out of the door, make me sign some papers and then release me back into the wild.

I am free for the first time in seven years. As soon as we are outside, the summer humidity smacks me right in the face, causing me to bead with sweat. I inhale the moist air slowly and smile into the sun. Then I look at Officer Mitchell like a lost puppy. "What now?

"Now we go," he looks down at his papers and reads, "to 441 Eastman Road," he looks up at me and notices my anxious expression. His face falls when he notices my trepidation. "Is that not right?"

"That's my father's house."

"Is that not where you want to go?" he asks, bemused.

I don't want to answer, but I do. "No, it is." That's the only place I have to go.

"On the way, I have some things to discuss with you," he says, making no attempt to look at me, but makes sure that I hear him, "Welcome to the real world, Genevieve."

"Ginny," I correct him.

"Ginny?" He scrunches his face up. "Why not Genny?"

I shrug because honestly, Jesse gave me the nickname and I never quite understood it myself.

I feel Officer Mitchell's hand guide me into the car after I almost lose my balance. I've learned to coordinate with my right leg after all these years of having a defective leg, but sometimes I get clumsy. Then he hops in the back with me when I notice that he has a driver. He whips out papers in a manila folder and hands me a few on where to find jobs, psychologists, and a small check from the prison. He sighs and closes his eyes, taking in the nice, cool air. "It's supposed to be one of the hottest summers."

"Figures," I sarcastically respond. "What are these?"

"The community service is mandated. You must do this or else it'll be reported to me and I will, well, just don't blow it off. There are some serious consequences," he warns. "Finding a job is optional depending on your financial situation. Seeing you have a pretty drastic limp, I'd suggest you find something sitting down," he rests his index finger on his chin and thinks for a moment.

"I know you saw one during your stay in prison, but I suggest that you see a shrink post incarceration. You've been in state prison with criminals and convicted felons for nearly a decade. You were locked up at a young age and experienced a tragic accident. I feel it'd be good for you to talk to someone."

I nod at his recommendations. "What type of work can a felon get sitting down?"

CHAPTER TWO

"Not much of anything. Maybe retail work," he responds and shakes his head. "I know, not exactly what you had in mind. I can help you with the job hunt at our next meeting in a couple days."

"Great, because I'll definitely need an income," I say.

"We'll find ya something, darlin'."

The drive feels longer than I remember. My body has a mini seizure at the thought of seeing my father again. Dad and I didn't have the traditional father daughter relationship. It was impersonal and quiet and tainted from the start. He was a bad alcoholic, yet he constantly tried to play a role in my adult life. In fact, he is the only person that ever visited me in prison; every time ending up horrific. He knew why I was in prison, yet that wouldn't stop him of reeking of beer and cigarettes when he came to visit.

He was okay to me as a kid but wasn't so wonderful to my mother. He would always push her around and smack the back of her head when he didn't like something she said or how she did something.

Eventually, my mother left him and his drunken bullshit behind.

She left me behind too.

With all my father's abusive tendencies, it was hard to completely shut him out of my life. He was all that I knew. It was just him and me weathering the storm together. I knew what he went through because I went through it with him. I had a turbulent childhood watching my mom and dad in the midst of World War 3, but then he moved on to his second wife, Jessie's mother Pam.

There was a short period of time when he eased up on the drinking while he was with Pam. We started doing stuff as a family and the bills were getting paid on time. Everything was smooth sailing until Pam got diagnosed with brain cancer. His drinking took a turn for the worse when Pam died. I'm imagining my incarceration didn't help his problem either.

My mind runs at full speed as I ponder all of these memories. Thankfully, the car comes to a halting stop. I whip my head up anxiously and notice that we're here.

I'm home.

I see the only house that I've ever known through tinted windows, dulling the life like experience. I feel like I'm dreaming, to be honest. The house looks the same; a little more beat up, maybe.

As I approach the front porch, I consider actually ringing the doorbell or to knock. This is a place where I used to live. This is the place where I grew up. I should feel comfortable here, right?

WRONG.

Instead, I open the door just a smidge. What I find is repulsive and all too familiar. I am welcomed into a pile of beer cans, which are decorating the living room floor for its own fucked up holiday.

Happy National Beer Day! We celebrate it big time here.

The foul smell is what has me gagging like a well-seasoned porn star. It smells of stale alcohol and dirt. You know what I'm talking about, the type of smell you would find at a bottle return place.

My face wears the deepest shade of crimson as I look at Officer Mitchell, who looks as if he's looking in on a murder scene. He pinches the tip of his nose in disgust as he looks back at me, waiting for answers. I hang my arm over my mouth and nose, trying to reduce the rotten smell and I just shrug. I wasn't necessarily expecting this either.

"I... what the?" I stutter. I honestly have no words. "I'm so sorry."

I quickly bend down and start picking up the beer cans.

"You can't stay here," His mouth is pressed into a hard line as he glares into the apartment. When his eyes dart to an area behind me, his face completely falls and turns to stone. It looks like he's just seen a ghost.

I turn around to another atrocious sight.

My father stands in the doorway wearing a raggedly navy blue robe and a beer in hand.

"Welcome home sweet pea," he slurs as he stumbles his way up to me. His uneasy feet shuffle relentlessly through all of the beer cans as he reaches me. The battered and bent cans prove how bruising his footsteps really are.

Then he does something completely unexpected. He gives me a tight hug.

It's almost too tight.

I pat his back not knowing what else to do. I am wholly dumbfounded. "Dad, you knew I was coming home today, right?"

"Of course!" He shouts in an exasperated tone and continues, "but I didn't know he would be here too," he scowls Officer Mitchell and takes a big swig of his beer. "Or else I would have done some cleaning."

He sounds anything but sincere.

"Dad," I shake my head. "What is this?"

"So it's a little messy. You've never seen a mess before?"

"I'm not talking about the mess!"

He snorts; his expression altering into something all too familiar. Anger.

"Well, you're obviously no angel either! Look at you, Ginny!" His tone is irate and defensive. He darts his eyes to Officer Mitchell and I notice they're having a pissing contest with their eyes, neither one of them backing down.

"You know I can't be around this!" I immediately catch his attention with my tone of voice.

"If you don't like it, then get the hell out!" He scolds.

I take a step back, my expression horrified as if I'd been slapped. I'm hurt. I'm angry. I feel anything but safe in this real world I've been dying to live in. The child in me wants to go right back to that prison cell where I had somewhat of a warm bed and shelter.

"Let's go, Genevieve. You won't be staying here," Officer Mitchell says as he steps in between my father and me.

"Oh trying being the hero. That's not a surprise," He spats, glaring at Officer Mitchell.

He tries getting closer to Officer Mitchell but I put a barrier between the two, facing my father. I glare into my father's eyes and reach a sense of familiarity, which makes me feel oddly content. He has hazel green eyes with a little ring of brown in the center, just like me. It's like staring into a mirror. It's like looking deep within my soul and reliving every good and bad memory of my child hood.

How could he be so awful?

How could I?

What happened to our family?

I'm snapped back into my unfortunate reality when I hear my father's whiskey cry. "Why in the hell are you here?"

I'm not so sure who he's talking to anymore. He's nose to nose with Officer Mitchell and I realize that I've lost my place between them.

Officer Mitchell lifts his hands up in a gesture to stop. Then he begins to repeat himself. "I am Genevieve's parole officer, Mr. Quinn. I was ordered to drop her off with you, seeing this was her home before incarceration. But, I clearly can't leave her here with you. She needs to stay away from alcohol and drugs," he explains slowly as if he is talking to a child.

"Drugs?" He hollers, "I am not a drug addict!"

Then he glares at me accusingly and spits, "What did you tell him?"

"I didn't tell him anything!" I shout. My eyes start to burn with tears as they dart to the ground to scan it. "But just look at these floors!"

"You're the felon here, not me," his harsh words burn through my body in the worst way. "Now get the hell out! Both of you!" He growls and points to the door.

"Come on, Genevieve. You don't want to live in this mess anyways," Officer Mitchell mutters, directing me towards the door with his hand on the small of my back.

Unfortunately, my father follows us out to give us an encore.

"And let me save you the energy. Don't bother going to his apartment. He doesn't want you either!" He shouts as we left the house. "No one wants you, Ginny! You're a burden to everyone! Everyone!"

I try not to let it happen, but the tears prickle at my eyes, begging for an opening. So I give them a chance and sob uncontrollably. I almost lose my breath when I think about what has become of my father. Did I make him even worse?

Before I know it, I'm hyperventilating.

The uninvited tears welcome themselves down my face as I try to restrain my cries.

My dad: 1
Me: 0

"Officer Mitchell?"

"Yes?" He looks up at me squinting as he tries to block the sun out of his face. At least he looks at me like a person. However, he is clearly anxious and trying to brainstorm. I can see it in his eyes.

"I have somewhere safe to go if you can just drop me off there. And I'd like to approach the place on my own. If that's okay."

Officer Mitchell takes a deep breath and exhales slowly. "How do I know you're telling me the truth?"

"You don't. But I'm telling you; I will be safe."

There is a long silence before Officer Mitchell says anything.

"Your father was talking about someone else. Someone not wanting to take you in. Is that where you want to go?"

"Yes," I confirm. "My step brother, Jesse. My father's opinions are inaccurate," I explain. How do I explain something like this without sounding like a creep? Or worse, stupid.

Oh, my stepbrother used to be in love with me. For all I know, he still is! He'll totally take me in.

I take a deep breath and continue. "He doesn't know the whole truth. My father, he doesn't know the real relationship that we have. Jesse would take me in a heartbeat, and I would feel safe with him."

It's then that my body begins to buzz with anticipation. Officer Mitchell shakes his head as if he's considered it and it's already a no.

"Please," I whisper. "I don't want to go to a shelter. I don't want to be homeless."

I don't want to be alone anymore.

Officer Mitchell sighs, followed by a light nod. I barely see it, but I do. He then gives me a reluctant look. He's still skeptical about it. "All right, get in."

I walk up to an apartment complex and room 180; Jessie's destination. I lift my shaky limb to the door and ball my fist. I fight myself just to knock, but eventually, my fist produces a mind of its own. I hesitantly knock on the door, bouncing in place to contain my nerves.

He never visited me in prison. I haven't seen him in seven years.

Before I can back track my steps and get the hell of his property, I hear the door unlock.

I quickly tuck my hair behind my ears and flatten out the wrinkly clothes I'm wearing.

The door opens just a smidge, and I'm given a look into a messy apartment. It definitely looks like his. His bong is out and wires from his video games cover the floor. I look up to meet his big brown eyes for the first time in seven years and almost faint on the spot. His ink black hair, which is messy and uncontained, is a reminder of the kind of man he is. Leaned back and relaxed. He looks like he's been bumming around all day and playing video games. However, none of that takes away from how gorgeous he still is. He looks the same; beautiful and youthful as ever.

He shoves a hand through his semi long hair as his thick eyebrows nearly hit his hairline. He gives me a quizzical look, making me lift an eyebrow myself. His face softens as he takes an assessing look at my whole body.

"Your hair got really long," he says.

"Hey, Jess," I smile.

CHAPTER THREE

Jesse takes an extensive look at me and nearly drops the bong in his hands. The shock is very apparent on his face as he reaches out for me. He holds me by the shoulders; not letting me escape from his tight grip.

To be honest, I don't want him to. I brush my free hand over his chest and take a second glance at him. I'd peak a thousand glances at him if I could.

He is smiling from ear to ear, too.

It's a moment I've been thinking and dreaming about for a very long time. It's finally here.

My lips lift into an eager grin as my eyes naturally burn into his.

"Get in here right now," he demands.

He grabs my hand, leading me into his apartment and then to his kitchenette. He doesn't have much; just a miniature kitchen and a living room, which seems to be the room he sleeps in. It looks as if he does have an actual bedroom, but the door remains closed. He was never one for keeping things tidy, but at least there are no beer cans on the floor.

After I'm done checking out the apartment, I turn to him and he's staring directly at me. If I thought it was possible, I'd say he's staring right through me. We stare at one another to absorb the fact that we're actually at the same place at the same time.

He is the first one to break the trance, making a bee line straight to the coffee maker. "If I still know you, then I know you want some coffee right now."

"That sounds great," I respond. I stand in the doorway and watching him brew coffee like it's the first time I've ever watched somebody do it. I catch his eyes a few times, but they don't stay on me for long.

I feel a sense of contentment come over me, followed by a wave of heat.

I've missed him.

"Sit down, Gin," he softly says.

"Thanks," I say, sitting down at the small table.

"Starbucks or Dunkin Donuts?"

"Is that even a serious question?" I ask, sardonically.

I see him suppress a smile as he works his magic. Before I know it, Starbucks starts dripping into the cup. The bitter smell attacks my nostrils in the best way. I'm thirstier than I thought.

The stillness in the room is over bearing. Jesse was never one to articulate much into conversations. I can hear the coffee drip into the porcelain mug, and the thudding of my heart beat; both of them pounding in sync. Everything seems heightened and it doesn't help any of my anxiety.

"How did you find me?" He breaks the awkward silence.

"Julia gave me your address."

He nods and runs a hand through his black tendrils. "She visited you?"

"No. I called."

"Oh," he says, looking at his hands.

I'd like to say I feel bad about the guilt that mars his face, but I'm not. He's the only one out of all of them that I wanted to see during those seven lonely years.

"I like your place," I say, scanning the room. Nothing like lame home decor talk to change the subject.

"I'm doing okay," he says as he delivers the cup of coffee to me. "Sugar?"

"Please."

He puts in two teaspoons of sugar and places the milk in front of me. "I don't know how much cream you like these days."

"Still none. Thank you," I smile.

"No problem," he says as he puts the milk back. I notice that he doesn't get a coffee of his own.

"So, when did you get out?" He prods.

"This morning, but my parole officer took me to Dads," I grimace, "It didn't end well."

He squeezes the bridge of his nose with his fingers and bleakly says, "It never does."

"There were beer cans all over the floor. My parole officer came in and saw everything," I frown.

CHAPTER THREE

"Gin," he softly whispers, reaching out to hold my hand. I intercept it without a doubt in my mind. I need his touch right now more than ever. He caresses it for a while as he looks at me with yielding eyes. Once I bite back my tears, I clear my throat and finish, "It was the worst I've ever seen him. What happened to him?"

"Dale has a lot of issues right now," he explains. It sounds more like he's defending him. Despite calling my dad by his real name, my father and he have always had a good relationship. When he notices that I'm irritated, he shifts in his seat uncomfortably and says, "Even I can barely get through to him."

"But at least you can."

"He will come around, Gin."

"Well, I don't know what I'm going to do or where I'm going to stay until he does."

"Stay here," he immediately responds.

I lift my gaze up at him and tilt my head. "You don't mind?"

He snorts. "I suggested it."

"I have nowhere else to go."

"Well, then it's settled. You stay with me as long as you need. We are family. You will get back on your feet."

I smile, appreciating the genuineness that is Jesse. He had always been able to cheer me up, even if I am distressed. He did it like it was his job.

Familiar feelings start to resurface, but I don't know what those feelings mean, so I suppress them.

I smile at him.

Since prison made me a morning person, I decided on delivering newspapers. With the help of Officer Mitchell, I found a good neighborhood to deliver in. Officer Mitchell then asked me if it would be too difficult for my leg, but I dismissed his worries right away. I figured the exercise would do me good.

On the other hand, I was only human and knew my injured knee would be my greatest challenge.

I received free medical attention in prison, but now I was living in the real world without any medical insurance. Being careful and safe was a priority.

I also had to attend mandatory AA meetings, which kind of sucked. I didn't want to attend them, but Jesse made me go.

However, he encouraged me with a blunt in his hand, so I couldn't take him that seriously.

After Jesse drops me off at the church, I immediately roll my eyes.

Of course, it's in a church, why wouldn't it be?

I walk into the church and see the directions to the AA meeting right in front of me. I feel my hands begin to tremble as I shake them ferociously and try to rid the annoyance. I scan my surroundings, looking for anyone that I know. Then again, I was glad to not see any familiar faces.

As I enter the room with the big welcome sign, I'm sure I've ended up where I'm supposed to. It's a small dimly lit room with six rows of chairs, complete with a podium at the front and center of it. I sit down towards the back of the room where no one will notice me.

Just when I am about to ditch this hell hole and never look back, a man approaches the podium. Everyone collectively becomes quiet and waits for him to speak.

Pin dropping silence.

He scans the room and smiles at a few people I'm assuming that he knows. I have to admit, he's a good looking guy, and I didn't expect to see any of them here.

I guess everyone has their issues, even the gorgeous ones.

He looks down at the papers he's holding, clears his throat and then looks up again. When he does, his eyes land right on me. Dark, translucent blue eyes drill into my own hazel ones, pinning me in a trance I can't break. He shoots me a warm smile and I almost look behind me to make sure it's for me. I feel a tinge of disappointment when he breaks eye contact first and clears his throat again.

CHAPTER THREE

A low baritone and raspy voice follows, "Hey everyone. I'm Benson and I'm an alcoholic," he lifts his eyes to me again and my breath nearly catches in my throat.

"I'm exactly one year sober today," he says as he holds up his bracelet. "I'm a single father, taking care of my sick father, and running a business all at the same time. Life can get stressful sometimes, and that's when I get my urges the most."

I'm almost sure that's how it starts, but I don't listen to the rest. I don't listen to anything else because I seem to have tunnel vision on those electrifying blue eyes. They're all I see, even from the back row. I almost forget to admire his dirty blonde hair that teases his dark eyebrows, sprouting in all directions from his head. Or the dark, five o'clock that shadows the bottom of his face. It compliments his lighter hair.

After he's done and sits down, not too far from me, I keep feeling his presence.

Is he looking at me?

But, why?

I slowly turn my head into the most intense eyes I've ever seen. It's confirmed that this man is looking right at me, seeing that a wall is behind me.

Just when it seems like I have all the strength in the world to ask him what the hell he's looking at, I storm out of there as fast as I can. I walk past the optional coffee and cookies that they have at the end. I walk past the big, scary crucifix, reminding me that this is all bullshit anyways.

That's right. I said it. It's all bullshit.

I walk out of that building and make a bee line straight home, which takes almost an hour.

My nights out of prison are quiet and alone. Even though I live with Jesse, he's out most of the time and working. I'm glad I'm not getting in the way of his life, but a little time with him would be nice. I curl up with a good book that night and fall asleep on the couch.

The next day, I wake up early for my paper route and get dressed accordingly. Each day has the same routine. I get up at five am, shower, get on my pathetic excuse of a bicycle, and ride up and down 8 blocks. It's a good exercise, to say the least.

I notice that I deliver papers in an upper, middle class neighborhood. Beautiful, tall, developmental houses stand like soldiers next to each other, with their respective lawns in front of them. There is not too much space between the houses since it's still in the city, but they're definitely nicer than the ones in Albany. It's amazing that if you go a few blocks down from here, you're back in the bad neighborhood.

Only a few days into the route, I find that for the pay this job contributes, it isn't worth it. I am entirely too exhausted and in pain all the time. I barely have enough money to buy myself a meal or get other necessities that I need.

Once I've saved up a week's worth of pay, I decide to buy myself a cell phone. Apparently, every person on Earth needs one of these or else life is ridiculously hard for them.

However, these cell phones are nothing like the cell phones we had in High School. These phones are bigger, flatter, and touch screen. They are called 'Smart Phones'. I hate the touch screen and just can't seem to get used to it. Whatever happened to a simple dial-up phone? Now, you can look up anything on the internet from where you are. I can see when you've read my messages when you're typing to me, when you're on your Social Media's, when you're in your underwear… okay, maybe not that last one. Still, it's basically a stalking device.

I decide on an iPhone.

The next morning I do my usual routine and begin delivering my papers. I decide not to take my bike today since it's about to spontaneously combust from being so old. Jesse had scraped it up for me at a garage sale he passed since he knew I couldn't drive.

"You really didn't have to get this," I say to him as we eat dinner.

He had surprised me with Chinese takeout this afternoon after he got out of work. I forgot how caring and thoughtful Jesse could be, but I was all being reminded of this again.

He looks up from his plate and looks at me for a few seconds in silence. I flicker my eyes down to my plate and push my food around with my fork a few times before I look back up. He still looks at me and I can't turn away from him. I was always a sucker for his big brown eyes and olive skin. Again, Jesse's absent father was Brazilian.

Before I know it, we're having an intense stare off.

What is he thinking of?

I drop my fork and tilt my head. I can tell he's brewing up something good in his head because I see a faint smirk spread his face.

"Do you remember when we went to prom and I beat the shit out of your prom date?" he asks.

I smile at the familiar memory as my insides begin to heat up.

Only he ever knew how to do this to me.

I nod. "I remember."

"Do you remember what happened after that?" He prods.

"You drove us home, except we got pulled over by a cop," I say, remembering the memories quite specifically.

"And I had an eighth of weed on me," he interrupts.

I can't help but start giggling. "You were freaking out."

He joins me laughing. "I tried hiding it under my ball sack, Ginny. Yeah, I was nervous."

Before I know it, we're both laughing uncontrollably. It feels so good to laugh like this. It feels even better that it's with him. We have so many good memories. Memories I've thought of repeatedly while in prison.

That very thought brings a sour taste to my mouth, but I swallow it down.

Silence follows our laughing and I begin to feel my nerves catch up with me. I keep my eye on my food, but I feel his eyes on me.

"Do you remember what happened after that?" He asks, his voice barely a whisper.

"We went home." No, don't you dare say it.

"And after that?"

You asshole. You're going to make me say it.

I don't answer. I know what he wants to hear.

I look up at him to see those eyes pinning me down in place. I feel like I have no room to breathe, let alone do anything else. Like, answer his question.

"We made love." I finally croak out.

He nods and adds, "Good memory."

I smile.

He smiles.

We both go back to eating after that.

It seems like only yesterday that Jesse consumed my every thought and action. Things are much different now.

After a few homes of elderly people, some that are downright, stone cold slytherin, I approach what could be a young father and his little daughter waiting on their front lawn. They are up rather early, but then I remember its late May so there's probably school today. The man is adjusting his tie on his front porch and watching after his young daughter, who is darting around like a ping pong machine. There is also an elderly man sitting in a rocking chair on the porch using his phone.

What the hell, even old people knew how to use these phones?

I'm assuming that he is the grandfather of the little girl since she goes over to him and sits on his lap.

After what seems to be some minor struggling with my knee, I incline my head and get another look at the man on the porch. A sense of déjà vu threatens my senses when he locks eyes with me. He looks at me with inquisition and nothing more.

I walk closer with his paper to get a better look at him, and I come to the conclusion this man is one gorgeous specimen. From head to toe, he's covered in tattoos. However, he's dressed to the nines in business attire.

Those eyes seem so familiar.

I think I've seen them before.

They're so dominant and dark.

CHAPTER THREE

So blue and liquid.

So electrifying and indifferent.

It's then when I notice that while they are indifferently intense, they're hidden with anger and regression. Impossible, you say? No. Not impossible.

These are not the type of eyes that are going to welcome you over for dinner and Monopoly game night.

"Hey! I'll take that!" A little girl snatches the paper from my hand. "Daddy likes it in the morning. You bring it on time," she observes. "I like you! Our old paperboy didn't bring it until Daddy was already at work. He would get so mad. Hey, you're a paper girl!" She chatters away as I smile absent mindedly and focus my attention on the man again.

He looks at me and something familiar rings in my ears. I can tell he is battling the same emotions from the way he looks at me. His nostrils flare and he quickly snaps out of it. "Annie. Come here right now!" he demands.

The little girl frowns at me and then turns around, skipping back to her father. He grabs her arm and drags her to the car.

I continue to walk when I overhear the man. "What did I tell you about talking to strangers?"

I stop in my tracks and turn around to him.

Are you kidding me?

This guy doesn't want me anywhere near his daughter? The curious side of me wonders why.

Does he know my history? Does he know who I am?

I go to take a step forward to apologize but then I realize something as I take a good look at him.

Intense blue eyes, check.

Dark five o'clock scruff, check.

Tattoos painting his sculpted body, check.

This is the same man that spoke at my first AA meeting yesterday. He's the one who kept staring at me as if I had a horn coming out of the center of my forehead.

My brow lifts at his comment. Stranger? Well, I suppose we are.

He wasn't looking at me like I was a stranger at our AA meeting the other day.

Without as much as a wave or explanation, he steps into his car and slams the door.

The next few days go by in a slow and tedious motion. I do my paper route, go to my AA meetings and see Officer Mitchell every Wednesday. However, I never saw the mystery man with blue eyes back at the meeting. Not after that run in during my paper route.

I continue looking for a new job but nothing catches on.

No one wants to hire a convict.

Until one unconventional day when I arrive around 9 a.m. at my meeting. Jesse drops me off before work again, this time giving me a kiss on the cheek before I get out.

He's been getting a little weird on me lately. He even tried to cuddle with me the other day while we were watching an episode of Naked and Afraid. I mean, really? Come on.

So here I am at my meeting. A meeting I don't even need to be attending.

Why the hell am I even here?

I'm not addicted to alcohol! I honestly can't even think of the last time I've had it.

Yes, I can.

I take a seat towards the back of the room.

After the people flood in, the talking seems to get louder and I seem to get more uncomfortable.

I weave my arms over my chest and tuck my chin in, hoping that helps me. It doesn't

Damn it prison for making me an introvert! Damn it all to hell.

Then, I see a big mass out of the corner of my eye. I lift my eyes to see just the man I was scoping out a few minutes earlier. The man I haven't seen in days.

The stranger with blue eyes.

"This seat taken?"

I look up at him and shake my head. I have nothing to say to him. No witty response here. I straighten my posture and move over a little in my seat as if it will help. It's not like he'll be sitting on top of me!

CHAPTER THREE

After he takes a seat next to me, he stretches his long legs and lets out a little sigh. I look straight ahead and cross my arms, trying not to look affected by how close he is, but I'm sure I'm radiating it.

At least he's not being a jerk right now.

"I'm Benson," he finally says to me.

When I don't answer, he continues, "I'm sorry about the other day. I can be a little over protective over my daughter sometimes."

Although I'm shocked he actually said something to me, I hide it the best that I can. I look straight ahead, trying my best to be indifferent. "No big deal."

"No big deal?" He repeats with a look of disbelief on his face.

I shrug. "Yeah, no big deal."

I then look over at him and flash what is probably the most hideous, ridiculous smile. Almost like that emoji that people misuse all the time. All teeth, no curve to it. The fakest smile ever.

"You're still mad," he observes. "Don't lie."

I gasp. "Me, lie? I'm not lying."

Silence fills the space between us as I accidently slip a real grin. I'm enjoying the banter a little too much. When I look up at him, he smiles slowly and sexy. "There's a real smile."

"How on earth would you know what my real smile looks like?"

He laughs and shrugs. "It's not easy to figure out. Why, are you scared?"

"Scared?"

He nods slowly. "That I can tell when you're lying through your teeth?"

I let out a bitter laugh and cross my arms again. I am terminating this conversation right here are right now. How dare this stranger think he knows even a little bit about me?

A few seconds of silence pass by when I finally speak up. "You were acting like I was a serial killer the other day."

He laughs at that and looks at the ground. It's probably the sexiest laugh I've ever heard. It's a real one too. I can just tell.

I look at him and catch his eyes staring at me. He then goes to open his mouth to say something, but we're interrupted by the head of the room.

"Hi, I'm Wendy and I'm an alcoholic…"

We then break eye contact and look at the head of the room.

For most of the meeting, we sit in comfortable silence next to each other. I catch him out of the corner of my eye looking at me occasionally.

When the meeting comes close to ending and Wendy tells us to grab some snacks and talk, I begin to feel really nervous. I don't want to talk to anyone. I don't want to talk to him. I can barely stand to even be here as it is.

"See you all next week," she says.

I fly out of my seat like a bat out of hell.

The next day, I do the usual routine of waking up and showering and tip toeing out of Jesse's apartment so that he doesn't wake up.

It's not like I'm dying to see that sexy stranger who always looks at me or anything. Okay, who am I kidding? I even wake up just at the right time so that I can bump into him. It's quite pathetic.

I decide to walk today, which may be a terrible idea considering after an hour my knee begins to bother me. The sharp pain radiates down my leg, making it hard for me to walk like a normal person. I'm almost done with my paper route and am finally approaching (or rather limping up to) Benson's house when I see his little girl approach me.

"Are you okay?" She asks, frowning.

"Annie! A deep and raspy voice shouts, sending an electric current through my body.

I lift my gaze and notice that he's giving me an unwelcome look from his porch. Then he does something that pisses me off, even more, he gives his daughter a set of cautionary eyes. He does it purely effortless as if he's warned people off his children a thousand times. And it's those effortless, unwelcoming eyes while he sets his cufflinks in place that sends me off the edge.

Who the hell does he think I am? More importantly, who the hell does he think he is?

I begin to feel my blood boil, causing my body to shake violently. I curl my fists until my knuckles turn white and bare my teeth at him.

"For the love of God, she's just asking if I'm ok!" I yell. I'm so angry that I'm heaving out of breath. "And I am." I begin to walk away, muttering under my breath, "thanks for nothing."

Maybe he's like this towards everyone with her.

He did say that he is very overprotective of her. He even apologized to me. But that doesn't excuse why he's being a dick right now.

Maybe he thinks you're the most hideous thing he's ever seen in his entire life.

The livid thought makes my bones harden and before I know it I'm snapping my limbs in motion, working them way harder than I should. Before I know it, my knee completely gives out and I'm on the ground, screaming in pain.

"Ohhh!" I groan in agony, immediately grabbing my injured knee.

I figure the rude man isn't going to come to my aid so I go to get up myself, but then something unbelievable happens. I feel another pair of hands on me, guiding me up. I turn around and there he is, standing eye to eye with me in all of his glory, wearing a concerned look.

Even when he's concerned he looks like a dick.

Oh great. On top of being hot and a dick, he is also a good citizen.

This also gives me a clear vision of his aqua eyes in the broad day light. I've seen them under the artificial lights of the church where our meetings are held, but this brings them to a whole new level. I'm speechless. I go to talk but nothing comes out other than a groan and few intellect vowels. I then bow my head in embarrassment and try to avoid eye contact with him.

He opens his mouth to say something but then snaps it shut. I notice I'm grinding my teeth because I'm so angry.

"Would you prefer I ignore her all together? Pretend she doesn't exist?" I ask with a hint of sarcasm.

He flinches at the stern tone of my voice and explains, "I told you I was over protective of her."

"I thought we've established I wasn't a serial killer." I spat.

"I know that," he says, irritated. "I couldn't see who she was talking to at first! And to be quite honest, I don't know you."

"No, you don't! Because if you did, you wouldn't be such a selfish, donkey dick!"

He looks at me like I'm speaking Spanish. His broad shoulders lift as he gives me a lazy smirk. "Donkey dick?"

I almost laugh that he is offended over that more than the other word I called him, but I hide my grin.

"Never mind," I say, limping away from the bastard.

Then I realize something. I'm letting this man, this donkey dick of a bastard get the last laugh. I bet if I turn around right now, he'd be laughing at my expense.

All of my years of reading books in prison and the best I can come up with is calling this undeniably rude man a donkey dick?

I turn around and my predictions are true. He has his hand covering the bottom half of his face, which is split into a smirk.

He's laughing at me.

At least he has the decency to cover his laugh, but I'm still pissed. So I scowl at him and turn back around to limp away again.

"You probably shouldn't walk if you have a bad knee. Maybe invest in a bicycle or something." The offer sounds empty. I look at him stunned. I can't believe this asshole.

My fast approach up to him again earns me a great look at his eyes. Not that I want to, but I'm scolding him and I'm not backing down this time.

Those eyes.

They're the darkest and most translucent eyes that I've ever seen. They are the clearest of blue, which remind me of the night ocean. I want to swim and get lost in them, never finding my way back home. My eyes then linger down a little more. His face is rugged, yet so beautiful. The dark stubble covers his flawless jaw, making his cheekbones appear even higher than I thought.

Before I lose my nerve, I shout at him. "I do have a bike. I didn't bring it today. Now if you'll excuse me, I have more important things to do than argue with someone that I don't even know."

This time, I do more than limp. I leap. Yes, I leap away. I try to get away from him as fast as I can. This should be very embarrassing for me, but the man is so rude that I don't even care how I look right now. I don't plan on ever seeing him again.

"Wait a second." I feel the light brush of finger tips on my bare arm.

How the hell did he catch up with me so fast?

I whip my head around to softer eyes than before. His features aren't nearly as hard as they were earlier. He seems a little more tolerable at the moment. He's actually even more gorgeous when angry lines aren't marring his face.

He then squats in front of his daughter so that they're eye level. I hear him whisper something to her but can't make out what he's saying. She nods and looks at him as if he's the center of the universe. Then she runs back towards their house, closing herself inside.

He clearly wants his daughter as far away from me as possible. I try to get to my feet but it's no use. I don't have the strength and honestly need his assistance. Knowing being stubborn won't do me any good, I sigh and hang my shoulders in defeat.

"Listen, I'm sorry. Are you okay?" He asks, checking out my knee delicately. The kind gesture sends a shiver up my spine, causing me to jolt away from him. His eyes snap up to mine, concerned.

Don't look at me like that.

"I'm fine. You really don't have to bother acting so concerned. I know you're not."

He laughs as if it's ridiculous and offers me his help anyway, but I twist out of his hold. "I don't need your damn help." I give him a scolding look, hoping he'll get the point. Then I walk away, fast, furious and... then my leg gives completely out. I fall to my knees, letting out a frustrated groan. Why can't I walk around this guy? Or talk? It's seriously annoying.

He approaches me with that asshole of a smirk on his face and helps me to my feet.

Just then, a soft breeze blows, giving us a cool-off from this summer humidity. He looks at me for a few seconds, and then delicately, he pushes a wayward strand away from my eyes so he can see them.

I steal another glance of his eyes because let's face it; I'm the president of their fan club. Not only does the man have striking eyes, but he also has the longest eyelashes that I've ever seen. I observe how they look against his sculpted, ridiculously high cheekbones when he blinks, and I nearly almost lose it.

I'm pretty sure he notices that I am gawking at him like an idiot.

He then scowls, ruining the moment.

I follow his facial structure, and tilt my head. "What?"

"Uh, you're bleeding like a faucet."

I look down at my knees, which are scraped and dripping with superficial blood.

Gross.

Attractive.

He breaks his silence and helps me to his front porch, "You need to put some ice on your knee before you go anywhere."

"I don't have to do anything."

"Just come in for a second, ice your knee, and go on your merry way," he shrugs.

Is he inviting me into his house?

"You, I... You're inviting me in your... house?" I scrunch my face up in confusion. He seems to find my inability to speak correctly entertaining because he's giving me that asshole smirk again.

Just then I notice that he's placed his hands under my elbows, helping me keep my balance.

How didn't I notice that this man was touching me?

Probably because I can't stop staring at those parallel orifices on his face, and I'm not talking about his nostrils.

"Suit yourself," he shrugs, taking his hands off me, which causes me to collapse again.

I yelp as my knee twists and then put my hands up in submission. "Fine! Fine!"

His eyes read satisfaction when I give in, causing my blood to boil all the more.

"If I can just rest for a second here, I will be on my way soon." I settle on his front porch, in the same chair the grandpa was sitting in the other day.

Then he does something crazy and unexpected when he reaches the top step. He flexes, putting his long arms to work as he touches the rain gutter above. I get a good view of his hard rock abs when his shirt lifts a little bit.

He smiles, knowing I'm gawking at him like an ape. He's doing it on purpose, not that I can blame him. His arms are thick and defined and colorful with tattoos covering them.

"Just come inside. I'm not a serial killer," he assures me. "You're not a killer, are you?"

I pause for a second. I think I like leaving him in suspense.

"No," I laugh. I try to sound confident; however, my heart is anything but. It's pounding so fast in my rib cage that it may spontaneously combust at any minute. "But sorry if I'm a bit confused by your... inconsistencies."

He places his hand over his heart as if he's internally wounded. "Inconsistencies?"

"You yell at your daughter if she comes within a five mile radius of me, yet you're inviting me in your home?"

He does something crazy again. He fans his shirt out, giving me a front row seat to his six pack. Now he's just playing dirty. "Can we go inside? It's so humid out here."

I go to interject, but he interrupts me. "Have you ever wanted to protect someone with your life so much that you'd do anything at all possible?"

"Well, I..." I'm not so sure what to say.

"You know where I'm getting at," He interrupts my confession. "She's my daughter. I'm just a little over protective. Stop being stubborn and come inside so I can help you. You know what help is, right?"

Now he's just being condescending. I liked it better when he played dirty.

My eyes turn into two little slits, which causes a ghost of a smile dancing on his lips. I could get used to this smile.

I finally give in and nod.

"Seriously, when is the last time you let someone help you?" He asks, holding the door to his house open for me.

"Hmmm..." I pretend to think. "Not since the Nazi's invaded Poland."

He lets out a burst of laughter and follows me inside.

After what seems to be a couple of minutes of more bickering, he wins and leads me into his home. I step in cautiously to a spacious hallway, where the living room is visible from on the left and the kitchen is straight ahead. His house is surprisingly clean for a man's house. Then again, his wife could be anywhere.

His house is spotless; he has to have a wife.

"Take a seat," he commands, gesturing towards the couch in the living room. I limp over to the couch and take a seat into the soft sofa. I immediately sink to it, feeling more comfortable than ever.

"I will be right back," he says as he turns on his heel and heads towards his kitchen. I hear him open the freezer and then close it. I look down at my knee, which is undeniably swollen with dried blood casing it. He returns with a bag of peas and showcases them in his hands. "This is all that I have."

I go to grab it, but before I can, he kneels in front of me and delicately sets the bag on my knee. I gasp as the cold plastic touches my tender skin, but after that, it soothes the burning sensation.

CHAPTER THREE

My eyes flicker quickly to him while he concentrates. There is something breathtakingly sexy about a man that kneels in front of you, and I can't quite pinpoint it. I suddenly realize I'm holding my breath and let out a huge exhale.

His dark blue eyes meet mine; his lashes fluttering upwards, and I swear I die. My body begins to betray me for lust. I break the eye contact when I notice that I'm sweating like a whore in church.

"Are you okay?" He asks, his voice barely a whisper.

"Yes," I squeak.

More silence fills the air between us, followed by his lips curving into a grin as he sets his sight back to my knee. It's like he can read my mind; all my erratic thoughts. It's like he can see right through me.

He then places the peas carefully back on my knee; his fingers brushing part of my thigh. I can barely feel the pain anymore because everything is over ridden by the adrenaline that I'm feeling. He's looking at me too, but I have no idea what he is thinking. He's quiet as a church mouse, but his eyes say enough to make me turn vermilion.

My eyes roam his living room and notice an abundance of pictures, which I am guessing are of his family. I keep seeing a lot of pictures of a flawless, dark haired woman. Almost the same color as mine. Hers may be a shade darker than mine. It's pitched black, actually.

She must not be home right now, or else he probably wouldn't be aiding to me on his knees.

"Does that feel any better?" He asks as he holds the bag to my knee. I figured he'd put it in my hands by now, but instead, he holds it there like a bomb's attached.

"A lot better, actually. I can take over," I say, as I intercept the bag from him and brush his hand momentarily. I feel a very painful, yet pleasurable spark ignite within my ribcage. I notice he jerks his hand away as if he'd been shocked, too.

He takes a seat next to me on the couch and juts his jaw at my knee. "How did you hurt it?"

"I was in a bad accident."

It's the truth.

"Ah," He nods, knowingly.

He looks down at my swollen knee and gives me that panty melting smirk. "You're too pretty to be a paper delivery boy."

I giggle even though I hate myself for it. He notices I'm blushing and looks away from me.

Wait, is he blushing too?

"You seem like a smart girl, why do you deliver papers with your knee like that?"

I shrug at his brutal honesty, and then we both begin laughing.

"It's just easy money," I say.

Oh yeah, and I'm a felon, but we won't tell you that today.

He looks at me concerned as if he can read my mind, then his expression transitions deep into thought. He begins taking a deeper breath and then lets out a huge sigh. I watch his muscles contract and I swear I'm drooling like a baby.

"Listen, I'm really sorry the way I've acted towards you," he softly says.

"It's okay. It's over with. Thank you for your help."

He sits there, soundless as if I took the words directly out of his mouth. "It really was nothing personal. I don't know you. It's just that... she's all that I have."

"I understand. I really do." I offer him a small smile.

"Well, let me make it up to you," he shrugs.

I laugh at his offer and then realize he's being serious. I tilt my head to the side and scrunch my face.

"How?" I ask.

He bites his lip in concentration as if I just asked him the question of the century. Then his eyes widen and the invisible light bulb goes off in his head. "How about I help you today with the rest of your route?"

I am stunned by his offer, and I really wouldn't mind spending time with this gorgeous man. On the other hand, he doesn't owe me anything and I am a felon, after all. I don't need to bring him or his daughter into my mess.

But it's just the rest of the paper route!

But... Jesse.

CHAPTER THREE

"I'm almost done for the day. There's no need." I say.

"You shouldn't be walking on it. Let me help you with the rest," he insists.

"I'm serious though! I only have like a street left. It's no big deal."

"You're exactly right. It's no big deal. We can grab a bite afterwards, my treat for being such a dick," he says. He actually looks excited, which makes me thrilled as well.

Because let's face it, this man is way out of my league and he wants to spend time with me.

"I just have to get my keys and we can be on our way," he calls out as he runs upstairs with a few sprints of his muscular legs. I go to say something, but he disappears before I can.

I sigh and turn my head to start looking at the pictures on the wall while I wait.

Maybe this won't be so bad. He's not so bad.

I let my eyes wander around the room as I wait for him to come back down, but a certain picture catches my undivided attention.

It's a picture of the woman with the black hair. The woman that is pretty much all throughout the house on the wall. She is stunning with long raven black hair and bright blue eyes that accent all of her features. She is smiling wide, with white and straight teeth. Her arm is propped up and is supporting her chin, revealing a golden charm bracelet.

It's definitely not the woman that catches my attention now that I think of it.

No, not at all.

It's the charm bracelet that looks oddly familiar. I'm pretty sure I've held it in my hands while bleeding and screaming.

I take a look at her again. I look directly into her lifeless eyes. The picture. Her face. That bracelet.

A golden charm bracelet with so much heartbreak and resentment added to it. A bracelet worth a thousand goodbyes and a seven year sentence.

Then, it hits me. I've seen this woman before. Not necessarily in person. I've never seen her in the flesh or while she was actually breathing.

Dead.

I've seen her dead on that fateful day and in my dreams ever since.

My blood begins to grow cold. My body is in complete shock, just like it was seven years ago when I hit her lifeless body. It's painful and raw, but I force myself to step outside to read the last name on the mailbox.

This can't be real.

I open the front door and check the name on the mailbox.

It reads "Daniels".

Angelina Daniels.

It confirms my worst fear and my darkest nightmare.

I'm in her house.

That gorgeous man upstairs is her husband. That little girl... *is her daughter!*

All of a sudden, I hear the stairs creak as he comes marching down the stairs. I can't see him, but I can hear him talking about my knee. In sheer panic, I turn around and run out the door as fast as I possibly can.

There is no way that I am staying here and letting him help me with anything.

Not after what I've done to him and his family.

CHAPTER FOUR

Finding out the handsome stranger that's been helping me was the man whose life I sabotaged just about did me in. What were the chances that I found my victim's widowed husband? How did I find him so easily? The fact that a seemingly perfect man like him attended Alcohol's Anonymous made much more sense now.

There were a lot of questions running rampant in my mind after I left his house, but the main one drilled into my core loud and painfully clear.

Does he know who I am?

I begin to wonder if this is the magical work of my parole officer, or if it was just over looked. I'm sure it was overlooked but who the hell would make a mistake like this? Sure, I didn't look like I did in high school anymore. The pink hair is now long, dark hair and the piercings on my face are no more. I've changed quite a bit.

For all intents and purposes, I'm a whole different woman.

Was this all one big and sick joke or something? Was the man upstairs sitting up there with a bucket of popcorn and a Cheshire smile right now? I sit and scold my television for the rest of the night, letting my brain take me away from my crappy reality.

I try to get his beautiful brooding eyes and ridiculously high cheekbones out of my head, but how can I when they're the most beautiful assets I've seen in my life?

Jesus Christ. I can't think straight.

I call in sick for the next two days and have another man fill in for me and my paper route. The last thing that I want to do is bump into the guy again.

The situation with Jesse turns a bit uncomfortable as time goes on. I try to avoid confrontation with him by leaving the house as much as I can, partaking in extra AA meetings and more hours of community service. I even leave the apartment before Jesse gets home from work and go visit Officer Mitchell.

Unfortunately, Officer Mitchell notices my dilemma. It doesn't take a rocket scientist to figure it out as I tap my knee relentlessly and bite my lip like I'm up next on America's Got Talent.

"So, you found a job?" Officer Mitchell asks.

"Yes. Thank you for the recommendations, by the way," I say with a grin that doesn't reach my eyes. "I'm delivering papers for now and residing with a family member."

"That is great, Genevieve."

"However, I am looking for another job already."

"You don't like it?" He looks disappointed.

I sigh. "I don't mind it."

"Well let me know if I can give you some more referrals. I see you did your community service this week and then some. That is awesome," he says, looking over the papers. "Have you set up an appointment to see a psychologist?"

I shake my head hesitantly, afraid of hearing his response. He doesn't look too impressed.

"Genevieve, it's very important that you talk to someone."

"Can't I just talk to you?" I protest.

"I'm not a doctor."

I don't say anything.

"Speaking of doctor," he says as he begins shuffling through his drawer, pulling out a plastic cup. "I do need a urine test."

"Wonderful," I say, dryly.

After two long and dreadful days pass by, I'm still worried that I will bump into him. I decided to take my bike just in case I have to make a run for it. For my first day back, I dress in a grey hooded sweatshirt and black yoga pants, with a pair of oversized sunglasses to cover my face. I'm not taking any chances.

I make sure to leave extra early so I don't run into any human interaction.

His interaction.

CHAPTER FOUR

Yeah, he won't recognize me when I look like that extra-terrestrial who eats Reese's Pieces.

I throw every paper fluidly as I peddle along to each house. The morning air is humid and sticky and downright disgusting. The fact that there's barely any light doesn't make it any better. My chest begins to cave as I approach his house. I battle the thick air to take a deep breath.

I also contemplate turning around right then and there, but something stops me from doing so.

He isn't outside, but what I find in front of his house is even more concerning. His daughter is on the porch, in her pale yellow nightgown and walking around aimlessly. She makes a habit to stay on the porch but walks in all directions that she can, reminding me of a hungry Pac Man.

I become extremely concerned when she walks over to the ledge. Her long, blonde locks curtain her eyes, blocking me from viewing her face. I stop my bike a little past her house and place it on the ground.

As I approach closer, I notice her eyes are closed as she walks. She's sleep walking.

I ring the door bell and try to help her avoid falling off the porch, but you know what they say, don't wake a sleep walker.

So instead, I wait for the door to open when she suddenly trips over a loose floorboard and falls head first onto the ground. This wakes her up as she observes her surroundings with befuddlement.

I help her up to her feet and she frowns. I can sense her embarrassment and it pulls on my heart strings majorly. Feeling anything for this little girl is heartrending. Now that I know who she is, I feel an unspoken connection to her.

I then notice her eyes roll in the back of her head as she falls limp into my arms.

Oh shit. Did she just pass out on me?

I immediately start slapping some color into her cheeks, trying to get her conscious and alert. I gather her in my arms and shake her vigorously.

Nothing.

I start to panic.

"Hey!" I rush up the porch steps with her limp in my arms. "Help!" I shout, kicking his front door. "Your daughter just fainted! Call 911!"

I watch him approach in a pair of low rise flannel pants and a wife beater, something that looks like he rushed to put on after his shower because his hair is gloriously wet and slicked back. I wipe the drool from my face and start to think maybe, A) I should tone it down a little bit, and B) I shouldn't have worn sweat pants today. I feel my face flame with embarrassment as I hold his child in my arms. I have to keep reminding myself not to drop her.

Don't you dare drop her, Quinn!

He notices the commotion but it doesn't rush him to the door; instead, he takes his sweet time. I offer to call an ambulance, but he just rolls his eyes and checks her pulse, then her temperature with the back of his hand.

"I'm calling 911," I insist, grabbing my phone out of my pocket.

"Don't bother. She's fine," he says.

I have the urge to slap this ape of a man in the face but instead, I hand her over to him. I notice his disinterest in the situation and it sets me on fire with piss and vinegar. It's as if this conundrum is ordinary to him.

"Your daughter just passed out," I remind him.

He looks at her and sighs. "She's fine."

He then turns around with no explanation and walks to his couch, settling her down with a blanket. The softness of his touch makes me think that maybe he does care. He takes his time tucking her in and that's when I take it as a sign to leave.

I battle many angry emotions in my head, the main one being that this man is the worst father on the planet. His daughter faints in my arms and he rolls his eyes as if it's nothing. The thought makes my blood boil despite the other feelings I feel.

Like pure, unadulterated lust.

I walk back to my bike when I hear rushing footsteps. "Wait a second."

CHAPTER FOUR

I had a feeling he'd follow, but I didn't anticipate the desperate tone to his voice. I turn around to him walking down the stairs and towards me. His muscles flex back and forth in his black dress shirt, which I'm sure he threw on just before chasing me. He has his hands shoved casually into his pockets and his sleeves are already rolled up, revealing his ink of flames. His hair is still slicked back from his shower; the sunrise bringing out his natural dirty blonde locks. My breathing falters as the sight of him sends my insides into a total frenzy.

Just as I'm about to make a run for it, he asks, "Where are you going?"

Is he stupid? Did those good-looking genes dominate his DNA, giving him no room for common sense?

"I'm getting the hell out of here before I get charged for endangerment of a child!" I shout.

He flinches and then relaxes his face. "Relax. I told you, she's fine."

He seems too tranquil. His smug face, I want to slap it.

"I'm getting out of here," I announce, throwing my hands up in defeat.

I turn to get the hell out of here, but his voice freezes me in time.

"Just like you did the other day?"

I let his words run through every nerve ending of my body, and all I feel is repulsion.

And maybe a little shame. I snap my head in his direction with my jaw hanging. If you could see the steam coming out of my ears, I could be mistaken for some sort of demonic force. "What did you just say to me?"

"You took off the other day. I came downstairs and you were gone," he says, soberly.

I wince, remembering my great escape. However, my face does not falter. I glare at him with every emotion that I'm feeling at the moment, which is currently livid-to-the-bone.

Then I'm reminded of his daughter when she lets out an uncent uncenemonious yawn, startling us both.

"You need to get her to a hospital."

"Don't change the subject."

I take in one deep and long breath. "Call 911 or I will!"

"She," he pauses, looking back at her again. I can tell he's trying to articulate what he's trying to say correctly. At least he's giving an effort now. "Annie has brain injuries," he says.

There's an awkward pause for a second, and I think he realizes my rage isn't subsiding because he inhales nervously. "Which has caused her a pretty severe case of Narcolepsy and a little sleep walking problem."

Oh.

Wait.

Really?

An awkward silence swarms the air between us as I let that sink in.

I break the silence, feeling the need to explain myself. "It's just… I didn't know she had a sleep walking problem or Narcolepsy. She fell into my arms and I just… freaked out."

I wait for him to say something in return, but he doesn't.

So it's not really a surprise when I turn on my heel to leave, I feel his rough fingertips brush my forearm. "Listen, thank you for being there. I've tried to do everything from locking her in her room to sedating her. It's no use. She's very fast and it's so hard to keep an eye on her. So I'm very grateful that you were there," he explains.

"I just wish I knew that before…" I cut myself off before I go any further.

"Before you judged me?" he asks, giving me a sheepish grin. "You must think I'm a pretty bad father."

Then I think of the worst. Did I do this to her?

"Hey, was… was she born with … it?"

"Yes. She's had these injuries since she was little," he says, looking at his daughter with adoration.

She was little? Maybe I didn't do this after all. She wasn't even born when I accidently killed her mother. Maybe this has nothing to do with me!

"Little? How little?"

"Since birth," he answers. "She was in a terrible accident while her mother has pregnant for her."

Well then, there you have it. All. My. Fault.

"I'm so sorry that happened to her," I choke back. I try to keep my cool, but I'm sure he can see right through me.

He grins. "It's not your fault."

A few seconds of silence take their toll as we have a stare off, both of us not blinking once.

"Oh wow," I mutter to myself. I look up at him and say the first thing that comes to mind. "What about an alarm bell?"

An alarm bell? Good job, you moron.

His mouth slowly splits into a grin as if he thinks it's the cutest thing he's ever heard. I cringe under his scrutiny because he's looking at me with tenderness like he would with his daughter. Not like he'd look at a twenty something year old woman with nipples hard as stone because it's freezing this morning.

I then realize what an ass I'm making out of myself and shake it off just like Taylor Swift.

Silence fills the air between us, reminding me that this is the perfect opportunity to run away. It's getting much lighter out and the birds are starting to chirp. I better get on with my paper route before I start to get customer complaints. I offer him a small smile and go to lift up my bike.

As much as I wanted to, I couldn't make friends with this man.

"Oh, about your knee," he points. "You ever think about getting a job where you don't walk around all day?"

I laugh and give a nod. "Oh, I've thought about it," I say. Then my attention deficits disorder attacks, reminding me to give him his paper. "Oh, here." I hand him his morning paper.

He looks surprised to see it but then tucks it under his arm.

I stare at our fingertips as they brush one another with the exchange. When he catches me gawking, he looks at me with inquiring eyes.

It eventually becomes too annoying to tolerate.

"Why are you looking at me like that?" I ask.

"Do you have any experience with nannying?"

"Nannying?" I squeak.

"Yeah, like babysitting," he explains.

"Babysitting," I repeat, enunciating each syllable. In all reality, I try to buy myself some thinking time. I really hope he wasn't asking what I thought that he was. "Well, I don't know who'd want me to watch their kid, but…"

"Annie," he drawls, rolling his eyes.

Annie. Angelina. Was she named after her mother?

"Oh," I nod, slowly. Then I start shaking it from side to side to make things even more confusing for him. "I'm probably not fit for that job."

"And you're fit for this one?" He looks down at my knee, defiantly. The way that he cocks his head is enough to fire me up.

"You really want a recovering alcoholic to watch your child?"

He thinks I'm cute because he's wearing that smile he wears when he looks at his daughter. A smile of adoration. He tilts his head to the side. "I'm a recovering alcoholic and I'm raising her."

"Touché," I say as I pick up my bike again. I notice the chain has come undone. "Shit," I whisper to myself, checking out the damage. "I must have slammed it down too hard."

"Is it broken?" he asks, hovering over my shoulder. He's so close that I smell his delicious aftershave.

"It's an easy fix. I think."

I had no idea what the hell I was talking about.

I put down the kick stand and assess my bike. I can do this. I didn't need his damn help or charity.

I don't even realize that he's running to his garage and back while I'm checking it out because when I look up, he's walking toward me with a tool box.

"You mind?" he asks, kneeling in front of the bike.

There he is on his knees again, looking up at me with those eyes. With tools in his hands. Doing things for me he doesn't have to. He wants to fix everything. He wants to fix my knee and my bike and my crappy work situation, and he doesn't even know me.

But I know him.

"That's not necessary. I can have my step brother fix it if I can't."

He laughs and looks up. "Really, it's okay. Annie's bike gets broken just about every other day."

I bite my lip and try to get used to his sincere side. I don't think it will be that hard.

I'm already glad the rude guy that wouldn't let me anywhere near his child is gone.

Not missing him one bit.

With a few clinks and clanks, he pops my chain back on its track.

"Voila," he gleams.

I can't help but smile. "Thank you. Really."

"It's no problem," he says. "Here, take this wrench. I have another," he adds, handing me his wrench. I grab it, feeling a little bit of him.

There's that shock again. It's so intense this time that I remove my hand as if I've been burned. The wrench ends up falling out of my hands and clinking against the cement, startling us both. He sees I'm flustered and goes to get it, but I beat him to it, grabbing the metal tool quickly.

I really must be looking like an idiot right now. If I open my mouth again I'm afraid I will become a blubbering mess all over again. So I quickly spew out, "Alright, well bye."

It was crucial that I kept my distance from this forbidden fruit, even though I was dying to sink my teeth into him.

I hop on my bike and begin peddling away when I hear his raspy voice.

"I'll see you tomorrow, Ginny."

I peddle away, melting into a big puddle on the way back to my house.

Then I wonder how the hell he knows my name. He introduced himself at A.A., but I don't remember telling him my name.

After the paper route and my dreaded, weekly AA meetings, where I don't see Benson, I'm so overtired that I find myself nodding off on the couch.
 I jump in the shower to wake up, slap myself a few times in the face, then park exactly where I was before and spend the rest of the evening watching Maury reruns. I haven't had this type of luxury in a long time, so I enjoy it way more than the average Joe.
 Seriously, how does someone not know who their baby's daddy is? That's just crazy.
 Watching this show makes me feel a little superior about my life, bearing in mind that I don't have much of one to begin with. It makes me feel grateful for the little I do have and that it's not too much.
 I take a brief nap and eat cereal for dinner. It's not what I had in mind but there's not much to work with. It looks like someone broke in here in the middle of the night and raided all of his kitchen cabinets. Not that I'm complaining, but Jesse could definitely benefit having a woman around.
 Jesse didn't grocery shop. Jesse didn't shop, period. The reason there was such a poor selection was no secret to me. Jesse cared more about his marijuana than his nutrition.
 Around 10 pm, I finally start dozing off.
 Around midnight, I faintly hear Jesse's footsteps enter the apartment. I lift an eye, peaking at him while he makes a bee line to his room. He is in there for about ten minutes, and then he comes and joins me on the couch.
 We're so close that is thigh lightly grazes mine. It seems Jesse has forgotten that I love my personal space, even though I've expressed it to him plenty of times. It's when he leans into me to grab the remote controller that I get a whiff of what choice of cologne he has on. He reeks of pot to the point where I'm pretty sure that I'm getting a contact high through my pores.
 He remains quiet, but his hand isn't afraid to brush up against mine. Jesse always had a habit of talking with his hands and not with his mouth. I kind of liked that little quirk about him.

CHAPTER FOUR

I feel his heated gaze on me, but decide to ignore it and indulge myself into the TV as an alternative.

I try immensely to avoid the sexual tension that is fizzing in the air between us, but I can't.

I can't control it. There's no use.

Whenever Jesse is within a five feet radius of me I feel my insides warm up. It's like Pavlov's dog; I immediately react. I start to fantasize about things between us that haven't happened in a long time. I long for his hands to be all over my body, making me feel good like he used to. It's a craving I'm afraid will never go away.

I zero in on how close he's sitting to me and think of how better it would be if he was closer. So I do something stupid. I move closer. He, of course, takes this as an invitation. Raising his arm, he places his big hand on the nape of my neck and starts to massage it. At first, I tense up.

But then the euphoria and comfort and addiction to Jesse's hands kick in. I tilt my head back and I close my eyes. His hands feel so good.

I relax my muscles and give into his touch. I let him pull the tension out of my neck. I loll my head, giving him better access.

Then I do something I immediately regret. I open my eyes and look into his.

They're gaping at me. Anticipating something. Badly wanting something.

He gently brushes a wayward strand out of my eyes, his stare never wavering.

I scoot closer because I can't get close enough. I know it's wrong but it doesn't feel like it is.

Our faces are so close now that I can feel his warm breath fan against my lips. I think we both know what is happening at this point.

Slow and steady breaths tickling my neck are my undoing. With hooded eyes, I watch his lips softly graze mine, before he starts kissing my jaw, cheeks, nose, and neck.

He kisses me everywhere on my face but my mouth, which annoys me because that's exactly where I want him the most.

Then he grants me my internal wishes. He looks at me, before fluttering his eyes closed and softly latching his mouth to mine. Warily, he tests the waters, exploring the inside of my mouth and eager tongue. Before I know it, his hands are cradling my face and his lips are bruising my face. Hard.

What he gives, I take. When I push, he pulls.

It reminds me of when we were in High School and would watch TV together late at night. He'd look over at me for a while, then back at the television. Then a few seconds later I would look over at him and smile, then look back at the show. We did this for a while until our eyes met in sync.

Then we'd make out until my dad came home from work.

But it wasn't like that this time. As soon as our lips meet, I begin to have my doubts.

Everything in me wants to curl up to him and tell him how much I've missed him. Another part of me wants to push him away and spit on him. They say there's a thin line between love and hate, and I truly believe that now.

There is an undeniable barrier between us now, and I'm not sure either one of us is strong enough to lift it back up.

Where was he when I absolutely needed him? Where was he when I was rotting away in that cell? Seven whole fucking years and I didn't see him once.

I withdraw my mouth and untangle my limbs from his. In confusion, he pauses and finally speaks, "What's wrong?"

"You never visited me," I whisper.

It takes him a minute to formulate a response. He wipes his red and swollen lips and then frowns. "I didn't think you'd want to see me."

"Are you serious?"

"Yes," he says, matching my sardonic tone.

"For seven whole years Jesse, you never visited me. Not even once!" I shout.

CHAPTER FOUR

It's not until I see his face that I realize just how badly I've scolded him. I take my voice down a notch and continue, "I missed you so much. I had no idea where you were, what you were doing, w-who you were with," I start to choke as my voice becomes thick with emotion; "You left me with nothing."

In true Jesse fashion, he keeps busy with his hands by rubbing his face but remains quiet.

"You have nothing to say." It's not a question. I'm talking to myself at this point.

He continues to sit in silence as he hides his face from me. I can't say that I was familiar with Jesse anymore, but the old Jesse would've folded like an accordion and told me everything he thought. This Jesse was so indifferent and so different from the boy I once knew.

I rise to my feet. "I'm just going to go to sleep."

He then lifts his weary gaze up to mine. His tone is a little desperate and astray, "No, Ginny please."

I place my eyes on his and to my surprise; he's looking at me instead of his hands. His lips are still red and swollen from my attack on them. I know I should be looking into his eyes but I can't take my eyes off of what I did. He looks so ripe and beautiful because of me. I hate to admit it to myself, but I love everything about flush Jesse.

"Please sit back down," he whispers.

I glare at him for a minute but then submit to his request. I sit back down, but this time at a safe distance. Or so I think.

He goes to reach for my hand but I slap it away.

He frowns.

Does this asshole still think I want to hold his hand when all I want to do is chop it off with a rusty axe?

As if he's really that hurt. You went seven years without me, buddy.

It's safe to say I've been a little bitter about this subject.

He exhales, speaking softly, "Gin, I was the most depressed I've ever been when you went away." He looks at me for permission to go on, and then continues, "There were some days that I didn't even want to live anymore. I missed you so much that it hurt. I tried to visit you many times, but I had to stop myself because if I was ever going to see you in a place like that, locked up behind bars, and without me," he stops himself and I see him vanish into his own thoughts.

    I gulp a huge chunk of air as I try to put myself in his shoes. It couldn't have been easy on Jesse either. He was the first one that went up to the lady to see the wreckage. He's probably traumatized by that.

    Then I was taken from him for a whole seven years. That couldn't have been easy for him.

    I hadn't thought of it like that.

    Things can never be the same," I whisper.

    "I know," he sighs, his eyes weary.

    The rest of the night, we curl up to one another and enjoy the last time we'll probably ever cuddle. He tells me tales of his life while I was in prison and I show him some of my drawings, which happen to be some of him. He tells me he's going to buy me new supplies.

    Scratch that, he promises me.

    It was a bittersweet night; and it only takes him a couple days for me to wake up to new canvases, different coals, oil paints, and colored pencils. There's a big yellow bow on top with a card that reads, "Draw and paint more. Love, Jesse."

    And with that, I remember why I fell in love with my step brother in the first place.

CHAPTER FIVE

    I wake up next to a sleeping and snoring Jesse. He must have started playing videogames when I fell asleep because the remote control is lying on his lap, upside down. I take a long look at his peaceful face before I quietly untangle myself from his long limbs. Then, I get up and turn off the game system and get ready to do my paper route.

    I decide to get some grocery shopping done because I notice Jesse has nothing in his fridge or cupboards. I go to the corner store hoping they have more than just junk food, but I'm not getting my hopes up.

    I put on my tennis shoes and pull my hair back into a high pony, and brace the scorching humidity. I would have gone to the bigger market, but there was that whole "I don't drive" thing.

    I enter the small market with a ding above the door. It looks like a ghost town in here.

    Good.

    I decide on a couple of soups and a few pieces of fruit that could be riper.

    "Eighteen dollars and twenty five cents," the cashier says, un-enthusiastically, may I add.

    "Oh man, really?" I really am surprised. Inflation was the last thing on my mind when I got out of prison. Things were more expensive, but not by much. I empty my pockets and look for any extra change that I can, but still come up short a dollar.

    He shrugs and looks at me like I'm a total idiot.

    "Okay hold on," I fish through my pockets. I'm sure the people behind me aren't too happy, either. God damn inflation.

    After finally giving him enough money for my ripped off dinner, I walk back home with a paper bag in my arms. There are worse places in New York, but Albany has its bad neighborhoods. The neighborhood seems worn out on the south side of Albany, but I keep to myself and walk at a fast pace.

Eventually walking at a fast pace has its price and my forehead starts to bead with sweat. Damn humidity. Damn summer. I forgot how badly I hated summer.

I can't wait until I get back to the apartment so that I can rip these pants right off and get in my birthday suit.

Suddenly, I spot something out of the corner of my eye. Trying my best not to be obvious, I take a peak. A car pulls up beside me and keeps a steady pace as I walk. I don't give them the satisfaction of turning to face them, but I still try to bend my eyes in ways they don't go.

I pick up the pace to try to get away from them, but it's no use.

Then I hear a familiar, deep velvet voice. "Looks like your knee is feeling better."

My posture straightens as I look over and see Benson, the hot dad, driving the car.

He's decked out in a crisp, white dress shirt and black tie that has been loosened around his neck. It looks like he's had a long day at work, but he still looks sexy as hell. His unkempt, sandy hair looks like he's put a hand through it many times today.

I approach the car with a smirk. "Sorry, I didn't know it was you."

"Hop in. I'll give you a lift home," he jerks his chin, indicating me to get in.

"It's okay, I…" I don't even finish my sentence due to the disapproving look that he's wearing. The air conditioner blasting my heated face is all the indication that I need to persuade me. I take a deep breath and hop into the beautiful, leather interior of his car, placing my grocery bag at my feet.

"You don't like when people do you favors, do you?" he asks, taking off into the street.

"You just don't owe me anything," I swiftly reply. I play with my hands nervously in my lap as they fidget with a mind of their own. I look over at him, sneaking a peak through my long tendrils and even after a long work day he still looks untouchable. Although his tie is loosened and his hair is a

CHAPTER FIVE

little messy, it works for him. He looks controlled as he turns the steering wheel, confident in where he is going.

"It's a nice gesture," he shrugs. "I am a nice person."

I silently laugh to myself and he catches that.

He looks over at me while driving and suppresses a grin of his own. "I'm not?"

"I mean, you weren't the friendliest when I met you, but I'll let that slide," I joke.

He remains silent, but his eyes seem amused by my verbal diarrhea. "I can be a bit rude sometimes without realizing it, I admit that."

"All is forgiven with this ride home," I joke.

"I had to make sure that you weren't a serial killer," he explains. "But then you came by my house with that creepy bike. It took a few days to finally figure it out. I have to be honest; I should have never given you that wrench. You have some sociopathic tendencies that you should really look into."

I gasp, and then quickly realize he's joking when he shoots me a sly grin. I hit his arm playfully.

He laughs and holds his arm mockingly. "See? You're priming me."

"Priming?"

"Hey, you're the serial killer, not me. Don't act like you don't know what priming is."

"You're the one picking up random girls you don't know," I tease.

He frowns. "You think I want to kill you?"

I laugh as if he's ridiculous. "No, of course not."

He smiles with satisfaction and then gives me a second glance. "Where do you live?"

"The Doorman Apartment Complexes."

He nods knowingly and then takes a right turn. I study his profile; his face is relaxed yet hard as stone. For a big, bad ass man with tattoos, his car is incredibly tidy. No thanks to my father and Jesse, I'm used to men being complete pigs. It's a refreshing change to be around a clean man.

Most of the drive is silent until he points to something near my feet. I realize he's pointing at the fruit in my grocery bags. "What are those?"

I look at the small, round fruits in my bag. "Clementine's?"

"Never had one."

"What?"

I am taken aback by his confession. Who the hell has never eaten a Clementine?"

"I just never got around to trying one," he shrugs, his face flushing with embarrassment.

"Well then here is your pay for driving me home." I hand him one.

He looks at the fruit like it is foreign to him. "Do I like, just bite into it?"

I knew he was too good to be true. He's dumber than a pile of bricks.

"No!"

"I'm kidding!" he laughs, shaking his head as he begins to unpeel the orange fruit with his expert hands. At least I'm guessing they are expert.

Then he throws a wedge into his mouth and chews.

I look at him for any reaction and then his eyes start to ease in total satisfaction. He chews and moans into the delicious fruit as his tongue darts around, savoring the flavors. He looks over in my direction and freezes in embarrassment.

I burst into laughter. *This guy is cute.*

"Oh man, that's good," he says; his mouth completely full.

I start to laugh because I find his appreciation for small things incredibly cute

"I can't believe you've never had a Clementine before," I mutter.

He grins and then lifts his head defiantly. "Oh come on, Miss Perfect. There has to be something you've never done before."

Miss perfect? My eyes transition into little slits as I shoot him a death glare.

CHAPTER FIVE

I sigh. "There are a lot of things I've never done, actually. I don't know, I guess I missed the boat on a lot of things but eating a Clementine?"

I watch his mouth twist as he tries to hide his amusement. He takes another right turn in silence.

"So, what have you never done before?" he prods.

Oh God, where do I start?

"Let's see," I say, tapping my chin in thought. I imagine all of the wonderful perks of turning 18; a luxury I never was able to experience. "I've never been to a casino, I've never been in an adult store, and I've never been to a bar." I list them off my fingers. "I've never bought a pack of cigarettes, not that I'd want to."

Slamming his breaks to a halt, he quickly glances over as his eyes widen. I flail my hands out to the dashboard and look at him in panic. "Oh my God, are you okay?"

He looks like he's seen a ghost. His dead wife, perhaps. "You've never been to a bar?"

"I, uh, no." I got nothing.

"You're a recovering alcoholic."

Of course, there's that minor little detail.

"I did most of my drinking at home," I shrug.

"Well, I wish I could bring you to a bar, but I can't."

I laugh. "Trust me. I'll pass."

"But I'll bring you to the next best thing," he says, steering back into the street.

And away we go.

"Hey everyone, it's this girl's 21st birthday!" Benson hollers to all of the patrons as we walk into the most colorful place I've ever seen.

It's not the type of bar that you'd think, but it definitely looks like a bar. Oxygen masks and tubes hang from the bar's ceiling with fluorescent lights shining down on signs that credit the oxygen flavors. The regulars are all young people, from my age to Benson's or maybe even older. They all wear their nasal cannulas and talk with each other as if they're already a 12 pack deep.

I'm at an Oxygen bar.

He looks at me, his eyes crinkled in excitement. "All right, let's get you hooked up!"

He places his hand on the small of my back and leads me to the bar, where a young woman stands behind it with tattoos covering her arms. The way she's looking at him makes me feel funny inside. It's a feeling I can't quite pin point.

"This is amazing," I gasp, smiling in awe.

It's hard to think just a week ago this man was giving me death glares from his front porch and prohibiting his daughter from going anywhere near me. Now I was hitching rides from him and he was throwing me pseudo birthday parties. We were becoming fast friends.

I begin letting my mind expand for the worse. This man is a forbidden fruit. He is my Clementine, and I will never get the chance to have a taste.

I already know him, and deep down he knows who I am too. This shouldn't bother me more than I let it, but it does. Every time I find the opportunity to walk away and never turn back, those pacific blue irises burn into mine and suddenly nothing matters but us.

He nudges me with his elbow, referring my thoughts into the now. "What will it be, Birthday girl?"

I lean in to look at the menu, but I end up getting two nostrils full of Benson. "Is there a choice of what type of oxygen I get?"

"Yes," he nods, pointing to the menu. "There are different Oxygen flavors."

"Mint green? Scented candles? Who makes these things up?" I ask, scrunching my face.

He laughs. "Bayberry is my favorite."

"I'll have what you have." I close the menu.

"Bayberry it is," he decides, closing his menu. Then he signals the bartender over who happens to be absolutely gorgeous and everything that I'm not. She has long, bleached blonde hair that reaches her butt with colorful tattoos covering her skin. When she reaches us, she leans into Benson closely, checking him out. He whispers something into her year and she nods eagerly, giving him a wink. She gives him another look over before walking away. As she gets our orders, I focus on the terrible feeling in the pit of my stomach.

I'm angry. I'm feeling territorial. Why the hell was she all over him?

I cringe when I realize it and then curse myself because I'm pretty sure what I just felt was jealousy.

All of the blood leaves my face, giving me a ghost like appearance. I wipe my sweaty hands on the front of my jeans and take a deep breath. He notices my unease and puts his hand on the small of my back. "Let's continue our game."

"Game?"

A game could be risky. Truth or Dare? Strip Poker? No way.

"Yes, a game," he answers. "Why, you scared or something?"

"I'm not scared!"

"So let's play a game!"

"We're so not playing a game."

He sighs as the sexy bartender brings our oxygen over. As much as I want a restraining order against her for Benson right now, I silently thank her for the distraction.

"How else am I going to find out things about you?" he asks.

"Why would you want to know anything about me?"

"Let's just say you have my interest."

"That's weird," I mutter.

"Why?"

"Uh, let's start with the fact that I'm not that interesting!"

A playful smirk ghosts his lips. "You look plenty interesting."

Screw the Oxygen; I want to inhale this man instead.

I sigh and relax my shoulders. "Fine, what game are we playing?"

I couldn't tell if he was coming onto me or just incredibly nice. I can't remember the last time someone has given me compliments without even giving me them.

"Never have I ever. Continuation from our ride," he says.

"We were playing never have I ever?"

"Well, kind of," he admits, grabbing the oxygen masks and handing me one. "One inhale equals one hit, okay"

I place the delicate cannula under my nose and immediately feel like I'm floating on water. My lungs feel fresh and my breathing is extraordinarily better. "Is this game healthy for, you know, people like us?"

"You mean alcoholics?"

I nod sheepishly.

He smirks but doesn't answer my question. Then unceremoniously, he places his nasal cannula under his nose.

We look at each other and start laughing at how ridiculous we look.

I decide to take the first turn.

"Never have I ever been to a place like this." I gesture around the room. Without thinking, I inhale deeply. It's the easiest breath I've ever taken in my life. It feels effortless. Then the high comes, but it's not the type of high I was expecting. A comfortable amount of euphoria pumps through me and I begin to feel a little light headed. I grab the edge of the bar for leverage.

However, it's very short lived. Within seconds, I'm back to normal.

"Weird," I comment.

It's just then that I notice he's watching my every move, a faint smile ghosting his lips.

"Okay, my turn," he says, clapping his hands together as if he can't wait. "Never have I ever eaten a Clementine before today."

After that, he smiles mischievously and measures my reaction.

"Hey come on, that's cheating!" I laugh and then inhale the fruity oxygen. "Who hasn't ever eaten a Clementine? Seriously?"

He shrugs. "Your turn."

I roll my eyes. "Never have I ever been a serial killer!"

He laughs and both of us just stare at each other without inhaling.

"Well, that turn sucked," I mutter.

He shrugs. "Sometimes monsters hide in plain sight."

I don't smile because he isn't. I don't think it's meant to be a joke.

"My turn." All humor has left his face.

"Only if you do an honest never have I ever!"

"Fine," he sighs. "Never have I ever," he pauses as he stares at something on my face. I think it's my eyes. He won't look away. "Never have I ever seen eyes that green. What color is that anyways?"

"Green," I shyly respond. "You're cheating again."

He shakes his head and laughs. "No, there's a yellow ring in the middle."

"If I said hazel, would that make you feel better?"

He shakes his head. "No, that doesn't do them justice."

I let him bluntly stare into my eyes as I melt into a puddle right in front of him.

"May I go again?" he asks in a deep, throaty voice.

I give him a timid nod.

"Never have I ever seen a girl who blushes so easily," he inhales.

As if right on cue, I blush vermillion. When I look up at him, he's chuckling. How dare he put me under the hot seat like this? I should make him turn vermillion, but I wouldn't even know where to start.

Never have I ever been the hottest guy alive.

We're interrupted by a few patrons, thank God. Because if I had to look into those eyes any longer, who knows what would have happened?

Afterward, A few people join us and we have a good time talking to them. It seems like the more talking Benson and I do, the more comfortable we get around each other.

We're not drunk. We're not stoned. We're simply high on life.

I can feel my body start to tingle with euphoria when I feel the tip of his hand brush mine. After the people we are talking to leave, silence takes over the space between us.

"It's good to talk to someone who knows what I'm going through," he says softly.

I look him in the eye. "Likewise."

"I don't really know you, so I don't know how you take a look at things. But, all I know is, being an alcoholic is a huge dark cloud hanging over me all of the time. People assume that's all there is to me. It's good to just have fun and not think about that sometimes."

"You're more than your disease, Benson." I urge, squeezing his hand once.

"I'm glad you see that. A lot of people don't, though. People like us, we're labeled for life."

"I know exactly what you mean."

He orders us another tank of oxygen and I choose Peppermint this time. He chooses Bayberry again.

"We need some music!" I feel like I just came up with the world's greatest idea.

Enough of the sulking. I'm going to spruce this party up again.

"Easy now, killer," he mutters as he stills me with a hand, making my body jolt. I look at his hand on my bare skin and begin to feel all of these urges. Urges that will do nothing but get me in trouble.

"Where's the Juke box?" I ask.

His beautiful blues rise to a spot above my left shoulder as he nods behind me.

"Be right back!" I inform him.

I scurry over to the music box and think of what to play. After what seems like a lifetime of fiddling with the screen, apparently they've done away with all buttons and you just touch the screen now, I settle on something a little more relaxing.

"Hey" by the Pixies.

The oxygen clears my head, yet I'm still unable to think straight. I begin to feel a little lightheaded from it and squeeze my eyes shut as I grab the nearest wall to steady myself.

That's when a hand curls around my lower waist. Whoa, is that Benson?

I open my eyes and turn around to an unfamiliar face. A good looking face, but unusual. He smiles from ear to ear, showcasing his overly white teeth. He has big brown eyes that crinkle at the corners as if he smiles too much. He's the definition of an all American boy. He looks like he belongs in a frat house, wearing pastel colors with a paddle in his hand and a cheap beer in the other.

"Hey, I'm Alex," he introduces himself, outstretching his hand.

"Ginny." I shake his hand, unenthusiastically. This guy is a red flag all over.

Why do I attract the red flags? But, you like Benson's red flag.

"You come around here often?" he asks, raking a hand through his auburn locks. This man looks like he spends more time in front of the mirror than I do. Maybe "man" is putting it too strong. He's a man-boy. Probably a gamer, too.

Please God, make this man boy go away.

Maybe if I tell him there's a Halo convention next door he will make himself scarce.

"I'm here with someone," I say, cringing.

There, that wasn't so bad.

"She's with her boyfriend," Benson interrupts as he anchors his strong and decorated arms around my waist. They feel heavy and comforting and safe. I become very aware that they are there when they start caressing the skin that's on show between my waistband and tee shirt. It's safe to say I'm nothing more than a bundle of nerves right now.

I look at Benson, dumbfounded. He grins, noticing the shock on my face.

It's a shit-eating grin too.

He lifts his hands possessively to my biceps and ghosts his fingertips up and down them. I shiver at his touch and for the first time in a long time, I'm really turned on.

So I play along by grabbing his hand that's currently slung over my shoulder. "Yeah, this is my... boyfriend."

In your dreams, Quinn.

Alex nods slowly, his eyes squinting with suspicion. "We're just celebrating our anniversary."

"Oh," Alex says, questionably. "How long have you been together?"

"Six," I start to say, but Benson cuts me off with, "Months. Six wonderful months."

He looks at me adoringly and plays with a strand of my raven hair, curling it around his long fingers. I'm not sure I'm going to be able to pick my jaw off the floor afterwards.

Alex nods and wishes us well, then stalks away with his head down. When he's gone, I instantly untangle myself from Benson's hard body and gasp at him. I look at him with disdain and shake my head. I still can't believe what he just did.

The longer I stare, the more my brain takes me away to a different land. That beautiful, perfect and decorated body was just all over me a moment ago. I snap out of it and nearly lift my brows up to my hairline. "Six months?"

"You were going to say six years," Benson mutters, but his eyes are on something else. He's making sure Alex is completely gone. After a few seconds, his big blues flicker back to mine.

"What's wrong with six years? That's a strong relationship!"

"Six years is long and boring. Six months is new and adventurous."

I can't help but to laugh and shake my head.

"He walked away from you, didn't he?"

I swallow a lump in my throat at his choice of words. A lot of people have walked away from me, but I'll save him the sob story.

"Thanks for the save." I nudge him with my elbow.

I try to think of how awkward I must come across to him. I put on a cool smile, but meanwhile, my blood rushes to my face thinking about how he had his hands on me.

CHAPTER FIVE

I wonder what's going through his mind. He seems so calm and collected. Not a blemish covers his sculpted features; not an inch of him is given away.

He looks just as put together as he was when he picked me up. How the hell does he do that?

As much as I've wanted to walk away tonight, all it took was our eyes colliding to defer that trigger. We leave the oxygen bar laughing over our horrible rendition of a couple in love when I see him going to get in the driver's seat of his car.

"I'm just getting your groceries," he calls, waving a bag. "Care to walk it home?"

"I'd love to." All of a sudden, it's easier to breathe after that. Even though we're not drunk or high, I'm relieved that we don't have to drive home. This means I get to spend a little more time with him.

"I don't know why, but I'm in the mood to walk today."

"Too high on life to drive?" I tease.

He grins. "That's exactly what it is."

The walk home is easy for me and all work for Benson. The first half of the walk is spent by Benson talking about all of the pretentious songs that people play at the oxygen bar. He has me laughing harder than I have in a long time.

I'm laughing so hard that I need to stop a few times to catch my breath. I am panting, breathless with laughter and loving every minute of it.

The second portion of the walk, I'm not proud of what I make him do. He notices that I'm limping on my bad knee, so he gives me a lift, piggy back style, all the way home.

This man constantly surprises me at every turn and I let him know it in my euphoric state. "You surprise me, Benson Daniels."

Shit, did I just say that out loud?

He suddenly stops to a halt with me still hanging off his back.

I wiggle off his back and he turns around with an inquisitive look on his face. Shit, did I say the wrong thing? What the hell is wrong with me?

"How'd you know my last name?" He's barely audible and his eye is arched with a notion.

I smile slowly. Then I show him his license that I slipped out of his pocket while I was on his back. "Drunken oxygen curiosity, we'll say."

However, let's face it, I already knew his name. I toss it back to him with a grin. "You better hide this more efficiently, because I'm pretty good at pick pocketing."

"So serial killing isn't your crime after all," he teases and laughs dryly.

I give him a mocking scowl, but its cut short because, without warning, he snatches me up and over his shoulder and starts running.

When we arrive at the apartment, he gently places me on my feet.

I internally frown, but on the outside, I shoot him a lazy grin. Two can play this game, acting like we're both unaffected by what's going on between us.

Maybe it's all in my head. I almost cry at the thought.

Thinking about the scary thought is enough to make my breath hitch. He notices and softens his expression.

He's the first to break the awkward silence and stare off. "Did you have a good night?"

I lick my lips nervously, not quite looking him in the eye. "Absolutely. But, you didn't have to…"

He cuts me off with a groan and rolls his eyes. "I didn't have to do that. That's what you were going to say, right?"

I give him a shy nod and absently bite my lip.

"I wanted to," he whispers, looking so hard into my eyes that it burns. I feel like he knows every little detail about me now, which scares me senseless. At this point, I knew better than to have relations with him. It wasn't in our cards.

But like I said, I'm senseless right now. So I stare at him back and hope the longing in my chest doesn't show in my eyes.

Of course, he notices. Once he sees it, he takes his thumb and reluctantly brushes it down my cheek, then to my chin, lifting it up. "What did I tell you earlier?"

CHAPTER FIVE

I don't answer.

"Your face gives you away."

I look down at my feet in embarrassment but then I notice something. I'm smiling.

I'm fucking smiling.

"You turn a beautiful shade of red when you're nervous," he observes. "It's quite adorable."

His expression turns into intensity and anticipation, his eyes dancing around my face. It's as if his eyes are magnetic to mine when they finally target my mouth and ask for permission. My mouth suddenly parts with a spat of anxious air, causing him to take a step back.

Shit.

So I do what anyone else would do. I just pretend it didn't happen.

"Thanks for the ride," I quickly blurt out. Awkward.

"Thanks for the apricot," he shoots back. He makes it sound like it was such a better gift.

"Clementine," I correct.

He stares at me for a few minutes without a word. I don't know how he does that. He's quiet as a church mouse but his eyes are screaming, saying it all.

"Will you make it home okay?" I ask.

He ignores my question. "Have you really never been to a bar before?"

"Honestly, I haven't."

"Well, I'm just sorry I couldn't give you a real 21st birthday. My addiction kind of gets in the way of that."

"Mine too," I lie. "It's not my 21st birthday anymore."

"I know," he grins.

I smile and go to turn on my heel when I feel his fingertips brush my arm.

Before I can turn around, he grabs my arm rather roughly and turns me himself. His eyes are intense as he reels me into him. Slowly and torturously, he pulls me in. He's going to finish what he started. I look at the contact of our skin through our hands, first, and then raise my eyes to meet his. They look cautious now, but none the less, he still wants something.

"Did you ever consider what I asked you?"

I let out a breath I forgot I was holding. This is not what I was expecting at all.

"I'm a busy man, and I'd be happy with offering you a job watching my daughter."

This is what he's been nerve racked to ask me. I should have known.

"You'd make much more money than at that God-forsaken Newsie's job you have now."

I let out a small snort, loving his reference. Newsie's job.

Jesus Christ, did I just snort in front of him?

I lift my head slowly to check out his reaction. He looks more amused than disgusted with my less than lady like actions.

I give him an inadequate grin. "I'm sorry, I can't."

"Oh, Okay," he simply says.

Wait, that's it?

"I don't really have any experience," I explain.

"It's okay. I understand," he waves his hand in dismissal. "It's just that Annie thinks highly of you, and believe it or not, she's a picky little girl. She's specifically requested you. And with your knee and all, it just seems like a rational thought. Forgive me." He smiles, but I hate the formality of it all. We just finished an extremely fun night and now he's being so business like.

I scratch my head in thought. "How many days a week would it be?"

I'm not quite looking at him, although I do expect an answer.

So, when he doesn't answer, I glance up at him. He's not looking at me either and he's very deep in thought. His dark brows perch and his full lips are in a tight line and barely showing.

"Benson, are you okay?" I ask, softly.

Then he takes a step back, robotically. It's as if a switch as gone off in his eyes and they're closed for the night. It's as if he just realized something he didn't want to know.

CHAPTER FIVE

"Benson?" I wave my hand in front of his face. "How many days a week?"

He looks up at me absent mindedly as if he's had an epiphany. "I'm sorry."

"Sorry for what?" I seriously have no idea what he's thinking, and he's starting to scare me.

"I, I don't know why I'm here. I have, I have to go." He says it so quickly and quietly that I barely hear it. I hope that he isn't thinking of who I think he is.

Me.

I take a step towards him and he immediately takes two steps backward.

"I have to go," he repeats, immediately turning around and walking as far as away from me as he can. No explanation, no nothing. He just turns around and walks away.

When he reaches the end of the street we're on, I could swear I hear him say, "I'll give you a call soon."

"But you don't have my number!" I shout.

I'm sure he hears me, but he doesn't turn around. Instead, he keeps walking.

Far, far away from me; exactly where he should be.

CHAPTER SIX

I swallow a hard lump in my throat as I approach his house the next day.

I need answers. I need to know why he ran like that.

Due to my father's ill reputation, I wasn't the biggest fan of lying. Omitting information is a form of lying and deep down I know that, but I feel it's the right decision in this case.

However, one thought keeps imbedding itself in my brain. Was he omitting any information as well?

What's behind those blue eyes? Why did he walk away from me the other night without so much of an explanation? I was dying to figure it out, so I told Jesse I was going for a walk and would be back later.

The sun is out and is blasting UV rays onto my skin; burning it a raw pink. The green grass is like a blanket in front of the tall, white house; groomed and level. The flowers are cropped and ready for pollination as I spot the only sign of life in sight. I duck my head as the buzzing sound gets louder and louder in my ear.

The bees swarm over their domestic masterpiece.

My eyes do a little swarming of their own as I glance at the driveway and notice he's home. I walk up to his door and hesitate to knock, thinking of all of the reasons that I shouldn't.

There's a window to the right and there he is, thinking hard, looking like a broody, beautiful bastard.

He can't see me, but I can see him.

When Annie catches his attention, his whole demeanor changes. His hazy eyes crinkle at the corners as he smiles and plays with her.

I'm actually thankful for the space right now. His eyes are my ruin, whether they're shining or dreary. Anytime they set on me, they are the black holes of my universe, recklessly sucking me in.

I sigh and decide I should probably leave.

He's avoiding me, and I'm willing to bet the reason why. He recognized something in me the other day. He

CHAPTER SIX

recognized me. He knows who I am and what I've done to his family.

My hair is completely different now. My once cropped neon pink hair is a long curtain of raven hair. My piercings are gone. My face has sculpted out of my baby face.

But eyes, they never change.

I turn around and start walking away.

I bring me and my bowl of cereal onto the couch and next to Jesse. Curling up, I try to get into a comfortable position and relax. I'm not proud of my stalking tendencies towards Benson and I'm sure it shows. I'm so stressed out about the situation that I forget to acknowledge Jesse.

As the couch sinks in next to him he shifts his positioning but doesn't acknowledge me either.

I am so not in the mood today.

I shoot him a glare but his eyes are reduced to two little slits and settled on the television. His posture is as straight as a stick all of a sudden; he's uncomfortable.

We spend some time watching TV in silence while I eat and he smokes. Then unexpectedly, I feel his eyes on me.

"Where were you yesterday?" I hear him ask.

I toss my bowl on the coffee table in front of us. It's after then that I realize I've done it too roughly.

"What?" I jab.

"I know you work, but I also know your paper routes are in the morning. Where were you last night?"

I scratch my head, purely annoyed by Jesse's innocent questions. Do I want to be the first to initiate a fight or do I swallow my anger and answer the questions? Before I can even think about it, I'm already marching to the beat of my own drum.

"You're not the boss of me, Jesse. What I do is none of your,"

He cuts me off. "It is, especially when you live with me."

This annoys every fiber of my being, so I get up and take my bowl to the sink. After that's done, I'm not quite ready to go back and face him, so I lean against the sink with my head bowed.

"What do you want, Jesse? You want me to not have a life again?"

"Of course not, but would it hurt you to let me in it a little?"

With that, I stay silent. He has a point, I have been avoiding him.

"I'd just like you to be honest with me."

"Honest with you? I haven't lied about anything." I feel like I'm being accused of something and I'm not sure of what.

"Are you seeing someone?" Ah, there it is.

The one simple question.

And I still can't bring myself to be honest with him.

"I mean, if you are its completely," he begins, but I cut him off with a bitter laugh.

"Definitely not!" I glare at him.

"Will you let me finish!" he shouts. He closes his eyes briefly, sighs and continues, "If you are seeing someone, I'm okay with it. Despite what you think, Ginny, I want you to be happy."

"I want that for you too," I whisper, suddenly feeling emotional. Jesse always brings out this side of me. He knows me better than anyone. He understands me better than anyone. And most of the time, I think he loves me more than anyone.

There is an awkward silence for a moment until I see Jesse's face split into a grin. That's all I need. Whenever I see that kind of smile from him, I know we're okay.

We continue to watch television a little until he has to go to work and I'm left home alone. I take a look around the chaotic apartment. I decide to do some cleaning while he's working because I cannot stand living in this kind of environment. I know it's a funny thing to say, but I always kept a clean cell.

CHAPTER SIX

I start in the kitchen. I wipe down all of the counters which are coated with sticky substance and pot leaves and twigs. I almost gag at the smell, which could be easily mistaken for vomit. It probably is vomit, but I continue washing his dishes and try to ignore the smell.

After all of the dishes are done and put away, I open the fridge and as usual, there's nothing to eat. I open the freezer and spot one lone bottle of vodka lay on its side. I shrug and take it out, twisting the cap off and gulp some of its contents.

Officer Mitchell did my urine test this week already so I didn't have to worry about being bombarded with another test. I station myself on the couch with the bottle in my hand, taking a swig occasionally as I fish through the cable.

By the time a quarter of its contents are consumed, my chest begins warming up; my head tingles with euphoria. I steal a picture of Jesse from his room and take my charcoals out that he bought me. This is what I always did to pass time in Prison. I guess old habits die hard.

A few minutes into sketching Jesse's shapely lips, I look at the joint laying in the ashtray on the table and think about picking it up.

Thank God I don't get far with that because a minute later I hear a light knock at the door. I stop what I'm doing and head for the door. Okay, more like stumble to the door. God, what if it's Officer Mitchell?

I start to think of the worst as I look into the door's peephole.

It's Benson and his big, distorted head. He even looks good with a distorted head. I really need to stop drinking.

Then another thought occurs to me. Its mother fucking Benson! Benson, who thinks I'm a recovering alcoholic. I open the door slowly to his inquisitive face. He wants something, but I'm not sure of what.

"You remember where I live?" I ask, genuinely surprised.

"I just walked you home yesterday," he reminds me. He at least seems more amused than irritated.

I shoot him a lopsided grin and stand to the side to let him in, but he doesn't move an inch. Instead, we're having an intense staring contest across the threshold of Jesse's apartment.

Even though a small breeze blows into the apartment and through my hair, I'm feeling warm inside due to the sight of him. He's here for me. I was on his mind. Me.

Then it's all accompanied by sheer panic. My palms begin to sweat and my shoulders are shaking vigorously. Where did I put the bottle of Vodka? Oh God, he can probably see it.

He must really think I'm a piece of work.

However, he doesn't seem to suspect anything as he stands in the doorway, big and tall. Towering me by almost a foot, he looks down his nose at me with his hands casually shoved in his pockets. I never realized how tall or big he is until now. He's actually quite intimidating when he's not wearing his trademark megawatt smile.

His dirty blonde hair is in all directions as if he just rolled out of bed. I'm not complaining, because it's sexy as hell. I can't stop staring. He's also wearing a brown leather pilot jacket with wool on the inside. It's very *Brokeback Mountain*.

I laugh at the thought.

"What's so funny?" he asks.

I shake my head once, wearing the tightest smile on my face. It seems I've turned into a mute in front of this man.

I try my best not to look like the wasted piece of shit that I am but I don't think it is working. He has the damn nerve to wear that knowing smirk as if I'm transparent. Although he looks amazing and unaffected, I can tell he's anxious; his hands balling into fists and then flexing back out. His hair reflects off the sun, which accent his butter cream highlights. However, what makes my insides tug is the dark stubble shadowing his jaw. I nearly have to remember to breathe because the contrast is so beautiful and perfect for him.

There's an eerily silence between us before his eyes dart past me and into the apartment. "Are you alone?"

My best bet is that he is wondering if I live with anyone. Just when I'm about to answer, he asks again. "Ginny. Are you alone?"

I shake my head obediently, giving him the answer he wants.

Then, I absorb his form. I've never appreciated the male form the way that I do with Benson's. His thin white shirt hugs his ridged abdomen and widespread shoulders just like I'd want to. I was in prison for years, so this is like free candy to me.

It takes me nearly infinity to peel my eyes away from his broad chest and back to his navy eyes.

Ultimately, my sexy daydream is ruined when I unceremoniously burp up an air pocket that reeks of alcohol. I immediately slap my hand over my lips as my eyes widen in embarrassment.

He lets out a robust laugh and shakes his head.

"Why won't you come in?" I ask, almost offended.

"Because I need to get back to Annie," he explains, raking a hand through his disheveled hair. "I just came to," his voice tapers off as his eyes settle on something behind me.

Shit, does he see the bottle?

Quickly, I look behind me, my heart pounding frantically and relentlessly. Nonetheless, all I spot is the unfinished sketch of Jesse on the coffee table.

"You're an artist?" he asks.

I turn back to him and grin. "I am."

"Where'd you learn to draw like that?"

In prison.

I shrug and shoot him a small smile. "Here and there."

He stares at the drawing, not uttering a word. The more he stands here with nothing to say, the more uncomfortable I become. With all honesty, I am ultimately confused by his presence.

He gets the hint and sighs. "What happened the other day?" He looks at me for permission to continue, so I nod. "Something happened to me that night. Something got into my head and... I didn't want to ruin our wonderful night. Remember when I told you I can be rude sometimes?"

I nod.

"Well, that was definitely one of those times. Sometimes I can get a little too lost in my own head. It's probably something you should know about me if we're going to be friends."

Friends? He wants to be friends?

He's apologizing for something that I've probably caused him

I wish I could tell him who I was. I wish I wasn't lying to my friend. My only friend.

I shift my stance because I've realized my leg is completely numb from putting all of my weight on it. Then, I play with the door handle and avoid all eye contact and human interaction. "It's no problem," I mumble.

There's that eerily silence again.

"You sure you don't want to come in?" I offer.

He portrays himself to look like he's in a rush, but I know he's not. "No, I have to go now. I left Annie with my dad and she can't be with him long."

"Oh okay."

"Well, see you around," he says noncommittally.

I watch him turn on his heel to leave when something takes over me. "Benson?"

He turns around immediately with a hopeful expression.

"Do, um, do," I stutter. "Do you still need a nanny?" I ask, awkwardly.

He looks taken aback by my bold question. Better yet, I think I see a sliver of excitement in his eyes. Maybe a little relief too.

"I do."

"I can do weekends."

A slow smile creeps upon his face. "So, I'll see you tomorrow at five pm?"

"Sure, I can do that," I respond a little too fast. He leans in the door way, eyes inquisitive, and then does something that catches me off guard. He hesitantly tucks a strand of my ebony hair behind my ear. After tucking it, he lets his fingers brush down the rosy skin of my cheek.

I wait for him to say something but he doesn't say a word.

I'm paralyzed by his actions. All I can do is gawk at him like an idiot. Apparently, I've lost my ability to speak and have human interaction with others. He notices the deep shade of crimson that I've turned with just the look of his eyes, and with that, he smiles, he turns, he leaves.

After he's gone, I'm left touching my sensitive and cherry skin where he touched it over and over.

After Benson leaves, I get more housecleaning done but am majorly distracted.

It's kind of hard to ignore what just happened. I'm officially the nanny to the daughter of the woman I killed seven years ago. I'm kicking myself in the ass the more I think about it.

What the hell was I thinking?

As I wage a war inside my head, I opt for the roof of our apartment complex with just my headphones and hindered spirit.

I figure I'd let the music do the talking tonight. I need to be as far away from human interaction as I possibly can. I just had gotten out of the loneliest place on Earth, and I was already running from anyone in sight.

I lay out a blanket and sprawl out until I am comfortable. As I tuck an ear bud in my ear, I hear a metal clanking against metal down below me.

At least that's what it sounds like.

I dart my eyes towards the ladder that I put on the side of the house and see it moving around.

I was correct.

In sheer panic, I stand up quickly and get ready to punch someone in the face. But instead, I see who it is and ease my stance.

"Julia." I put down my fists. The presence of her makes me somewhat speechless.

Julia was one of my best friends growing up and she was in the car with me on that tragic night. I haven't heard from her in seven years. She still looks the same. Same light brown complexion and slender figure. Her chocolate hair is a little longer if anything.

She looks at me with her big brown eyes and smiles.

Julia was the top of our class and I heard she went to California after we graduated to become a doctor. I can't necessarily blame her for not being there for me. While I was rotting away in prison, she was making something of herself.

"Hey Genevieve, Jesse told me you were up here," she says, walking up to me. At first, I take a step back because I'm shocked to see her, but then I charge forward and give her a big and awkward hug. It's been a long time.

"Julia." I can't get the shock out of my voice.

"It's so good to see you," she says.

When I don't say anything, she adds, "I'm sorry I never visited you."

"Don't be sorry," I whisper. Sitting down on the cold shingles, I pat the space next to me. She sits down and takes a good, long look at me.

"You know, Jesse and Lacey didn't visit me either," I tell her. "I mean I'm living with Jesse now, but I came to him." I take a deep breath and continue, "Haven't heard from Lacey either."

I look at her and then notice that there is something heavily weighing on her mind.

Something is off. She knows something that I don't. "What is it, Julia?" I prod.

She gives me a sympathetic smile. "This is not why I came over. I came here to apologize for my lack of friendship and my hopes to rekindle it. But now I have to tell you something."

"Tell me what?"

She bites her lip. "You can't freak out. Promise me you won't be mad at me for not telling you sooner. I felt guilty."

"Just spit it out." I'm starting to get annoyed.

CHAPTER SIX

"Lacey and Jesse didn't visit you probably because they probably felt guilty too."

"Because of the accident," I assume. I flash her a smile, thinking that will somehow change her response.

She shakes her head no. "I wish it were that simple." She looks at me with consideration, biting her damn lip nearly raw. "They got together not long after you went away, Genevieve."

My heart drops into my stomach. What did she just say?

I scratch my chin. "Like, to hang out?"

"No." She shakes her head. "They fell in love. They were together for five years."

My smile begins to fade as the proverbial ball from outfield smacks me right in my face.

What?

Later that night, I walk into the apartment with a vengeance; stomping my heavy feet and brows low like a caveman. I fly past Jesse, hoping he doesn't so much as say a peep to me. I'm suddenly in the mood to castrate him.

He inhales the smoke out of his bong while playing video games. What the hell is new? Is this all he ever does?

He lifts his drowsy gaze to mine and shoots me a lopsided, goofy grin. He tries to pass the bong to me and I give him a disgusted look, yanking my ear buds out.

He tilts his head in confusion.

"I get drug tested every week, you know that," I hiss.

He wedges his bong between his legs and lifts his hands in surrender. "Geez, I'm sorry."

"Like hell you are," I spat.

His eyes widen in disbelief as he takes another hit of his bong. Then he sets down the glass cylinder and reclines back on the couch. "What's the hells the matter with you?"

"Nothing the hell is the matter with me," I mock him.

"Are you on your period or something?" He puts on a suspicious look.

An eerily silence fills the room as my eyes transform into little slits.

Would you get a load of this guy?

I feel like slapping this prick in the face, but I make the careful decision not to. Instead, I turn around and stalk into the kitchen to get a drink of water. I take a sip and then I hear him walk up behind me.

Feeling him behind me feels familiar, but I don't let him know it. I don't even give him the satisfaction of turning around, face to face.

"What's wrong with you, Gin?" The guy actually sounds concerned.

I slam my water down and turn around, my furious eyes meeting his. "Why do you even care?"

"I thought we were over this!"

I interrupt him and place my hands on my hips. "Correction, you're over this. You're moving on with your life and that's great for you!" I choke back on my tears, continuing to shout, "But me? You don't know what I went through, and you will never! So stop trying to act like you do!"

He glares at me for a second before saying anything. He looks like he is starting to get offended. I can't say I blame him. I realize this all is coming out of left field, but it feels so good to get out in the open and let him know how I feel.

"I might not know what you went through, Ginny. But I do care. A lot. Or else you wouldn't be here," he says, cautiously.

I sigh and roll my eyes. "Never mind, Jesse."

I begin to walk away when his curious voice stops me. "Do you need to be fucked?"

My eyes pop open. "Excuse me?"

"Listen. Just because I haven't seen you in seven years, doesn't mean I've forgotten how horny that you get around the time of your period," he mutters.

I swear I can feel the steam blow out of my ears. I can't believe this is the same Jesse that I fell in love with many years ago. He thinks he knows everything about me after all these years, after not visiting me once? The nerve.

"I don't need you in that way anymore, Jesse," I say, deadpan. I know my words cut him deep, but I can't help but to feel enjoyment in seeing him flinch from them.

What was once satisfaction quickly turns into a pang of guilt in my chest that I can't get rid of. I suddenly am unable to look him in the eye.

This time when I turn around to leave, he doesn't stop me.

I've decided I'm going to sleep on the roof tonight.

The next day at five p.m. sharp, I stay true to my word and show up to nanny for Annie Daniels, daughter of Benson Daniels. Benson, the man who I have made unlikely friends with. Benson, who I can't stop obsessing over like I'm still a thirteen year old girl with rainbow colored braces.

His beautiful indigo eyes light up like a Christmas tree as soon as he spots me at the front of his door. To my surprise, he doesn't seem to be apprehensive like I am. I'm shaking with anxiety from my head to my toes. My breath hitches as soon as we lock eyes; he looks stunning, as usual. His long legs are encased in a fitting pair of black slacks and topped in a sinister purple dress shirt. His dirty blonde locks are in all directions, but it works for him. I've never met anyone with a better case of bed head.

I have to nearly pick my jaw off the floor and rehinge it back into place.

I become aware of a few tattoos that peak out from underneath his sleeves that I hadn't noticed before, propelling little waves of excitement down my spine. One particularly stands out to me. It is the name Angelina with a pair of wings weaving around the letters.

He shoots me a knowing smile that doesn't reach his eyes. We'll call it a grin.

"You look pretty good for someone who is deathly hung over."

I look at him like a deer in headlights and feel all the blood travel to my face. Then, entirely too fast, I say, "I'm not hung over."

He gives me a 'don't be stupid' stare. "Ginny, I may have not said anything when I saw that bottle of vodka out in the open yesterday because I was there to apologize to you, but today I need to say something."

I look at him for a moment and notice the concern etched across his face. His blue eyes are softer than usual and his forehead is crinkled. I don't like this side of Benson at all; it's very unsettling. I wonder if he's as hurt as he really looks.

I completely hate the thought of it.

"It was a one time thing. I had a bad day," I whisper.

"I get it, I really do," he pauses, measuring my reaction. "Ginny, one bad day can ruin our lives. Don't you get that?"

I give him a tight nod and look down at my feet. I feel like a small child being scolded by a grown up. I want to tell him once and for all that alcohol is not my problem. I want to tell him his wife practically walked into my car and killed herself and sent me to prison during the most pivotal years of my life.

However, that just wouldn't be the truth.

"I know. It was a one time thing. I promise." I look up into his eyes and after a solid moment or two, he nods. I can't tell if he believes me or not; he has no reason to. However, he doesn't know that.

He leads me into his spacious living room. It doesn't hit me as hard as I thought it would. I keep good on my facial reactions when I see her picture hanging on the wall. I keep my gasps inaudible when I look at that familiar bracelet dangling on her wrist. However, the whole swallowing a lump in my throat thing I'm doing too loudly.

"Are you ok?" he asks.

I smile and offer him a lone nod. Then I hear his footsteps approach me slowly, stopping right behind me. He's not touching me but I feel the heat of his presence. It feels too good, but I force myself to step away.

CHAPTER SIX

Then something else catches my attention. I notice a hutch right outside of his living room. In the hutch reveals the largest collection of knives that I've ever seen. My eyes widen and shock floods my features as I look in Benson's direction. He's a knife nut?

"That's a BC-41. It was used by the British commandos during WW2," he walks up beside me, an appropriate amount away.

I nod slowly and look at another. It's a small, silver little one with sharp ridges hanging off of it.

"That's an SOG Seal," he states a matter-of-factly.

I look at a few others and feel a wave of regret come over me. What if these were illegal knives? I can't be around anything illegal. What if he's psychotic and uses the knives on me? Worst yet, what if he's used them already on someone else? Every single horrific possibility runs through my head.

Maybe I shouldn't be here. I had no idea who this man was at all.

"You collect knives?"

He laughs darkly. "It's more than a collection. I love them."

Deep in confusion, I stare at his horrifying collection. I'm not quite following.

"Why?"

He shrugs. "Why do you love painting?"

I remain silent, feeling defeated and a little frustrated. I liked painting because it made me feel good. It made me feel accomplished. Did he like knives for the same reason? The thought petrified me.

A startling jolt runs through my body as a piercing voice shouts behind me.

"Ginny!" A small girl races towards me and throws her arms around my lower half, squeezing me tightly.

Oh yeah. His daughter; who could forget? A daughter that he takes amazing care of and would never hurt. A seven year old, innocent little girl. Maybe his knives are just part of a collection after all. Maybe I'm letting my paranoia get the best of me. It wouldn't be the first time.

"Hey, little cutie," I mirror her tone, speaking in a higher pitch than I was formerly talking in. "How are you?"

"Can we play Pictionary tonight?" she blurts out. "I know you like to draw too because Daddy told me! I don't have school tomorrow either. We can stay up all night!" she says in almost one breath.

"Take a breath little lady," Benson says. Is that a shade of red I see forming on his cheeks?

He squats down to Annie's level and meets her eyes. "Annie, Sweet heart, let me talk to Ginny for one minute. Will you let me?"

"Fine, but I get her tonight!" She demands. Then she grabs her drawing board and runs up the stairs faster than a bolt of lightning.

She listens well. That's a good sign.

But then something else comes to my attention. Does he know something?

My paranoia, which wasn't fully gone to begin with, has come back full throttle.

I wait for him to give anything away when I notice him staring at something below. I instantly look down at my hands and realize they're trembling.

Great, now he thinks I'm scared. I just need to break eye contact for one moment. His eyes are too intense. I just need a minute away from them, that's all. I snap my head in the other direction and meet the other eyes on the wall. Not just any wall. The wall with the picture on it.

She's glaring at me. Judging me.

She's telling me to get the hell out of her house and away from her family.

What the hell was I thinking by taking this job?

"Ginny," Benson calls in a tone that's almost a whisper. He's standing directly behind me, a thread from touching me. I can feel his breath fan my neck, although I don't think he means to. I don't think he realizes how close he is to me. He feels so close that if I turned around, our noses would touch.

CHAPTER SIX

I nearly soar out of my own skin when he places his hands on my waist and turns me around. He's caught me looking at her pictures. I feel instantly mortified.

"I'm sorry," I whisper.

"That's my wife," he answers.

He assumes that's what I'm thinking about, but it couldn't be further from the truth. I actually cannot think of anything else but his hands on my waist.

I nod and look directly at my feet. I refuse to make eye contact with him. I can't.

"She," he pauses and exhales deeply. I continue to stare at the square tiles while he gains his composure. "She passed away seven years ago. She was killed by a drunk driver."

I can tell that this type of honesty is very hard to come by for him. I appreciate him telling me, even though I already know.

"That's," I whisper, placing my hand over my heart. I try to continue but I feel like I'm running out of air. The room starts spinning and I feel like I've suddenly been drugged. I try to finish what I'm saying but it comes out thick and throaty. "I'm so sorry, Benson."

The more lightheaded I become, the more my legs happen to be too weak to stand on. If I don't sit as soon as possible, I'm going to collapse right in front of him. I search for a seat immediately and plop myself down on the couch, sighing.

He looks at me bemused, so I feel the need to give him an explanation. "Sorry, just felt a bit dizzy for a second."

"You're nervous," Benson observes. He moves over to the couch and vigilantly takes a seat next to me. "Did the knives freak you out?"

"No," I nervously laugh while shuffling my quivering hands around my bag. "I think it's just my blood sugar."

Then he does something that takes me by surprise. He takes his two hands and shells them over my own, which are currently and frantically making a mess in my purse.

"Slow down," he says, softly.

I close my eyes and take a deep breath, feeling overcome by his presence. I can't look at him. I'm terrified to find out what he may think of me if he really sees me.

What the hell, Ginny? He's not a mind reader!

"You're right, I'm nervous," I admit.

"There is no reason to be nervous. All of those knives are locked up and have never been used. At least by me," he assures.

That's not why I'm nervous. "Benson, that's not why I'm nervous."

"Annie is crazy about you. What else is there?"

I'm crazy about you. I killed your woman. I almost killed your kid. I had sex with my step brother. I just got out of prison. You know nothing about me. I'm your worst nightmare.

I feel all the blood rush to my face, exposing my crimson cheeks. I'm pretty sure he notices, causing him to stifle a grin. "Relax, you'll do fine."

I let out a big sigh and shoot him an assuring smile. Then I nod even though my heart rate has gone through the roof. I'd give him the illusion that I was fine when I wasn't. I didn't know this man nearly enough to let him inside my head just yet.

It's not until I lower my chin that I realize his hands are still on top of mine, gently cradling them. Not only are they shelling my hands, but they are actively caressing them. He must have forgotten too, because he looks down and quickly removes them, clearing his throat.

"So, I can drive you home later on," he changes the subject.

"I can walk," I shrug.

"You already know that's not happening."

I throw a curveball at him. "You're not going to kidnap me away to another Oxygen bar, are you?"

He stifles a grin. "Is that what you want?"

Suddenly it's all I want, but I don't let him know that.

It seems that I have nothing clever to say whenever I am with this man. He literally makes me speechless. It was unfortunate because I was sarcastic at my finest. I was a funny girl. But this man made me a blubbering mess.

I guess that was a good thing, considering I had an overbearing secret about myself that he could never know.

"So, do you live alone or with a roommate?" he prods.

"Roommate."

"So you do have a boyfriend." It isn't a question.

"No," I respond; a long pause following. I have to think exactly how to articulate this sentence before I say it out loud. "I live with my step brother."

Knowing what I know, that was not an easy thing to say to anyone.

"Oh, that's good." He cocks his head in thought, seemingly a little baffled. "I think."

Don't figure it out. Don't even try.

He suppresses a familiar look that I get from many people whenever I mention Jesse. It's a mix of bemusement and disgust. "Saving money?"

No, that wasn't it.

I nod quickly and shift uncomfortably in my seat.

"All right. Give me your phone," he demands, his hand stretched out.

"Why?"

I see him hold back a smile as he keeps his hand out. "Rule number one if we're going to be friends. Do not ever question me."

Well, alright then you caveman.

I cautiously hand him over my phone. He snatches it unapologetically and begins tapping the touch screen. I can't see what on Earth he's doing and it bothers me. On the thought alone that he finds anything embarrassing on it makes me feel queasy. He lifts his head up from the phone screen and smiles, handing it back to me. "Now you have my number."

I sigh in relief and take my phone back, glaring at him.

"Call me at any hour if you or Annie need anything at all."

I mouth the words, "Okay."

"Or you can use it any other time. If you ever just want to talk." His eyes linger up to mine, curiously. He actually looks apprehensive, but it's quickly saved by his sexy grin. I internally melt into the seat of his couch and am almost confident that it is going to eat me whole. He just gave me his number.

Because of Annie, you fool.

I nod and toss my phone back into the back pocket of my jeans. He must notice how uncomfortable I am because he deliberately snickers at my cringe worthy state. I shoot him an embarrassing smirk and then cover my face because his eyes are burning a hole right through me.

Oh God, can he see how red I am right now?

"Don't," he whispers, removing my hands from my face. "You have nothing to be ashamed of. It's a beautiful face." His bold blue eyes are demanding and blaze into mine. Gone is the man blushing just a moment ago.

Now it's me who's doing the blushing.

I notice that our once appropriate amount of space away from each other is now, well, an inappropriate amount. My coy smile is now stripped from my face as we drink each other in for a moment.

Our intense staring contest comes to an end when the front door swings open. "Honey, I'm here!"

An obnoxious whirlwind of caramel brown hair spins in, carrying a bunch of designer name bags and a big black pair of Gucci sunglasses resting over her eyes.

Wait, who is this?

Both of us are jolted in our seats, startled, as we slide over from one another quickly. I look at Benson, waiting to see if he says anything with his eyes, but he doesn't. I feel the blood immediately drain from my face.

Of course, he has a girlfriend. Why wouldn't he?

I assess the girl in front of me. There is no doubt that this girl takes care of herself in every way possible. She is the definition of prim and proper. Probably around her early thirties. She is dressed in a beautiful knee length cream colored pencil dress with white stilettos that accent her tan, sculpted legs.

CHAPTER SIX

He was just being nice to me by bringing me to a bar. He was just being nice by giving me a job. It was all in my head. I should have known a guy like him would have a girlfriend.

Her facial expression changes immediately when she sees me. Her face scrunches up, and she instantaneously looks ten years older.

"Honey we're going to be late," her tone is snappy. She walks in and throughout the house like she owns the place.

"Janet, this is Ginny," he ignores her to introduce us. This can't be normal. He can't think that this is even remotely okay.

Part of me thinks that he is a dog, and the other part thinks that maybe I was reading too much into yesterday. That he did this all to get me to nanny for him. I feel used in the worst way and think about leaving. But then I think of Annie.

"Pleased to meet you. I'm Benson's girlfriend."

Fuck.

CHAPTER SEVEN

I think I sit in the chair in his living room for way too long. It feels like an eternity, honestly. My hands fidget and rub one another, over and over. My tell-tale when I am nervous.

I have to be honest; Annie distracted me from getting too angry over Benson having a girlfriend. Yes, I hate to admit that it bothered me, but it did. In the little time we had spent, I thought something more was there. He was unfortunately just scouting me out to be his child's nanny.

I was thankful to have a distraction such as her. Not only did I have to be on my best behavior, but I actually enjoyed my time with her. She even stayed completely still for a while and let me sketch her. When I was done, she snatched the drawing from me and hung it up on her fridge so that her father could see it.

Her father. He has a girlfriend. A really pretty one.

Next time he brushes my damn hair out of my face I'm going to smack his hand. Hard.

So for now, I will continue to watch his daughter. The little thing is a spitfire, bundle of energy. She happens to be one of the only friends I have right now, so I will tough it out.

Here goes nothing.

While making myself a cup of morning coffee, I think about the rest of the night spent at Benson's while babysitting Annie.

Towards the end of the night, I kept hearing footsteps upstairs and started to freak out because I had just made sure she was asleep. I kind of had to text Benson even though I didn't want to.

I am not proud of how scared I was at that moment.

Moments after texting him, his name popped up on my phone.

It read "Hot dad." I really had to change it to Benson.

Hot dad: Remember when I told you that Annie sleepwalks?

CHAPTER SEVEN

He had come home alone that night and had wanted me to nanny again the next day, but I declined. I told him I had family engagements. I didn't want to see him right away since I was being such a delicate little flower. I thought pretty hard about not babysitting anymore in general; about telling him that I couldn't do it, but I couldn't bring myself to say the words.

Fast forward a week later and it is Friday again. That's when I receive a call from him again.

As I expected, his tone over the phone is casual and unaffected. It's as if we've been talking all week. Or as if he didn't touch my face and introduce me to his girlfriend in the same breath.

I decide to get dressed up a little; nothing too crazy. I choose a pair of tight blue jeans and a black tank top. My long, dark brown hair is styled up in a ponytail, just how he likes it.

After a bitter second of thinking about it, I pull the rubber band out of my hair and mess it all up. I'm not letting him dictate how I wear my hair. I don't care if he can't see my face. I'm not his. Let Janet wear her hair in a damn pony tail, I'm going with my hair down and comfortable.

I do my makeup and wing my eyes with black eyeliner. I actually feel good and pampered for once, aside from the crazy hair.

I almost feel sexy.

Just when I'm about to head out the door, my phone goes off. It's him.

Benson: Haven't heard from you. Still coming tonight?
Me: Leaving now, Be there in twenty minutes.
Benson: I'll come to get you. It's like Jumanji outside right now.
Me: Don't. I got it covered.
Benson: You'll just never let me do you a nice gesture, will you?
Me: Nope.

When I arrive, Janet is sitting in a chair with impeccable posture and her legs crossed. It takes me a moment to realize she's sitting right under a picture of his wife. I can't help but compare the both of them. Even with her make up all done, her hair flawlessly straight, and the expensive designer clothes, she still doesn't hold a candle to Angelina Daniels.

I walk in the entry way sopping wet, take off my raincoat and offer Janet a nod. I don't get much of one back from her. Just a forced grin and judgmental eyes. When her eyes roam over my monsoon-like appearance, they grow even wider. I follow the path of her eyes and realize that they're on my chest.

My nipples are in two hard points, saying hello to Janet and the world.

Damn rain.

Benson stampedes down the stairs and notices pretty much right away, his eyes glued to my chest. I immediately fold my arms over one another as Janet lets out a warning cough towards her boyfriend.

He snaps out of it with a quick shake and shifts his embarrassment over to Janet. He looks like an animal caught in a booby trap. A booby trap. Oh man, I crack myself up.

He slows down and smiles. "Thanks for coming."

"I told you I would."

I feel as if my voice comes out way more formal than I tend it to. However, pretending I'm not affected by this is all exhausting.

I need to face the fact that I'm jealous. This is his girlfriend. I am his nanny. End of story.

He shoves his hands in his pockets and looks at me attentively. I haven't had anything to eat today so my strength is not one hundred percent, including my intuition. But my intuition is telling me that he wants something from me; maybe it's in his eyes.

I somehow get the impression that Benson feels guilty about something. Guilty perhaps for the information that he omitted from me.

Or maybe it's me who feels guilty.

CHAPTER SEVEN

I lock eyes with him, freezing for a moment, taking him all in. Submitting a small smile, I divert my eyes back to Janet who is scowling at us both. Apparently even looking at the man above the neck is unacceptable. Give me a break.

"There are some sick people out there that wouldn't think twice about hurting you, Ginny. Rejecting my offers to drive you home is over and done with," Benson orders.

I suddenly feel all of the blood rush to my face, blushing scarlet.

Janet chimes in, and it's not long before I notice that she's out of her seat and standing directly behind me. "The bus line has a very good schedule too if you want to check that out."

I smile, but don't show any teeth. I'm afraid if I do I will come off like a rabid dog.

Thanks, bitch.

Benson turns to Janet and then looks at me. He's probably wondering the same thing. What in the hell just happened?

"What?" she asks, exasperated. "It's not your job to drive her home, Benny. She's an adult."

Benny?

I don't take my eyes off of her as she insults me. In fact, I'm trying my best not to spontaneously combust, freak out, lose my shit, etc. I could go on.

I squeeze my hands into tight fists, almost cutting off the circulation. It's my only source of an outlet at the moment, honestly. That and grinding my teeth. Once I feel like I'm in enough control, I reply in my most sarcastic tone that I can muster up. "Thank you so much for that incredibly useful information. You should be a motivational speaker."

He lets a chuckle slip and Janet immediately renders him speechless with an evil eye.

Benson sighs. "Okay, we better get going. Janet, why don't you start my car?"

She smiles at him. "You're going to let me drive?"

"I'm only letting you start it. Don't even think for a second that you're driving it."

She rolls her eyes, snatches the keys and struts out the door like her shit doesn't stink.

Once she leaves, Benson shakes his head and looks at me, his cheerful face gone. He looks worried. I give him a confused look and shrug. What does he want?

"So...a family engagement, huh?"

I'm confused for a moment but then remember that is the excuse I used last week when I told him I couldn't babysit. I nod, "Yep."

I'm not elaborating for this guy. He doesn't know a thing about me.

He tilts his head sideways. "With who?"

"My dad," I say as if I've said it a thousand times.

"Don't lie to me. It's not very Christian."

"It's a good thing I'm not Christian then." I mean it as a joke, but he doesn't laugh. He tilts his head in confusion and thinks for a moment. Probably thinking of whether he should believe me or not. Silence fills the air between us until he breaks it. "You'd probably benefit from God. You don't seem to be doing too well without him."

I roll my eyes at him. I'm probably not as hurt as I should be.

"Something tells me you're not much of a daddy's girl either," he adds.

"You don't even know the half of it," I huff.

"I don't," he says, almost too quietly. Then he heads for the door, giving me a hint of a smirk. I'm glad he does because I don't want him leaving on a bad note while I'm in his house.

"Call me if you need me," he says softly, walking out.

Then - he's gone, and it leaves the worst taste in my mouth.

Once he leaves, I take a few deep breaths. That was intense.

However, as I sprawl out on the couch and get comfortable, I can't help but plaster a victorious smile on my face. Benson's girlfriend doesn't like me one bit, but better than that, I'm not too sure if Benson even likes her either.

CHAPTER SEVEN

As I curl up and start reading a romance novel, I begin to imagine Benson as the alpha hero of the book. He's a good Christian boy who takes confessions at the altar by day and a bad boy stripper who takes dollar bills on the stage at night. I immediately become irritated when I picture woman throwing themselves at him on that imaginary stage.

I'm tremendously irritated. In fact, this book really sucks.

I slam the book shut and go upstairs to see what Annie's doing.

She's lying on her belly with her feet in the air and moving in all directions. She has a plate of baby carrots in front of her that she's snacking on. I sit next to her as she concentrates on the movie. When I sit on her bed, she leans up against me and offers me the bowl of carrots.

"Carrots?" I ask, picking one up and throwing it right back down. "How about some pizza tonight?"

"Sure," she sighs.

I notice something is on her mind. She isn't her perky, usual self.

I place my hand on her back. "What's wrong, Annie?"

"I don't like her," she bites out.

"Janet?" I question. Of course, it's her.

She ignores me and dives right into it. "She's mean. I don't want her here. She steals my daddy from me all the time. I hope she doesn't become my new mom."

"She's not your mom. I can promise you that," I pet her hair. I know this is totally wrong, but I prod anyways. "So, how much time does your father spend with Janet?"

"More time than he spends with me," she mutters. "But she usually never comes here. When she does, she goes to his room."

From what I just got from a seven year olds innocent explanation, Janet was Benson's fuck buddy.

"How is she mean to you?" I pry.

She shrugs and takes another bite of her carrot. "She never talks to me and she yells at daddy a lot. They fight a lot. I once heard him say that if she wanted flowers, she should go visit a green house."

I can't help but stifle a laugh.

With Annie being put to bed, I can't help but want to doze off myself. My mind begins to wonder where Benson is right now with Janet. Is he wining and dining her? Are they at a hotel? Are they at a bar? Of course, they're not at a bar. Benson has a drinking problem.

After what seems like forever, I get myself calm enough to close my eyes. I rest my head on the arm of the couch and begin slipping into a sound slumber.

After what feels like hours, I feel an arm brush up against me in the most sensual way.

I squint one of my eyes open and look around the living room.

No one is there.

I close my eyes and slip into another light doze, and that's when I feel it again.

A couple fingers brush against my upper arm in the most torturous way, gliding over my clavicle and then to the side of my neck. I open my sleep deprived eyes and there he is right in front of me.

Benson's royal blue eyes are spearing into my sleepy ones and he's wearing a shit-eating grin.

It's not until he starts caressing the side of my stomach that I realize he's kneeling over the couch and on top of me.

I lay in silence for a couple minutes, soaking it all in.

Why would he just hop on top of me while I'm sleeping? Not that I'm complaining.

Every part of my body is hyperaware when it comes to Benson's hands roaming and exploring it. I squeeze my eyes shut as he continues to touch my sensitive skin all over.

"Do you like that?" he whispers, brushing the skin below my navel, so delicately that it hurts.

What the hell?

CHAPTER SEVEN

He then moves his hand down to my cleft, teasing but not going inside. He just lightly brushes over my jeans, making me go insane.

"Yes." I don't even sound like myself.

"How about this?" He slides his hands inside my waistband and brushes the lowest possible part of my abdomen. Fucking tease.

I let out a frustrated groan and he laughs, watching me wiggle like a piece of spaghetti. He looks like he's enjoying it way too much.

"Just tell me what you want," he teases.

"I want you to touch me," I say, with my eyes closed.

"Where? He whispers, brushing his full lips against my sensitive ear. He's totally doing that on purpose.

I then slide my hand down to my heat. "Here."

Half-conscious, I begin moving my hips due to all of the blood rushing down below. I need relief in the worst way, but I'm not fully awake to give it to myself.

Then, with one swift and sensual touch with what feels like lips to the most sensitive part of my body, I wake to my arousal.

I look around the room in a haze, realizing that Benson is standing a few feet away, staring at me, his broad shoulder leaning against the entry way molding.

My eyes widened; mortified. I straighten myself up on the couch and squeeze my legs shut, placing my hands on my lap. It's just then that I realize I was dreaming.

It felt so real that I find myself questioning it still.

Did he just watch me have an orgasm in my sleep? Or did he actually really give me one?

The thought of both of them humiliates me.

"Are you alright?" he asks softly. He appears fretful.

"I was just dreaming."

"Was it a good dream?" he asks, smirking and sitting down beside me. His hand brushes across my thigh and makes me think of my reverie again; just when I was beginning to forget. I shut my eyes and tilt my head back, feeling completely unhinged. Was he doing that on purpose?

"Is it Midnight already?" I ask in my sleepy voice, rubbing my eyes.

"Not even close," he grins.

"Why are you home so early?"

"Change of plans," he shrugs nonchalantly.

I look at him, bewildered, and still half awake. He lifts his hand to my right eye and gently wipes the sleep from it. "Missed a spot."

I cringe at the thought of him picking my sleep boogers but he just looks amused by it.

"Thanks," I mumble. "Change of plans?"

"It gets old going out all of the time. Especially with people you have nothing in common with. I go out with a couple of friends and I obviously don't drink. I can usually watch them drink and be fine, but today, I couldn't wait to get out of there," he tells me. His eyes are intense but not on me. He's in profound reflection. "You know what I mean, right?"

I feel a tinge of pain in my chest and just nod. I can stare into those passionate, translucent eyes all night if I wanted to, but now is not the time. Not when he's feeling so vulnerable.

I squeeze my eyes shut again as I struggle to regain my composure before the long walk home.

I suddenly become more awake after I stretch my limbs and straighten my posture. "Well, I should go."

"Yes, of course," he pauses, broodingly staring straight ahead, his shoulders hunched in defeat.

I've seen the irritated Benson. I've seen the cocky Benson. I've even seen the insecure & nervous Benson who stood up in front of all of those people at AA. However, I've never seen the Benson that looked so lost for words. So defeated.

He looks at me for permission to continue, his face etched with worry. "I saw the way Janet treated you earlier, I should have said something."

"It's okay. I'm a big girl," I assure him.

"Yeah, but I didn't like it," he says sternly.

"I don't think she likes me very much." I laugh light heartedly. It's supposed to be funny but it just upsets him even more.

"It doesn't matter what she thinks," he retorts. "I like you. That's all that matters."

I smile but don't respond to that. In fact, I never want this moment to end.

"I'm sorry," he whispers. I shift my gaze to him and he wears a serious expression. He actually looks like he is truly sorry, or else he is a really good actor. I wonder what he's sorry about.

"Sorry for what?" I mumble.

He continues, "We had so much fun together that telling you I had a fuck buddy, well, it wasn't really on my mind."

"She said she was your girlfriend," I grin, noticing he's a little embarrassed by that.

"She is well aware that she's not," he warns. I laugh because he's being so serious and I'm trying to keep the conversation light.

"Hey, it's completely fine. You don't have to explain anything to me, Benson," I assure him, but then immediately dodge his eyes and look at the lamp shade next to me.

"Did you know when people lie they tend to look to the left?" he retorts.

"Hey!" I poke him because I know he's implying that I'm lying.

Then his smile is gone and he shrugs. "It's just... I don't like lies. It won't happen again."

"It's not a problem," I dismiss. I then shift on the couch and square my shoulders up. "Actually, while we're on the topic," I pause and try to articulate the sentence in a way that won't offend him. "Annie mentioned earlier that she doesn't like Janet."

He doesn't look surprised. "I figured."

"She misses spending time with you."

He smiles to himself and then looks at me with warm eyes. Then, he says something that takes me by absolute surprise. In fact, it's so quiet that I almost miss it. "I enjoy talking to you, Ginny."

A warm, ticklish feeling comes over my body. I should feel grateful, but all I feel is flustered and at a loss for words. So I ask the only thing that I can think of. "Why?"

"I feel like I can tell you things," he admits, placing a hand over mine. "And you just proved to me that you can tell me things too."

Checkmate.

I inhale deeply as I stare at our connected hands. I smile at his confession, which releases the metaphorical butterflies throughout my whole stomach.

According to the large, antique, maple clock that sits in the corner, it's only a few minutes that we sit in comfortable silence.

After what seems like an eternity to me, I rise to my feet.

"Could you take me home?" I ask. I know it's a shot in the dark, because I'm always turning down his rides, but I actually want the extra few minutes with him, although this is something I'd never admit.

He sighs, looking almost disappointed that I'm not staying longer, but also relieved that I actually ask for a ride home. "You got it."

The drive home is not the same comfortable silence we sat in at his house. We both don't have anything to say. It's not that we are closer to each other than we were at the house, but the car makes the air feel compact and the tiny space more prominent. It feels more personal being in such a small space with him and inhaling his every day scent.

I just stare out the window, watching the lights dot my skin as we pass the city. I wonder if Benson can actually see what is under my skin. Perhaps a liar or a murderer.

I shake my horrible thoughts and switch to another agitating one. I wonder what a beautiful man like Benson was doing with a woman like Janet.

She's hot. She's easy.

CHAPTER SEVEN

We finally reach the apartment complexes, but I don't feel like getting out just yet.

I can feel his heated gaze on me as I turn my head to meet his inquiring eyes.

"Okay, well, thank you," I say quickly, trying to get out of there as fast as I can, but his voice stops me before I even open the door. "Are you angry with me?"

I put on my best baffled face. "No!"

"You don't like Janet. I get that," It's not a question, but a very correct assumption.

"What?" I spit out. "She's not so bad. She... she's..."

The more I lie about her, the more I feel the anger ejaculate out of my body. It just feels natural to hate her in every way. Why hide it?

He smiles to himself but avoids eye contact with me. Then he comes to the exact realization that I was afraid of. "You're jealous."

My eyes widen in embarrassment. "What? No!" I say in a defensive tone.

"Ginny... you don't want anything to do with me," he tells me, his tone is raw and vulnerable. "You're so young and,"

"Stop. You don't have to explain anything to me. And as for me not wanting anything to do with you, I think you've got that the other way around," I say, with my face deadpan. "You don't know anything about me," I say before I go to get out of the car for good this time when he shuts it on me, trapping me in.

"You keep saying that," he grits out, frustrated.

"Saying what?" I match his tone.

Well, this conversation escalated a little too quickly.

"That I don't know a thing about you," he stares me square in the eye before continuing, "The more you say it, the more I want to know."

I just stare at him because it's all I can do in the moment.

He stays leaned over me and whispers in my ear. "For what it's worth, Ginny? She's not the one that I think about every waking moment."

I look at him, a few raw inches from my face. I try to hide the shock from it but I'm sure I'm radiating it.

I stutter as I try to respond to him but he just shakes his head and squeezes his eyes shut. "I know I'm telling you more than you need or want to know, but I don't want you to think I'm some womanizer or something. I actually care what you think."

"You do?"

"With Janet, our relationship is casual and consensual. I was looking for someone with no strings attached, and she claimed that was her thing too. But I don't think it's like that for her anymore." He looks tormented by the situation. Pausing in thought, he spares a glance at me. "Then she saw you in my house. And I think she got jealous, too."

I just keep looking straight ahead silently, letting it all sink in.

"She just feels a little threatened by you I think," he admits, shaking his head and silently laughing, as if the God damned thought of that is so ridiculous.

Instead of getting mad and defending my own honor, I join him by letting out a quiet chuckle and shaking my head too. "Threatened by me?"

He nods.

"Why on earth would she be jealous of me?" I continue laughing, but notice he stops.

"Oh wake up, Ginny. Look at you," he insists. He turns the rearview mirror in my direction so that I can see myself. "You're stunning," he says it like it is general knowledge. "Your eyes are the perfect almond shape. You don't need makeup with those eyelashes. And your lips, you'll never need to invest in a lip stick because they're permanently stained cherry red. Your adorable, springy nose."

It wasn't general knowledge to me. I didn't wear makeup often because I was in prison for a long time. When you have just enough money to buy things like tampons and toiletries, makeup doesn't quite make the cut. My hair was a bland dark brown and I felt often that my face was mousey looking. I could definitely afford to put on a few pounds. I didn't have the curves I wanted. I was the definition of a plain Jane.

However, the more I look at myself in the mirror, I knew that he wasn't just saying this all to make me feel better. My lips were redder than usual, probably from blood flow. My lashes are naturally long. I used to think my springy nose was a curse, but it turned out someone liked it.

I shrink in the passenger seat and feel my cheeks burn scarlet red. I feel like a baby Gazelle running for its life in the middle of the African Savanna. This beautiful man was giving me attention that I didn't deserve.

When I fix my eyes back on him, he continues looking at me and drinking me in. It's then I realize that our faces are only inches apart. He darts his eyes down to my lips, studying them intently. I nervously lick them under his scrutiny and feel his eyes blaze even hotter.

Then he does that thing with his index finger again. He unapologetically traces the slopes and contours of my face, finally resting them at the bow of my lips. He softly traces the outline of them, never taking his eyes off them. I'm so anxious to see what he does next.

Instead of waiting, I take it upon myself to seal that fate. I nip his finger between my teeth and suck it in my mouth. When I pull his single digit out of my mouth with a pop, his eyes flare like wildfire.

Within a blink, we are jolted by the slam of a door. Jesse walks outside and stops in his tracks when he sees us in the car. He has a bag of garbage in his hand and walks to the cans across the street. Every sound he makes is forceful and exaggerated. It's almost as if he's angry.

As if he saw something he didn't like one bit.

We stiffen up in our seats and slide far apart from each other as we can until Jesse walks back inside, slamming the door behind him.

"I thought that you said you didn't have a boyfriend?" he asks.

"That's my stepbrother."

Oh brother.

CHAPTER EIGHT

In the aftermath of Jesse witnessing me getting too personal with another man, he pretty much ignores me every option he gets. I don't remember Jesse ever being the jealous type, but I never really gave him the motive.
In high school, I generally stayed away from boys because there was only one on my mind. I only had eyes for him; my stepbrother. So here we are, seven years later after being seven years apart, and we already have complications.
What he told me the other day still weighs heavy on my mind. He had expressed that he wouldn't be upset if I moved on and wants me to be happy.
So why was I getting the cold shoulder?
It seems like every night he comes home from his job at the hardware store, he grabs his bong and then makes a bee line straight to his room.
It's not only Jesse's bullshit that upsets me. It's what Julia told me the other night that currently has my head spinning like the exorcist. I know I was gone for a long time, but I can barely breathe knowing that Jesse was with someone else other than me. I desperately want to confront him on what I hear regarding him and Lacey. I try so hard to not let it trouble me, but the truth is that it does. It bothers me terribly.
Later that night, I head over to Benson's to watch Annie for the night. He warns me that he'll be a little late, but it's already midnight and I haven't heard from him at all.
I dim the lights and turn the volume down on the television as soon as Annie knocks herself out. We lay on the couch, sprawled out and tangled, limiting my access to move. Being pinned down makes it so much harder for me because I am forced to look at the damn pictures on the wall, reminding me that I ruined this man, woman, and child's life. So I keep my eyes focused on the book I'm reading. I'll do anything but look at these walls. Anything but that.
Keeping me conscious was a priority because apparently, I had wet dreams.

CHAPTER EIGHT

I'm reading Jane Eyre for the countless time. Not only is it my favorite book of all time, but I can relate to it. Sometimes I feel like my whole existence is based on a Bronte girl's novel.

A Governess and her handsome Master; a nanny and her hot boss.

Wuthering "I'm in love with my stepbrother" Heights is another one.

My phone buzzes to life as 'Hot Dad' appears on my phone's screen. A burst of warm energy flows through my veins as I snort over the name. I also notice that I'm smiling ear to ear like a damn goon. I poke at my phone, slide and unlock, and then quickly change his name back to Benson.

Benson: Hey Picasso

I keep grinning like a fool as I try to think of something witty to say back, but then my inner voice chimes in. He's thinking of Annie, you fool. I roll my eyes and wipe the smirk off my face. Before I can type a reply back, another message pops up.

Benson: What's your favorite color?

That's a good question. What was my favorite color? Better yet, why?

Me: Why do you want to know?

Benson: It's for science.

Me: Well then I just have to answer, don't I?

Benson: ☺

After a minute of thinking, because honestly, I loved all colors, I was an artist. Except for orange, the color of my jumpsuits for seven whole years.

Me: Yellow.

Me: Why?

He doesn't respond back.

I put down the phone and consider why the hell he wants to know what my favorite color is. I also wonder if Benson has any dark secrets of his own. Any that happen to be comparable to the one that I'm burdening. My mind roams more when I start to question if Benson is the perfection that I thought that he was. After all, he's only human.

I throw my phone and book on the coffee table next to me and gape at the picture of his wife on the wall. A chill runs through me.

The torture eats me alive to the point where the large space in the house isn't even enough. I feel the sudden urge to get the hell out of here.

I can't breathe.

I untangle myself from Annie's petite body as gently as I can and toss a blanket over her. Then I tip toe outside onto the porch and opt for the porch swing. My lungs fill with fresh air and I suddenly feel so much better. I push my foot off the ground and start swinging back and forth, slipping into my own little world.

The sun is starting to peak over the horizon, shedding light onto the porch and the sidewalks. I wonder why Benson is so late and then groan when I realize he's probably stayed the night at Janet's.

Just as my frustration starts to settle down, I see a car quickly pull into the drive way. Not even a minute later, the driver's door swings open, revealing Benson and his gigantic grin.

Even after a long night, his skin was still glowing and is as gorgeous as ever.

Although I am feeling a little bitter, I smile back at him out of instinct. How can I not?

With a few big leaps, he makes his way up the porch and towards the swing. He looks too youthful at the moment to be a full grown man and father. I find it hard to scowl at him, which was my original plan.

But it's not long before the unpleasant feeling smacks me right in the face. The unfamiliar feeling stirs within my gut, making my stomach feel unsettled. What is this uneasy feeling?

I was jealous because someone else put that beautiful smile on his face.

I void all emotion from my face once he's close enough to see it. I examine him carefully as I scoot over and allow him to sit. Stillness fills the air, allowing him to lean back onto the swing with me, his long legs sprawling out.

Oh great. My hands are trembling again. I quickly shake them to get the blood flowing when he puts his hands over them lacking a second thought; almost as if it's second nature by now.

Yep. He notices.

This guy must think I'm a real weirdo. I was constantly quivering like a battered puppy whenever he came around. I continue to think these negative thoughts to myself as I observe our intertwined hands.

Then I remember who he was with.

Without warning, my body heats up in a silent rage as I quickly vacate my hands from his. I cannot touch him like this when I am having an internal melt down.

All I want to do at this moment is punch him in his beautiful face, especially when I get a whiff of a certain aroma.

He quickly grabs my hand again as if I never pulled away. I look in his direction and his brows are pointed, his mouth pouty.

"What?" I still.

"You're angry," he observes. "Why are you angry?"

"I'm not angry," I deny.

"You are."

"Am not."

"You're disappointed in me," he accuses.

"I didn't say that!"

"Maybe you didn't say it, but you're thinking it."

He's right. I'm very angry. I'm thinking about how pissed I am that he broke his six month clean streak. I smell it on his breath.

"You're an alcoholic, Benson. How could you? " I remind him, my voice small.

"I didn't drink," he says, his voice defensive.

"It's none of my business."

He pulls his hand away and suddenly I feel bottomless. "Let's make it your business for just a second then."

"I can smell it on you."

"Janet. That's why you smell it," he says, his voice bold and to the point. I can tell he regrets telling me, although I can also see he's glad he's spared me the details.

"I'm telling you the truth," he tells me, grabbing my hand again and clinging to it like a lifeline. "And I have a surprise for you."

"You do?"

And just like that, all my anger towards this man is shattered to smithereens.

He grabs my hand and leads me down his porch steps, luring me over to his car with a huge grin splitting his face. When we arrive at his car, he pops his trunk, slowly pulling out a brand new, pale yellow bicycle. It has a basket in the front and reflectors all over it. It kind of looks expensive. Why would he buy a bike?

"What's this?"

"Yours," he gloats.

I'm flabbergasted that he would even do something like this for me. It takes me a second to articulate a proper sentence. "Y-you got me a bike?"

He nods with a cheek splitting grin. I look at the cute, yellow bike and then back up at him again. Two of the most beautiful sights I've ever seen, but I don't let him know it.

"You don't like it?" he frowns.

"I love it. But…Benson, I can't accept this."

"You can and you will," he sternly tells me. "You're old one is a death trap on wheels. You're done riding that thing." He pushes the bike towards me. "Want to give her a test spin?"

Okay, I give up. I'm at a loss for words. Why would he do something like this for me? I ponder the thought for a few seconds before I smile, flying my hands up in defeat. "Fine!"

The first thing that I look at is the leather seat that has sunflower printing all over it. I never mentioned to him that it was my favorite flower. It amazes me that even though he barely knows me, he knows what I like. "It's beautiful," I whisper, almost sadly.

He stands there smiling ear to ear and with his hands shoved casually into his pockets. I imagine it's what he'd look like if he's watching Annie open up a gift on Christmas morning. He looks genuinely happy that I love his gift.

"No one has ever done anything like this for me before," I say, hopping on the bike and looking at him before I take off fluidly, riding in a small circle. I put my feet down when I'm in front of him again and beam at him.

We stare at each other for a moment before I come to a realization. I can't accept this. There was no way. Benson didn't owe me anything. I already took so much away from him and he didn't even know it.

"I should go home." I hop off the bike in one fast motion and kick down the stand.

He shifts anxiously and puts his arm up to stop me from walking away. "What?"

"Benson I can't take this. It's wrong."

He squints his eyes. He doesn't understand because he has no idea. I can tell I've pushed him off balance.

"I'm going to go now. Thank you for this, but I can't take it."

"Let me at least drive you home," he offers.

Ignoring him seems like the best option at the time, so I stalk away from him.

"Is your step brother mad?" I hear him call after me.

Like clockwork, he has me sucked into his black hole again. I turn around, giving him exactly what he wants. "What?"

"He seemed pretty angry the other night when I dropped you off."

"No, of course not," I respond, my tone defensive.

"He looks like he cares a lot about you," he takes a few vigilant steps towards me.

"He does." I meet his steps.

"So, does he always get that mad when you bring a guy home?"

I laugh at his remarks as if they are ridiculous. "I told you! He doesn't care."

"Good, cause that would be weird."

And just when I realize that we were having yet another awkward stare off, I break it off by changing the subject. "I told you I have to go. Why can't you just respect that? Why won't you let me go?"

He shrugs. "I'm not physically keeping you. You can go whenever you'd like."

"Yeah but," I sigh and melt when I see his compromising eyes.

"You could just walk away."

"That would be rude!"

"What's rude is that you don't accept my gift," he mutters; hands on waist.

God, he looks so hot when he does that. Why does everything he do seem so hot? He certainly warms the cool, morning air up. The wind is kind to him, softly blowing through his blonde strands, making me nearly drool.

I look down at my feet in silence as I stir for a response, but I have nothing. I can see him staring at me out of the corner of my eyes, assessing me. I then look back up at him with a defeated look. "Thank you, Benson."

"You're very welcome."

An awkward silence fills between us. He's the first one to break it. "Although I wouldn't have pegged you for a yellow fan."

My posture shoots up as I swiftly respond, "Just shows that you don't know much about me."

"I guess so," he mutters.

"Disappointed?" I challenge.

"Not even a little bit."

We both start to silently laugh at each other. It's a beautiful moment full of understanding and acceptance. I don't ever want it to end. Then his eyes start to droop. He seems lost in his own thoughts again. He begins scratching his dark ginger scruff in confusion.

"I'm sorry," he says, snapping out of his trance. "It's just… you're an enigma to me. I know very little about you and I want to know more," he looks at me with a genuineness I'm not used to. "I'd like to know more about you if you will let me."

My nerve endings ignite and I shyly respond, "Well, what would you like to know?"

Let's see what good ones he comes up with. Let's see what he's got.

"Do you like breakfast?" he asks.

"Who doesn't?"

"What do you say we hit the morning AA meeting together and get breakfast afterwards?"

CHAPTER NINE

We take his car to the a.m. meeting for AA at our local church. Getting out of the car together, I notice some of the members staring at us. Some people are whispering and a lot of them are out right talking. They're not even trying to hide it. Great, now we're going to be the talk of this place.

Benson says hi to all the members as if they are long lost friends, giving them hugs that I wish he could give me instead. Benson calls me over while he is in the middle of a conversation with an older lady. She smiles as I approach.

"Ginny, this is my sponsor, Catherine."

The woman smiles wide and outstretches her hand. "Lovely to meet you, Ginny. Is that short for something?"

Shaking her hand, I say, "No. Just Ginny. It's very nice to meet you."

She's an older lady with shoulder length white hair. Dressed to the nines, all of her rings are evidence of a rich husband or significant other. Or maybe she's the rich one. Who am I to judge?

Catherine talks about Benson as if he's her own son. Meanwhile, my eyes dart in different directions and take in the holier-than-thou architecture. He even seems embarrassed at some point of the conversation when Catherine admits what a good looking man he is and how all of the ladies want him. He blushes and I suddenly understand why he loves to see me that way. It's a beautiful sight.

When the meeting starts, Benson nudges me. "Want to go up there?"

"Heaven?" I joke.

He grins and points to the podium. "No. Up there."

At the podium, a young woman currently talks about how awful of a mother she is thanks to Vodka. I look at him and the back at the podium. "Hell no."

He scratches a temple at my choice of words. I immediately slap my hand over my mouth when I realize where we are. Sorry, God.

"Why not?" he laughs, challenging me. "It feels good afterwards, I promise."

"I'm not going up there!"

"I'll get you to go up there eventually," he warns me with a wink.

I roll my eyes.

After our meeting, we make a bee line to the restaurant across the street. We get our food served to us hot and quick by a young brunette that has an eye wandering problem. Or maybe it's just a lazy eye. Whatever it is, her eyes can't seem to stay off Benson.

I watch Benson devour his waffles in only a few bites. I inspect his full lips and the whiskers that surround them. His lips are lush, somewhat feminine, soft and perfectly shaped. I find myself staring at them for way too long.

I start to wonder what his lips would feel like against my own. Or moving towards the insides of my thighs and to the most pivotal part of me. I squirm at the thought of it. Are they firm and soft? Rough and manly? I slowly transport my French toast into my mouth as I try to stop myself from gawking like a fourteen year old virgin.

He clears his throat, breaking my obsession with his lips. I drop my fork like it's hot and raise my eyes to meet his. He shoots me a shit eating grin. "Reading Jane Eyre, the color yellow, French toast."

I grab my fork and shove a massive piece in my mouth, giving him perplexing eyes. I don't quite get what he's saying, but I want to hear more of his beautiful baritone voice, so I keep quiet.

"Oh, and art," he adds. I give him a quizzical look as he shoves another fork full of eggs in his mouth. "Things that I know about you so far," he clarifies and chews. He puts his fork down and gives me his undivided attention. "Tell me more."

I make the quick decision that I'm not giving him anymore rope. "Well, I'm a nanny."

His shoulders slouch and he raises an eyebrow. "Technically, my father is the nanny right now," he teases.

I smirk and put my hands up in submission. "Fine. I'm a total Star Trek geek. I love all of the movies and shows."

He cocks his head back in surprise. "You're a Trekkie?"

"I'm a Trekkie," I confirm, proudly.

"So are you one of those fans that dress up in Princess Leia buns and goes to those conventions?"

I drop my fork and roll my eyes. "That's Star Wars."

"So, you don't dress up? Like as a sexy Vulcan or something?" He's just teasing me now.

I give into his shenanigans. "No! Not that there's anything wrong with that."

He throws his head back and laughs robustly.

I huff and puff and cross my arms as he continues laughing uncontrollably. I can't believe that we're sitting across from each other like this so comfortably. It's as if we've known each other our whole lives. It's as if he already knows everything about me. On the other hand, he doesn't even know the half of it.

Somehow he gets himself to stop laughing and sighs. It's probably the cutest sigh I've ever heard but I don't let him know that.

"Well, there's got to be something you're into that's not so… nerdy?"

I mock offensiveness and then lift a strawberry off my plate and throw it at his head. He catches it with ninja like reflexes and pops it in his mouth, never taking his eyes off mine. Suddenly, I feel like all of my air has been taken away from me. How does he do that?

"So, do you have any family besides your step brother?" he prods, stealing another strawberry off my plate.

I shrug and avoid eye contact. "There's not much to know about my family. I don't want to talk about me. Let's talk about you."

"Nuh-uh. We came here to talk about you."

I sigh in defeat and put my utensils down. "I have an alcoholic father, my mom left us when I was a kid, and my step mother died of brain cancer when I was in High School.

Oddly enough, she was really the only one that I liked out of the whole bunch."

"That's a lot to know."

"A lot of bad things," I correct him.

"They're still things. I'm sorry about your step mother. And your mother," he says.

"Thanks." I shift in my seat uncomfortably.

"I had a step mother too for a little while. She was horrible and didn't last long. My real mother died a long time ago when I was a kid. Overdosed on pills. I barely remember her."

"I'm sorry Benson," I say. "I know what it's like not to remember your real mother. Pam may as well have been my real mother."

"I know," he sympathizes. He then lifts his arm to touch my hand which holds my fork. The touch is so intense I have to pull away. This makes things much more awkward.

"So that's your step brother's mom, right?" he says, not affected the least.

I nod.

"Did they get along?"

"We all got along. We were a real family." I start to get lost in my own thoughts.

"You haven't had that in a long time, have you?" he asks, his intense stare catching my eyes like wildfire.

I feed his intense gaze, putting my fork down and inhaling deeply. He's cracked me open like an egg and he doesn't even know it. I'm not usually this open with my family let alone a stranger.

"Ginny, is that you?" I hear a soft voice.

I look up and see a slender woman around my age with strawberry blonde hair. Right away, I recognize her. She looks just as surprised to see me.

Well, there's a face I haven't seen in a while. A face I haven't seen since High School Graduation. A face that I wanted to smack harder than a loose wired Television set. A face that had the pleasure of enjoying my step brother the whole time I was locked away.

Lacey was one of the friends in the car with me on the night of the accident. She's also the friend that Jesse hooked up with after I was locked up in prison. It's safe to say Lacey isn't a friend anymore.

I clear my throat and offer her a weak smile. I sense a little anxiety from her, which is kind of relieving because I feel it too. I also feel a little anger. Scratch that; I feel a whole hell of a lot of anger.

This is it.

He's going to find out who I am. Either she is going to say something or I am going to completely lose my shit in front of him.

"Lacey," I greet her with an anti-climactic tone.

She looks at Benson uncomfortably, as if she's interrupting something. "Sorry. I just wanted to say hi." She immediately looks like she regrets approaching me. "I'm sorry."

"It's fine," I say.

An awkward silence fills the air between us, but then she finally breaks it. "How are you?"

I don't appreciate the sympathy in her voice at all.

Looking over at Benson, I notice that he's beginning to think something's not right.

"I'm doing great. Very, very great." Real smooth, Ginny.

His face lifts in suspicion.

When she finally gets the hint that I'm not in a talkative mood, she takes a step back and sighs. "Well, it was good seeing you."

I nod and look down at my empty plate. I really didn't have a word to say to her. I close my eyes and inhale, hoping that when I open them it will just be Benson and me again.

When I open my eyes a minute later, my wish is granted and she is gone. He waits for an explanation, more or less looking amused by all of it.

"So, that was my friend from High School," I say, pushing my empty place aside.

CHAPTER NINE

"You don't like her very much, do you?

I confirm his assumption with a certain look.

"Bad friend?" he asks.

I give him another look and he throws his napkin on his plate and looks at me with mischief. "Why don't we get out of here?"

It's really amazing how much you can communicate without words.

After we leave the breakfast joint, we decide to walk the bike home and talk. The humidity is rising and my hair takes an embarrassing turn for the worse, resembling something along the lines of a Chia Pet. I keep brushing it out of my face while we walk when I swear I hear a snicker escape him.

I gasp. "Are you laughing at me?"

"A little," he admits.

"It's the humidity," I explain, blowing it out of my face.

He flashes his beautiful smile. "You have Macho Man hair."

"Macho Man hair?"

"You know, The Macho Man Randy Savage?"

I shake my head in confusion. Who the hell is The Macho Man? And why am I macho to him?

He gasps. "You're telling me you know what the r2d2 and cp30 droids are but you don't know who Macho Man Randy Savage is?" He then clears his throat and transitions his voice into a raspy and low mock. "Snap into a Slim Jim!"

"Once again, that's Star Wars," I say, dead pan.

"Who are you?" he asks.

I smirk. "I'd tell you, but then I'd have to kill you."

"I knew it. You're a part of the dark side, aren't you?"

I lean in closer and whisper, "I am the dark side."

He takes in my devious smile and smirks. "But seriously, were you born under a rock or something? You don't seem to know a lot of modern things." His eyes light up like a Christmas tree. "Wait, are you a time traveler?"

"No! I mean....yes!"

He ignores me and goes on. "I knew it. I mean, it'd be a little more awesome if you came by a Dolorean time machine, but whatever, semantics."

I gasp, stopping in my tracks. "Your compliment talk is a bit rusty, you know."

He walks up to me with a menacing look in his eyes. When he reaches me, it softens and he says in a low voice, "Macho Man Randy Savage is a Pro Wrestler from the '80s... with crazy hair. Kind of like yours. You really need to learn your wrestlers of the twentieth century, babe. Knowing your cyborgs but not pro wrestlers? Come on."

I roll my eyes, knowing very well he's messing with me. "I'll keep that in mind."

He gently moves a strand of my Macho Man hair out of my face. I can't look away if I tried. I love this care free Benson. The man that looks so boyish and playful. The jokester.

His fingertips ignite a spark across my forehead as he gently brushes them transversely over it. My breath catches like a knitted sock on a nail.

It suddenly becomes deafly silent. I look up to see him staring at me with a longing I have not quite seen before. To be completely honest, it's kind of bothering me. He has a girlfriend. Or 'fuck buddy'. Either way, he has someone and it is not me.

"So you're going back home to your step brother now?" he asks.

I shrug. "I don't really have anywhere else to go."

I'm actually surprised that he even acknowledges Jesse. He says "brother" with such piss and vinegar that I have to wonder if he's jealous or just teasing me.

"You watch my kid. You could stay with me for a little bit,"

"No," I nervously laugh. I realize I'm a little too quick to reject his offer and instantly regret it. "I mean no thank you."

He seems taken aback by my answer. This man must be used to being told yes by every woman he's ever known because right now he doesn't look happy. I can't tell if he's going to smile and shrug it off, or start world war three.

I start to get a feeling within my gut that this isn't just a friend to friend conversation. He has a bitter look on his face and the conversation no longer seems light.

"I don't think Janet would be okay with that," I add, trying to lighten the load.

Or did I just make it worse?

"It's not Janet's decision. I don't belong to her, therefore,"

"But you do," I interrupt, bitterly laughing. "You say that you two don't date, but she's… you're her… you guys are together."

"But we're not exclusive," he corrects me. "You're young. Haven't you heard of casually dating someone?"

"Of course I have," I say. Great, now I'm getting defensive.

In all honesty, I was just trying to make him shut up about it. Even though I hated the fact that he casually dated anyone at all, I didn't want to fight about it.

"You never cared before. When did she become so important to you?" he asks, his head tipped in confusion.

That's it. The claws are coming out.

"First of all, I'm not jealous," my voice rises.

"I didn't say anything about jealousy," he retorts.

"Yes, you did! The other day," I remind him. "Now, you implied it."

"Sorry that I want to be your friend despite what my fuck buddy may think," he says, his voice stinging me.

Fuck buddy.

Two words coming from his mouth, and they burn me alive.

"Don't you think that would confuse Annie just a little bit?"

His jaw drops but he snaps it shut again.

Yes, Ginny! Insult his intelligence. Make it personal! Men hate that.

"Believe it or not, this doesn't have anything to do with your fuck buddy!" I shout, making him flinch. "Did you ever stop a second to think of Annie? How confused she may be when tons of women cross the threshold of your home?"

His face is so red it may just explode. "Well if this doesn't have anything to do with her, then why the hell...wait." He stops himself as if he just had an epiphany. He absently rubs his newly grown in scruff, silently thinking. "You're right. This has absolutely nothing to do with Janet."

"What?"

"It's because of Jesse, isn't it?" he prods

No. Please stop.

God damn it, why does he have to always be right?

"Excuse me." I step away from him, hoping he doesn't say anymore. Hoping he gets the hint that he crossed the damn line. My voice is surprisingly calm for how pissed I am. "You don't know anything about me or my situation. Please stop assuming that you do."

He smiles to himself, but the gesture anything but sincere. After a few seconds of awkward silence and one loud sigh, he inclines his head to mine and says, "You're right. It's none of my business."

CHAPTER TEN

Later that night, I meet up with Julia and go to a house party she's invited me to. I figure that I could use a mindless good time seeing that I was trying to stay away from anyone with a nut sack, or at least the ones I knew.

I wear a black lace dress that stops just above the knees and pull my hair into a high ponytail. I slide into my suede slouch boots while going through Julia's makeup. What the hell was a contouring kit and how on earth do you use it?

I don't own much of anything besides a few outfits. The lace dress isn't even mine, hence the reason it's a little loose around the hips. Julia has curves in all the right places that men drool over.

My argument with Benson currently weighs heavily on my mind, but I'm determined not to let it ruin my night. I'm not in prison anymore. It was time to live it up.

Carpe Diem.

Yolo. Or so I've heard.

I take a swig of the shot Julia hands me and silently hope that Officer Mitchell doesn't surprise me with a piss test tomorrow.

About a half hour later, we arrive at the small party with familiar faces from high school. What isn't familiar is the modern music that blasts through the speaker systems. I had some catching up to do in that department, seeing that everyone knows the words but me. Julia is in the corner with her mystery man, who is wearing the lamest clothes that I've ever seen, complete with a trucker hat.

Those things were still popular?

I'm on a couch next to a couple who can't keep their paws off each other. The guy, whose name is Evan went to high school with me but I've never seen the girl before in my life. It's quite interesting watching people age. Evan used to be the palest twig, but now ink covers his arms and his once boney shoulders have muscle mass. I try not to let those tattooed muscles remind me of someone else, but they unfortunately do.

Evan looks over my way and gives me a cocky grin.

"Evan, how are things?" I ask him.

He unlatches his mouth from the young looking brunette and looks my way. "Ginny, when'd you get out of the slammer?"

Cut right to the point, why don't you?

"Oh! I didn't get out. I escaped," I smirk, giving him a pair of crazy eyes. He laughs and I continue to say, "What are you doing with your life, Evan?"

"This is my girlfriend, Ashley," he says, looking at her adoringly.

We nod at each other when a guy in tight boxer shorts races across the living room, singing at the top of his lungs.

"What the hell was that?" I ask, exasperated.

"That's Patrick McLaughlin! You don't remember him?"

"Wait," I say, taking a better look at the tall and slender man dancing in his underwear. "Is that Fatty Patty?"

Patrick was an overweight boy at our high school who made us all laugh like it was his job. Instead of being the unpopular kid who felt the need to defend himself constantly, he was the popular linebacker of the football team who made light of his weight. He was also a good friend of Jesse's, who is the one who invented the nickname. I'm almost positive.

"He lost a lot of weight," I say.

Evan nods and then starts making out with his underage girlfriend again. I roll my eyes and take a look around the room. Aside from Fatty Patty hauling his newly renovated ass across the living room, it is way more relaxed than a high school party. For starters, the room is not compact and most people are sitting. There is also a lot more alcohol and weed out in the open.

I raise the bottle of vodka to my lips and let it fall down my throat like a waterfall. And suddenly, I'm having déjà vu. I'm back in high school drinking at a party, except someone is missing.

Before I know it, a quarter of the bottle is already gone.

Julia walks by me like she is on a mission to mars. She's leading the ape of a man she's with upstairs. She

CHAPTER TEN

glances at me and then to my empty bottle, but decides not to comment on it.

Good choice.

"Think you'll be okay for 10 minutes?" she asks.

The guy holding her hand looks purely offended. "Babe! More like a half hour."

"I'll be fine," I tell her.

"Okay. Jesse should be here soon," she mentions.

My eyes widen and the vodka decides to spurt out of my mouth instead of going down my esophagus. "You invited him?"

"I told him to stop by. He usually comes over to these things anyways. Why? Is there a problem?"

I shake my head and keep on drinking. I'm not even going to entertain Julia with the drama before she gets laid. Maybe Mr. Trucker Hat deserves that, but she certainly doesn't.

She flashes me a clueless smile before disappearing upstairs with her eager and waiting guy. I take it that she has no idea how sour things are between me and Jesse right now. Not many people knew about us, anyways.

I engulf another long swig of my bottle until there is no more left and then tip it upside down.

"Well, that's the second biggest tragedy that's ever happened to me," I mumble to myself.

While I'm waiting, a few people I recognize from High School pass by and wave. Some don't acknowledge me at all. Some go as far as even giving me the stink eye. I opt for the spot in the den where no one will find me, along with the bottle of cheap Gin that I stole from Evan, who didn't even notice because he was busy sucking face.

Now I hear Jesse enter the house and everyone sounds so happy to see him. I roll my eyes at the thought and self-medicate some more.

After what seems to be a few minutes of self-loathing, followed by another few minutes of waiting for Julia to finish up, I get up and walk around in my drunken stupor. I try to find the bathroom but then realize it's in the room Jesse's in. I'll have to walk right across him to get to it.

I stroll into the room that Jesse's in to him wearing a headset and cursing at the flat screen. There are two other guys that I don't recognize who are playing videogames with him. His bong sits on the coffee table; smoke residue coming from the foul smelling instrument. I spree across the living room at a rapid pace, hoping the Gin has given me Flash-like abilities.

"Where were you today?" he asks, his face glued to the flat screen.

I notice his buddies are snickering and that pisses me off even more. I stop right in front of the flat screen and cross my arms. "I had breakfast with a friend this morning."

"Was it with that guy?"

I look at him like he is certifiably insane, which he might be if he's asking if I'm seeing someone again. I can't even believe the balls Jesse has grown since I got put away. "Can we talk about this is private, Jesse?" I sigh.

He bitterly laughs as the guy next to him says, "you're in the dog house now, man."

He lifts his head and decides to put on a show. "Nah, we'll talk right here." He continues playing his game, eyes glued to the screen and leaving me with my jaw hanging.

Then finally he looks at me. In his most casual tone, he asks, "So. How'd his fingers taste?"

The room goes silent as my eyes blaze into his. They're more than blazing; they're watering. My fists are so tight that I'm sure all the blood flow is gone and they're about to fall off. "What did you just say to me?"

"What? No need to be secretive. We're all friends here," he shrugs. His voice comes off as mocking. A taunt. This isn't the Jessie that I know or love, but I already knew that the second I showed up on his doorstep.

"I'm not seeing him!" I shout.

"Could have fooled me!" He matches my tone.

"What I do now is none of your fucking business, Jesse!"

The room remains silent and I see Jesse turn a shade of crimson that I've never seen him wear. He stops pressing the buttons on his game controller and throws it to the ground in anger. Then he looks in my direction with wide eyes and flared nostrils. I think I've finally set him off, and I immediately regret it.

He gets up and aggressively grabs my upper arm to lead me into another room. I hear the whole room collectively gasp and laugh as we leave.

"Oh shut up you losers!" I yell from the other room, ignoring Jesse's iron grip and iced over eyes.

He slams the door behind us and looks at me with irritation. "What the hell is your problem?"

"You're the one that decided to start a God damn spectacle out there!" I scold him. "I'll say it again, Jesse! Not any of this is your God damn business, and I certainly don't want the world knowing it either!"

"You're right! I'm sorry!" he shouts in my face. "But you can at least have the decency not to parade it around right in front of me!" He slams the walls on both sides of my head, making me jump. "Did you ever think of how that makes me feel for one second?"

If I was a cartoon right now, my ears would be blowing steam accompanied by train honking. I fight the urge to say what's on my mind, knowing it will make things worse, but I blurt it out anyways. "Oh, you'd rather I kept it on the down-low like you and Lacey did?"

Oops.

He cocks his head back in disbelief and doesn't say a word in return. After a few moments of loathing me with his red framed eyes, he softens his facial features and closes the space between us. "Who told you that?"

"It doesn't matter!" I hiss.

"Lacey?" he pries, gripping my arm as if I'm going to start running.

"Nope!" I pop with a sarcastic tone and jerk my arm away.

"Julia," he grits through his teeth, coming to realization. "It was Julia."

"At least she had the balls to tell me!"

"I was going to tell you, Ginny," he tells me, his voice cracking.

I let out a bitter laugh and give him a crazy smile. "I thought we were through with this. I thought we were starting over! But you've been lying to me since I got out!"

"Gin," he cages me between the door and him, not giving me much wiggle room. His heavy breathing engulfs my every nerve ending, making me feel sensations I'm not used to.

I squeeze my eyes shut to avoid his sad stare.

He continues with a whisper, "Lacey was beautiful and smart and everything I should have wanted. We could have made a great fucking life together and a beautiful family. I could have had money and I could have left this family behind without a second thought," he grits out, his voice getting angrier with every syllable. Before I can blink again, he's smashing his fists against the wall again. When I let out a cry, his face softens a little again. He hangs his head low for a moment and then lifts it back up; his eyes drilling mine. "But you're missing something, Ginny. It's the same exact something that was the reason Lacey and I never worked out." Those eyes, those lips, that voice, I'm melting. "She wasn't you, Gin. She was never going to be you, either."

An unwanted tear makes its selfish way down my face, making me feel raw and wide open. He smothers his face into my hair and inhales deeply. I start to thaw within his embrace.

"Don't," I whisper.

He doesn't stop. He cups my face, forcing me to make eye contact with him.

"I'm not going to lie to you. I'm never going to lie to you again. She made things easier for me. She took care of me and picked up the pieces when you went away. No matter how much you hate her, I owed her for that."

Oh hell, I can't listen to this.

I go to turn my head and tune him out when he grabs me by the chin again and forces me to look at him. "But she wasn't you, Gin. She never made me feel the way you made me feel."

CHAPTER TEN

"Please don't do this," I warn him, tears in my eyes. I'm too weak right now.

I want him too much. He needs to be the strong one.

"We will never be over, Ginny. So you should stop fooling me, yourself, and especially that man."

I feel defenseless and spent. So when he leans into my face and our lips touch, I don't have the energy to pull away. I don't have the energy to stop crying. So I let the tears fall, and I let him kiss me. I let him hold me and whisper sweet nothings to me. Because I don't have anything left in me to stop.

When his hands start to wander and his tongue makes an appearance, I figure I should be enjoying this rather than feeling like I want to die. That's when I suddenly come to the decision that I need to get the hell out of here.

Pulling his hands off my face, I pull my head away from his and make sure to look him directly in the eye when I say what I want to say next. "Leave me alone."

I get the hell out of that house as fast as I can, forgetting to give Julia a heads up. Then I pull out my phone and dial the first person I can think of.

I catch the silhouette of his beautiful profile which is other worldly due to the simple fact that I'm seeing double. I'm not sure if I'm dreaming or if the alcohol is finally doing its job. I keep one eye shut and my other on the window reflection of him.

Instead of asking him how the hell I got in his car, I croak, "Water."

As the car slows down, I notice him inhale deeply. He's annoyed.

"What, who are we doing?" I sit up, feeling disoriented. I feel like I've been hit by a truck full of bricks. I rub the sleep from my cloudy eyes when I see his house come into view. He effortlessly pulls in the front and turns the car off, making the atmosphere pin-dropping silent.

"Where are we going?" he corrects me. His voice is laced with a sarcasm that I'm not used to with him. It takes me a couple of moments to realize that he's being an ass and picking on my drunken vocabulary.

Let me try this again. "W-what happened?"

"You called me," he tells me.

"I know," my voice is barely above a whisper. I remember that much.

What I don't remember is him picking me up or the car ride home.

"I'm sorry I called you so late. I actually just needed a ride home."

"I was going to bring you home," he explains. He's tracing the steering wheel with his finger, following it with his dreary eyes over and over. "But you begged me not to. You said you didn't want to be around Jesse."

I do the only thing I can right now; I laugh it off, but it's short lived by Benson's fists violently slamming into his dashboard. "God damn it, Ginny! Why'd you have to drink? You were doing so well!"

"I'm fine. Really," my voice comes out small.

He provides me a glare that says 'no you're not', then sighs as if I'm the most annoying creature on the planet.

"Seriously, Benson, I'm fine."

"You're obviously not if you're calling for me for help."

"I just wanted a ride home, Benson. If it was too much trouble, I could have asked someone else."

"Who else?" he asks and it truly stumps me. I remain silent and smothered in misery until he speaks up again. "I mean, do you even know what happens to people like us if we let go? It ruins everything, Ginny. Everything!"

"Stop it!"

"Are you having a hard time telling the truth, Ginny? Because that's the impression I'm getting!" His face is so close to mine but it's not how I pictured it being. If he's trying to intimidate me, it's working.

"I don't remember anything I said, Benson! Enlighten me, please!"

He shakes his head and dismisses my question with the wave of his hand.

CHAPTER TEN

"Please. Whatever I said I didn't mean. You can take me home!" I insist.

He smacks his hands on the steering wheel out of anger. "I'm beginning to think you like making me this frustrated."

I stare at his angry profile. "Benson."

I start to feel my chest tingle with embarrassment. He knew something that I didn't. I must have told him something in my drunken state that I don't remember. And he must've not liked a word of what I told him.

"Benson? What did I say? "

He finally directs his gaze towards me without looking like he wants to rip my head off. However, it's still not the look I prefer. This one is full of sadness and defeat. Almost as if he's already given up. "It's none of my business. Remember?"

His eyes are sunken in more than usual and his jaw is clenching hard. For a man that seems perfect on the outside, today is certainly not his day. He looks malnourished and sleep-deprived, but the killer part of it all is that he's doing nothing to hide it in front of me.

All of a sudden it feels like an elephant is sitting on my chest and I can't breathe. Before I know it, I'm choking on air and sobbing out of breath. I'm fucking hyperventilating. I reach out for anything but the closest thing I find is the dashboard. I smack it a few times until I get a release.

Alcohol-fueled tears glisten down my face as I continue to panic in his car, which suddenly feels smaller. I lay back in the seat, unable to care that he's witnessing the shit show from hell. I pull my legs up to my knees and wrap my arms around them; rocking back and forth in the fetal position.

I keep on sobbing, mortified and spent.

But then I hear Benson get out and slam his door shut, walking over to my side of the car. Opening my door, he tugs me out and lifts me by the waist. Before I know it, he's carrying me like a princess towards his house. My head lolls on his chest, and that's where it stays.

I manage to inhale his scent which actually soothes me. Between the tears, I take a peek at his broad chest and see his determined face. He looks pained and really pissed off. This man barely even knows me and he's already saving me from myself.

When we get inside, he heads for the kitchen and sets me down on the counter. Then he trails off to the living room, only to come back with a blanket for me. Once he drapes it over me, he heads over to his cabinet and pulls out his tea and hot chocolate. He has one in his left and the other in his right and shoves them in front of me, insisting that I choose one. I tap the hot cocoa box and see the corner of his lips twitch into a little smile.

I watch him work around his own kitchen in silence. It's unusually silent, but then again the seven year old isn't up. I glance at the clock; it's three in the damn morning.

"Why are you so nice to me?" I blurt out. Damn unfiltered thoughts.

I see his posture stiffen with my question. He stops what he's doing but doesn't give me the satisfaction of turning around. After watching his broad shoulders rise and fall a few times, he shrugs. "Because you take care of my daughter?"

"Oh come on. A real answer, please."

"Because I like you," he sighs.

I take a deep breath and match his sigh.

"You wouldn't like me so much if you knew me better."

He stops what he's doing again and turns half way around, meeting my eyes. "I could say the same."

"I'm twisted."

In response to that, I see his lips twitch into a grin. Once he's completely facing me, he continues, "We all have a past. We all have to deal with it. Give yourself a little more credit." He looks like he is pondering a question to ask me. His mouth opens to speak, but then he snaps it shut and looks away.

"Spit it out," I tell him.

CHAPTER TEN

He smiles cautiously as I see a hint of pink form in his cheeks. "This may be too personal, but just a shot in the dark. Are you still in love with him?"

I'm sure it only takes a few seconds to really answer him, but it feels like a lifetime. The truth is that I don't have a concrete answer. I slowly shake my head from side to side. "I, I don't know."

He seems a little let down by my answer. He turns back around and finishes boiling the hot chocolate.

"Put it this way. If I could go back in time and do it all again? I don't think I would."

"So you've made some decisions that you regret. It doesn't mean they were wrong or didn't mean anything."

"I just feel so guilty and," I trail off; searching for the word I'm looking for. It comes out, unfiltered, "dirty."

He seems taken aback by my choice of words. "I understand the guilt. But why dirty?"

I look up at Benson and feel my face flush. "He's my step brother. It wasn't supposed to happen."

"Could be worse," he mumbles.

"How?" I challenge, poking out my chin and chest.

"Hmm, let's see." He tilts his head in thought and then gives me a smug grin. "Well, he could be your real brother."

I roll my eyes and actually crack a smile. "True. Okay, you win."

"Nothing's perfect," he sighs. "You think my life with Angie was perfect? Hell, you think I'm the perfect father? I'm not going to sugarcoat it; Annie went to school with no socks on the other day. I have no idea what I'm doing."

"Have you ever felt guilty for loving someone?" I blurt.

He blinks. "If you didn't feel guilty for loving your step brother just a smidge, I'd really have to question your mental status."

I go to agree with him when interrupts me. "But Ginny? Not any part of you is dirty. Don't talk about my friend that way."

Emotions flood my face, causing my cheeks to flush cherry red. He winks and shoots me a warm smile. Without warning, a selfish tear makes its way down my face, followed by another. And another.

I didn't want to love him.

"I didn't want to love him," I sob.

"Hey, hey," he murmurs, engulfing me into his arms.

"Damn it. I hate crying," I choke as he takes the pad of his thumb and wipes a tear away.

"I'm sorry for earlier, Benson. I never wanted you to find out these things about me. I hate that you know them now."

"We're friends now Ginny, aren't we?"

I look up at him and nod.

"Do you have a sponsor yet?"

I shake my head, confused.

"Maybe you don't need help right now, but you will need someone to talk to when things get rough. You'll need a sponsor, and it will be me," he says. He doesn't offer it, he demands it.

"You will?" I ask, wiping the stray tears. He chuckles and nods, stroking my hair as I lay into his chest. When I look up at him he is staring at me adoringly with a stifled smile. He strokes my hair and looks at my face as if it's his most prized possession. Then he slowly slides his hand from my hair to the tender, red skin of my cheeks, rubbing them gently.

I'm so focused on his hands touching me that I barely hear him whisper, "Beautiful."

His fingers trail down my jaw and over the crown of my upper lip, delicately tracing them and watching me shudder. It looks like he's enjoying watching me by the incline of his lips. I'm definitely enjoying the unfamiliar feeling between my legs.

It's right then and there that I feel the desperate urge to feel his lips on mine. It's the way the inaudible gasp escapes them, tranquilizing me to no return.

I hop off the counter and lift up to my tippy toes, assessing his reaction before I place a small, dry kiss onto his full lips. As soon as we make contact, he stills completely.

CHAPTER TEN

I turn almost as red as him when we part and gage his reaction. My eyes grow even wider when I realize he's the one that parted the kiss first.

He looks like he's just seen the ghost of Christmas past.

Did he not like it? Is he angry or upset or regretting it already?

My face blushes with all of these embarrassing possibilities.

"I'm sorry," I finally whisper. I go to open my mouth again to say something, but am quickly pushed up against the wall, one arm around my waist and one hand firmly over my throat; lips sealed over mine.

This kiss is more firm and desperate. Testing the waters, we coax our lips against one another timidly. I snake my arms around his neck to bring him closer. It's like my body molds to his like a piece of clay. Wherever I tug, he goes. Wherever he pulls, there I am. He starts to back me up against the kitchen counter and then grabs my thighs, lifting me. I wrap my legs around his waist as he sets me down on the counter.

We continue getting to know each other's mouths with our tongues, our needy hands searching for something to grab onto.

There's a scientific term called Fight or Flight, which is a physiological reaction that happens during a damaging event, attack or threat to survival. So when Benson slides both of his hands up my neck and applies pressure again, this time painful, I quickly push him away and take a few steps back.

His eyes widen in a mix of shock and lust. "Did I hurt you?" he asks; his breath heavy and laced with concern.

"I should go," I pant, backing away from him.

"Ginny. I didn't mean to," he panics.

"It's okay," I dismiss. "I have to go." I quickly walk to the door and he follows. He's calling out my name and telling me to wait, but all I can think about is his hands around my neck, squeezing the life out of me. Before I walk out the door, I turn to him and what I see is disheartening. Worry and fear are etched all over his face.

"Benson, it's okay. You didn't hurt me." He didn't hurt me, but the action just felt wrong.

"I didn't mean to squeeze so hard," he whispers.

It's right then and there that I realize he's telling the truth. That it's a kink he likes but it went too far.

"I know," I say. "Let's forget about it, okay?"

CHAPTER ELEVEN

I wait for Benson's call the next day, but it never comes. In fact, I wait a whole two weeks before I hear from him again. Fourteen days, four AA meetings without Benson present, and two appointments with Officer Mitchell later, I finally get a text from him asking if I can watch Annie tonight.

Like the idiot I am, I agree.

When I arrive, I'm disappointed to see Janet waiting in his car for him. He must have done that on purpose so I didn't have to interact with her. I don't give him any beef about it, because let's face it, I'm nothing to him. What we did was a huge mistake. So I smile and engage in pointless chit chat with him until he leaves.

Once I get Annie to bed, I lay on the couch and try to read, which turns into skimming, which eventually turns into my eyes closing.

There is something quite unsettling about falling asleep in someone's house that you killed. My eyes immediately open back up when I think too hard about it.

I slam my book shut and go check on Annie. When I see she's fast asleep, I head to the kitchen and make myself a peanut butter and jelly sandwich. When I stroll back into the living room, I become aware of a bookshelf hiding behind the kitchen door.

That's weird.

It's out of sight and tucked away in a corner where people can easily walk past.

Being the nosey person I am, I brave a peek at what's on the shelf. There are tons of burned discs and DVDs with labels on them. I start shuffling through them when I realize that these are a bunch of home videos of Angelina, Benson and Annie.

I grab the one labeled, "Angie and Ben, Christmas vacation, 2005," and I walk over to the flat screen. I pop it in and make myself comfortable on the couch.

Why I am subjecting myself to this kind of torture, I have no idea.

What I witness next is beautiful yet utterly heartbreaking. I've never seen a man look more in love than Benson looks in this video. His blonde hair is longer and brighter in the sun, flopping over his tanned skin. His smile is bigger, his eyes are brighter, and his whole aura is healthier. You can tell that Angelina took care of him and made him happy.

Not only does his physical appearance look dissimilar, but his personality is too. He seems more carefree and content with life, and is obviously is much younger.

He is almost unrecognizable. A different person.

All of a sudden, Benson picks her up and throws her over his shoulder. She laughs freely as she tries to wiggle out of his playful hold.

I stop the DVD, throwing the remote on the floor in frustration. I don't need to see anymore to know that Angelina is the love of Benson's life. I wonder what would have come of me if I never went to Prison and ruined a family. Well for starters, I would have never met Benson at all.

I guess fate has a funny way of showing itself, sometimes.

What would have happened to Jesse and me?

I then think of my father. Would he not be the piece of shit that he is today?

I sit back on the couch and shut my eyes, trying to erase all of the frantic thoughts burrowing through my head. I start thinking of happy thoughts. Images of Benson and Annie and I raid my brain. The fantasy allows me to drift into a content slumber, despite my efforts fighting it.

Riiinggg!

My phone buzzes to life, startling me back into the sitting position.

I look and it's a text message from Jesse.

Jesse: Hey, can we talk?

I go to respond to him but am interrupted when the door flies open causing a deafening blast to my ear drums. I nearly wet my pants when I realize someone must have entered Benson's house. I hastily shove my phone back in my pocket, figuring I will respond to Jesse after I see who it is. If I'm still alive.

When I see its Benson, I push out all the excess air that I was holding in. Even though Janet is present and I can tell something's off with him, I'm relieved. He staggers in with his head hanging low, his movements sloppy and uncoordinated. When he spots me, he squeezes his eyes shut and starts to sway off balance.

After I get a waft of his scent, the assumptions I have made are confirmed. He is drunk. Belligerently drunk!

"You're going to fall," I warn him, quickly jumping to my feet and running towards him. That's when I see a tiny figure flashing down the stairs. Annie.

I turn to her when Janet forcefully bumps into me, pushing me to the side. She's drinking some sort of liquor still, a full bottle in her hand.

"What the hell are you guys doing awake?" she slurs, just inches away from my face. I nearly gag at the foul smell that lingers on her breath. I steady her when she loses her balance, but I think about just giving her a push instead.

That's when I hear Benson growl behind me. "Don't you dare talk to them like that!"

The thunder in his voice takes me by surprise, but I'm guessing she's used to it because she doesn't even blink.

"Don't you fucking yell at me you asshole!" she shouts, bumping chest to chest with him.

I feel Annie squeeze my hand tightly; holding onto me for dear life.

Janet takes a huge gulp of the contents in her bottle and then proceeds to throw it directly at Benson's head.

Holy. Shit.

He ducks quickly as the glass shatters all over the floor. I swiftly snatch Annie close to my side, making sure that she doesn't step into it. She is clinging onto my side like a koala bear in a tree, her body shaking with anxiety. I'm kind of wishing that I had someone's whole body to hold onto, too.

I turn my attention back to Benson, and it doesn't look good. His eyes are about to bulge out of the orifices of his skull.

"You are one crazy bitch!" he growls; the center of his eyes tiny pinholes.

Annie looks terrified, as if she's never seen anything like this before in her life. I feel relieved in knowing this because that must mean she's not used to it. If she's not used to it, then he doesn't do this often or in front of her. Thank God.

Instead of punching Benson directly in the nose like I really want to, I turn to Annie who is sobbing and holding onto me for dear life. I squat in front of her and softly murmur, "Annie, go back up to your bedroom, okay? I will be there in a minute to tuck you in."

"I'm coming too," I hear Benson slur, stumbling past me and to the staircase.

"Not a good idea right now," I warn him, putting my hands on his chest to stop him.

"I agree," Janet says obnoxiously. "Come back out. You know you loved it." She then hooks her index finger in the front of her low-cut shirt and pulls it down even more, teasing him.

Great. This woman was going to be the death of him.

I immediately turn Annie around, escorting her upstairs and into bed. This is a side of Benson that she had absolutely no business seeing.

As I lead Annie to bed, I hear Janet and Benson bickering. He's saying he's going upstairs to tuck his daughter in and Janet is saying every curse word in the hand book.

"That is my fucking daughter!" Benson bellows.

"Stop using your daughter as an excuse to see that whore upstairs!" I hear Janet shout.

"Don't you ever fucking call her that!" Benson roars, accompanied by a glass shattering. I take notice of the loud slam of a door, followed by pin dropping silence.

Good. Let them take it outside.

CHAPTER ELEVEN

As much of a good guy Benson is, he sure seems on the violent side sometimes. I shut my eyes, trying to restore my sanity before I tuck Annie into bed. She's crying under her pillow and stuffed animals.

"You okay, little chicky?" I ask, brushing her hair out of her face.

"What's wrong with Daddy?" Annie sobs. "I don't like Janet, Ginny. I don't like her one bit. He changes around her."

"I know, honey. But, he's still your daddy and he still loves you," I assure her, stroking her cheek. I stroke her blonde curls and let her cry it out. "Close your eyes sweetie."

When I'm positive that she isn't going to wake up, I murmur, "I'm sorry for what I did to your mom, kid. You have no idea."

Then as quietly as I can, I tip toe out of her room and fly down the stairs. He isn't in the foyer or the living room like I thought he would be. I search for him everywhere else in the house. He's nowhere. I go back up the stairs and hear a ruckus coming from one of the rooms. I peek in Annie's room just to make sure she hasn't woken up.

I walk towards the thrashing and screaming as the sounds get louder and louder. By the sound of it, it's most likely glass objects being shattered into smithereens and heavy objects being thrown around. When I peak my head in his room, I realize I'm not wrong, and that it's the source of Benson's mental breakdown.

He's pacing the room when he notices me, but then immediately finds another object to throw at the wall. This time it's his alarm clock.

I charge through the door like a bull ready to take out a torero, watching all of the objects fly around the room. He's throwing anything he can get his hands on and watching it crash against the wall.

He then sets his sight on his nightstand and looks at the only object left on it. He snatches it in his hands and winds it up, ready to throw, and that's when I see it. It's a picture of him and Angelina hugging each other.

I quickly run and steal it out of his hands without much of an effort. I tuck the picture away in one of his dressers and then return to face him. He's sitting on his bed, his head hanging on by a thread. He meets my gaze slowly and gapes at me in his drunken stupor.

I make sure my irritated face is doing all of the talking. My nose is flared and jaw is painfully clenched shut. We have a face off for a moment, but it's interrupted when he bursts out laughing. I shut his bedroom door behind me. If he wakes Annie up again, I'm almost sure I'll castrate him.

I open my mouth to shout, but then I decide to go a different route. Yelling at a drunk can be pointless or can escalate circumstances. "Could you stop that?"

He continues to wail, holding his belly as if I'm delivering the world's best comedy show. I truly begin to question his sanity when he almost falls off his bed because he's laughing so hard.

I'm also feeling a little insulted that he finds my 'I'm pissed at you' face funny. I go to open my mouth again, but then sigh. It seems the angrier that I get, the more laughing he does. Eventually, his happy oblivious mood rubs off on me and I start laughing along with him.

If you can't beat them, join them. Right?

"You can't be mad at me, can you?"

When I meet his eyes, they're blazing into mine with an intensity that wasn't there before. His new demeanor is nothing like the flirty, light voice like before. I feel my chest constrict with his raw, intense gaze. I steal a glance away from him, trying to gain some composure.

"Hey, want to pick up where we left off last night?" he chuckles.

I know he means it as a joke, but instead, my smile vanishes and all I feel is a flash of fury. "Don't flatter yourself."

His eyebrows bend and he tilts his head at me like I'm the crazy one.

"Oh, get over yourself, Benson!" I shout, surprised by my own tone. Then, I whisper yell, "You give me all these lectures about staying clean but you're so piss drunk right now you can't even stand up straight. On top of that, you just woke your daughter up at three in the morning. She was crying pretty hard. But you didn't have to take care of that, I did!"

He gradually stops smiling and just stares at something across the room that isn't even there. I notice his face harden as he starts to realize what he's done.

Panic. Despair. Regret.

After what seems to be a minute or two of self-loathing, he finally mumbles, "She'll get over it."

The rage I feel in the pit of my stomach dives head first even deeper, making me feel violently ill. I need to watch what I say, but somehow my filter forgets that I'm in someone else's house.

"No. She will not get over it," I spat, my voice strained. "She will remember this, Benson. She's old enough now. She's not a baby anymore. She will have memories of this!"

"Says the girl with daddy issues?" he mocks.

My jaw almost unhinges to the floor but I snap it shut and take a deep breath. I'm starting to feel my emotional walls crack. It's safe to say I hate drunken Benson. He's not a nice guy.

He's not the same guy.

As I struggle not to cry over his mean remarks, I can't help but notice he looks somber. Almost as if he regrets what he said. Good. He deserves to feel like shit for what he said.

When he lifts his gaze, his face noticeably softens when I hurriedly wipe away a few stray tears. He does not get to see me like this. Not today.

My conscience decides to make an appearance tonight, reminding me that this has been enough action for one night. Instead of telling him I'm leaving, I just do it. I turn on my heel and begin to walk out of his room. It takes less than a second for him to intercept me into his arms, grabbing me by the waist and reeling me into his chest.

With my back to his chest so forcefully, I feel him there in every way. My body is very aware of his fingertips skating over my skin and how close his lips are to my neck.

He grabs my hips firmly and turns me around to face him. When he pulls me into his warm embrace, I cling onto him as well. This was the type of attention that I craved from Benson, not the asshole brand.

"I'm sorry," he whispers, smothering his face into my neck, sending shivers down my spine. As we stand in the middle of his room, clinging onto each other for dear life, I completely dissolve into him. I'm fully aware of how close his beautiful and full lips are to my skin.

"I'm never going to do that again, I promise," he adds.

Promises, promises.

He hooks his finger under my chin, lifting it so that our eyes are aligned. I realize this is it. We are going to pick up exactly where we left off last night. His lips are inches away from mine, breathing air from his lungs into mine, reviving my insides, and kickstarting my heart.

The carefree part of me tells myself to let him do whatever he wants to me and that I've been waiting for this since I met him. On the other hand, the logical part of me comes bursting out into flames, taking my free will away from me. I place my hands on his chest and softly push away from him.

There is only one word that I need to tell myself when I need this to stop.

Angelina.

"I can't nanny for you anymore, Benson."

CHAPTER TWELVE

"What?"

"I can't do this," I break loose from him, back up a few steps and hug myself.

"But... I need you," he whispers, his voice strained.

I steal a glance at him and notice he's balling his fists and looking at me with determination. However, his focus has an edge to it that I can't quite put my finger on. He looks like he might explode at any given moment, so I attempt to tread lightly. "You don't need me. You don't even know me," I sigh.

"What?" he asks tilting his head to the side with confusion. "No, like, I really need you," he explains. "You have to help me get this piece of glass out of my hand. When Janet threw that bottle, I somehow got this." He walks up to me impatiently and holds out his hand.

I look down at his hand, which is palm up and in my face. In his hand reveals a one inch laceration that looks like it may need stitches. I'm relieved that he didn't actually need me, but at the same time, I'm entirely disappointed. I look at him and groan, grabbing his hand in mine and studying the affected area. Then I mutter, "You guys are quite the pair."

His mouth curves into a sloppy grin. "I'll tell her you said that tonight."

I drop his arm like it's hot. "You're going to her house after all this?"

He seems to enjoy my distress, but not in a mean way. More like he loves that I'm jealous.

Grinning, he asks, "Why, you don't want me to?"

"Did I say that?" I walk over to his bathroom and raid the medicine cabinet.

"You implied it."

I let out a low, bitter laugh and shake my head to myself. He notices and walks over to the bathroom. "Why is that funny, Ginny?"

I ignore his question, scanning the cabinet for a pair of tweezers. Once I find them, I walk over to him but don't settle my eyes on him just yet. I'm more than happy to avoid that question. I take his hand in mine again, digging gently under the surface of his skin with the point of the tweezers. He seethes when I dig too deep, jerking his hand away quickly.

When my eyes dart up to his, he's looking at me quizzically, like I'm the fucking weird one.

"Give me your hand," I command.

He stares at me for a beat too long. Then his whole face changes and it looks as if he's just figured out the math equation from hell. "You don't like me with her, do you?"

I don't answer; instead, I stare at his hand and play with the tweezers in my hand. I take a deep breath and choose to be honest. "No, I don't. Now give me your hand."

When he doesn't, I do myself a favor and grab it myself. I continue to poke him with the tweezers and ignore his intense eyes. He's silent for a few solid minutes, but then he takes his other hand and tilts my chin up to meet his.

"Do you want me to stop seeing her?" he finally asks, his voice tender. Everything about it is inviting and I want to say yes.

I don't answer him. I go to grab his hand yet again. He leans in so close to me that I can feel his hot breath and whispers into the shell of my ear. "Is that what you want?"

Goosebumps invade my body. I space out for a moment with his interrogations, then quickly grab his hand and start hunting for the piece of glass again. I focus all of my attention on that, hoping that I can block out his voice. He pulls his hand away again and looks at me with caution. "Ginny?"

My eyes slowly meet his. I don't know whether to bluff or be truthful. Something tells me that if I'm honest that I'll be disappointed.

"What do you want?" he prods. He scans my face, accessing me like I am the most complex thing he's ever seen in his life. To be truthful, I am completely overwhelmed by his questions. I go to speak, but the words don't come out because I don't know what to say. I look back up at him and he's waiting patiently for a response.

CHAPTER TWELVE

"I don't know!" I explode and head to the bathroom, setting the tweezers on the counter. My frail arms support my weight as I lean against it. I don't have the strength to do this anymore. I need to leave while I still can.

"Yes you do," he encourages me.

"Fine! You know what I really want, Benson? I want you to surround yourself with people who make you feel the need not to drink! Jesus Christ!"

Liar, liar, pants on fire, Ginny.

"Are you saying Janet drives me to drink?"

I roll my eyes. "That's one way of putting it. She's just no good for you, and you know it."

"So you do want me to stop seeing her," he teases, the corner of his mouth quirking up.

"I don't give a shit what you do, Benson," I say, throwing my hands up in the air in defeat.

"Can you just admit to me what you can't?" he yells, starting to get annoyed.

"I don't know what you're talking about!"

"What do you want?" he bellows. I jump at the tone of his voice but a sliver of a thrill runs through my body at the same time.

"You!" I shout and then back up, putting a huge, imaginary barrier between us. I cannot believe I just said that. Silence fills the air and I gesture the space between us with a wave. "But it can't happen. I want you, but it can never happen."

"You're afraid of me?" He frowns.

"I'm not afraid of you, Benson," I lie. I am so close to giving up on this fight and letting him take me right here on his bed. Or maybe I should just come clean with him since this lie has gone on too long. I take another long inhale of air and hold it while I think of what to say to him. "I'm afraid of myself."

I notice he's walking towards me again like I had given him the green light. I put up my arms in an attempt to stop him. "No Benson, Stop."

"Why?"

"Don't you get it?"

"Not at all." He looks like he's ready to pounce.

"We're a disaster waiting to happen."

He places his hands on my hips before I can stop him. "Well, there's really nothing you can do to prevent natural disasters. You just have to let him run their course."

I'm deathly afraid of Benson Daniels. So I do the worst thing I can do to get out of the situation. I say the absolute wrong thing.

"Yes, there actually is." I swallow a hard lump in my throat. "Instead of trying to get my pants, maybe you should check on your daughter." I immediately regret my words when I see how hard they hit him. I make a bee line to the door but am stopped by his voice again, and it's laced with resentment this time around. "Don't you ever tell me how to raise my daughter," he growls through gritted teeth.

The words shatter me to my very core, causing me to bend over and hold my abdomen. I feel like I'm going to be sick. When I steal a glance at him, his eyes say it all. He looks like he is ready to kill. I sigh, "You're a great father, Benson. I guess I just thought that you'd have the decency not to drive drunk. Isn't that how your wife died?"

His eyes widen as he focuses on something on the carpet. "Yes. That's exactly how she died," he mumbles. "She was walking on foot. She didn't stand a chance."

"But you do."

"Don't go. Please," he begs.

I'm shocked by the quick change in his demeanor and desperation towards me. I'm also shocked at what I'm about to say next. "Don't go to Janet's house."

"Okay." He stands up, interrogating me with his beautiful blue eyes. He gives me a once over, up and down, and starts to walk towards me like a predator. With each step he takes, I step backwards, bumping into a solid wall behind me. When he is so close to me that you can't even fit a pencil between us, he sets his forehead to mine softly. "I'd do anything you ask me to."

"You're drunk."

"I'm being honest. I'm an honest drunk."

CHAPTER TWELVE

If I were being completely honest, I'd do anything he'd ask me to as well.

"Tell me more," I finally whisper, melting into him.

I can't believe I just said that. He can't either. He looks at me with confusion.

"More honesty," I prod.

"I am a single father," he whispers. "I've had to be a mother and a father to Annie," he gets lost in his own words, staring at the contact of our skin. "And while I had to do that, I've had this burning hole eating away inside me the whole time. It's been there since Angelina die, and nothing has fixed it." He tilts my chin up, forcing me to look at him. "Then I met you. The hole doesn't feel like a hole anymore. It certainly doesn't burn anymore. It's just… there. A scar. It reminds me of those times I wish I could forget, but it doesn't hurt anymore."

"Whoa," I exhale.

He nods. "I have a lot of demons, Ginny. More than meets the eye."

I lift my head to see that his eyes are blazing into mine, and suddenly my stomach feels unsettled. I think these are what they call butterflies. A rush of euphoria hits me like never before, and the need for Benson grows even stronger.

"How's that for honesty?"

I nod, unable to speak properly. "It's good."

"If it means I get to have you, I'll always be honest with you and I'll never lay an eye on Janet again." He says so low that I almost miss it.

I feel so overwhelmed with emotions right now, but once I hear her name, all it makes me feel is angry and bitter.

"I should go now," I whisper.

"Okay," he agrees but doesn't move. He scratches the scruff on his chin in thought and I have to wonder what he's thinking. It dawns on me that he didn't listen to a word I was saying. Not a word, at all.

"If that's what you really want," he adds, burning and burrowing his way through my head.

My butterflies fly south with the lone intensity of his stare. I feel the sudden urge to have his hands all over me, every single inch, every slope, and every single valley. I straighten my posture and get ready to make a run for it; however, both of his hands have me caged to the wall.

"One more thing," he adds, his lips nearly touching the shell of my ear. I pulse my head away from his touch, because if he comes any closer I might just let go.

I nod and look into his eyes. They are so close that they're all that I can see.

"You remind me of her."

Four simple words. One complicated sentence. I swallow, hoping that he isn't referring to who I think. Realization hits me out of nowhere when I come to the conclusion that's exactly who he means. Her dark hair, check. Her pale skin, check. Her husband, check.

The only thing I'm missing is her damn charm bracelet.

I stiffen my posture, more aware than ever of his desire for me. For the first time tonight, I begin to feel uncomfortable with it. He gazes at me, waiting patiently for a reaction, but then continues, "I can't explain it, but some of your mannerisms. Your hair. I don't know if that's a good thing or a bad thing but I've thought it from the first second that I saw you."

He lifts his hands and cradles my cheeks, almost having me sold.

Could we make this work with me knowing I'll never amount to his wife and him knowing I killed her?

Could we get passed this? The sliver of hope makes me think we actually have a chance.

The realistic part of me knows there's no chance in hell.

I take both of his wrists in my hands and pull them down. I'm putting a stop to this right here, right now. "It's probably a bad thing. I'm nothing like her."

"I know this because you're actually here!" He grabs onto me extra tight, knowing at any moment I will escape. "I can touch you," he whispers.

CHAPTER TWELVE

I don't tell him that there are actually many more differences between us. I leave that one alone.

I take a step back so now he can't touch me. I don't know how I feel about his confession. I don't want to be a replacement for his wife. Still, with a few feet between us, he stares at my lips, looking ready to pounce.

"I'm not a replacement, Benson. I never will be your wife. I'm Ginny. I'm the woman you met at AA."

He quickly pushes me up against the wall, leaning his body completely into mine and I can feel him poking into my stomach. "Do you feel that?" he whispers. "This is what you do to me. Not her. Not Janet." He has me in the ultimate trap, physically and emotionally. I let him toy with me and he nuzzles his nose against the most sensitive part of my neck. "You."

He grabs me by the chin, forcing me to look at him again. "Stay with me tonight."

He hesitantly places soft kisses on my neck, under the fluttering pulse, and I moan in response. He traces torturous kisses up my jaw line and makes his way to my ear lobe, biting it hard. This causes my knees to buckle and give out beneath me. He catches me in his arms, holding onto me completely.

I feel his hands start to roam my body with urgency, feeling the softness of my skin. He lightly grazes my nipples, making them come to life, hard and visible through my t shirt.

Finally, his lips make their way over mine, brushing over them tauntingly. I moan and buck my hips, needing them to be on me. He softly chuckles, enjoying me at his mercy. At last, he gives me what I want, sealing his full lips over mine, soft and gentle. As soon as we are connected, his lips and tongue immediately beg for more access.

I feel the urgency in him more than ever.

Now, it's my turn to tease him.

I feel his demanding hands on my thighs and hips but don't stop him. I let him go crazy, refusing to feed him my tongue just yet.

"Open for me, Ginny," he growls in the pit of heat and desire. "Give me your tongue right now." His tongue peaks out and swivels my neck, jaw line, and lips. "What will it take? Coming while sleeping on my couch, again?" I feel his lips curl into a smile knowingly against mine.

That's all it takes for me to lose the rest of my inhibitions and open my mouth for him. As soon as I do, I feel his slick, greedy tongue slide right in, exploring mine and taking what he wants.

I clutch onto his dirty blonde hair and kiss him back desperately, passionately, and demandingly. I know I've had them just once before, but this time is different. His lips are soft and full and everything I've imagined. His beard scuff massages my raw face, awakening every nerve ending on my body.

His needy hands slide down my abdomen and curl around my waist, clutching it hard. It doesn't take long for his dancing hands find the zipper of my jeans, pulling it down and slipping his hand inside. His eyes dance over mine mischievously before he slides his hand down my panties, touching me right where I need him to. Gently, he brushes his fingers over my overly sensitized nub, rubbing in a circular motion. When his two fingers find my slick entrance, I see a pleased smile on his lips. He continues tormenting me with two fingers, sliding in and out torturously slow, his eyes never leaving mine.

"We shouldn't," I shudder.

"We definitely should. Tell me what you need, baby," he coos and continues to rub me just right. I think he's enjoying my sex coma way too much. I moan and shake my head in response.

"Do you want me to stop?" he taunts, taking out his fingers little by little.

I arch my hips forwards, taking more of his fingers and giving him all the approval that he needs. He starts teasing me again with his fingers, leisurely. When I begin to swell inside, he picks up the pace, sliding in and out of me hard and fast. I feel his lips smile against my neck as he continues his sexual torment. "You really enjoy being finger banged, don't you?"

CHAPTER TWELVE

"Oh God, don't you dare stop," I moan into his neck, gripping onto his biceps.

The temperature between my legs is rising quickly as I get ready for my big finish. He notices this and picks up the pace with his hands.

I'm so close. I just need a few more circles of those expert fingers. I'm almost there. I blow out a gasp of air and throw my head back in pleasure. "I'm gonna come."

I'm on the brink when a high-pitched sound goes off in my pocket, followed by a quick vibration. It's my no good, son-of-a-bitch phone. I think about smashing it across the wall and getting back to it.

It's Benson who hesitantly unlatches his mouth from mine and removes his hand, resting it on my stomach. I quickly shuffle into my pocket, not taking my eyes off his, until I look to see who it is.

Jesse: I know it's none of my business, but I'm worried about you.

Jesse: Just tell me that you're okay.

I stare at my phone for a good moment until Benson chimes in. "Who is it?"

"Jesse." I can't quite look Benson in the eye, so I look pretty much anywhere but at him.

"I have to admit something that I'm probably not going to remember in the morning." He nuzzles his face into my hair and takes my phone away from me, placing it on the table. When he turns back around to face me, he's in full cuddling mode, wrapping his long limbs around me. "I don't like seeing you with him, and I'm willing to bet that I wouldn't like seeing you with any other guy either." He dips his fingers into my mouth and then slowly pulls them out, forcing me to taste myself.

Then, I say something stupid. Really stupid. "He's family."

"We all know that doesn't matter to either one of you," he says, deadpan.

"Stop it," I whisper as I wiggle out of our intertwined bodies.

"I'm being honest. Honesty is what has got us here, Ginny."

I lift to my feet and walk across the room to retrieve my shoes, ignoring him. I'm not responding to that even though my crimson face says it all. He notices my embarrassment, grabbing me by the arm and turning me around.

"Hey," he says softly. "I'm sorry but after what you told me, all I can picture is him putting his hands all over you. I just don't like it. It's … repulsive. Can you blame me?"

I want to tell him to fuck off, but I'm the one in someone else's house. I want to get so loud and furious, but Annie is in the other room. Just when I flair my nostrils and squeeze my fists so hard that my knuckles turn white, I notice something in my peripheral vision.

He seems different. His stance, his whole being is not the same.

I watch him blink a few times and he suddenly straightens his posture.

"I'm… I'm sorry," he tells me.

He looks pained. Thwarted. Even though his blood alcohol level is through the roof, he looks as sober as ever.

I'm stunned by his response. I open my mouth to retort, but hastily snap it back shut.

He distances himself by backing up a few steps and clears his throat. "You should go."

I suppose I was hoping he wouldn't say something like that.

"What?" I'm confused. I'm frustrated. Anything but this.

"You're Annie's nanny," he informs me, his voice soft but firm. "I'm just really drunk right now. This is my entire fault."

"Benson." My heart drops to my stomach. I feel like I'm losing him when I've never really had him.

"This was a mistake, Ginny. Please, you should go," his voice gets firmer by the end of the sentence.

CHAPTER TWELVE

I reluctantly nod and go to exit his room but stop short at the door. I have to get this off my chest. I need to say this to him, at least. "Please don't go see Janet tonight."

I don't turn around to assess his reaction. He doesn't even give me a response, which makes me think maybe he didn't even hear me.

"Don't sleep with her, Benson," I repeat.

After what seems like a lifetime but has only been a few minutes, I finally hear him speak. His voice cracks and is laced with pain and emotion. "You know I can't promise you that."

I swallow a large lump in my throat and nod. I am so upset to my stomach that I don't even reply. Instead, I hold back the unwanted tears that intrude my tear ducts. I give him a soft nod to hide my grief, and then leave.

This time he lets me leave, no questions asked, no big arms intercepting me.

Walking into Jesse's apartment as quietly as I can is a horrible failure. After accidently shutting the door too hard, I lean up adjacent to the wall and squeeze my eyes shut. I really hope he didn't just hear that.

Oh, but he did. He stands like a tower in the doorway of his bedroom, leaning against the molding. I don't want him to see me sniveling, so I dart right to the couch and cover my head with a pillow.

Real mature, Quinn.

I hear his bare footsteps pad their way towards me. He remains quiet, squatting beside me and softly petting my hair. Of course, he knows something is wrong; it's Jesse we're talking about here.

I peer through the pillow and see his concerned eyes. His beautiful big brown eyes. He knows something's wrong and he knows it has nothing to do with us this time. I sit up straight, putting some space between us. The text messages he sent me earlier tonight come to my attention.

"Are you okay?" I hiccup.

"You look horrible. Shouldn't I be asking you that?"

I can't hold it in anymore. Before I know it, I start to sob and throw myself into his waiting arms. He gently shushes me as he strokes my hair, letting out a little chuckle.

Wait, did he just laugh? Just when I'm about to pretend it never happened, I feel his chest vibrate against my face. I lift my head to see his face splitting into a grin.

He notices I look irritated and explains, "Sorry. This just reminds me of high school all over again with your heart getting broken and me picking up the pieces."

"I'm sorry. You don't have to do this."

"Stop," he whispers, rubbing his hand up and down my arm. "I want to."

His eyes search mine before he takes a profound breath. "Sleep in my room tonight. You need a good night's rest."

"No. I'm fine here. I slouch down the couch to get comfortable. Within a split second, I'm lifted completely off my butt and slung over Jesse's shoulder. He carries me to his bedroom, holding me like a sack of potatoes.

What the hell does he think is going to happen? Does he think we're going to sleep in the same bed? Because if he does, then he's sorely mistaken.

I attempt to wrestle out of his hold, not getting very far.

"NO!" I shout. "I am not sleeping with you! It's disgusting. We can't do that anymore!"

He looks as if I slapped him across the face. "Sleep with me? Who said anything about sleeping with me?" His voice is undoubtedly defensive. "I was going to give up my bed for you!"

My face softens. "I thought…"

"Get over yourself," he cuts me off. He tries to get away from me but I pull him back onto the couch. He takes a deep breath in defeat and looks straight ahead like a caveman. He won't even look at me now.

"You thought wrong," he finally says.

"Jesse please," I whisper as I hesitantly reach out my hands and cradle his face in my hands. "I've had a terrible night. I'm so sorry. Please don't go."

CHAPTER TWELVE

Jesse was just trying to comfort me, and I was such a bitch to him. I steal a glance at the only man that I ever knew. Sure, he wasn't always there, but he's more than making up for lost times now.

The otherwise dark room allows a luminous streak of moonlight to peak through the curtains, coloring his face at just the right angle. I can't help but remember how beautiful Jesse has always been to me.

Especially his dark and thick lashes that flutter against his sharp cheekbones. God, he could be a male model if he really wanted to.

He sighs and flickers his eyes shut, looking pained. He looks tired. I don't want to bother him, but I can't help myself. I reach for his hand and cradle it in mine, holding it tightly.

I just sit there and devour Jesse's indifferent beauty. From his careless fashion to his hair that he doesn't even have to style to look amazing. I often wonder what he thinks of himself and if he knows how beautiful he really is.

I suddenly feel my inhibitions escape like wildfire, getting hungrier by the minute. It's too late to catch my conscience which has flown out the window as soon as he licks his lips. Everything I do now is out of pure instinct.

I watch a single tear fall down his smooth, olive-toned skin and carefully catch it with the tip of my tongue. After licking it away, I intercept his mouth with mine and latch on softly. He graciously accepts my invitation and wraps his arms around my waist, pulling me into him as if he is starving for me.

I need comfort in the worse way tonight, and Jesse is going to give it to me.

CHAPTER THIRTEEN

I wake from a fulfilling sleep the next morning. The first thing that I recognize is all of our clothes scattered throughout the floor like a tornado hit it. Both of the clothes Jesse and I wore the previous night are here, there and everywhere. They're on the lamp shade, the dresser, and the night stand. Basically, anywhere my eyes go; there's an article of clothing.

Oh, and there are my panties shamelessly hanging out on Jesse's lampshade.

Wait a minute. Jesse's lamp. Jesse's room.

I jump up when I realize that I am in his bed. I also notice that I am completely naked.

Squeezing my eyes shut, I groan and pull a pillow over my head.

I remember now. Jesse and I had Earth-shattering sex last night. I spot a broken footboard leaning up against the wall that wasn't there yesterday, yet somehow the bed's symmetry is fine. I grin at the thought of our rough adventures.

Then all of the vivid memories come back to me.

"I knew you needed to get laid. I just knew it," he groans through heated kisses and licks. His body roams every smooth plane and crevice of my body as if he's been dying to do it his whole life. He's rough and demanding, yet sensitive and tender; just as I remember him.

I know this is wrong but it feels way too good to stop. I've been reduced to a panting and breathless mess.

"This can't happen again, okay?" I moan.

"Shut up Ginny. Just shut up," he groans, intercepting my mouth right after. I'm assuming he does it because he wants to and not because he wants me to actually shut up.

"God, you feel so good," I whimper.

He enters me slowly, stretching me for the first time in seven years. I bite my lip through the stinging pain, knowing very soon it will bring me unrelenting pleasure.

CHAPTER THIRTEEN

"I love you more than my own life, you know that right? I love you so fucking much," he chants. His lips dance across my damp body like a ritual.

I close my eyes, letting Jesse worship my body like it's his temple. I let him take the pain away. To my recollection, I may have even asked him to. And he does. Jesse takes the pain away the only way he knows how. He unforgivably loves me with his hands, his lips, and other parts of him until I'm in tears, begging him for mercy.

My breath hitches as I remember the escapades from last night.

The sexcapades.

It felt too dream-like to be reality, but it felt too real to be a dream.

My questions are answered as soon as I hear voluminous voices outside the room. I instinctively curl into the fetal position and pull the sheets over my body as if it's a shield. I also note that there is more than one voice and that they're arguing.

One I definitely identify as Jesse's voice. The other voice is familiar but seems frustrated and hard to comprehend.

I know that voice. I've heard it in my nightmares.

It's my father.

I quickly get changed and open the door to them bickering in the living room across from one another. They seem to be in the middle of a heated discussion, their hands flying in the air. The argument is all but short of them throwing punches and objects at each other.

"What are you doing here?" I interrupt, coldly. I stand in the doorway, against the molding with my arms crossed like it's actually protecting me from them.

"Gin, sit down," my dad dismisses.

I abandon my sanctuary and walk towards them with my fists squeezing so tightly that they almost bleed. I can't believe Jesse would invite my father here when he knows our history.

"Fuck you, Dale," I spit at my father, using his real name for a change. Then I fix my eyes in Jesse's direction. "How could you?"

He sighs. "Ginny, I had to."

"Why?" I shout. "What was so important to call the last man I'd ever want to see?"

"You guys need to work things out," Jesse grits through his teeth, seemingly fed up. "I can't be the middle man anymore!"

I let out a bitter laugh. "You can't be in the middle anymore?" I huff. "But you'll be other things that are convenient, won't you?"

Jesse's eyes widen. He looks terrified.

Good.

Although he had never mentioned it, I believe my father had a suspicion all along that Jesse and I screwed around. In hindsight, we didn't do a good job of hiding it. And in all honesty, I didn't care if he knew it either.

"I'm the last man you'd ever want to see?" my father growls. "Really?"

I nod manically. "Yeah, Father dearest! The last person on Earth! Maybe second last, now." I shoot daggers at Jesse.

"What about Benson Daniels?" My father's taunting voice makes my ears perk.

I think I've heard him correctly, but I ask anyways. "What?"

"Where is he exactly on your list these days? I thought for sure he'd have me beat."

The room goes eerily silent; not one of us saying a word. I blink once, my nostrils flaring in pure and unadulterated rage. My fists are back at it again, flexing and then tensing into a tight ball. And I don't think I've blinked in the past five minutes at all.

I try to hide the shock off my face. How did he find out? I start thinking of all of the possibilities, but the most obvious choice is the one I was hoping wasn't true.

"Who told you?" my tone is angry but surprisingly even.

CHAPTER THIRTEEN

My dad rolls his eyes. "I'm not an idiot."

"He dropped you off the other day," Jesse chimes in.

"Shut the hell up, Jesse," I snap, keeping my angry glare on my father.

And that's when I realize my suspicions are correct. Jesse told him everything. That he dropped me off the other night, that I've been babysitting his daughter, that I've been spending most of my time with him.

"It's a small town," my excuse of a sperm donor adds.

"That's not how you found out!" I shout. "It has nothing to do with this shitty small town. This is all you!" I glare at Jesse. "You told him everything. You're jealous because I chose to spend my time with him and not with you. You're a jealous bastard."

"We all know!" Jesse bellows, pulling at his hair with frustration. "And soon he will too. It's just a matter of time, Ginny!"

I snap my head back, shocked by Jesse's demeanor. I'm so pissed off that I can't even look at him. Grabbing my stuff, I head for the door. "I'm never forgiving you for this."

"Ginny wait," Jesse pleads.

I go to leave the apartment when my father's mocking voice stops me. "Just out of curiosity Ginny, what did Jesse do other than help you?" he asks. "You ungrateful little whore."

I can practically feel my blood rush to my head through my ears. I can hear the fucking ocean. I snap my head in my father's direction. "Excuse me?"

"You heard me," he calmly says. "I raised a little whore of a daughter. No dreams or aspirations, other than anything that moves. That's probably what you've been doing with this Benson guy, yeah?"

My face sobers as I listen to this man I used to call my father. I can tell that Jesse is completely blindsided by all of this, and didn't mean to take it this far. I take a couple predatorily steps towards my father and scowl at him. He is so lucky that I hated prison, or else I'd be going back today.

"No, no. You didn't raise me. You didn't raise me at all," I take a step closer and give him a mocking smile of my own since he's such a fan of them these days. "And you answered your own question. What did Jesse do other than help me? He banged me," I shrug. "That's what he did- in every position, on every surface of your home."

Silence fills the room. Jesse has turned a shade of white resembling a ghost. He looks like he's about to pass out. However, my father is another shade completely; red as a tomato.

"Oh, and remember your car that we totaled senior year? That's because I was giving Jesse head so good that he ran into a thruway exit sign. It –was–that–good." I emphasize every word.

Then within the blink of an eye, his hand raises, giving me a hard and stinging slap across my face. My jaw drops and my initial instinct is to grab my face. Jesse stands there stunned but doesn't do anything. The coward doesn't say anything let alone help me.

However, I'm not as stunned as I seem. I use to see him do this to my mother on a daily basis. I suppose that I almost anticipated it.

My dad seemingly doesn't regret a thing and that fails to surprise me either. If you look deep into his whiskey eyes, you'll notice he may have even enjoyed it.

I hold my sore face and glare at Jesse, hoping he'll chime in again just like he had been doing. But he doesn't. Unwelcome tears start to raid my face, but not because of what my father did. It's Jesse that I'm disappointed about this time.

Running out of the house is when Jesse storms out the door and follows me.

"Ginny, please!" he shouts, catching my forearm in his tight grasp. I immediately pull out of his hold and shoot daggers at him.

"Don't you ever touch me again!" I scold him.

"I had no idea he was going to do that to you, Ginny."

"You did nothing!" I scream at him, tears pouring down my cheeks.

"I wanted to help you. I did." His voice is regretful, but I don't buy it.

CHAPTER THIRTEEN

"Oh, you did?" I sass. "Well, where in the hell were you?"

He shrugs. "I'm sorry. I was in shock. I'll go in there right now and punch him in the face if that's what you want. I'll do it."

I laugh bitterly. "Yeah, okay Jesse," I dismiss him.

When I turn my back on him, his voice stops me in my tracks. "Yesterday meant something to me, Gin."

I look at him dead pan, my heart feeling as black as coal. I touch the swollen, stinging cheekbone that my father gave me and shudder. I'm not ready to forgive him and I don't know if I'll ever be.

I want to tell him that I don't love him and will never love him again. I want to tell him that part of our lives is far over with, and I have found more to live for than him. I go to open my mouth to confess these things, but as I look into his watering eyes, I start feeling a hint of remorse.

"Please, leave me alone. Not for a day, not for a week, not for a month. Not for seven years." I swallow a large lump in my throat and an unwanted tear makes its way down my face. "Leave me alone forever, Jesse."

This was going to leave another mark.

I knock three times before turning around to leave. That's when I hear the door creak open.

"Ms. Quinn," Officer Mitchell calls from behind. He sounds surprised to see me, but I detect it laced with relief.

I turn around slowly when he notices a big black and blue bruise that surrounds my right eye. He covers his mouth with his hands. "What happened to you?"

I swallow hard before trying to find the right words to respond with. "My father happened to me."

He nods knowingly. I watch him swallow hard as he tries to process his next words, but instead, I cut him off by clearing my throat and saying, "Hey, do you still have the number to that homeless shelter that you've been raving about?"

"Come in, Ginny." He holds the door open for me.

I walk in his big suburban home, scanning my eyes around the white leather furniture and six foot tall plants that sit the corners of the room. Then I look at where their seventy-two inch flat screen is and to the right, I see his wife rapidly pacing on the treadmill. She stiffens when she sees me and looks at her husband with curious eyes. I take off my hood so that she doesn't think that I'm a suicidal terrorist or something. God knows she hasn't had someone like me in her house before.

I didn't picture Officer Mitchell with a little petite blonde for some reason. He seemed much too dark and twisty to have such a peppy wife. I guess opposites really do attract.

"One of my kids," he tells her. "Hold my calls, Laura." Then he turns to me and says, "Let's go to my office and talk, Ginny."

I follow him down a narrow and bland hallway to his private office, where he gestures me to sit in front of his desk. He sits down across from me and crosses his arms with a sigh. "Tell me what happened."

I slouch down in the chair with my arms crossed and absolutely nothing to say. For some reason, I suddenly feel shy about airing my dirty laundry out to him. It's not that I didn't trust him. He had treated me well since I've gotten out. Despite my faulty actions in the past, he saw the good in me. So I explain my situation to him the best way I can without giving everything away.

"I'm homeless," I shrug. "That's what it comes down to."

"And your step brother?"

I shake my head, insinuating that's no longer an option.

"Well, you're not alone, Ginny. There are many women in your shoes. I know a home for women down in Pittsfield; it's on the outskirts of Rochester, New York. I know it's a little bit of a drive, but at least you would have a safe place to be with a roof over your head. They help you get back on your feet."

CHAPTER THIRTEEN

I nod vigorously. "Okay. Just give me the address and I will be on my way."

"I'll call them to let them know," he tells me.

He picks up the phone off the cradle to dial the number and I can't help but notice he knows the number by heart. We wait in silence for a few minutes before someone answers on their end. His tone is very formal and persuasive, knowing exactly what to say and when.

After he ends the call, he gently places the phone on the cradle and looks at me. "Tomorrow, first thing in the morning they will be expecting you. They lock the doors after a certain time and we'd never make it in time now."

He notices the look of dissatisfaction on my face. "You can stay here tonight and crash on our couch. Tomorrow, I will bring you myself."

"No way," I immediately object.

He smiles softly and knowingly. "Shouldn't I be the one worried?"

His sarcasm charms me and I flash a genuine smile. "I can't stay in your home. It wouldn't be right."

"No, it wouldn't," He drawls as he plays with the cord of his phone. "But I'm going to make plans for you today anyway with Dr. Lee and then a meeting at AA. You'll barely be here."

Oh, God.

I groan and slide down my seat like I'm in school and he's giving me lunch detention.

"Relax; it's only a half hour long. But, you're appointment is in an hour so you should start to get ready."

"Who is Dr. Lee? You're killing me," I mutter.

"Look, this is the deal. I want you to talk to someone. You get these things done; you get a warm bed tonight. Then tomorrow, I will safely bring you to the women's shelter in Pittsfield. Deal?"

I sigh. "Fine. Deal."

CHAPTER FOURTEEN

    I should consider myself lucky that my own parole officer is willing to take me under his wing, but who the hell does that? Nothing seems right about it and my mind starts to wonder if he is harboring some messed up obsession with me or something. I am so completely fucked up sexually that I'm even considering sleeping with him for a roof. He's not the worst looking old man and he certainly takes care of his body.
    I snap out of it abruptly when a slender Asian woman takes a seat across from me. She's pretty but the gray hairs surrounding her temples give her true age away.
    "Why are you here, Genevieve?" Dr. Lee asks, tapping her pencil against her arm rest. She looks a little nervous, too.
    I inhale and cross my arms, securely. "My parole officer seems to think I need to talk to someone."
    "Well, do you think that you need this?" She tilts her head.
    I divert my eyes from hers, my finger trailing over my jean clad legs over and over out of boredom. I'll do anything but look into her eyes and give her honesty right now.
    "I may need therapy," I sigh. "But I sure as hell don't need AA meetings."
    "You really think that?" she challenges me. "We don't just end up at AA, do we now? There's a reason why you're there."
    I cross my arms impatiently.
    "Tell me about your AA meetings," she prods.
    I laugh because it's funny. I knew she'd get to that question eventually. Tell me about this and tell me about that. How does that make you feel? I feel like throwing this lady off and filling her in on my whole life. But who was she to trust if I didn't even trust the closest people to me?
    "You're thinking something right now, I can tell. What are you thinking?" she asks.
    "Within my whole lifetime, I've probably gotten drunk about three times," I pause, gauging her reaction. She looks

a little confused but waits for me to continue. I count off my fingers, "One out of those three times, I drove home drunk and accidently killed a woman. And you know what they say... it only takes one time. Went to prison for seven years and here I am."

She nods slowly as if she understands. She never could understand, but I let her do her little part anyway.

"You have a lot of regrets," she softly says.

I smile slowly, regarding her. But all I want to tell her is that's not the part I regret. Then she thankfully changes the subject. Pointing with her pen, she asks, "How did you get that bruise on your face?"

I falter with a response, touching my fingers to the swollen flesh. "My father did that."

"Did you call the cops?" she asks, furtively.

I laugh bitterly. "I'm the convict out of the two. Who do you think they would believe?"

She nods. "You still should have. You were assaulted, by a male none the less."

I shrug again and look out the window. "Not really an option when you're desperate for a place to live."

"Well, there are a lot of women homeless shelters in the area, but the one that specifically helps women get back on their feet is quite a drive from here. I heard Mr. Mitchell made some calls for you, so you will have a spot there. I can't tell you how lucky you are to know Mr. Mitchell. He's a great man for doing this."

"I know," I say so softly I barely hear myself.

"Genevieve. A lot of women are in your position," she says, placing her slender hand over mine. "You have to keep a strong mindset and do what you need to do to take care of yourself. You need to be strong."

Once she's done, she reclines back into her chair and looks at her notes.

I begin crying unexpectedly. She looks up from her notes and takes off her glasses. I shake my head as she offers me a facial tissue. When she shoves it in my face again, I take it from her and dab my unwanted tears.

"You can do this," she encourages.

"I can't do this anymore!" I shout, almost too loud. I take a deep breath and place my hand over my chest, willing me to calm down. When I do, I continue in a softer tone, "I forget what it's like to be strong. I sat in a prison cell for seven years with not much interaction. I didn't want it then. But I do now, and no one is making this any easier on me. The only person who makes it easier... he doesn't even know my situation."

"Who else besides your father doesn't make it easy?" she prods.

"My step-brother," I answer softly.

"Does he hit you too?"

"God, no. He's in love with me." I roll my eyes and wipe the tears off my cheeks.

Although Dr. Lee looks calm and collective on the outside, I can't help but notice the surprised look in her eyes due to my confession. She wasn't expecting that.

"It's okay to react," I say.

"Listen to your own advice." She smiles warmly. "If your step brother is a problem, maybe it's time to cut him out of your life. Who is this person that doesn't know your situation?"

I shake my head. I'm not ready to tell her, let alone anyone else that part yet.

"Ginny, we're not going to get anywhere if you don't tell me everything."

"I can't." I look down at my feet, which are scuffing Dr. Lee's polished marble floors relentlessly. I lift my head up after a few minutes of thinking. "Is all the information I tell you truly private?"

She nods. "Absolutely. I cannot disclose any information that you tell me, except if you want to harm yourself or someone else. Doctor/Patient confidentiality," she smiles.

Her beautiful, tight smile has me lifting my own lips into a weak smirk.

"Okay." I exhale air I didn't realize I was holding and look at her waiting eyes. "The pregnant woman I accidentally hit with my car after graduation, have you heard the basics?"

CHAPTER FOURTEEN

She nods. "I believe so."

"So then you know that she left behind a husband, and her baby survived?"

She nods. "Some say it was a miracle."

I ignore her and continue, "Benson Daniels and Annie Daniels. She was named after her mother."

Dr. Lee sighs. "It's natural to be curious about these types of things, Genevieve. It sounds like you may have a touch of survivor's guilt."

I shake my head. "No, that's not it."

She remains quiet, stunned that I interrupted her.

"I… I know them. Personally." I watch her face fall and continue, "I'm in current contact with Benson Daniels. I kind of nanny for his daughter; the miracle baby. I say kind of because… well, I plan on quitting now."

She drops her pen on her notepad and looks at me though her little lenses. Then she crosses her legs smoothly and shoots me a befuddled look. "You mean the woman's husband that you…"

"Correct." I don't let her finish.

"Does he… does he know?" she asks. She's wearing the same face that I assume everyone else would wear while finding out this type of information. I can't blame her for judging me for this. It's wrong on so many levels. Even I know that.

"He doesn't have a clue."

"So why quit now?" she asks, clearing her throat.

"I think I'm in love with him."

"Wow," she says to herself. Lifting her head, she looks at me for a beat too long.

I sigh. "Yeah."

"How did that happen?" she asks with amazement. It almost sounds like I'm talking to a friend at this point and filling them in on a horrible night of sex. She's intrigued. Curious.

"Alcoholics Anonymous," I laugh bitterly. "Can you even believe it? Oh, and I am a paper girl. I deliver papers because it's one of the only jobs that would hire me. I delivered to his house every morning. One day, my bad knee gave out and I ended up in his house with a pack of frozen peas on my knee," I breathe in and out, carefully. "That's how I found out who he was. I recognized a picture of her on the wall."

"I see," she mutters. "And he just swept you off your feet while you gave him the Sunday paper? Help me out here."

"That's pretty much the size of it," I say, picking at my nails, and already feeling regretful about telling her.

"How'd you avoid telling him this whole time?"

"It never came up," I tell her. "He doesn't recognize me at all because, in high school, I looked completely different. I had short pink hair and piercings all over my face. I wore different clothes. My face was different. I was still a baby," I reminisce. "My full name was in the papers and on the news, but he only knows me by Ginny, my nickname."

She smiles almost as if she is impressed and throws her pencil back on her desk. "We're going to need a second session."

The ride from the doctor's appointment to my AA meeting is in complete silence. Officer Mitchell drives me like the gentleman that he is, going the exact speed limit and getting me there punctually. Since he lives in the suburbs, we go to a different location for the meeting. I'm kind of relieved when he tells me because that means I won't bump into Benson or any other familiar faces.

He pries a little and asks a few questions about the meeting. I answer him honestly but am short with him. There's only so much that he knows. When he notices I'm not in the mood to talk, he stops asking questions and keeps on driving. He pulls up to the church where the meeting is held and I immediately hop out and thank him.

When I get inside, I don't see any familiar faces as suspected. I take a seat in the second row, which is unusual for me. But I figured I'd take advantage of this meeting since no one knows me.

They've been through what I've been through. Labeled. Misjudged. Stigmatized.

CHAPTER FOURTEEN

Now that I'm paying attention to everyone's stories, the meeting isn't as painful as I thought it would be. Eventually, my mind begins to drift off somewhere else. I start thinking about the time Benson and I went together to a meeting together. He went up to the front and made a speech like he did every time and then he had tried to get me up there but I refused. Then he had made a comment that he will get me up there sooner or later.

Snapping myself back into the present and without thinking, I raise my hand.

"You," the woman says, looking at me. "You're a new face. Why don't you come up here and introduce yourself?"

I nod; standing up on shaky legs and will myself to move forward. When my legs won't budge, I pinch my eyes shut and think of Benson again. Here I was going up there to speak and he wasn't even here.

Finally, my legs start moving toward the front of the room.

When I reach the podium, I feel a rush of anxiety as I look out at all the people. There are more people here at these meetings than the ones at home. A lot of older people. I kind of appreciate that part more. It makes this all easier knowing they've been through what I have and then some.

I clear my throat and start and look at all of their waiting eyes.

"Hi. My name is Gin, um, Genevieve. I don't necessarily think I'm an alcoholic."

Deafening silence.

They all look at me like I've just grown a horn in the middle of my head.

"With that being said, alcohol ruined my life." I look at the crowd again and a lot of them are nodding their heads in agreement as if they understand. It inspires me to keep on talking. "I'm mandated to come to these meetings for a crime I committed the night of my graduation, seven years ago. It was supposed to be the happiest day of my life. Instead, it was a nightmare that I will relive every night for the rest of my life," I choke out, beginning to feel emotional. I squeeze the tears back as I look out to the crowd for more assurance.

Sure enough, the woman that picked me to come up here nods for me to continue.

"I spent the last seven years of my early adult hood in a state penitentiary thanks to alcohol. I missed college. I missed making friends and boyfriends. I missed a crucial part of my life that was supposed to be a building block for me. I was looking forward to that. I was depending on it, and now I'll never get that back.

"I'm a convicted felon thanks to alcohol. I've ruined my family and another's thanks to alcohol. I've taken a women's innocent life thanks to alcohol. Therefore, I have a problem with alcohol, and I do belong here after all. I may not be addicted to alcohol, but I certainly need this program just as much as anyone else. I belong here as much as every one of you. And I'm glad I'm getting the help that I need finally."

I look down at the podium for a moment and take a deep breath before saying, "Thank you."

The whole room erupts in collective applause and the woman, whose name tag I now read as Francis, comes up and gives me a big hug. I hug her back, realizing how much I've needed this all.

My heart feels warm and less heavy. When we finally part, I shoot her a smirk with a scarlet red face and feel much better than when I walked in.

As I am leaving the church, I slip into the bathroom before my ride shows up. All the stalls seem to be taken so I take a detour to the mirrors to look at my appearance. I smooth out my clothes with my hands to rid the wrinkles and wipe my smeared eye liner from a few tears shed during the speech.

"So you're a felon. Who would have known?"

I stop what I'm doing and look into the mirror. There, I see a familiar face behind me.

"Surely not Benson," she adds, a shit eating grin plastered across her face.

It's Janet, and her eyes are practically rolling at my presence.

CHAPTER FOURTEEN

I shove my trembling hands under the faucet in a hurry to wipe them clean.

"Genevieve Quinn," she rolls off her tongue. She must have looked into the sign in book and put two and two together. Or maybe she overheard me introduce myself to other people. Or maybe she googled me. Which one was it?

I feel all of the blood leave my face, giving me the appearance of a ghost.

"It's such a beautiful name. Why do you go by Ginny?"

I decide to cut the bullshit so that I can leave. "It's just easier."

"You are an easy girl, aren't you?" She flashes me the fakest smile. I want to rip it off her stupid face.

"To one guy particularly," I swiftly respond.

She ignores my jab. "He broke up with me today. Have any idea why?"

I shrug and decide patronizing is the best way to go. "Oh, I'm so sorry. I'm sure it wasn't you, it was him. Or maybe he's just not that into you."

Her eyes squint into little slits. "Enjoy my leftovers."

I flash her sarcastic smile. "I fully intend to."

I quickly shake the water off of my hands and go to leave the bathroom.

"Oh, just one more thing," I hear her behind me. I turn around and lean up against the door. The last thing I need is someone witnessing this bullshit.

"I wonder what Benson would think if he knew he blew off this," she gestures herself, "for a convicted felon."

I'm nearly busting at the seams with hate for this woman. Not giving her the satisfaction, I quietly push the door open and leave.

I don't think I've ever run away so fast in my life.

It's not towards Officer Mitchell's house I run, it's towards Benson's.

CHAPTER FIFTEEN

By the time I approach Benson's house, the sun has set and I'm left in the dark with my second thoughts. I'm also sweaty and out of breath from all of the walking I've done to get here. A bus only took me so far. To be honest, I'm exhausted and ready to face plant onto the ground. I forget why I even came here.

Oh yes, to tell Benson the truth.

When I reach his doorstep, my second thoughts only grow needier and I feel that white, hot ball of anxiety willing me to walk away. What if he already knew everything? How much did he know? Why the hell was I going to try to justify this whole thing? He's going to hate me after he finds out, anyways. It's no use.

Sure, Janet heard my speech, which was my whole heart and soul poured out for everyone to see. But she didn't confront me for taking a life like I admitted in the speech. She confronted me about being a convicted felon. I truly wonder how much she listened to the whole speech. She really wasn't the smartest crayon in the box.

But I need to be honest with him and tell him everything. I owe him that because I think I love the guy. I decide that's exactly why I came here as I look out at his lawn. I will tell him the truth tonight. I will tell him everything.

But then I picture the first day I delivered papers to him. Annie was playing hopscotch and Benson looked as gorgeous as ever in his button up collared shirt, going to… whatever job he had.

God, what did he do for a living? I didn't even know the answer to that.

There were so many things that we didn't know about each other. So many major details.

I lift my hand, bunching it into a shaking fist and resisting the urge to knock on the door. I drop my hand, feeling overcome by all of my thoughts and just stand in front of his door.

What if this is the last time that I ever see him?

CHAPTER FIFTEEN

All of a sudden, I see the lights flicker on and the door creaks open. I erect my posture, tuck my hair behind my ears and try to look as presentable as I can.

And there he is, in all his Benson glory. In low rise flannel pants and a wife beater to match. He looks amazing and nothing less. His tattoos are all visible and his stubble is coming in more than usual, all down his neck as if he hasn't shaved in days.

Why the hell does this guy even like me? I ask myself that every day.

When my eyes make their way back up to his, I notice he looks a little surprised to see me. However, behind those navy blues, I can also see a hint of relief.

"Um, what do you do for a living?" That's my big opener?

His broad shoulders stiffen with the sound of my voice as he grows taller in front of me. I can't tell if he's still mad at me or wants to smother me. I look at him sympathetically, begging him to say something with my eyes. Hoping he can miraculously read me telepathically.

Before I reveal anything to him, I need to at least know how he feels because the truth is that being without Benson was beginning to kill me.

He opens the door the rest of the way and stalks towards me with purpose. I stand where I am and watch him saunter up to me. For just one moment, I think he may actually throw me off his front porch.

"Ginny," he whispers as he engulfs me in his arms. I immediately throw my arms around his taut abdomen and bury my face into his thick chest. He returns the affection and nuzzles his face securely into the crook of my neck, not letting me go. I feel his wet kisses trail down my neck and to my collar bone. I close my eyes and melt into him. My anxiety paralyzes me thinking of how this is probably the last time he'll ever show me affection. He catches my chin with his index finger and looks into my eyes tenderly. "I'm a chef. I work at Grand Cannoli's."

My expression becomes bewildered. That was the biggest and most popular restaurant in downtown Albany. I was thinking pretty much anything but a chef. Usually, chefs didn't wear suits to work.

"Wow. A chef," I mutter to myself. "I thought you were a business man or something."

He curves his lips into a beautiful half-smile, and seems charmed. "Well, you're not too far off. I also own the place."

I smile at my feet, thinking of how down to Earth he can be. He owned the most popular restaurant in our city and I didn't even know it. He tilts my chin up again, forcing me to make eye contact with him. "Ginny, I'm so sorry."

I shake my head. "Benson, I didn't come here for an apology. We have to talk. I have to tell you something."

"I know," he says, squeezing my hand tightly. Worry floods me when I start to question if Janet has already told him. "Come inside. My dad was just about to leave with Annie to go see his friend."

I give him a shy nod and walk in, spotting a very hyper Annie and her tired Grandfather trying to get her ready.

"So, your dad has a friend?" I turn to Benson.

"Yup, a lady friend," he waggles his brows.

I laugh when I'm interrupted by a high pitched, squeaky voice.

"Ginny!" Annie calls out, running up to me. She's ready to leave with her little leather jacket on. At her tail is Benson's father, looking like he just ran a marathon.

Benson gives his daughter a kiss on the forehead and talks to his father briefly before sending them out the door. Once they are gone and so is the madness, he shuts his front door and locks it. Then he zeroes in all of his attention on me.

We look at each other for a moment in silence, selfishly soaking each other in. Carefully and slowly, he cups the sides of my face with both of his hands; as if I am the most delicate thing he's ever touched. Within a blink, his perfect lips are pressing against mine and begging for access and permission. At first, I welcome the soft caress, hanging onto him like a bad habit. When he nips my bottom

CHAPTER FIFTEEN

lip, my hormones run wild, leaving me panting and out of breath. We are eventually smothering each other with our lips, passionately and curiously. Our hands are groping anything we can get a hold of. I can feel the affection in his kiss, the desperation in his hands, and the possessiveness of his grip.

I want him more than ever now. More than I've ever wanted anything in my entire life. I want every inch of his inked skin on me, over me, under me, beside me. I want his full lips that leave me panting and hungry every time. I want to devour him. I hug him tightly, every inch of him that I can grab; inhaling his manly scent and warm embrace.

"I'm so sorry," I breathe into his mouth.

"You're sorry? Everything was my fault," he says, breathing me in, kissing every surface of my face. I can barely breathe from his smothering assault, but I'm not complaining.

"It was mine too," I say. He really has no idea.

"Baby, I haven't seen you all fucking week. Just kiss me, please. Apologize to me with these incredible lips," he murmurs, catching my lips with his again.

My lips mold into his like a piece of clay when he abruptly stops. He grabs me by the shoulders and takes a step back, assessing my face. His face transitions from lust to anger a matter of seconds as he brushes his thumb across the swollen flesh of my eye. "Who did this to you?"

I notice the disgust in his eyes when I don't answer him. "Did your step brother do this to you?"

"What? God no!" I touch the heat of my cheek, forgetting it was even there for the world to see.

"I'm going to kick his ass!" He goes to walk past me and I block him with my whole body. "Stop, no!"

"I knew he beat you. God knows what he's done to you," he growls.

I say nothing because I cannot hold a poker face worth shit anymore. Jesse has done many things to me, but abusing me physically definitely wasn't one of them.

"Did he touch you, Ginny?" Benson barks. "Did that burnt out little shithead hurt you?"

"No!" I shout. I continue blocking him from running off this porch and murdering Jesse. I'm practically using my entire body as a human shield.

"He's a dead man."

"He didn't do this!" I shout.

"I don't care if he did or didn't. I'm still going to bust his face in," he yells as he slams his fist into the siding of his house. I catch a peak of his knuckles, which are a bloody mess. He doesn't even seem to be phased by it. I don't think I've ever seen him this angry. This definitely beats his drunken fit, and he's not even drunk right now. At least, I don't think he is.

"I see the way that burn-out looks at you and I don't like it."

"Jesse and I had a consensual relationship. You're the only person I've ever told this to. Ever. Please don't make me regret that," I choke.

Oh shit, maybe that wasn't the best thing to say when Benson's about to kill Jesse.

He frowns, his face softening. "Then tell me who did this to your face. Please."

"It wasn't Jesse. He would never hurt me," I reply.

"Have you guys had sex?"

To my surprise, I notice Benson is actually thunderstruck and a little insecure himself. I remember him making little comments about Jesse and me during our last fight; I know that I wasn't imagining it. "What kind of question is that?"

"One I'd like to know the answer to."

My vocal chords struggle to vibrate and give him an answer back.

"Well?" he prods. "Do you guys still fuck?"

"We don't do that anymore, Benson. I don't want Jesse anymore."

I soak up his face, which is wearing a familiar glare that I've seen many times whenever mentioning Jesse. He hates the name Jesse and his revolted face shows it.

"It's over. We're over. I don't want him that way anymore. I haven't in a long time," I explain, knowing damn well that I'm a hypocrite. I'll always have a place in my heart for Jesse, but he is the past and Benson is the future.

Benson grabs my shoulders and gives them a little shake. "Swear to me. Tell me you're not in love with him any longer. I can't do this if you love someone else."

This I can at least answer with the truth. There is no question about it. "Jesse is my step brother. I'm not going to lie and say he doesn't hold a special place in my heart. But Benson, since I met you...since the first day, it's been you. I haven't even thought of Jesse like that. I'm not in love with him anymore."

"But, you were?" he prods. Why can't he just let this go?

I take a deep breath in defeat. What I really want to do is roll my eyes, but I refrain. "He was all that I ever knew. I know this sounds crazy to you..."

"I should beat him until he's ganja on the ground," he paces his front porch.

"Benson." I try to snap him out of his angry trance, but honestly, seeing him this worked up with his balled fists and puffed chest, it's kind of hot.

"How can I be sure that he won't put his nasty hands on you again?" I see his nostrils flair with anger. His lips are in a thin, hard line and his eyes are wide and terrifying.

"Because I wouldn't let him. I don't crave his touch and attention anymore. I crave for yours!" I take a deep breath as I place my hands on his bulging biceps. God, they're hard and smooth and bite worthy.

All that I hear is the pin dropping silence that surrounds us as he soaks up my confession.

Does he like what I said? Does he hate it? Say something.

He exhales first, his eyes darting to the ground in thought. I'm hoping this oddly relaxing look on his face is relief and not indifference. He gently removes my hands from his arms and holds them in his own, grazing softly with the pads of his thumbs. "You won't be seeing Janet around anymore, either."

"I know," I murmur.

"You know?"

I nod and look at my feet. "Saw her today," I clear my throat and continue, "She told me to enjoy her leftovers."

A shit eating grin plasters his face. "Enjoy her what?"

I sigh. "Don't make me say it again."

He doesn't look me in the eye, but I spot a glint of enjoyment in them as he takes in everything but me. Is Benson blushing? I don't think I've ever seen such a beautiful sight.

He nods with understanding as he intercepts my hands into his and grazes calloused fingers over them. At this time, I take in the difference of his breathing. It's heavier and faster than usual. His cheeks are flusher and his hands that hold mine are unsteady.

I'm surprised when he whispers, "Will you be enjoying them?"

"You are anything but leftovers, Benson. But even if you were, I'd be glad to have any part of you at all."

His broad shoulders relax at my admission, and I swear I see him stifle a smile. Our mouths are so close to each other that I'm pretty sure we're breathing the same recycled air.

Now is a good time to ruin my world. Not because I want to, but because I owe it to him. I need to tell him who I am before Janet gets to him.

Awareness hits me like a bulldozer. "Wait. Did you break up with her for me?"

"Isn't that what you wanted?" His voice is barely above a whisper, but he doesn't miss a beat. When I raise my gaze to his fiery blue eyes, I can feel the heat bouncing off of them and seeping into my every pore. I don't answer him, which causes him to anxiously shift his stance. Cupping my face with his big hand, he asks, "It's not?"

"Of course it is," I whisper, placing a hand over his on my cheek. I slowly lean into him and rise to the tip of my toes, placing a small and chaste kiss onto his. When we part, he almost looks pained by it.

I tilt my head in confusion.

CHAPTER FIFTEEN

"Please tell me who did this," he whispers as he trails his fingers over my shiner.

"My father."

"I'm going to kill him."

"No. Please, Benson." I squeeze my eyes shut. "You're making this so hard. I came here to talk to you and tell you something."

"We will talk, but you are not going back there. You'll stay with me," he demands.

He notices I'm hesitant and takes a step back.

"I need you safe, Ginny. What do you not get about that?" he snaps. "You've had me worried sick this past week. I," he trails off, becoming lost with one swipe of my skin. "I missed you like crazy."

I shudder at the skillful hands that roam my body. I'd love more than anything for him to continue what he's doing. I'd also love more than anything to keep feeling this way, but I need to be a good human being and tell him the truth.

"Benson, there are so many things you need to know about me."

That's it. Say it before it feels too good and you can't stop. Tell him the truth, Genevieve.

"I could say the same," he replies, tracing his fingers across my clavicle. I lean into his embrace and close my eyes for a moment. When I open them, he's looking at me like I'm the center of the universe.

I shut my eyes hard and shake my head. "I can't do this."

"Do what?" He traces his fingers on the soft flesh behind my ear to the sensitive part of my neck, destined for my collarbone. I feel every blood vessel and capillary come to the surface of my skin, begging for another swipe of his hand. I catch him studying my lips vigilantly as I dart my tongue out and lick my lips intentionally.

Within a blink of an eye, his lips are sealed over mine and claiming them as his own. It's different from any of the other kisses that we've shared. This one is short and sweet and tender enough to cut with a knife. I keep my eyes shut when his silky lips leave mine, hoping that when I open them I won't be dreaming.

When I open my eyes, I exhale. Benson is still right in front of me in all his glory. It all seems like a dream to me. I still can't believe he likes me the way he does. To say that Benson is out of my league is quite the understatement.

"Benson, what I have to tell you… it's really important."

"Can it wait?" He seems more interested in the touch of my skin than what I am actually telling him. I guess I have soft skin going for me.

"No, it can't. You may not want to touch me anymore after I tell you this."

"It's okay," he whispers, "I already know."

What the hell did he just say?

CHAPTER SIXTEEN

An electrical current raids my scalp when he tells me he already knows. The confession gives me the brain zap from hell, that's for damn sure.

Looking over at him, I notice he isn't smiling, but he also doesn't look like he wants to kill me either. The poor guy wants a little honesty. Who can blame him?

He already knows.

Oh my God. I'm dead. I'm a dead woman.

RIP Genevieve Quinn.

He lifts his hand to my shoulder and squeezes it affectionately. It's the type of response that I'm certainly not expecting. I'm so distracted by his touch and confession that I just stare at him with perplexity. I'm not sure whether to respond or cry or throw myself in front of a bus.

"Y-you know?" I clear my scratchy throat.

He nods and softly murmurs, "Janet paid me a visit today."

"I tried to get to you before her," I say it to myself even though I'm talking to him.

"So… you're a felon," he says, his voice casual. He doesn't seem angry, but he doesn't seem happy either. I'm too busy trying to stop the wheels spinning in my head for just one minute rather than figure it out.

I nod. I can't even look him in the eye.

Was that all she told him?

My estranged mother's voice pops into my head right then. She would always say to do everything in small doses. Do everything in small doses, that way you aren't too surprised or overwhelmed at the time. It was ridiculous to think, but should I tell him all my lies in small doses? I mean, how many lies could the poor guy handle? I have kept quite a few from him at this point.

Nothing.

"I ran into Janet at a meeting in Clifton Park," I mumble.

"Makes sense. She lives there."

I lift my head to his, looking him square in the eye. "What else did she tell you?"

"Is there more?"

I cock my brow back.

"She said that you're a convicted felon," he shrugs. "What on Earth did you do?"

"Shhh, she didn't t-tell you?" God, I'm so nervous I can't even talk correctly.

He shakes his head. "She didn't seem to know the answer to that. Trust me, I asked."

I look down at my feet and hate myself for feeling the relief flood me. Because the truth is I wasn't ready to tell him just yet. I was just getting acquainted with his lips and hands and body, and I wasn't ready to lose him the way I was about to today. "I'm sorry, I should have told you."

Damn it, Quinn! Way to go, you lying son-of-a-bitch. I mean daughter of a bitch. Definitely daughter of a bitch and asshole.

He gives me a tender look and brushes his hand down my cheek. "You should have. I'm more understanding than you may think."

"I didn't know how to tell you."

"You still haven't answered my question."

"Well, that's why I'm here. To tell you everything."

These damn awkward silences are going to be the death of me.

"Are you a murderer?" he asks.

I look at him for a moment, my answer coming a bit too late. "No. Of course not."

He noticeably sighs and asks, "Child molester?"

"Are you serious?" I leer at him. He's really beginning to annoy me.

He notices that I'm getting wound up and hurriedly grabs my hand, squeezing it. "How did a beautiful girl like you end up in jail, Ginny?"

Prison, actually.

Oh man. This is it. I'm never going to see this guy again. Don't cry too hard when he chops up your heart with his knife collection.

I open my mouth to respond, but he interrupts me. "We all have our own issues, Ginny."

CHAPTER SIXTEEN

No.

"You obviously care about me and Annie."

No. Stop.

"And I can also tell this is hard for you…"

Please. Don't.

"I'll give you the time you need because I understand what it's like to have skeletons…"

And just like that, I don't tell him what I planned to. "Okay," I whisper.

"But I need you to promise me something. Promise me you didn't do anything cruel or pre meditated. That you're not a threat to me or Annie."

I lock eyes with him. "I would never hurt you guys."

He gives me a nod as his phone buzzes to life.

Relief floods me for the second time today when it doesn't have the right to. He stares at his phone for a brief moment with worry before flipping it open, making me ponder who is on the other end.

"Hello?"

More torturous silence fills the room. I've just about had enough of it for the day.

I nudge him. "Everything okay?"

He ignores me and continues talking to the person on the other line. "What? How could you let this happen?"

More silence.

"I'll be right there!" He quickly snaps his phone shut and looks at me anxiously. "It's Annie. She needs stitches. She was sleep walking again and fell down the stairs this time. Banged her chin wide open," he cradles his head into his hands. "My dad forgot to turn on the hall light for her again. He's really forgetting things, Ginny. He's forgetting a lot."

I take his hand in mine and lift them up to my lips, kissing them softly. "Let me go to the hospital with you."

"Okay."

When we arrive at the hospital, Benson's father is snoring in a waiting room chair, causing Benson to roll his eyes.

"She's probably already in a room. I have to go find her. She must be scared," he says, going up to the secretary's desk. I wait behind and sit next to Benson's resting Dad.

I hear her high pitched giggle from the other room, making us both snap our heads in the direction of the sound. She gets wheeled out by a medical technician who is seemingly enjoying her company. Her right hand is all bandaged up but she seems to be smiling ear to ear.

"Hey Ginny, will you draw on my cast?" she asks, exasperated.

I force myself to smirk. "That's not a cast, silly. That's just a bandage! But sure."

She beams back, and her concentration then focusing on her father. Her face falls. "Daddy, I fell. I'm sorry."

"Don't you ever be sorry," Benson says with relief laced in his voice. He bends down to hug her in the wheelchair and she giggles. "You're coming home with us, baby."

"Is Ginny coming too? Can we have a sleepover?"

I shoot Benson a furtive glance. A smile escapes his lips although I don't think it's meant to.

"You deserve some ice cream." Benson changes the subject, feeling for his wallet. "Oh crap, I forgot my wallet. I was such in a hurry to leave when I got the call that it slipped my mind. What do you say we go home and I'll go buy you a carton of your favorite, Cherry Garcia?"

She squeals with excitement as the medical technician chimes in, "There's an ice cream vending machine downstairs in the cafeteria. I can bring her. My treat for being one of the best patients we've had today."

"Thank you so much," Benson says to the girl. The way she's ogling at him right now makes me want to yank her stethoscope off and choke her with it.

"No problem," she says as she takes off with Annie.

Benson sits down in a chair next to me and cradles his head into his hands. He looks worn out and not in the mood to talk, so we sit in silence for a while. The only sound

CHAPTER SIXTEEN

detectable is the loud snore of his father, which may as well be a chainsaw.

"So," he says, tepidly interested. "Ready to tell me yet?"

Even though I sense sarcasm in his tone, I know it's still something he's dying to know.

What comes out of my unfiltered, blubbering mouth next even surprises me. "Alcohol and drugs. Duh. I met you at AA."

He nods knowingly, letting it sink in. Then he gives me a sympathetic look and squeezes my hand. "I don't care what you did, Ginny. As long as you're not a danger to us."

I can feel like heart capsizing the more he talks about it.

No more questions. Please.

"I know one thing for sure, and that's that I would never hurt you guys."

"And I believe that," he responds. "We all have a past, as much as we hate to talk or think about it."

I nudge him. "So, you don't hate me?"

He gives me that million dollar grin. "No. I don't hate you. I've been through the ringer with my past, too. I guess that's why I'm trying not to hound you so much. You will tell me when you're ready."

"So, you have a past too?"

A curve teases the edge of his lips. "Why, you think I'm this forgiving all the time?"

"I'm going to say no."

He nods. "You'd be correct. If I told you everything at once, you'd be running for the hills."

I snort, nuzzling myself into the curve of his side and placing my hand over his restless thigh. I look up at him from his chest and say, "Please. I can't see myself ever running from you. Even if you were a crazy person."

He looks at me deadpan and says, "Be careful what you wish for."

I slap his arm. "Come on. Tell me something."

"Let's see. I'm a widow and am a lousy drunk, but you already knew that."

I nod and encourage him to keep talking by staying quiet.

"I lost my wife to a drunk driver," he adds.

I stiffen on instinct but then nod again. He absently rubs my arm as we sit in the uncomfortable waiting room chairs, his dad still snoring like a motorboat.

"It took me a long time to get over that. I felt more guilt than I should have," he says with pain in his eyes. His head is dropped low and his eyes are squeezing shut. I want to get closer to him but it's impossible without jumping on his lap. I don't think that'd be appropriate in an emergency waiting room, so I stay where I am.

"There's something about Angelina that a lot of people don't know."

"Benson," I whisper.

"She was bipolar. Was often institutionalized for it."

I let out an absurd gasp and cover my mouth immediately. "Oh my God."

"So sometimes I wonder things I shouldn't. Things I have no right to wonder."

"Like what?" I prod.

He pauses. I can tell he doesn't want to tell me, but he does anyways. "If she loved her life as much as she claimed she did."

Realization hits me. "Wait. Did she..."

"- Want to be hit? - Jump in front of the car?" he finishes my sentence, but then shakes his head. "I don't know. I guess I'll never know. I can't seem to understand why she'd do that to our own baby, but we were fighting really badly before she left the house that night."

I swallow a thick lump. "I don't think she wanted that, Benson. I don't think she wanted to be hit."

"You would think. But... I can't help but wonder sometimes."

He takes a deep breath, enough for both of us. I can tell this is reasonably hard for him. He has every right not wanting to tell me. In fact, he didn't have to at all. I'd still be here. I'd still feel the same way about him without knowing. It didn't change anything for me.

CHAPTER SIXTEEN

"At first, I thought her illness was a blessing," he says, breaking me from my thoughts. "I had my own skeletons since I was a boy. No one knew about them, really. But, any time I got close to a woman, I'd bring them out to test the waters. I would just end up scaring them away. You probably think I'm exaggerating, but I'm not. When I met Angelina and found out about her illness, I felt I found my match. We were perfect for each other. Two injured souls becoming one. Two imperfect people, perfect together."

Not long ago, I remember him saying something like that about us.

"When did it all go wrong?" I ask.

His eyes slide down me and back up again. "When my addiction got worse."

I roll my eyes. "God I hate alcohol."

He laughs bitterly. "I actually had never touched the stuff up until Angelina's death, and that's the truth." He sighs. "Okay, here it goes. I have another terrible addiction, Ginny. And I'm not talking about the alcohol. This one is much worse for me."

"Drugs," I say to myself. "Benson, I will never understand what you went through and what it took to get your mind off of things." I grab his hand and squeeze it.

He could have told me. I would have understood. It wouldn't have changed a thing.

"I'm not a drug addict, Ginny." He looks ashamed and embarrassed. He exhales loudly, looking me directly in the eye. "Sex."

I freeze up all my muscles when awareness hits me right in the gut. "You're a sex addict."

Then, I get really unreasonably mad. He's a sex addict and he's never even initiated sex with me. I stand up and clear my throat. "I must be hideous to you or something."

He hurriedly grabs my hand and pulls me onto his lip. "Hey, hey. Just the opposite. You're stunning and I think you're much better than me."

Everything begins to make sense now. The way he looks at me like he wants to eat me like a three course meal.

The way his eyes assault me with a sensual tenderness that's soft enough to cut with a plastic spoon. The way that his fingertips are completely obsessed with my skin as if it's magnetic.

"I've had it under control for years, until recently."

I look down at our intertwined hands. "I had no idea."

"How could you? I'd never expect you to deal with this," he admits. "Thing is, I'm having a hell of a time controlling myself these days. More than ever." He slips his arms around my waist and pulls me into him as if I'll run. "The last thing I want to do is scare or hurt you."

"Do you see me running?"

He shoots me a crooked smile and keeps holding me. We sit like this for a few more minutes in silence. My guilt festers to an unbearable limit as I look up into his aqua eyes. They are somber and hollow and swollen, but there no stray tears visible on that perfect skin of his.

The second he squeezes his eyes shut, I take it upon myself to kiss him. Then I kiss his nose because I can't help it.

In a way, I guess that you could say that I was an addict too. He was my drug, and I was helplessly obsessed with him in every way.

"When my wife died," he begins. "I guess in a way, I did too. I was out of control for a while. I risked it all," he says quietly, broodingly. I can tell he's very embarrassed by his admissions. "When I mixed the sex with alcohol, it was the perfect cocktail. I felt like I was on top of the world. Like no one could stop me. I felt in control, even though I was spiraling out of it. It was the only time I wasn't in pain."

He pulls me up into the standing position with him and starts to pace the waiting room.

"At one point, it was so bad that Annie got taken right away from me. I finally got her back two years ago with the help of my father. That's why I reacted so horribly when we got into a fight about her. I was worried that you thought I was a bad father."

"I understand, Benson. You don't have to say anymore." I lift to my feet and wrap my slender arms around

CHAPTER SIXTEEN

his tight mid-section. It turns out that I need some comforting of my own. He notices that I'm pleading for his touch, so he gently pushes my back to the wall and sets his hands on each side, caging me in. He touches his nose to mine, so close that his blue irises are all that I can see.

"I kind of feel horrible sometimes. The impulses that I get around you? They're no good, Ginny. They're no good at all."

"What do you mean?"

He silently asks me with his face if he really has to say it out loud.

I bite the bait. I hesitantly raise my hands to his biceps and squeeze them. "What... what would you do?" Did that really just come out of my mouth?

"A lot of things that would not be helping my addiction," he smirks.

Well, this is not as fun as I'd hoped.

"Let's make a deal," I propose. His navy eyes settle on my forest ones.

I approach him slow and steady. It takes everything that I have not to pounce onto him like a wild animal. What I say next is meant to be a joke, but it comes out a little more seriously than intended. "I will help you as much as I can with your addiction, but only after you tell me what you want to do to me."

"You're bad," he stifles a grin.

"Don't have to tell me twice," I wink.

"Okay," he smiles at my initiative. "But it would require us getting out of here as soon as possible."

I giggle when he brushes his lips over the most sensitive part of my neck. I giggle. When have I been reduced to a snickering, little school girl?

As we stare into one another's eyes, I should be feeling rainbows and butterflies, but all I can think of is Benson never letting me make love to him. He notices my worry and squeezes my hand. "What's wrong?"

"You know Benson, it is okay to feel the way that you feel. The feeling is mutual. It would mean something to me."

"Hey," he whispers as he grabs my chin. "I've just had a lot of women that I regret, and you're special." He rubs the soft skin of my upper arm, quite mesmerized by it. "I just want our time to be right."

I nod, knowing deep down inside that I want him to take me right now on this gross, waiting room chair. No matter how bad of an idea it is. "Well then waiting it is."

"But you should still come home with me tonight." His eyes are set on my long, raven hair as falls through his long fingers.

"I can't," I tell him. "My parole officer has given me a place to stay. He's been extremely helpful."

"Why are you staying there?"

"I'm leaving tomorrow, Benson."

"What?"

"I'm moving away."

"No. No, you're not."

I nod." Yes, I am. Officer Mitchell found me a group home for homeless women. He's bringing me on a four hour trip there tomorrow morning. He says it's a great place for women like me to get back on my feet."

"Ginny, you can't," he says, his voice strained. "You can't leave me. Not now."

"I have no where…"

"Don't say what's not true. You have a place to go. You can stay with me until you get back on your feet, Ginny."

"It wouldn't be right."

"It's exactly what feels right. You moving away is the last thing I want."

Before I can answer, a whirlwind of blonde hair is detected out of the corner of my eye. We both catch a glimpse of the commotion.

"Daddy!" Annie runs down the hallway with a chocolate ice cream cone. "Want some, Ginny?" She shoves the cone in my face and I take a lick just to make her happy.

Benson's father wakes up with a loud grunt, looking disoriented and disheveled. Annie walks up to him and shoves the cone in his face too. He mumbles something to her that doesn't sound pleasant and Benson laughs.

CHAPTER SIXTEEN

"Alright guys, let's head home."

His dad and Annie head out first holding hands while Benson grabs my hand and pulls me back inside.

I look at him expectantly when I realize he's nervous. He takes a deep breath before murmuring, "Give me tonight. Please. If you still want to go tomorrow, then fine. But stay with me tonight."

I know I don't have a choice in the matter when he grabs my face in his hands and kisses me. How could I move away from him? How will I ever live without this man, now?

"Alright. I'll stay with you. But just tonight."

He smiles big and kisses me again, this time harder. I pull him into me and squeeze him around the waist, which is like hugging a Greek statue.

"You still like me now that you know what a fuck-up I am?" he asks, fixated on my swollen lips.

"I like you even more," I respond. It's the absolute truth.

He snorts. "How's that even possible?"

"Maybe because you're almost as fucked up as I am," I whisper.

We all walk out of the hospital together and I close my eyes and shudder. Although the guilt saturates every fiber of my being, it doesn't stop the blood from rushing below my belt.

Just like him, I am an addict after all.

CHAPTER SEVENTEEN

I'm led into his bedroom where I've been once or twice before. However, this time it's so much different. I'm not forced to come in here to calm an irritated and drunk Benson down. And I'm certainly not chasing Annie in here and telling her she can't be snooping on her father. This time, my being here is a choice.

Not only is it my choice, it's our choice.

I notice my hands are trembling so I stick them in my pockets, hoping he doesn't notice.

The mood is quiet and the air is full of expectations. He walks past me and immediately draws all of the blinds and curtains shut. I study the bold, black drapes that dangle over his only window. It's almost as if it's meant to wedge the rest of the world out. His bed is neatly tucked to a tight crisp, and everything else is in its rightful home. His room is incredibly clean for a bachelor's room, but I could've guessed that by seeing the rest of his house and car.

Out of the corner of my eye sits the framed picture of him and Angelina propped up on his night stand. It's the same picture he almost threw the other night before I stopped him.

Part of me is disappointed because I put it in his drawer after he tried to shatter it. That means he put it back on his night table. In the picture that is still intact thanks to me, he holds her around the waist; a feeling I'm all too familiar with. I wonder if she felt the same way that I do whenever he held her like that.

The picture isn't supposed to upset me, but it does. It's the untimely reminder that Angelina will always come first to him. No matter what.

He leaves me for a moment, giving me a soft peck on the cheek and telling me he's tucking Annie in real quick. I silently thank him for the privacy because I need it right now. I situate myself by the window, opening the curtain to look at the night sky.

Anything to get my mind off the fact that Benson is a sex addict but doesn't want to have sex with me. Anything but waiting for this whole situation to tumble down like a perfect game of dominos.

I can hear his voice lingering down the hall as he tucks Annie in, his sweet and soft voice lulling me into a trance. The next thing I hear is the door closing behind me, causing me to shut the curtains and instinctively stiffen.

I feel the swipe of his callused hands wrapping around my waist and pulling me in. I feel him from his chiseled chest to something notably long and hard, relentlessly poking into my back side.

Although that's a distraction, I focus on his generous hands. It's as if his hands are the last missing piece to my body's puzzle. I wish he had a thousand hands so that he could touch me on every inch of my body. Two of his hands just aren't enough.

After a few minutes of silence and getting used to each other's presence, he buries his head in the crook of my shoulder and neck. He traces small and soft kisses down my neck and then makes his way up to the lobe of my ear, tugging it gently with his teeth.

Spinning me around like were dancing, he forces me to face him. I take a moment to admire his beautiful body, taut and sculpted in all the right places. Every muscle is perfectly defined and tightly encased by inked skin. He's straight out of a warrior movie, adding a modern twist with all of his tattoos.

I think about our conversation at the hospital.

Benson is a sex addict.

It all makes sense now. All of the touching and wandering hands that reduce me to a puddle on the ground. Those sex starved eyes, hooded and looking at me like a three course dinner.

Guilt hits me in the worst way as his blue eyes drill mine. I innately stare back, realizing something new but unsurprising. Even with his addictions and misfortunes, he is still the most beautiful and sincere man that I've ever met.

"Are you hungry?" he asks, whipping me back into reality.

Yeah, for you.

I shake my head no and look at the ground. Why am I all of a sudden feeling so shy?

He grabs my chin with his thumb and index and forces me to look him in the eye. "Tired?"

I shake my head no again and give him a soft smile.

"Nervous?" he asks, knowing he hit the nail right on the head. I've been trying my best to hide it, but of course, I'm translucent whenever it comes to him.

"Jesus, Ginny. You're hands are trembling again," he whispers. He's observing my frantic hands, front and back, and then kisses them delicately.

"Yes," I clear my throat, unable to look him in the eye. "I'm nervous. But mostly just scared."

"Scared?"

I can tell he doesn't like that, but he has no idea how scared I really am. I'm so scared that I'm scared to tell him how scared I actually am.

My eyes flicker to his, locking in place with the dark blues that never fail to bring me to my knees.

"Good kind of scared," I assure him. "I've wanted this for a very long time, Benson. I guess I still can't believe it is happening." It's true. I thought a lot of things when I found out who Benson actually was. Falling for the man was not one of them.

He places his forehead to mine and says, "Well, you better start believing…because it's happening."

"I still have things to tell you."

"I know," he responds, shooting me a tender look. "We'll get to it. But for now, don't worry about the past. I want you here in the now. Can you do that for me?"

I sniff my response and nod.

"I can tell it's difficult for you," he says, sympathetically.

"It is," I admit. "But I'm going to try, okay?"

He kisses my forehead and looks me in the eye. "Whatever it is, we'll get through it. Okay?"

I nod again but am unable to look him in the eye. Something tells me that omitting the truth is the worst thing I can do. He catches me off guard when he grabs my hand

and silently leads me to his bathroom. I wonder what the hell he's up to when he surprises me even more and grabs me by the waist, lifting me on the counter as if I weigh nothing.

Not that I'm complaining, but my brain is at full capacity with questions when I watch him walk to the tub and start running the water.

When he turns around, he shoots me a smile that could only be described as devious.

Furthermore, my body's reaction to that smile makes me question my wellbeing.

"Bath time?" I try to play it cool even though I'm dying to jump and hump in that tub with him.

"Hot tub time," he corrects me. "It will relax you. These jets are the shit. You'll love 'em."

"Benson, I'm fine!"

He gives me a 'don't be stupid' look. "Being nervous is one thing, but I never want you to be scared around me."

Feeling suddenly bashful, I change the subject immediately. Swinging my legs off the counter, I give him a bashful look and ask, "So what does this hot tub time entail?"

I watch him wander around the room, grabbing some necessities and can't help but to smile. I've never had anyone treat me like a queen before. I try to keep it in my pants when I notice that he grabs two white and fluffy towels.

Then he reaches to the top shelf and snatches a bottle of dove soap. Although the happy trail on his hard abdomen does nothing but distracts me, I also can't help but wonder if he kept it here for any other "guests".

Or far worse, I hope it's not seven years old.

He laughs when he spots my eyes widen with apprehension. "It's Annie's. It's the only soap she isn't allergic to."

I shoot him an embarrassing smile, feeling my ears turn redder by the minute. My heart is beating faster than an African drum.

He turns off the bath water and sits on the ledge of the tub, delivering me a look that could only be described as mischievous. Silence and steam pollute the air as we soak in the warmth of each other's eyes.

"Come here," he orders.

My tormented heart pounds as I walk up to him, my tummy and his face level with each other. He slowly lifts the hem of my shirt and gives my stomach one small, chaste kiss. My hands betray my brain's better judgment as I run my fingers through his sandy hair, petting and tugging it.

"Turn around," he commands. I oblige and he slowly grabs the bottom hem of my shirt. "Hands up."

I do as I'm told and before I know it, my shirt is off me and flung onto the floor.

I'm bare from the waist up and I curse myself for not wearing a bra today. Not that I need one anyways with my little B cups.

"Jesus Christ Ginny, you're more beautiful than I thought," he whispers, cupping my breasts into his hands and squeezing them firmly.

Unexpectedly, he stands up, towering over me and larger than life.

Right after giving me a peck on the forehead, he turns away and walks towards the bathroom door.

Wait, where's he going? He's leaving?

"Where are you going?" I try to keep the desperation out of my voice.

"I'm giving you some privacy," he turns around at the threshold of the bathroom entrance, his hand propped up on the molding for support. He looks suddenly pained.

My body is currently suffering a level of physical need that is unfamiliar to me. I am willing to get on my knees and beg if I have to. I glance down at my small B cups and then back up to him again. "Really?"

He smirks and goes to leave again. Just when he reaches the door again, I shout, "Wait!"

He turns around, his eyes inhibited.

"I thought you were going to take a bath with me." That's it. There's no hiding it now. I'm totally pathetic.

However, he smiles as if I'm adorable, a slow smile creeping upon his face as he walks back to me. I become more excited with each step that he takes and my erratic breaths show it.

CHAPTER SEVENTEEN

I look down at my feet, embarrassed. "Sorry. I just thought…"

My mind begins to litter with upsetting thoughts such as the information I'm omitting from him. An awkward silence passes before he tilts my chin up, forcing me to meet his gaze again. He cradles my face in his big hands and studies every curvature of it.

"We need to be slow." His words shoot down my spine, triggering a burn to my already diminutive ego.

I nod, detesting the fact that I'm coming across desperate again. Every bone in my body feels brittle, every muscle under my skin aches for him. "I know."

"But there's one thing I'm going to remind you over and over throughout all of this."

My eyes light up as we make eye contact.

"I…" He kisses my nose. "Want…" He kisses my neck. "You…" He kisses my lips, soft and slow.

I welcome the kiss, devouring it before he can pull back and change his mind. I even slip my tongue in and, thank God, it's intercepted.

We kiss, pull, bite, and tug for a few more minutes until he breaks the connection first.

"I don't think you understand," he shoots me a panty melting grin. "You're not helping when you look at me like that, or when you kiss me like that."

I kiss the palm of his hand the second he settles it on my flushed face. "Too much pressure?"

He chuckles. "It doesn't feel like the worst pressure in the world, I'll tell you that much."

"I just want to show you how I feel."

He smiles and gives me a soft, closed mouthed kiss. He's teasing me without even trying and I hate him for it. I want him to give into me like he would with a one night stand. As I press myself against his body, his hardness is more than enough proof that he ultimately wants that as well.

But I have to respect his wishes.

"We have plenty of time for that, Ginny."

Before I can say anything else, he walks out of the room and leaves me alone in the steaming bath room. I take a step back and lift one foot into the scolding hot water, hoping it will relax my body and let the blood rush some other places.

Lord knows it needs to.

I make myself as comfortable as I can on Benson's king size bed, sinking into his sheets and pinning them under me like I'm in a straitjacket. It's the only way I can sleep, ironically.

Benson had told me I could have his bed tonight, another disappointment since he insisted he slept downstairs on the couch. I didn't want to come across as desperate and ask him to stay again, so I reluctantly watched him leave.

Once I find myself comfortable enough to feel like I'm sleeping on a bed of clouds, I inhale the sheets and pillows like a creep. Something about the aroma imbedded in his sheets gives me an obscene thrill. I smother my face into them some more and grab them tightly, pretending that they're his torso. I suddenly notice that I am grinning ear to ear like an idiot.

I'm in his bed.

I look at the clock and it reads 11:42 pm. Every time I attempt to shut my eyes, I'm bombarded with another distracting memory.

The Flowers in the Attic situation with my step brother. Benson's sex addiction. Lying to Benson. Basically, anything that has to do with Benson.

Is that even a BAD thing?

It could be.

All these thoughts weigh profoundly on my mind for the next couple of hours. By the time 3 am hits, I'm tossing and turning like a fish out of water.

I sit up abruptly and shake my head as if that will clear my head.

It doesn't.

Placing my restless feet on the ground, I get out of bed and head to the chair by his window.

I guess I'm just hoping that a change in scenery will clear my head so that I can get back to sleep. But I know that's not happening anytime soon. I think about everything in that chair, everything but telling Benson the truth because allowing myself to think that makes me feel uneasy in the worst way.

I steal a glance out the window when I feel a heated gaze on me. It's not just anyone's heated gaze, either. It's so scorching hot that I might just disintegrate into ashes on the ground. I turn to the doorway where a bare-chested Benson stands in his low rise flannel pants, revealing the mother of all six packs.

I attempt hiding how obvious it looks, but I'm pretty sure I'm just drooling like an idiot.

"How long have you been standing there?" I whisper.

"A few minutes." His expression is soft and yielding.

He stands near the door way as if his bedroom's floor is made of lava. He seems so far away. I want him closer. I'll walk across the fire to get to him if I have to.

"I didn't even hear you come up."

"Well, I heard you moving around downstairs. I was just checking to see if you were okay."

I flash a reassuring smile. "I couldn't sleep."

"Neither could I." He bounces off the doorframe and walks into his room. He takes a seat on the edge of his bed, facing me. Sighing, he joins me and looks out of the window. Then he says something that's a bolt from the blue, "How did a beautiful girl like you get into drugs?"

"What?"

I heard him just fine. I'm just bidding myself some time.

I swallow hard and lift myself to my feet, suddenly feeling the urge to walk out. Instead, I pace the area in front of him. Some may think what I say next is wrong on so many levels. "Addiction."

Good one, Ginny. Throw his weaknesses right back in his face to make him feel bad for you.

He nods and looks at his feet. "I'm just trying to wrap my head around it. I guess it's hard to believe."

I know, right? Because it's not true! Benson's smarter than that.

I clear my throat. "Listen, I want to tell you everything. I really do. I just... I'd like to do it when I'm ready. And I don't feel ready right now."

He nods. "Of course. Not tonight."

I'm sorry, Benson.

Before I know it, he grabs me by the waist and yanks me onto his lap. "Promise you will tell me soon, though? Everything?"

I brush his scruffy cheek and stroke it, knowing I can't go back at this point. "I do, Benson. I just need a little more time. A lot of the memories are still fresh. Painful."

I hate myself for lying to you.

"I'm sorry for prying." He strokes my arm and lifts my hand to his lips, giving the back of it small kisses. "But I should have known better that you didn't do anything harmful. You never could."

My heart literally hurts. What the hell am I doing?

My conscious is screaming at the top of my lungs and begging to be heard, but I somehow maintain my composure. A generous tear finds its way down my cheek as I give him a soft smile. He wipes it with his thumb and kisses my cheek.

"I guess I'm just curious what's going on in that beautiful head of yours."

"You deserve to know everything."

"You won't ever have to carry the burden alone again."

"I'm sorry."

He kisses my forehead. "Don't be. I can see it's hard for you. We both have tales to tell, and we'll tell them when were ready. Okay?"

I nod and sniff my response.

I'm inches away from this beautiful man's face and I feel like I can hardly breathe. His eyes are careful and soft but conflicting at the same time. I could tell that he was fiercely battling his addiction at the moment.

I straddle his thighs and feel all the proof of his arousal for me that I need.

CHAPTER SEVENTEEN

He sighs, his face suddenly contorted with pain. "I can't seem to say no to you."

"Don't," I murmur. I slide my hand across his stubble, taking my time with probing fingers. "Would it be such a bad idea if you touched me?"

"I am touching you," he says, his hand dancing under my shirt.

I lower my head to his ear and tickle it with my lips, loving the reaction I get when he squeezes my bottom. "Yes, exactly like that," I urge him.

"I want more. Trust me." He sounds like he's getting flustered, but I refuse to back off. I continue assaulting his neck with my eager lips. He shakes his head regretfully and softly nudges me away. "Just not tonight, Ginny. Trust me on this."

"Why not?" I back away and sit across the bed from him. I am officially flustered.

He keeps stroking a tendril of my hair, his eyes hollow and absent. I'm almost positive he didn't hear my question. I go to open my mouth again but he places a finger over my lips.

He heard me.

On an exhale, he says, "Ginny, I don't make love."

But he's a sex addict. That requires lots of... it. *Doesn't it?*

Baffled to the point of no return, I wait for him to continue.

"For a girl like you, I can be your worst nightmare. I have to be honest with you, Ginny. I'm really afraid of what will happen. Much like with drugs, I tend to spiral out of control," he tells me.

Worst nightmare? Afraid of what will happen to us? Spiral out of control? And here I thought I won the lottery.

I let out a huge sigh, slumping my shoulders. "Throw me a bone here, Benson."

"I mean, when I say that I am a sex addict, it doesn't mean I'm a sexual person, or that I even like sex. In fact, I usually feel shameful or regretful afterwards almost always. I feel powerless to sex. Like, I can't control myself. For you or any person I want to be with… it can be very detrimental," he pauses for a second to maintain his composure, then on a deep exhale he continues, "Sex isn't a big deal to me like it is to other people. I do it like a crack head does what they need to do to get their next fix. I do it for the high and to get it over with."

Silence fills the room as I try to soak in what he's just confessed. Then he lets out a faint and aching sigh.

It finally dawns on me that he seeks sex like a crack head seeks their next hit.

"Would you cheat on me?" What a female thing to say.

He laughs bitterly and looks at his feet. "I've cheated if that's what you're wondering."

"On Angelina?"

He doesn't say anything which answers that. For some reason, he cheating on Angelina offends me just as much as if he would cheat on me.

"You can't control yourself? Is that what you're saying?"

He nods and looks up. "I want more than anything to be with one person. I want more than anything to be with just you. But I need the right support. We need to do this the right way. You need to understand my disorder. If you don't understand it, then this won't work."

I get what he's saying, but I can only help so much. "Are you seeking help for this?"

"I see a therapist twice a month and a go to the support group sometimes."

"Good." I look at my feet. "As long as you're trying to change, I will do anything in my power to help you, Benson."

He sighs with relief. "That's all I want."

He sits across from me a few inches away, and all I can think about is touching him all over. Straddling him. Kissing his neck. Sucking on those swollen, red lips that I assaulted earlier.

Get your mind out of the gutter, Quinn.

Instead, I grab his hand and squeeze it.

"I'm all in," I whisper.

But I'm not. Not really.
I accidently killed your wife.
I'm that careless teenager.
I love you so much.
I never intended to.
It just happened.
I was afraid to tell you.
Now, what's the point?
I love you.

"Do you think we will ever sleep together?" I ask. Seriously. What is wrong with me?

"God, I hope so," he smirks. I see a flicker of regret in his eyes. "Sometimes I can get very carried away like any addict would. You won't like me like that, I promise you. I need you to know me thoroughly before we go there. I need you to understand me. I need you to trust me."

"I trust you already, Benson. I trust you with everything I am." I grab his hand and he snatches it slowly, letting it fall on his lap.

"If you trust me that much, then I need you to trust me on this."

After a beat, I finally say, "Okay."

"Okay," he murmurs.

And that's the end of the discussion for now.

It's a while before I make eye contact again with him. I mean, how can you look the guy you love in the eye when he doesn't even want to have sex with you?

I figure it's a shot in the dark, but I ask anyway. "Will you at least lay with me?"

Instead of replying, he lay on his side and pulls me into him like I'm his favorite stuffed animal. I wrap my arms around his torso and melt into him. Looking up into his eyes, I arch an eyebrow and bite my lip.

This isn't exactly what I had in mind. "Hmmm..."

He looks at me and tilts his head in confusion. "I thought you wanted to..."

"I was kind of hoping that I could hold you," I clarify.

He looks genuinely surprised and points to himself. "You want me to be the little spoon?"

I grin. "That's right."

"Fine," he submits with a chuckle. He turns away from me and lets me wrap my arms around him. Turning the lamp off, he then places his hands over mine and caresses them in a circular motion.

I suddenly hear laughter. "This is actually nice."

I laugh along with him and shut my eyes. It is nice. We lay in the dark and comfortable silence for a few minutes.

"What's your favorite movie?" he asks, startling me. Such a simple question compared to the conversation we just had.

I snuggle into him more. "Um, Gone with the Wind. You?"

"Pulp Fiction," he whispers, caressing my stomach. "Favorite band?"

"That's a tough one. I like a lot of them."

"Name a few," he insists.

"Let's see. Coldplay, Pixies, Taking back Sunday, MGMT...what's yours?"

He smiles into the crook of my neck. "MGMT. What's that?"

We laugh together silently. "It's a band, silly."

"I forget how young you are sometimes," he jokes. "Color?"

"Whatever color those flannel pants you wear are," I joke.

He tickles me and I can't help but to yelp. Hovering over me, he says, "I thought it was yellow. Remember your bike?"

"I guess it is."

"Mine is the color of your eyes."

I smile to myself and burrow my head into his back. "Like, the color of poop?"

"What?" he asks, exasperated. "They're green, with a yellowish brown ring in the center. They're amazing."

I sigh. "Never thought of it like that."

He squeezes me tightly. "Ginny?"

"Yeah?"

"Goodnight darling."

"Goodnight Benson."

It's come to this. Benson and I sleeping in the same bed together. I wanted so much more, but I didn't want to push him. I wanted to know everything about him, including his life with Angelina. I wanted to be with him all of the time, every second of the day. I needed to.

Benson was quickly becoming the best friend I never had. I smile at the thought.

"Benson?" I murmur.

"Yeah?"

"I'll stay with you until I get back on my feet."

"Good baby," he yawns.

I think of how I'm currently the luckiest girl in the world at the moment. That, along with the smell of his soap-scented skin allows me to drift into the most peaceful somber.

CHAPTER EIGHTEEN

The following weeks with Benson and Annie are amazing, to say the least. I feel like I have an actual family again. They are so amazing that I fail to attend my AA meetings or community service.

Which makes someone very unhappy. I'll give you a hint. He's a parole officer.

Officer Mitchell glances up through his glasses with a look of disappointment that causes me to feel like I'm five years old. I raise a suspicious glance at him and that's when he decides to dart his eyes back to his clip board.

What the hell?

Before I can even ask him any questions, he answers them all for me in one sentence.

"You missed an appointment last week. No call, no show," he says offhandedly.

I shift in my seat uncomfortably. "Yeah, about that. I'm really sorry…I,"

He interrupts me in an even tone. "You could get into a lot of trouble for that."

"I know. Please let me make it up. You know I wouldn't just skip these things," I explain.

"Why did you skip it?" he asks, taking his glasses off.

"I had to leave Jesse's house because I no longer felt safe. Woke up one day with my father there. I've been laying low at a friend's house."

"A friend?" he prods. "Which friend are we talking here?"

When I don't answer, he looks at me as if he's caught me in the lie.

"Which friend, Ginny?"

"I don't have to tell you that."

"And I don't have to help you," he snaps, throwing his pen down on the clipboard and looking back up. Instead of asking him how he suspects such personal information, I refrain because he's my parole officer and it's probably just his job.

CHAPTER EIGHTEEN 211

"Then why are you?" I shrug. I've truly had enough of everyone telling me what I can and cannot do. Everyone needs to get off my back once and for all. I didn't realize I was in prison anymore, so why did it feel like I still was?

I'm afraid to look up and see how angry I've made him. Instead, I play with the loose thread of my sweater, wrapping it around my finger and thinking of all of the things I wish I could do without people reprimanding me.

When I raise my eyes to his, he looks at me as if I should already know the answer. Then on a deep exhale, he explains, "Because I don't want to see you fail. But you are going to if you continue with this kind of behavior." He then lifts to his feet and raises his voice even louder, "I offered you my gratitude with a safe place to stay and you walk out in the middle of the night without calling or with not so much as a note." On his way out of the room he tosses the clipboard on his desk and says, "Don't forget your community service today. It's mandatory."

After the unanticipated argument that I had in Officer Mitchell's office, I feel a little more beat down than usual. I stroll into Benson's house feeling cumbersome and not one for conversation. I provide him a faint smile and walk past him when his voice stops me by the staircase.

"You're brother called," he casually says, glaring at the television.

You'd be baffled for a second if you focused on the way his hands gently run through Annie's hair while she sleeps on his lap. But his eyes, that glare, explain everything.

I turn around, annoyed that I even have to say what I say next. "Step brother."

He has to know that bothers me.

"Yeah," he grumbles, yet his hand holds a graceful set of movements within Annie's hair.

"Wait, I have my phone on me." I pat down my pockets and feel the little device in my pocket. "Did he call you?"

"Yes," he mutters and I catch a faint rolling of his eyes.

What. The. Fuck?

I throw my hands up in surrender. "Whoa. I don't know how he got your number but…"

"Relax. I know why he called and I know exactly where he got it."

"Well, you got me beat there. What did he want?" I pry.

He sighs and retreats his attention to me. "I guess we should put all the cards on the table, shouldn't we?"

My heart drops into my stomach. What the hell did Jesse tell him? What does he know?

"Jesse called to threaten me," he explains, a bitter laugh escaping his throat.

I shoot him a baffled look and wait for him to explain more. "You're going to have to explain more than that, Benson. I don't know why he would threaten you. I haven't seen any of them…"

"Yes. I know you haven't seen them. But I have," he gently moves Annie and gets off the couch, stalking towards me.

No… he didn't.

I'm too shocked to even say anything. I just walk backwards until the wall hits me.

"I paid your father a visit today."

Shit.

"What did you do?" I ask, with my heart in my throat. I feel my pulse quicken and my heart bang against my rib cage like an African drum.

He approaches me slowly, chest to chest, nose to nose. I glance at him and am surprised by what I realize. It's not at all how he usually looks at me, which is usually adoringly. He's pissed and his beautiful face is marred with tension and creases I didn't know he had.

"Benson, what did you do?"

"Nothing," he says indifferently. "Just shook him up a little. He will never hurt you again."

Unbelievable.

"Are you crazy?" I shout, my hands flailing in the air like a windmill.

CHAPTER EIGHTEEN

Benson looks at me alarmed and with a touch of anger. I can tell this isn't the response he had hoped for.

"I wasn't going to just sit back and watch your dad give you a black eye!" he growls, pointing his finger painfully into my chest. I don't think he realizes the strength he actually puts into it.

"I told you to stay away from him! Wait, was Jesse there?" My paranoia seeps in, making me sound completely suspicious. I snap my jaw shut before I spew out anymore garbage. "You said he's the one that called... why did he call and not my dad?"

Oh hell! Just shut your mouth, Genevieve!

Benson shakes his head like a wet, confused dog. "I defend your honor and you're thinking about that guy?"

"Jesse didn't do anything!" It's my turn to point at his chest.

"Oh, he didn't do anything? How about he's a sick fuck who took advantage of his sister! How about that?" he spats, turning his back to me.

"Benson I told you to stay away from that man. I don't want anything to do with him!" I'm referring to my father.

"Then why was he at your house?" he asks.

Silence.

"If he was such a bad man to you, why was he there?"

"Jesse let him in." I shrug. Hey, it's the truth.

His shoulders straighten out, his wide back still facing me. Then he slowly turns, his livid eyes drilling into mine and never leaving. "I'm not a fool, Ginny. Don't you dare play me for one!"

"I'm not!"

"I know you still feel something for Jesse," he accuses. "Oh, and by the way, he wasn't even there. Because if he was he'd be missing all of his front teeth. I wonder how hard it is to get your munchies on with no teeth after smoking a big fucking fatty."

That almost makes me laugh.

"I don't feel anything for him," I deadpan, completely ignoring his threat. I wouldn't answer it like such a smartass if it wasn't my millionth time saying it.

"I don't believe you," he matches my tone.

"What do I have to do, Benson?"

He doesn't answer that. He doesn't even look at me.

"What can I do to prove to you that you're the only one?"

"Can you," he pauses and takes a deep breath and tries again. "Can you please cut the bullshit, Ginny? Please?" he asks with the saddest tone.

We have a stare off for several moments, neither one of us wanting to back down. There are so many things I want to say but I keep my mouth shut because I don't want to make things worse. He has his reasons, but so do I. I may be omitting a lot of information and even lying to him, but I wasn't lying about this.

It was only Benson. Only him.

I don't answer him. Instead, I shoot him a melancholy smile and nod. I nod because it's the only thing I'm able to do or say at this point without him looking at me like that.

Yet he's still looking at me that way.

I dash up the stairs as fast as I can before I allow him to see me reduced to nothing but a blotchy face and a mess of tears. When I reach his room, I slam the door shut and sprawl myself out on his bed, throwing a pillow over my head.

I lie there all night and even hear him put Annie to bed when the time comes. Yet, he still doesn't make an appearance in his room knowing I'm there.

I hear him go right back downstairs and that's when I realize he's still mad and maybe it's me who should be apologizing.

We were not going to get anywhere if I was always being paranoid and irrational. He was only trying to help. He doesn't know the whole situation. This is your entire fault, not his.

This. Is. All. Your. Fault.

Benson has done nothing but help me, and to be honest, I was aching for him so badly right now that I couldn't even walk straight. I think this is what withdrawals must feel like.

CHAPTER EIGHTEEN

I get up and walk downstairs as quietly as I can with nothing but his shirt on. I think better of it as I hit the bottom step, pausing for a moment and pulling it down.

He's still sitting in front of the television, looking as miserable as ever. His eyes flicker to me briefly when he notices I'm standing there, yet they return right back to the TV. I can tell he's still angry with me so I do what's best for the both of us at this point.

I make my way over to him and stand in front of him until I have his full attention. This surprisingly takes a little while. He really doesn't want to talk to me.

When his eyes finally transfer back to me, I grab the remote from him and turn off the television, letting the silence between us soak in.

He looks at me like I just confiscated his favorite toy.

I sigh and allow my eyes drill into his with regret. Maybe even a little sympathy, too.

"I'm sorry, Benson," I murmur.

He looks up at me with those beautiful indigo eyes and it brings me back to the first time that I ever met him when he nursed my knee back to health. He looked up at me through those long, fluttering eyelashes and I lost my ability to speak.

I was sold.

Screw it. He had me at hello. He had me the first time he blinked, even.

"I'm not used to being taken care of," I tell him. I hesitantly reach my hand out, slowly raking my fingers through his hair. I can't help it. He has such a beautiful, full head of hair.

I feel the need to do it again, so I do. This time I catch him shut his eyes and enjoy it. It's so faint that you wouldn't really notice it if you weren't looking hard enough.

I take that as permission to do more. I straddle him on the couch with one leg on each side of him, because I can't help that either and he doesn't seem to be protesting it.

He looks a little baffled by my actions but quickly reciprocates by placing his hands on my upper thighs and pressing me into him. I'm completely opened to him now and can feel how rapidly he is getting aroused.

He's not the only one getting aroused. I'm sick of this waiting game. His eyes scream that he's not ready for this, but it's all one big, fat lie. I feel the proof right beneath me. His body tells me a different story, an undeniable one.

"I want to take care of you in every way, Ginny," he says, fixated on my lips. "No one will ever hurt you again. Not on my watch."

God, if that isn't all the indication that I need to do what I really want to do. I bring my head forward; my lips embracing his tentatively. Before they make contact, he nips at my lower lip, licking along the bow of my lip. I take this as an invitation and seal my lips over his in the most agonizing kiss that I've ever experienced. His lips are soft and warm and inviting. It's so tender that you can cut it with the dullest of knives. His tongue comes out first, tangling with my eager one. A warmness quickly rushes below my belt and I know I should stop it out of respect, but instead, I bite his lip harder and grind against him.

God, I'm an animal.

My audacious actions set him off completely. Before I know it, his hands are moving all over me like he's discovered a brand new world. He fiercely pulls me into him, gripping my hips painfully tight. We moan into each other's mouths and grind into each other shamelessly. The heat is rising so quickly that I'm ready to take off my clothes, but before I can, he grabs me by my arms and pulls away.

"Wait."

Wait? I've never loathed such a word in my life.

I stop what I'm doing, panting heavily with pleading eyes.

Great. I've finally reduced myself to a dog.

He is panting as well but shakes his head. "We can't do this. Not like this."

I slump my shoulders and groan. That's not what I expected to hear. Still, I place my hands on a safe zone; his shoulders. But they're so masculine and square, and that's sexy and it's making me hot. So really, how safe is it?

CHAPTER EIGHTEEN

"I know," I mumble.

"You know I want to."

"I know. Me too," I sigh, placing my forehead to his.

But then I feel the firm effect I have on him below and my hips start stirring again. He noisily exhales and flabbergasts me when he digs his fingers into my hips to roll them harder. It's like the previous words he's shared with me don't even exist. I know he's having a rough time controlling it because his hands are trembling and he's biting his lip.

God, help me!

Not only is he having trouble with control, but watching him biting his lip has to be the hottest thing I've ever seen. The more I rub against him, the more I feel like I'm going to explode.

"Please Benson," I plead. I grind against him not caring about the repercussions what so ever. I feel too close to stop.

His forehead drops to where my shoulder meets my neck and he shakes his head.

He's in agony.

"I'm so close, Benson," I warn him. Just a couple more rubs back and forth and I'll feel like I'm on the best drug on Earth.

Benson Daniels.

"Ginny," he groans in frustration as I work myself against him.

"Please, Benson. I need you so bad," I whine.

He slowly looks up at me with pensive eyes and that's when I see it.

He's considering it.

With the devil on my shoulder in full affect, I roll against him once more and this time I almost come to orgasm. I look at him to see if he notices, and of course, he does. His eyes are on fire.

I bring my lips to his ear, barely touching. What I say next is more than a threat than anything else, and I don't feel sorry about it what so ever. "I almost just came. I need to sit on you right now."

Please.

He looks at me for a moment, fire in his eyes and then unbuckles his belt with quick precision. I help him with the zipper because waiting a minute more seems impossible, now.

With a quick pull of his pants, his thick cock juts out and lands heavily in my hands. I take a moment of silence to just look at it. You would think I had just discovered the Holy Grail.

It looks angry; red and thick and ready to explode. It's bigger than I imagined. It puts any of the others that I've seen before to shame, not that there are many.

"Today, Ginny," he warns me, his voice stern and flustered as hell.

I immediately wrap my fingers around it and hear him seethe through his teeth from the contact. The expression makes me feel in control and I love it. I let him shamelessly rock his hips into my hands a few times and I get to know him. After a few pumps, I look up at him and notice he's smirking.

Just like that, he's in control again.

I quickly shift onto my knees and adjust myself over him. Avoiding eye contact for the sake of any second thoughts on his end, I brace my hands on his shoulders and guide him into me, lowering slowly until my ass meets his lap. I drop my head into his shoulder as we both gasp for air and adjust to one another. I have to close my eyes for a moment because the relief of him inside me is so overwhelming. My hypersensitive body is in overdrive as I begin to grind against him.

When I feel his big hand cup my face and tilt my chin up, I meet his eyes for the first time. They are filled with lust and flames, threatening to burn me alive. Then my eyes dart to his red kissed mouth, daring him to make a move.

And he does make a move, dipping his head in first and allowing our lips to crash together hard and relentlessly. We swallow each other's moans, my tongue reaching every surface of the inside of his mouth. Any further and it would literally be down his throat.

CHAPTER EIGHTEEN

I can't think. I can't speak. All I can do is suck his full bottom lip between my teeth as I have the most intense orgasm of my life. I rock out the waves, greedily taking what I've wanted all along.

This orgasm puts all of the other orgasms I've had to shame.

Before I can even process my post coital bliss, he lifts me off him and sets me aside. It's then that I realize he hasn't finished. I reach out and say, "let me,"

"No," he quietly says, pushing me back and buckling up his belt.

What the fuck?

His wide chest rises up and down, sucking in and blowing out too much air. His cheeks are an unfamiliar flushed pink, making him look so beautiful post-coital. Not to mention when he licks his pillow lips and runs a hand through his copper hair. Unfortunately, that's not the complete center of my focus for once. I witness it happening, but the only thing I can think about is that we broke his cardinal rule of no penetration.

And he's regretting it.

I ruined it all for the most amazing feeling I've ever had in my life. ...And screw it. I'd do it again and again, too.

"Why don't you head to bed," he tells me, not sounding the least bit convincing. He stares off into blank space and scratches his chin. I can tell he's back to being broody Benson. He is going over every worst case scenario in his head and playing it on repeat.

And here I am trying to calm my damn hormones.

You know what? Screw this. It was his decision just as much as it was mine. Surely he won't put the full blame on me.

"Why won't you let me help you?" I ask, annoyed.

"I don't need help," he retorts.

I flinch at the sudden sternness of his voice. "You know what I mean. As soon as I came, you threw me off you like I have the plague. Do you really feel that bad about fucking me? You didn't do anything wrong. What we did was okay. Better yet, it felt good, Benson."

"No Ginny!" He bellows, and the room goes eerily silent. He squeezes his eyes shut and I know exactly what he's thinking in this very moment. He's hoping he didn't just wake his daughter. He breathes a few times, in and out, and then he scowls. "It didn't feel right to me. It wasn't a moment. It wasn't beautiful. Maybe for you, but for me, I was just feeding my addiction."

I place my hand over my heart. His words are like a sucker punch straight to my rib cage.

"How could you say that?" I choke out. I'm so hurt that a single tear sneaks its way out of my ducts and down my flush face. I feel like the most pathetic scum of the Earth. I feel stupid and so very used. I don't like this version of Benson. I'm not sure that this version of Benson even likes me.

"Stop it," he orders.

"What? You got your fix and now you're done with me? You can't even talk to me right now?"

He stares past me; his face looks like it's made of stone.

"You can't even look at me," I whisper.

He ignores me and continues to stare at the wall behind me.

I hit his chest and push him hard because I'm so angry. "Answer me, Benson! What's the deal? Are you done with me now?"

I sound psycho, but everything coming out of me right now is nothing compared to what I feel in inside.

Inside, I am bursting at the seams.

He strides towards me until we're nearly nose to nose. He seems to be on the brink of an emotional break down because his fists are squeezed together so tightly that his knuckles are white. His eyes are popping out of his skull, making him look like Igor from Young Frankenstein. "No Ginny. I'm not even close to done with you. You've woken up something inside of me that you will soon regret. You don't know what you just got yourself into."

His words sound downright lethal, and a lot like a threat.

CHAPTER EIGHTEEN

Before I can refute my response, he inaudibly says, "Go to bed, Ginny. I'll be up in a little while."

Feeling like an adolescent and having no legitimate response, I turn on my heel and head for the stairs. I shoot up them faster than a flash of lightning and find my solace in the sheets of his bed. I nestle my face into the scent of his pillow and allow myself to shut my eyes.

It's not long before I hear his heavy footsteps and the door creak open into the silent night. I'm not facing the door, but I know without a doubt it's him. The bed dips in next to me and I feel a jolt of confidence run through my veins, warming my body with anticipation. I hear the clanking of his belt buckle, following articles of clothing carelessly being scattered around the room. I'm almost positive he thinks I'm sleeping, but I am very much conscious and waiting to feel his warm hands all over my body again.

It's almost as if he reads my mind when his hand slips over my bare stomach and he pulls me into him, forcing me to feel him again. I hold his hand in place and raise it under my breasts. Quickly, he turns me over so that I'm facing him and pulls me into him until we're nose to nose. We snuggle into each other in silence. He's caressing my thigh as I run my hands through his small beard he has grown.

There's so much I want to say to him. Where do I start?

Pulling away, I say his name. It carries a sad tone that I can't get rid of if I tried.

"Ginny, no," he interrupts. "No talking."

Again, he turns me so that I'm facing him and cups my cheek with his big palm. I notice right then that his eyes are red and harsh as if tears have threatened to fall from them. I can't picture Benson crying, yet somehow I've seen the proof of a few aftermaths. I wish I hadn't.

"No, don't," I whisper, brushing my thumbs over his eyes and wiping away the excess tears. I scoot closer until were chest to chest and kiss his damp eyelids. When I look him in the eye, he grabs my chin between his index and thumb and leads me to his lips, kissing me softly and tentatively. A warm buzz ignites my body and I realize I could live off this kiss.

So much that when he pulls away, I give him a pleading look not to stop. After teasing me with his eyes, he finally gives me what I want and kisses me again. This time it's longer and with some tongue.

This time I pull away because I need to know what he's thinking.

Before I can even figure it out, we're kissing again, fast and passionately. We become a tangle of limbs and heavy breaths, rolling over the tangled sheets until we can't anymore. In one fast movement, he lifts my hands above my head and settles himself on top of me, his big erection digging into my stomach. When he pushes it in to my center, I sigh from the contact, moving my hips in a circular motion and trying to seek relief. He trails open mouthed kisses down my jaw and neck, to my collarbone and the swell of my breasts. He still has my arms above my head but I find a way to squirm all over anyways.

"This is going to be a problem," he whispers against my lips.

I'm a little too turned on to decipher what he is talking about.

"I will want this all the time," he says. As if it's a bad thing!

"Take me whenever you want," I instantly respond. I reach for his belt when he grabs my wrists and pulls them away.

"You're not going to always want it the way that you do right now. It's not always going to be like this, Ginny."

I take my hands back and place them on his face, cupping it. "Hey, I want this. Just as much as you do. Don't make it ugly, okay?"

He ignores what I just said. "It will be a lot."

"Okay."

"You won't have time for anyone else."

Oh no he didn't. "There is no one else."

CHAPTER EIGHTEEN

He shuts me up before I can say anymore by sealing his mouth over mine. As if he can't wait another minute. Good. I was sick of waiting.

Yet, what he does next somewhat shocks me.

Roughly grabbing me by my wrists, he pins them above my head with one of his hands. His eyes turn black, showing no emotion what so ever. It's like a switch has flipped. Before I can ask him what he's doing, he quickly turns me over onto my stomach and slaps my ass so hard that I'm almost positive it's bleeding from the impact.

He roughly rips my panties off, not even bothering with my shirt. I smile at his eagerness.

No foreplay. No warning. I let out a squeal as he enters me with one hard pump. You would think I'm being forced from an outsiders stand point, but that's definitely not the case.

He lifts his weight off of me while he's still in me, attempting to at least give me a moment of recuperation.

Then he's thrusting again, aggressively gripping my hips as I cry out and grab the bed rails for purchase. I'm certainly not used to having sex like this, and at some moments, I think about telling him to stop.

"Benson, a little easier, please?" I ask in a voice I don't even recognize.

He shuts his eyes, presumably blocking out the way I'm peering over my shoulder at him. He then pulls out of me, turning me back onto my back and then puts all his weight on me as he slides back in. He places his hand gently on my face and looks at me with concern. This time, his thrusts are gentler but he still takes what he wants until he finishes.

When we're done, he turns over so that his back is facing me and shoves his head under the pillow. He stays like that for a few minutes until I notice that his shoulders are shaking.

"Benson?" I whisper.

When he doesn't answer, I place my hand on his shuddering shoulder and it stops.

"I hurt you," I hear his muffled voice.

"No, you didn't," I assure him. "You just got a little carried away."

He removes his head from under the pillow and I notice his eyes are red, wet, and swollen. "We can't do that again, okay?"

I broke a promise. I disrespected his wishes. I broke Benson.

I swallow a lump in my throat. "Okay, Benson. It won't happen again."

We lie there for a long time before either one of us falls asleep.

The next day I am woken by Annie jumping on the bed. The slightest motion attacks my heightened senses, bringing me to the realization that I'm sorer than ever. Every limb aches and the apex of my thighs are on fire. Great. I have fire crotch, literally.

I lift one eye only to see Annie's tilted little head, her small features scrunched in confusion.

"Daddy, I think she's dead," she yells.

Then, I hear Benson's voice boom from downstairs. Jump some more!"

Bastard.

It's then I get a whiff of the scrumptious air that is circulating into the room from the kitchen. It smells amazing.

I smell bacon. I smell pancakes. The chef is at work.

I sit up in Benson's king sized bed and smile at the cutest little girl in the world. "Good Morning Princess."

"I wish," she mutters. "Daddy made us breakfast!"

The smile on her face is genuine and pure. She really loves when her daddy cooks for her.

"Okay honey. Tell your dad that I will be right down. I just need to get dressed."

"Okay!" she says, bouncing off the bed and out of the room like a rocket.

Once I make sure she's gone, I get out of bed in nearly nothing but my underwear and a silk night top that is just for Benson's eyes. I shuffle my feet over to his closet to

CHAPTER EIGHTEEN

see what I can cover up with that would be comfortable. I find a robe on his door and slip that on.

I enter the kitchen to the most beautiful scenery I've ever seen.

It's not the stunning sunflowers that surround the kitchen windows or the table full of delicious breakfast food. It also isn't the content smiles on everyone's faces this morning.

It's the shirtless Benson in low rise flannel pants. I stand in the doorway for a moment, appreciating the muscular V that sculpts his hips and disappear into his pants. That's what I am appreciating right now.

He has a spatula in his hand and a white half apron draping over his pajamas, but that doesn't stop him from being a total DILF. Oddly, it makes him look even sexier.

I look over at Annie, who is oblivious to her shirtless father and my eye ogling. She's way too busy stacking the sugar packets into a castle to be concerned with that.

"Good Morning, Captain Snoozie! Coffee?"

I hear a high pitch giggle next to me as Benson comes around with the steaming coffee pot.

I smile at Annie and then stick my tongue out at him. "Please."

He pours me a cup of coffee and hands me it. "Sit down and relax, you two. Let me serve my two favorite girls in the world."

I glance at Annie and she is all smiles, seemingly in on a secret I don't know about. She keeps looking at her dad and laughing, and vice versa. I ignore it for the time being and take a long sip of my hot coffee.

There are eggs, bacon, pancakes, crepes, croissants, assorted fruits and flowers covering their entire kitchen table. This is something that you would see straight out of a movie, but instead, this is my life right now.

And I did absolutely nothing to deserve it.

But I take a scone anyway.

"It looks and smells amazing," I compliment, taking a seat across from Annie so that she can sit next to her father.

"This is nothing," he mutters, flipping the pancakes one last time before turning the stove off. "Wait until you see what I'm doing for dinner tonight."

"Dinner?" I look at Annie and then back at him. "You know anything about this?" I ask Annie, and she giggles, shaking her head.

"I'm going to Grandpa's girlfriend's house tonight."

"We're having a date," Benson announces.

"A date?" I ask. "We are? Doesn't the other person have to give consent in order for there to be a date? Surely people don't go on dates alone."

"Hmmm," he hums, staring me down with a look that just screams mischief. After serving Annie and me our delectable plates of food, he turns to his daughter and asks, "Would you get a load of that, Annie? She says she needs to give consent to go on a date with me!"

Annie laughs. Her little voice music to my ears. "Just ask her then, daddy! She'll probably say yes!"

I can't help but to laugh and blush scarlet red.

Benson walks around to my side of the table and gets on a knee, making a big spectacle out of it. Annie's giggle is all I can hear in the background.

"Ginny, I really don't want to go on our date alone and I'd really like if you were there. Will you go on our date with me?"

A burst of excitement seeps through my pores at the very thought, but then something brings me right back down to Earth. Making him wait, I take a bite of the delicious food and think about my community service tonight. Officer Mitchell has been on me about missing it.

But maybe if I just miss it one more time...

I mean, how much trouble could I get in for missing it one more time?

"Yes, Benson. I'd love to go on our date with you."

I'm getting a few things for our date tonight at the grocery store when I walk out to the parking lot alone. The sun has gone down, leaving a beautiful orange after glow. I

CHAPTER EIGHTEEN

take a minute to watch it set before walking the rest of the way to my car.

Benson pleaded with me not to go until he got home from work, but of course, I ignored his request. I wanted to surprise him with everything for when he got home, insisting I'd bring one of his knives with me just in case. Not that I know how to use any of them.

Usually walking in the dark doesn't spook me, but tonight is different. I just can't get over the fact that I'm being watched.

I have a sinking suspicion someone is behind me but I don't turn around, instead, I walk even faster down the street. The faster I walk, the faster I hear the footsteps behind me.

At this point, I'm terrified to turn around.

"Ginny?" I hear a soft, deep voice.

I turn around with my bags and what I see next utterly shocks me.

An unmistakably disheveled Jesse. He doesn't look anything like his normal state as he stares at something past my shoulder. I'm not even sure he realizes I'm there yet.

I take in his appearance. I barely recognize him. His hair is greasy and there are stains all over his shirt. He definitely didn't look like that a few days ago.

"Jesse?"

He lifts his somber eyes to mine and nods hesitantly. Outstretching his arms, he says, "Let me take those for you."

Before he can snatch them, I pull them out of his reach and stare at the inside of his fore arms. Something completely takes my attention and it's not the dirt stains all over his clothes or his unwashed hair. However, those were a close second. I could smell him from here.

Track marks. Bruised needle marks pepper the inside of his forearm, all the way up to the inside of his elbow. Jesse has been shooting up.

He sees my face transition into anger and quickly goes to grab me as if I will run away. I'm so angry that I swat his hands away. "I'm fine."

He gives me a pleading look.

"Heroin, Jesse? Really?" I say way too loud.

A few bypassing people look our way but I ignore them.

He doesn't answer me. He won't even look at me. The only thing I notice is that he is picking at his skin, which looks a lot worse than it did the last time I saw him. His failure to make eye contact or talk to me confirms what I'm already dreading.

"You followed me here." It's not a question. It's a statement.

"I had to get you alone and away from that guy."

"Away from that guy? What do you have against him other than the fact that he's with me?"

He doesn't respond to my jab but sighs, defeat stiffening his posture. He takes a few tentative steps closer and that's when I get the unfortunate whiff of his aroma, and it's not the least bit pleasant.

"Jesse, you know I can't be around you when you're like this. I'm on probation."

"I know," is all he says. His voice isn't his own. It's defeated and laced with regret. I wouldn't recognize it if I didn't see him talking right in front of me.

I shrug irritably and ask, "Why are you hurting yourself? Why now?"

He looks at the ground, at a loss for words. "I… I just really hate myself for what I did to you all these years. I made you nonexistent for my own happiness. I wish I could do it all over again. I'd visit you in prison. I'd be a good boyfriend. I'd… I'd be a good brother."

"We were never meant to be, Jesse. You were just supposed to be a good brother."

"I don't feel that way, Ginny. I regret letting you go."

"I know, but its better this way," I whisper, looking at the ground with him.

"Now it's my turn to struggle. I deserve everything that's come my way."

"When's the last time you showered?" I grimace, changing the subject.

CHAPTER EIGHTEEN

"A few days ago," he mentions, off handedly. "Are you happy with him?"

I have to be careful how I answer that. So I just I nod and say, "I am."

He nods and we have a brief stare off, neither of us wavering. Even in his disheveled state, he's still the most beautiful person I've ever laid eyes on.

How does he do that?

He suddenly grabs his chest and holds on to the nearest parked car so that he doesn't fall.

I quickly realize he's not being dramatic and that something's really wrong.

"I don't feel so good, Gin." He slowly loses his footing and begins to drop to the ground in slow motion. I set my bags on the same car and jump into action, holding him up by his arm. "Jesse, how much did you take?"

"The last few times I've taken it, it didn't do anything. So I just took a little bit more."

"Jess, we need to get you to a hospital."

"No!" he shouts. He looks around the parking lot, his eyes wide saucers. It's then he realizes how loud he was with me. He shoots me an apologetic look and sighs. "Just take me home. Please."

I hesitantly nod and we get to his car, where I drive for the first time in seven years.

It really is like riding a bicycle in a way. I may have ran a stop sign or hit a curb or two, but we made it back to his apartment in one piece.

Once we get to his apartment, I prop him up on a kitchen chair while I make him a bed on the couch. Used needles and soiled baggies are littered all over the coffee table and floor. I make it a note to get rid of all of those next. Once I tuck the sheet into the cushions, I grab a limp Jesse by the arm and carefully lay him out on the couch, pulling a blanket over him.

"Is this all you have? What's on the floor?" I prod.

He looks at me as if he doesn't understand what I'm saying.

"Heroin, Jesse. Is it all gone?" I say in a more stern voice.

He hesitantly shakes his head. He knows I'm not about the back down so he reaches into his back pocket and pulls out the last of what he has, handing it to me. "This is it," he whispers.

I look at the harsh brown powder in a baggie and go straight to the toilet, tossing it in the water and immediately flushing it. "No more, Jesse. No more of this shit, do you hear me?" I shout from the bathroom. "You need to get clean starting now. Unless you want to die."

When I walk back into the living room, he's snoring with one eye half open. I can tell by the steady rise and fall of his chest that he's in a deep sleep but not dead, so I let him sleep a little while I watch some TV and make a call to Benson.

The phone rings twice before he picks up.

"Gin?" His voice sounds desperate as if he's been looking for me.

"Hey," I say after a beat.

"Where in God's heavens are you?"

"I didn't forget our date. I," I pause because I want to say the next sentence as smoothly as I can. "I was at the store getting some stuff and ran into someone that needed help."

"Someone that needed help?" Even though I can't see him, I can picture him arching that perfect black eyebrow at me.

"Yes, I'm just staying a little to make sure he's okay. Then I'll be back."

Silence. My heart is racing a mile a minute.

He knows. He's not stupid.

"Just tell me it's not him and I will be okay with it," he whispers in the calmest voice he can muster up.

I don't have a response, a correct one anyways.

"Benson, come on,"

"Tell. Me. It's. Not. Him!" he snarls.

"Fine! It's not him! Are you happy? You want me to lie to you? Fuck, that's what you're forcing me to do! You're

CHAPTER EIGHTEEN

forcing me to lie to you!" I realize I'm rambling on and it's too late when I stop myself. I've already said too much.

Before I can apologize for my childish behavior, the line goes dead. I look at the phone as if it's his face and grimace. This is going to be a long conversation that I don't want to even have.

Instead of calling back, I let him cool off a bit and go to make myself a pot of coffee.

What happens next is a whirlwind of blurry movements, causing me to snap my head in Jesse's direction. He sits up quickly, projectile vomit spurting out of his mouth exorcist style and splattering all over the carpet. He hunches over, retching everything he's eaten within the past few days. I drop my phone and quickly rush to his aid, sitting down next to him and rubbing his back.

We'll call that a natural reaction.

It's only after he completely empties out the contents of his stomach that he starts to dry heave.

"Shhh. It's okay," I whisper, trying to comfort him. I continue rubbing his back and whispering assurances into his ears.

He cradles his head in his hands once he's done, nearly busting at the seams from the whole experience. His ink black hair curtains his face, giving me no clues as to what he's thinking. I lean in to get a better look at his face when his shoulders begin to shake.

Tears fall generously from his eyes as he tries to cover his sobs with his hands. I rip them away and force him to look at me. "Jesse, when did you start doing heroin?"

He shakes his head, seeming a bit groggy and disoriented. "I don't know. A week ago?"

I give him a harsh shake. "It stops now, okay?"

Tough love, baby.

He nods eagerly as if we're on the same page. I hope that is the case.

I rub his back a little more as we sit in silence. He takes a few deep breaths before he finally says, "I'm so sorry, Genevieve. I've failed you. I've failed everyone I've ever loved."

"Stop it, Jesse. We've both failed. We can't dwell on the past. We need to move forward. That's all we can do."

He lifts his head, his ink black hair falling into his eyes, reminding me why I fell in love with him in the first place. God, he's beautiful.

I notice his features are more swollen than usual, his face red and raw and angry. His amber eyes are blood shot more than usual. "I don't want to move on if it's without you."

I stand up, wanting to terminate this conversation whole heartedly. He notices my uneasiness and grabs my hand, pulling me back down. "Please, just sit. I'll stop talking about that. I promise."

I sit back down slowly and stare at the puke stains on the carpet. That's going to be a real bitch to clean up. I can't believe Jesse had been turning to heroin instead of the help he needs. Maybe if I was here and leading him in the right direction, he wouldn't have gotten to this point.

Tears threaten to pour from my eyes and he notices. He slings an arm around my slumped shoulders and reels me in. "Don't cry for me," he whispers into my ear. "I don't deserve your tears."

"I don't want to see you like this," I sniffle.

"You're my best friend, Genevieve."

I snort my response and then cry even harder. Sobbing, I ask, "Will you stop then? Please?"

"Okay. I will."

I don't believe a word of it and my eyes show it.

"Chalk it up to a really bad decision, okay?" he assures me. "I only used a couple times. It stops now. I promise."

I whimper and nod. Of course, Jesse would be comforting me when he needs me the most. Standing up abruptly, I wipe my tears. "Let me clean this up. Why don't you go lay in your bed for now."

Without saying a word, he raises to his feet and gives me a subtle nod. When he reaches his room, he turns around and looks at me. With his hand on the door knob, he says, "Ginny?"

"Yeah?"

CHAPTER EIGHTEEN

"Do me a favor?"

I nod.

"I know you have to leave at some point. Don't go until I'm sleeping, okay?"

I smile softly. "I won't leave until you're fast asleep, Jesse."

He nods, his face showing a contented glow before he shuts his bedroom door with him inside it.

I slip inside the door and to my disbelief; he's not waiting for me like I expect him to be. In fact, I can't even see his face. All I can see is his strong back, the muscles clenching with uneasiness. He's in the kitchen frying something up on the stove. I tip toe into the room when Annie comes into view, sitting at the table while waiting for her grilled cheese.

This isn't going to be easy.

"Hey." I barely hear myself.

He turns halfway with a spatula in his hand and nods, not even making eye contact with me. Then he turns back around.

Okay then. I should have known it wouldn't be that easy.

"Sorry. I tried coming home as soon as I could," I explain, sitting next to Annie. I know it's cheap on my part by sitting next to his little girl so that he can't curse me out, but I do anyways. She looks up through her blonde locks and smiles her little smile and I can't help but smile back.

He gracefully moves around the kitchen, placing the grilled sandwich on a paper plate and placing it in front of his daughter. "Take this to your room," he softly orders.

She snaps her head up to his, taken aback. "But you said no eating in the…"

"I'm revoking the rule for today," he cuts her off.

She looks at her father for a beat before grabbing her plate and flying up the stairs.

Shit. I knew I couldn't use Annie for a shield for that long. Pathetic.

Now that we're alone, I brace the inevitable. However, as soon as Annie scurries up the stairs, I expect something much worse than what I receive. He's not screaming in my face as I expected. He's not even making eye contact with me but is hunched over the sink, his strong arms holding himself up for support. His head is hung so low it looks like he doesn't even have one.

Silence saturates the room as I take in his broad shoulders rising up and down, calculated and measured. I'm afraid if I say anything I will awaken the beast. At any moment I expect him to turn around and reprimand me. Instead, he starts cleaning the stove.

I watch him for a little bit until he turns around and leans up against the counter. "I didn't make us the big dinner you wanted because I didn't think you were coming home."

"Benson. I'm really sorry, I…"

He shakes his head and puts his hand up. "Don't."

I snap my mouth shut and look at his falling face. Why the hell isn't he angry and screaming at me? He certainly should be.

"Just wear something nice tonight. We're going out to meet a few of my friends."

That's it? "Okay."

"Okay," he says, looking at me for a beat before leaving the room.

What the hell just happened?

Later that night, I keep my promise to meet his friends despite the unusual mood he's in. To be honest, it's rather scary. I know deep down inside he's angry with me, but you can't see a shred of it. He hides it so well.

We stride in to a beautifully dimmed club, adorned with elegant white lights and silver fixtures. I've never seen anything like it in my life. When I think of a dance club, I think sleazy, sweaty and sexy. However, Benson assures me that you have to be a member to even get into this club, and on Fridays, you're allowed to bring a guest.

CHAPTER EIGHTEEN

The bass is so earsplitting that I feel the blood in my ears gyrating to the beat. I sense Benson brush his hand up against mine, as light as a feather. As soon as we make eye contact, he clasps it and then raises my knuckles to his lips. He doesn't kiss my knuckles but gently skims his lips across them back and forth.

I think he can tell that I'm nervous to meet his friends and he softens his posture because of that. I'm relieved knowing that I have the power of peeling back his layers, even at the worst of times.

What made me completely nervous about getting to know Benson better is the fact that he would get to know me better. He will get to know my body language better. He will be able to tell when I'm truly happy when I'm pissed, or in this case…anxious.

He was already starting to catch on.

"Ginny, you know you can drink tonight. Don't feel weird about it just because I don't."

"I don't need a drink," I say.

"You're trembling. I think you do," he jokes.

"I am?" I look at my hands and sigh. "Okay, maybe one. It won't tempt you?"

He raises his head and gives me a shit eating grin. Somehow, I don't think we're talking about alcohol anymore.

I playfully shove him in the chest as he leads me by the hand to a table full of well-dressed people that all look around his age. They look like they range from their early to late thirties; most of the women looking younger.

There are two females and three males, not that I'm counting. They all stand when they see Benson and me approaching. They seem a bit surprised to see him, almost as if they hadn't seen him in a while.

"Here's the motley crew," he says, referring to his friends. They all look pleased to see him and all provide him with hugs. Some are a simple pat on the back and others are big, bear hugs. He seems to be a very likeable man. Seeing how much his friends like him makes me adore him even more.

"This is Melanie, Greg, Nick, Tina, and Joseph Broseph," he introduces them.

They all wave and I wave back, feeling the scarlet shoot right up my spine.

"Everyone, this is Ginny." He raises our intertwined hands into view like we just won a two-legged race.

"Sit down over here!" Melanie offers, patting the empty seat next to her. She's a little petite blonde with a vibrant personality. It seems like her and Greg have something serious going on.

I reluctantly unlock my hands with Benson's and go and sit next to her.

"So where are you from?" Tina shouts over the music. She's a little taller than Melanie and curvy in all the right places. A luscious red head. In fact, Joseph Broseph cannot take his eyes off of her.

"Here!" I shout.

She nods with a smile. "I hope you're ready to get hammered because you have no choice."

"Is that right?" I ask with a smirk.

"We've tried moving our outings somewhere else like a bowling alley or something," Tina explains. "But Benson wouldn't have it. The amazing bastard doesn't drink and still manages to have fun."

Melanie points to the dance floor. "I hope you're ready to dance."

"Oh god, no! I don't dance." I state as a matter-of-factly.

"You don't dance, or you can't dance?" Melanie asks. My face flushes. "Both."

"Well, you're going to learn tonight!"

She wasn't kidding. For the next couple of hours, we all take shots and talk about everything from how we "met" to what all of us did for a living. Everyone seems shocked that Benson brought a girl to meet them tonight. That means they've never met Janet. I wear a big, shit eating grin for the next few minutes knowing that little piece of information.

The boys take over talking, each taking turns busting Benson's chops.

CHAPTER EIGHTEEN

"Women love him but it's like he's allergic to them," Nick says.

"Poor Benson. So many women, so little time," his friend Joe chimes in.

Benson sits there, stirring his soda, blushing the whole time. I've never seen him look so innocent. Vulnerable. It's as if he thinks he doesn't deserve all of the attention that's on him. I think it's the cutest thing I've ever seen to be quite honest. I squeeze his hard thigh and pat it gently.

By eleven at night, we are all jumping and swaying on the dance floor. I'm pretty sure that I have no rhythm but the liquor flowing through my blood stream makes me want to try. Melanie and Tina grind on each side of me in their euphoric states. I steal a glance at Benson who is leaning up against the bar and facing me, watching me. They seem to be talking to him but it sure doesn't look like he's listening. He's too focused on me.

He nods his head at his friend as if he's listening, but never takes his eyes off me.

So I start swaying my hips from side to side and close my eyes. To tell you the truth, I have no idea what I'm doing. I observe how the girls next to me move and copy their lead. It seems to be working because when I look up, Benson's eyes are like a deer in headlights. His eyes are two fireballs burning into my body, overheating me with lust and desire. When I see how turned on he is, I maintain eye contact with him and follow the synthetic beats, snapping back and forth like a belly dancer. It all of a sudden feels so natural.

He seems to be mesmerized by the swaying of my hips, so I keep doing what I'm doing and let the girls dance on me. I close my eyes and move to the rhythm, letting the alcohol take all of my inhibitions away. When I open my eyes, he has a shit eating grin plastered across his face. God, he's never looked so deviant. I love him this way.

My heart drops into my stomach when he puts his soda down and starts walking through the dancing crowd... in my direction.

The crowd splits for him naturally as if he's Jesus or something. Or maybe it's just the alcohol talking. The room is spinning just a little bit, but I don't let that ruin my good time. I don't let that stop me from what happens next.

Finally, in front of me, he places his hands on my hips and sweeps me off my feet, literally. In one swift movement, he spins me in the air, my hair curtaining us both as we stare into each other's eyes. As soon as my feet hit the ground, he firmly presses me up against him. I can feel what I do to him because it's poking me hard. He bucks his hips forward and it isn't an accident. He really wants me to feel it. I suddenly feel all the nerve-endings in my lower extremities, leaving me aroused in the middle of a room full of dancing people.

Towering over me, he touches his nose to mine and stares into my eyes. He's so close that his lust filled eyes are all I can see. We're in our own little world, standing in the middle of a crowded dance floor and panting into each other. He slowly lowers his lips to my ear and nips the lobe, causing me to visibly shudder.

"I think I've waited long enough to taste you," he says, his voice throaty.

I look up at him, my jaw slack. I can't believe the words that just came out of his mouth.

"Can we go somewhere?" I eagerly ask him, my finger nails digging into his forearms with excitement. I want to leave before he changes his mind.

He growls and squeezes my hips so hard I almost yelp.

"Let's get out of here," he growls.

I feel my heart flutter, then aimlessly crash into the deepest portion of my stomach.

"Okay, I say, barely able to speak.

During the ride home, we can barely keep our hands off each other. More like I can't keep my hands off him. His right hand rests on my thigh, groping any part of it that he can. The left hand is on the wheel, unfortunately.

CHAPTER EIGHTEEN

I am rubbing him down and kissing his throat, chin, and chest. Basically anywhere I can reach without disturbing him from the road.

Okay, let's be honest, he's swerving like he's had a few six packs. Sadly, that doesn't stop me.

He moans as I reach the most sensitive part of his neck, right near the bottom of his ear. He has some trouble parallel parking, but masters it none the less. The man is perfect at almost everything he does.

Except controlling his sexual appetite.

We burst into his room while in the middle of a make out frenzy. He forcefully pushes me on the bed with a playful smile. It seems as if all of the conversations about abstinence he's drilled into my brain are irrelevant now that we are finally in his room with no interruptions. I smile and lay on his satin sheets as I slither up to the headboard like a snake. He slowly creeps onto the bed and sneaks his left hand up my right calf. With one touch of his callused hand, it's enough to make all of the blood rush to the center of my body. Then, he makes his way to the top of my thigh highs. He grips onto the thigh high, and with one swift motion he rips it off.

"God, your thighs are so fucking sexy. Has anyone ever told you that?" He heavily breathes. Then without warning, he gives them a hard smack. It's enough to leave me panting as well.

I might be a slender woman, but it's not the first time someone's told me that I have nice legs. They are a bit bigger compared to the rest of my body. A little thicker than the rest of me. I was always self-conscious about them, but apparently men like thick thighs.

I don't tell him any of that though, because nothing good could come of him knowing that Jesse thought the same thing.

The center of his attention goes back to my slender, yet thick contradiction of legs; sliding his hands up them until he reaches the apex of my thighs. He begins moving his fingers in a circular motion against the cotton of my panties, zeroing in on my face. It seems the more that I arch my back in pleasure, the more that he teases me. My aching pelvis begs for release as I arch my core into his hand. He notices I'm close and keeps going like he's trying to win a race.

I let out loud, shameless moan and he slows down enough for me to notice.

"Don't you dare stop, Benson," I pant, arching my hips into his hand, riding out the waves of impending pleasure.

"Tell me what you want or else I will stop," he demands, calmly.

My eyes test him, and he slows down again.

"Taste me," I order.

He grins wickedly. "Taste you where?"

"You know where," I grit out.

He pulls away from me. "Tell me where. I want to hear you say it."

He kneels in front of me and places his hands on his lap. I can't believe he's pulling this shit right now. He shoots me a teasing grin because he knows I'm starting to get frustrated by the loss of him.

"Down there," I growl.

"Now is not the time to be coy, Ginny..."

I cut him off with a groan, "Jesus Christ, Benson! Lick my pussy! Please!"

Apparently, I'm not above begging.

When my eyes connect with his, I'm taken aback. His eyes are so intense; broody and sensual. Yet he's wearing the smuggest grin. Closing the distance between us, his lips lustfully collaborate with mine, bruising them completely. It's different from the other kisses he's given me in the past. This one is more urgent, needy.

Part of me wants him to do me hard and animalistic like he did the other night. Part of me wants him to go slow and take his time with me. I want him in every way.

Suddenly he slows down, stops moving his hips, his lips, his hands...

Hey, don't stop! Wait!

He sits up with a sober face and stares ahead of him. He looks like a deer in headlights.

What the hell, dude?

CHAPTER EIGHTEEN

I look at Benson, who might as well be a Macy's mannequin at the moment. I turn my attention to where he's staring and see Annie at the door with her Olaf stuffed animal propped in her arm.

I quickly grab the covers over me and Benson does the same to become decent.

I observe Benson for a minute because he seems to be the more disturbed of the two. He goes to open his mouth and then snaps it shut. He's at a loss of words.

"What's wrong sweetie?" I intervene.

She just stands in the door way with vacant eyes, not even looking in our direction. After a few seconds, Benson chimes in, "She's sleep walking."

I exhale a puff of air I didn't realize I was holding in. Thank God. She won't remember any of this.

Either that or she is traumatized.

Benson looks at me and sighs. "Be right back."

I nod understandingly and sink into the bed. Poor guy cannot get a break. No wonder he needed a nanny.

CHAPTER NINETEEN

I wake up in the middle of the night feeling insanely aroused. It's the strangest sensation. I had no prior dream leading to this point, so I'm a little confused by my sensitive state.

Benson is lying next to me in the complete dark, his back leaning against the headboard. Although I'm having trouble seeing, I can tell he is very much awake and that his focus is on me.

Then I feel his feather light touch. His finger drawing circles dangerously low on my stomach. Was he doing this while I was sleeping? That would explain everything.

I feel like I might be having an anxiety attack, so I sit up in the bed and instinctively place my hand over my chest to calm my pounding heart. A few inhales and exhales and I finally start to relax.

"Bad dream?" he whispers, softly caressing my bare abdomen. After he left to go put Annie to bed, I shamelessly stripped down to my bra and panties and then fell asleep while waiting for him.

His nurturing hand allows me to lie back down, but my heart is still racing. I shake my head, letting him know it wasn't a bad dream. Letting him know I'm just cursed with random panic attacks, even during my REM stage of sleep.

Benson reaches over me to turn on the light, but I stop him. "Don't."

"Are you sure?"

"Just hold me?" I ask, my voice sounding unrecognizably raw.

He pulls me into him, tucking my head under his chin and intertwining his legs with mine. We drown in the thick silence that pollutes his room. We're as close as we can possibly be at the moment.

It's not enough. I want to be closer. I need to be closer.

This man who has been through so much has taken me into his home where he and his daughter live. He trusts

CHAPTER NINETEEN

me with his life, and it's all for nothing. He shouldn't trust me at all.

I feel like the worst human being on the planet.

I wonder if the lies are worth the anxiety that sledge through my veins on a daily basis. If it's not him actually finding out who I am, it's the constant fear of knowing he will eventually know. It's only a matter of time.

What an amazing feeling it is to be loved. A pang of anxiety accompanies that sensation knowing that if he finds out who I am, it'll be over. Those two thoughts go hand in hand, unfortunately. It's always on my mind, every single day, every torturous minute.

"You fell asleep when I came back," he whispers. "Maybe it was a good thing."

"I wish I didn't."

"Fall back asleep?"

I nod. "I was finally having my way with you."

He smirks at the thought. "You've already had your way with me."

We just lay there caressing each other and cuddling like it's our last night on Earth. In some ways, I feel like it is. It won't be much longer until this guilt eats me alive and forces me to confess. We can't be this ignorantly happy forever. It's not fair to either one of us. It's not fair to Annie.

It's getting harder and harder to lie to him, and easier and easier to love him.

"Benson?" I whisper.

"Shhh," he soothes me. Staring at me in the pitched darkness, he studies every curvature of my face.

He brushes his fingertips along my cheekbone and trails them down to the back of my neck. He gently grips the hair at the nape of my neck, reeling me in and latching his lips to mine. It is simple and tender; not necessarily picking up where we left off. When he pulls back to look at me, I feel the loss immediately. However, it's replaced by the intensity of his panty soaking stare. That just about does me in.

Before I can blink, he reconnects his lips with mine and our tongues shamelessly collide and wrestle together. His hands are more daring than usual, impatiently touching any part of my skin that he can get his hands on. When a little whimper escapes into his mouth, he shifts one of his thick, hard thighs between my legs and rhythmically rubs it onto my sex. He lowers his mouth to my erect nipples, teasing them by nuzzling the hard peaks with his nose. I stifle a moan and he takes his time to shoot me the wickedest grin. He knows exactly what he's doing.

He lowers his mouth down to my tummy, his eyes never leaving mine. Then he teasingly trails his tongue around my navel. I close my eyes and arch my back, writhing beneath him, hoping he will never stop.

"Benson," I whimper.

He lifts his head; his big and broad shoulders heaving with his beautiful blue eyes on me. I can tell that his patience is wearing thin. So is mine.

"I know I'm not being supportive right now," I breathe. "You have an addiction and told me to respect that."

"Don't you think that's a little redundant now?" he trails soft kisses on my lower abdomen.

"But you..." Oh God, never mind.

"How do you like to come, baby?" he asks in between kisses.

Oh my God, just touch me.

"Err, what?"

"What do you like? Want me to tongue you? Or suck on this swollen clit?" He flicks my clit through my cotton panties as he says the word.

Jesus Christ.

I mumble out a string of incoherent words and writhe like a worm, and that's when I feel his lips head south. I arch my back when he hits the sensitive skin on the inside of my thigh. He is so incredibly close to a place that no one has ever been. Sure, Jesse and I have had sex, but he never went down on me. This is new grounds for me. Part of me wants to run. Part of me wants to cut to the chase and shove his head in between my legs.

He rubs his hands up my thighs, stopping at my panties and grabs onto the hem line. He peels them off slowly, his eyes never wavering from mine. Then he discards them on the floor.

"Benson," I whimper. I'm squirming all over the place and he hasn't even touched me down there yet. I don't think I've ever been this worked up in my entire life. Then he latches his mouth to my clit and I completely lose it. I arch my back as the amazing sensation takes over my entire body. The suction of his lips brings warmth to every nerve ending of my body. I realize when I grind into him, the feeling gets even more intense.

He mixes it up by trailing his tongue down to my hole, in and out relentlessly.

Jesus Christ. This is what I've been missing?

I can't believe he's tonguing me, and he's good at it. Of course, he'd be good at it. He's a little too good at it because I'm grabbing all the sheets I can gather and arching my back like a Russian gymnast.

When I'm pretty sure I can't take it anymore, he simply laps my clit with the flat part of his tongue and I let go. Ecstasy takes over my body as I moan out another set of incoherent words; this time there's a lot of four lettered curses.

It's beautiful. It's agony. It's everything I've ever wanted and needed.

Nearly comatose, I lay there as he laps up the rest of my orgasm. I'm afraid to get up since my legs have turned to jelly. I'm pretty sure my arms are useless, too.

If it wasn't for the slight shifting of his bed, I wouldn't have opened my eyes.

But I have, and he's now pacing the room with a hand over his mouth.

Uh oh.

"What's wrong?" I ask, pulling the covers over me. I suddenly feel too naked in front of him.

"I just need a minute," he says. In one swift movement, he's out the door and shooting down the stairs.

I ask myself a few questions.

Did I do something wrong? Why is he so flustered?

We already sealed the deal. We both just received the most amazing orgasms; you'd think he'd be ecstatic.

Instead, it looks like he wants to pull his own hair out. What the hell is his problem?

I decide to find out, slipping on one of his baggy shirts and following him downstairs. It's probably not the best decision since he needs some space, but I don't let that stop me.

I find him in the kitchen opening a bottle of vodka. Oh. Boy.

"What are you doing?" It's all I can really ask. My tone comes off condescending as if I'm talking to a child. Normally I wouldn't be shocked if someone was drinking post coital, but Benson is a recovering alcoholic.

"I'm sorry I'm drinking in front of you," he says.

This pisses me off. "I'm not the alcoholic, Benson. You are!"

"Huh," he says to himself while looking at the label. Then he shoves the bottle towards me. "Want some, then?"

I remain silent and he says, "Since you can handle it and all?"

He's being a total smart ass and not the man I know. I don't like it.

"What's your problem?"

He puts the bottle down and leans against the counter, but doesn't say anything.

Is he trying to make me angry? Because it's working!

"Benson, sex is a vital part of a relationship. What we did is okay." I'm assuming this is all about that.

"Not for me, sweetheart," he mutters. He paces the kitchen, laughing and cursing to himself. I don't know this version of Benson. This man is cold and unapologetic. This man looks like he resents me.

I want to tell him to go fuck himself. I want to tell him I'm leaving and not putting up with this shit. But instead, I walk up to him. His broad back is facing me as he grips the counter. I warily wrap my hands around his abdomen and to my surprise, he lets me.

This man is more complex than The Matrix.

CHAPTER NINETEEN

It takes a moment, but I begin to feel him sigh as he relaxes against me. I rest my head against his back and we stand like this for a few minutes.

After several minutes of silence and holding each other, he turns around and snakes his hands around my waist, his eyes trailing from my breast to my eyes. When I get a good look at his eyes, I noticed they are red and a little swollen. There's a vein that is sticking out on the side of his forehead.

"Please Benson," I beg. "Tell me what's wrong. Tell me how to fix it."

"I don't want to hurt you," he whispers. "And I will."

I immediately see remorse in his eyes.

"You're hurting me now."

"I know. I'm not trying to. I just think we need to cool it."

"Cool it?" I ask. "It's a little too late for that, don't you think?"

"Ginny, it's not the same for me as it is for you. After we had sex, I felt... I felt disgusted with myself."

"How can you say that?" I whisper yell. He can't be serious.

He shakes his head and runs a hand through his golden hair. "It'll get ugly if we keep this up. You'll hate me."

I put a finger on his full lips to silence him and then whisper, "Never. I will never hate you. We are going to get through this. We're going to be able to do this without you feeling the way you do now. We just need to work..."

He cuts me off by pulling my hands from his lips and holding them in his. "I hope so Ginny. I really do." He gives my hands desperate kisses all over.

I pull my hands back, surprised by his nervousness. Before I can take a step back, he grabs me by the waist and pulls me into him, regret immediately creeping on his face. "I'm so sorry, Ginny. I'm so sorry."

I melt into him.

This is good. I think.

We hold each other for a few minutes in silence. When I find it's appropriate, I say, "I never felt like making love to you was a bad thing. I don't think I ever could."

"You would if you knew what was going on in my head afterwards."

"Well, tell me. So we can work it out."

"No offense, but you're not ready for that."

"I'm an adult, Benson. I can handle it."

He sighs deeply and looks at the ground, seemingly regaining his bearings. When he looks back up at me, he shoots a knowing smirk.

"Fine," he sighs. "After we had sex, I was thinking about how badly I wanted to bend you over the night table and do you again. Partially because I was still hard, but the real reason was because I wanted to do things my way and pound you until you were in tears. Fucking you so hard that it boarded on the line of pain and pleasure. I want to hear you scream like the little slut I know you are."

Silence.

I stand there frozen and at a loss for words.

I don't let his words affect me like he wants them to. I don't even blink.

Wait. Never mind, I just did. *What the hell does he mean by that?*

"You… you weren't satisfied?" I clear my throat, trying not to sound upset.

His face softens. "Of course I was."

I look at him, absorbing what he just said to me. I can do this. I can adjust. I can meet his ridiculous needs.

I quietly wrap my arms around his torso and brush my lips against his, barely touching them. "Then do it."

"Come again?"

"Fuck me like a slut," I whisper, shyly batting my lashes. He laughs at my attempt to be sexy. The funny part is that I think he does find it sexy.

But I don't laugh with him. Instead, I give him a suggestive look and firmly grab his crotch.

His smile disappears really fast. He lifts me up and in one swift motion, my legs wrap around him and my body

CHAPTER NINETEEN

slams into the nearest counter. Without a word, he bends me over the counter until I'm completely flat and bends with me, whispering in my ear, "You like this, don't you? You like being told what to do; just like a good little slut."

I want to nod eagerly but don't get the chance to because he roughly pulls my head back in place, forcing me to make eye contact. His other hand teases my bare nipples under the night shirt I slipped on before chasing him downstairs.

Then he pulls his hand away and I immediately miss its warmth. I hear him pull down his pants and drop them to the ground. One minute I'm empty; the next I'm generously full as he slams into me.

He slaps his hand hard over my mouth and roughly whispers, "Shut the hell up! You're going to wake up Annie."

All I have left to communicate with are my eyes, which widen with shock. His roughness towards me does not go unnoticed, but I'm too turned on to care.

He starts pounding me hard and fast, rhythmically. It's hard and unapologetic, unlike all of the other times we have done it. It's beautifully desperate. It's almost as if it's not enough.

A tear falls down my eye uncontrollably as I come to orgasm. He then squeezes my hips as tight as he can, his head buried in the crook of my neck and shoulder, biting on it. He releases inside me and begins to slow down. When he's done he doesn't pull out right away. We just lay there for a while. I feel glorious; however, he doesn't. He looks as if he's feeling a lot of remorse.

The next few days are spent with my new family. It's refreshing and a nice change from the family that I'm used to. Annie and Benson are nothing short than the closest thing I've ever had to family.

I guess that's not counting Jesse.

Jesse.

As the days turn into weeks, I develop a better understanding of what Benson meant about sex being a bad thing. As amazing as I think our love making is at the time, I always end up feeling used afterwards.

I was fooling myself when I thought sex would be magical with the man that I love. In place of that magical feeling are confusion and regret. I always find myself asking the same question, over and over. Why doesn't he feel what I feel when we're together?

I can tell the guilt is eating him alive. Guilt for using the woman he loves. Guilt for making me one of them.

I assure him that everything is going to be okay and not to give up on us. He rubs my back and keeps whispering in my ear how sorry he is.

When I try to cuddle with him, he reluctantly rejects me. It hurts, I won't lie.

So we sleep with our backs facing each other, both looking in opposite directions. He faces his doorway and I face the window. If I could guess what he is thinking about at the moment, it would be the same exact thing I am.

How long would it take to flee out this window? Or in his case, the door?

Which brings us to today.

I'm in a weird mood today. Saying I'm depressed is pushing it because I am happy to be here. However, something just doesn't feel right.

It feels as if everything may crash and burn at any second now. I'm more agitated than usual and my jittery hands show it. I'm aware of my surroundings more than ever.

I think I'm paranoid.

Later on, Benson walks through the door after a long day of work. Annie and I are in the middle of an intense game of Apples to Apples. He flashes us his bright smile and makes his way to both of us, giving us each a kiss on the cheek. Then he walks to the kitchen where I hear him pour himself a glass of water.

The rest of the night we lock ourselves inside his room and thank the God's that Benson's father was feeling good enough to keep an eye on Annie.

CHAPTER NINETEEN

You'd think that it'd be an amazing night. At least it sounds like it'd be on paper. But there's just one miniscule problem. One I'd never notice if he didn't just shove his tongue down my throat.

That water he poured earlier? Well, it's definitely mixed with Vodka because I smell it every time he brings his lips to mine.

Still, I don't say a word. I silently watch him drink his choice of a thirst quencher as he becomes more flush and happier by the minute.

The one thing I do appreciate about the Vodka is that it's great as a truth serum.

As a matter of fact, I'm learning a few things about Benson in his less than stellar state.

His slight southern drawl is due to the fact that he was born and raised in Texas. I would have never known this if he didn't admit it to me tonight because Benson hates the South. Says there are too many bugs and it's too hot.

This explains his next confession. Benson is deathly afraid of spiders and says he will make me kill one if it is within a ten foot radius. I laugh at this. For hours.

"Now that I know everything there is to know about you, I think I'll catch some sleep. Well, that is after I check the whole house for bugs," I tease him. Then I unceremoniously try to get up, but he pulls me back down with him.

"Stay a little more."

We originally determined that it would be a good idea to sleep in separate beds for Annie's sake, but that didn't stop us from creeping into each other's rooms after hours. Ultimately, he let me take his bed like the true gentleman that he was. However, he took that same bed most nights too.

I found myself sleeping more sound whenever he was next to me.

Sometimes we'd talk each other's ears off in bed while sleep pended.

Sometimes we didn't fall asleep until the sun came up.

Tonight seems to be one of those nights. His courage juice is kicking in because his hands are wandering and becoming more frantic by the minute.

"Alright, Mr. Wandering Hands! That's enough," I laugh, swatting his big paws away.

He's in his signature flannel pajamas and I'm in nothing else but a Grand Cannoli's t shirt and my underwear. His hands absently rub up and down my naked thighs.

He gives me a smoldering look that makes my smile disappear. God, he's so sexy. How can I ever be mad at him?

Sure, I want more than anything to have a talk with him about his problem, but where will that get me right now? Maybe I'll just wait until he's sober.

Yes, that's it.

Just when I'm about to give in and tackle him like a linebacker, he tickles me relentlessly until I can't breathe. I try to wiggle out of his playful hold but as soon as he puts all of his weight on me, it's a lost battle.

He gently cups his hand over my mouth and applies a gentle weight to it when I laugh too loud.

"Give that jaw a rest. I want you using it later," he whispers.

My eyes widen as he squeezes my cheeks with one hand.

Benson is a dirty talker, plain and simple. I've heard all of his crude comments while we have had sex, and sometimes they even turned me on.

But right now? Not so much. There's just one little problem and it's in his hands; in liquid form.

After taking a few deep breaths, I glance back at him to see his face stretched into a crooked grin. That's all it takes for me to give him a smile back. He looks so youthful and carefree at the moment that I forget about our age difference. I even forget he's piss drunk.

"MUHHHHH," I yell into his cupped hand, but it's just muffled gibberish.

He sarcastically cups his ear with the other hand. "What was that?"

CHAPTER NINETEEN

He finally removes his hand from my mouth and places his index finger up to my smiling lips instead. I know the reason he's being like this is the alcohol, but I love this playful version of Benson. I really love it. Our eye contact stays connected and I almost forget how inebriated he is because his eyes look abstemious for once tonight.

"My friends want to see you again." He brushes a strand of hair out of my eyes and grins.

"Really?"

"Really."

"They actually liked me?"

He looks at me a second before letting out a snorting laugh. "Of course they liked you."

"I have some very annoying qualities," I joke.

"It's just a little get together." He says it as if I still need to be convinced, but my mind was already made the second he told me that they wanted to see me again.

"I'd love to," I whisper.

I become nervous under his scrutiny; his face only inches away from mine. His beautiful mouth stretches into a happy grin.

"And wear a sexy dress?" He waggles his eyebrows.

I giggle. I actually fucking giggle, and I'm not proud of it either.

"I want to show you off to my loved ones. I want everyone to see how happy I am and for them to understand why."

"I will find something. Although Benson, I'm almost certain they will not see the same thing that you see."

"Yes they will," he whispers, nudging his nose into the crook of my neck. His movements become a little too much because I notice I'm forming getting goose bumps all over my body. "Do you need my card?"

"I don't have to buy a new dress," I roll my eyes. "I hate shopping, anyways. It gives me anxiety."

He disconnects our limbs, moving away to get a better look at me. He's glaring at me like I said something wrong. He's gawking at me like I have two heads. "You are unlike any other girl that I know, Ginny."

One minute he's smiling at me, the next he is in wonder. "Hey, what's your last name?"

"What now?" Oh, I heard him. Loud and clear.

"What's your last name? I can't believe I've never asked."

It's a simple question. What is my last name?

It's also a simple answer, but it's one of the very few answers that I can't be honest about right now. It would ruin everything. It would end us, and I'm not ready for that. I don't think I will ever be.

He sits up and grabs both of my hands; his undivided attention on me. I'm almost positive that he notices I'm scared or hesitant to tell him. "I think that I deserve to know the last name of the girl I am crazy about, don't you?"

I nervously laugh and then clear my throat. "Ah, um, it's Mitchell."

Officer Mitchell.

"Ginny Mitchell," he tests. It rolls off his tongue smoother than silk. He almost makes me want to change my name.

My eyes land on his full lips, and I do the best thing I can think of at this moment. I change the subject. Gently caressing his lips with my index finger, I say, "These are so fucking sexy."

He quickly catches my finger with his teeth and pops it in his mouth, sucking on every last inch of it.

I shoot him a sly grin and continue, "Every time I look at you, my eyes go straight to them and all I can think about is getting a taste of them." I trace my finger along the seam and watch him shut his eyes blissfully.

They stay shut for a while as I continue my assault on his lips with my finger. When he opens his eyes, they are blazing into mine. "I love you."

It's so soft and quiet that I almost miss it. I stop my wandering hand and drop it to my side.

He nervously laughs. "I know we haven't known each other long…"

"Say it again," I croak.

CHAPTER NINETEEN

I need to hear it again. I don't think I've heard him correctly.

"I... love... you... Ginny Mitchell. I love you so much."

I close my eyes, letting the sweet words absorb into my blood stream and set fire throughout my body.

I curl into his body and squeeze my eyes shut, knowing there will not be many moments like this sooner or later. Our love will implode when he finds out who I really am. It was only a matter of time.

Benson admitting he loved me should have made me feel like the best girl on Earth. So why did I feel like I wanted to be buried in it instead?

CHAPTER TWENTY

Nothing makes me smile more than seeing the way Benson takes care of his daughter.

Early Friday morning, the sun has barely come up and he's getting Annie ready for school. With my warm cup of coffee in my hand, I observe their morning ritual. I watch as he carefully moves his sculpted arms around Annie's hair, putting it into a simple pony tail. Such a big man but he's so delicate when it comes to her. I laugh when he observes his final masterpiece and shakes his head with disappointment. He's not happy with it.

"Too crooked," he explains. "She looks like Punky Brewster."

I laugh. "Punky is adorable."

My words go in one ear and right out the other.

He takes it back out and tries again. He brushes all of the hair to one point on top of her head and ties it. His feather light touches don't interrupt her from watching a cartoon on her tablet.

He wins Father of the Year for that one.

A beautiful feeling comes over me as I watch him care for his little girl. He touches her like she is the most delicate flower on the planet. He handles her how Annie is currently handling her tablet; with care.

Benson. Hot Dad. Family Man.

Not to mention it's sexy. I mean it. There is nothing sexier than a good father.

Once she's off to school, he shuts the door while glaring at his sleeping father. "This is what I'm talking about. How is he supposed to watch my daughter if he can't even remain conscious?"

I stand up and walk over to him. "That's why you have me. I'll help you with Annie; you know that."

He sighs and pulls me into him. "I know that, but you shouldn't have to do that. It's not your job."

That actually offends me a little bit.

"Not anymore, at least," he corrects.

CHAPTER TWENTY

I'm still not laughing. "As long as we're together, it's my job. Whether or not I'm getting paid for it. Especially if I'm not getting paid for it. Especially if I am here living in your home."

"Really?" he asks, gently. I don't think I've ever seen him look so vulnerable.

I grin and give him a small peck on the lips. "Really."

He pulls me in again and his lips land on mine hard and relentlessly. I slide my arms up to his chest and around his neck, reeling him in and holding him tightly. I mold into his hard body like a missing puzzle piece.

Nibbling his red hot ear, I whisper, "Relax. I will do these dishes and clean up. You're already late for work."

"Is this real life?"

I grin.

He tucks a tendril of my raven hair behind my ear, dragging his index under my chin and lifting my head to meet his eyes. "You know, it's been Annie, my father and I as long as I can remember. Annie is my child, so naturally, I take care of her. My father is getting old, so I feel obligated to take care of him. I know how horrible that probably sounds."

"What are you getting at?"

He rubs my upper arms. "It's just nice having someone look out for me. I forgot what it feels like."

My heart melts like butter when he says that. Also, guilt bleeds out of every pore in my body, but thankfully he doesn't notice.

He turns around and cups my face with his hands. His thumb grazes my dry lips, rubbing them back and forth as his heated gaze soaks them up.

Then his mouth is on mine before he leaves me in his house, all alone.

I make sure to really do myself up good tonight. I paint my lips a bloody red and curl my long dark locks. I slip on the sexiest thing I own, a simple pale, yellow sundress. I put on the only heels I own which are a brown and low pat and leather heel.

As I glance into the mirror for a moment, I find that I'm biting my lip with anxiety. I smooth my hands down my dress, flattening out the wrinkles and give myself the nod of approval.

I wobble down the stairs in my heels feeling like a baby giraffe.

I look up and notice that everyone in the room is staring at me. I flash one of my clumsy smiles and hold onto the railing for dear life.

"Maybe I should have gone with flats."

"No," Benson is quick to say. He looks very satisfied according to the dimples that peak out of his weeklong scruff-age. Annie is smiling ear to ear. Even the cranky old man looks pleased.

"She looks nice," Benson's dad says entirely too loud. I don't think he's heard a word we've said.

Benson and I smile at each other knowingly.

The car ride is about twenty minutes of us listening to the radio in silence. We are not angry or irritated with one other, but enjoying each other's company in peace. With it being back to school for kids, I take time to notice the trees changing colors. Upstate New York is gorgeous in the fall.

Suddenly, he turns off the radio and looks at me cautiously.

I rake my brain, wondering what the hell his problem is, but he darts his eyes back to the road.

After a long pause, he says, "I forgot to tell you a pretty important detail about tonight."

"Are all your exes going to be there?" I tease.

"All of them, actually."

I squint my eyes and he nearly busts a gut laughing. "I'm kidding."

I smile with relief and lean over him. I start raking my fingers through his dirty blonde locks. "What is it then?"

His face hardens to stone but his eyes remain on the road. I have an inkling that I'm not going to like what he says next.

CHAPTER TWENTY

"I told you we were meeting up with my friends, and we are," he rushes out. "I just didn't tell you everything."

I give him a glare and wait for him to continue.

"You remember Melanie and Greg, right?"

I nod. "I figured they'd be there."

"We're not going to the club again, Ginny. We're meeting up with them for dinner."

"Cool, where?"

"Her parents."

"Okay. You lost me. Why her parents?"

He takes a deep breath before sparing a glance at me. Something is way off. I can tell by the way he's gnawing off his lip.

He takes a deep breath and looks over at me. "Melanie is Angelina's little sister."

And just like that, all the blood drains from my face. I'm almost positive I'm dead.

"Which makes her parents," my voice cracks, but cannot finish the sentence.

"My in laws," he finishes. "I want you to meet my in-laws."

I try to absorb what he's saying, but it's going as good as an ADD person in The Labyrinth.

How the hell could he do this to me?

"We've remained close over the years and when I told them I was dating someone new, they wanted to meet you. To be honest, Ginny, they've been more of parents to me than my own."

I'm frozen in time. I can't move my face, let alone feel it.

I clear my horse throat before speaking. "Why didn't you tell me about them if they're so important?"

He shrugs. "I didn't want to freak you out."

"I'm not freaking out," I snap.

"Hey, calm down. Please," he says, placing a hand on my thigh.

I nod and look at his fingers tapping relentlessly on my lap. It almost seems like he's anxious too. This makes me livid. He knew this was a big deal, yet he waited to tell me on the way there?

He cocks his head back to get a better look at me. "You… you're not mad, are you?"

"Stop the car!" I bellow. "Stop the car, now!"

Although my voice comes out harsher that I've intended it to, I am still furious. Make no mistake about it. I feel trapped and let's not forget betrayed.

He pulls over, wearing a forlorn expression.

I immediately grab the door handle and open it, shifting uncomfortably in my seat. Before I get out, I look at him with bewilderment. "Why didn't you tell me this?"

"I don't know! Maybe because it's not a big deal to me and it doesn't affect you at all?" He's getting more defensive by the minute.

"Doesn't affect me? Are you for real?" I shout, panic mode taking over my body.

"And maybe because I was afraid you'd react like this!"

"Bring me home, Benson," I order.

"Will you just calm down for a second?" I can see him trying to diffuse the situation. I know this means a lot to him, but I just can't go through with it. I take a deep breath and spare him a glance.

"They all know about you. They're ecstatic to meet you. I just didn't know how to tell you about them. I didn't want you to think I'm living in the past or something. These people mean a lot to me. They're my family, even now that Angelina's gone. You don't turn your back on family."

Yeah, except if his name is Jesse.

"I can't go," I say.

He glares at me and I swear if it was fire, I'd be ashes on his car floor. Before letting out a huge sigh, he grips the steering wheel and hugs it. His forehead rests on the top of the wheel; his eyes squeezed shut in pain.

That's when my sympathy finally kicks in.

"Benson," I sigh. "I'll go. I'm sorry."

He doesn't move. He is clearly upset with me and I can't blame him. Although I'm upset that he failed to

CHAPTER TWENTY

mention this to me, he didn't do it maliciously. He was worried about what I would think. Which is exactly what I do think: I don't want to meet his dead wife's parents.

I mean, why would I?

I killed their little girl.

Maybe because they are important to him. Maybe because I am important to him.

"Please forgive me. I didn't mean I didn't want to go. You just have to understand that this caught me off guard," I tell him, softly.

I guess my main problem was that I worried people would recognize me. With my long dark hair, maybe people wouldn't notice. It's quite the difference from my once short, bright pink hair and facial piercings that gave me a look to remember. Seven years and one very hard lesson later, I was a much different person. Superficially.

I spare a glance his way and find that he's looking at me with the same hope in his eyes that he did before he told me. I offer him a small smile and nod. He finally takes a few deep breaths in silence and begins driving again.

Driving towards my Karma. He just doesn't realize it yet, but I do.

We arrive at a stunning home, with bright, white lights draping over the molding like melted icicles. It's the nicest house on the block, with the healthiest body of grass that I've ever seen.

With the sun setting, it provides the posh home and landscaping with an aluminous glow.

Angelina's parents are rich.

I glance down at my Target dress made of cotton and let out a silent groan, flattening out the wrinkles with my hands.

I don't hold a candle to these people.

Benson hops out of the car and comes around on my side to open the door. When I grab his hand and hop out, he gives me a once over and smiles. I wonder what that once over really means, but before I can identify it, I'm being led up to their door and my heart accelerates.

It's then he notices my hesitance and stops in front of me right before we hit the stairs. He places his big hands on my shaking shoulders and gives me a tender look. "It's going to be alright. They're going to love you."

I let out a nervous laugh and keep my eyes trained on the pristine ground. Jesus Christ, even their cement ground is clean and elegant.

He rings the doorbell and clasps my hand to his. I glance over to him and he's adjusting his collar with his other hand. I think it's cute that he wants to be a certain way around them. But it also fills me with jealousy. He never fixes his collar for me.

As much as I feel bad about it all, I am still furious with him that he would lie to me about something like this. Here I thought that I was just meeting up with his friends again because they really liked me, but instead, I was meeting his deceased wife's parents. It was safe to say that I felt shanghaied.

I was starting to think that this was one big, sick joke.

He squeezes my hand as I direct my eyes up to his. I'm afraid he can see right through me at the moment. All my truths, my lies, my fears. I'm afraid he can see everything.

However, he just gives me a reassuring smile and softly kisses my knuckles. "They're going to love you just as much as I do."

I doubt that, but I nod anyways.

All it takes is one ring and then a slender, fair-haired woman who looks about sixty is standing in the doorway. She wears a cream colored pant suit that fits her like a glove and her chin is held high.

"Benny!" she cries out, hugging my boyfriend as tight as a virgin butthole.

Benny?

This must be Angelina's mother. Either that or it's Angelina reincarnated, because the way she's looking at my boyfriend makes me want to pour something over her head,

CHAPTER TWENTY

preferably something slimly and hard to get out of that expensive hair style.

When she's done getting her fill of my man, her eyes land on me and they crinkle in the corners.

She's smiling at me. I think.

For the hell of it, I smile back.

"It's lovely to meet you, Ginny. I've heard so much about you," she says, reeling me in for a stiff hug. It's nothing like the hug Benson received, but it's still nice.

I hug her back and look at Benson over her shoulder. He's laughing, that asshole.

"I'm Miriam," she says to me. "Come on in, you two."

As we slowly enter the posh home, our rubber necks turn in every direction. I get my fill of Angelina's first home, letting it all sink in. Large, pristine chandeliers hang from the ceiling; the crystals so blinding that it lights up the spacious room. Not a thing is out of place or on the floor. Everything is shined to perfection, not a piece of dust in sight.

I can tell even Benson is impressed. He must not come here often. That gives me some relief, believe it or not.

Classic music plays softly in the background, the soft notes bouncing off my ears. It renders me relaxed for the moment. My lungs open, inviting more air into my lungs.

There is no turning back now. I squeeze my hands into fists and hope for the best. The best scenario is that I meet them and they don't recognize me. We have a good time and then go home. Before I can catch my breath, it gets caught in my throat and blocks my airway. I hurdle over in a choking frenzy when Melanie spots us and charges towards us. She looks startled to catch me in my currently troubled state.

Benson rubs my back. "Are you okay, Ginny?"

"I'm okay," I croak, straightening up to my actual height.

Melanie smiles and comes in for a hug. "So happy you came, Ginny! Let me introduce you to my parents!"

"I just met your mom," I tell her.

Please. No more parents.

"My Dad's probably smoking out back right now. My mom hates it so he sneaks out. When he comes back I'll introduce you two. For now, do you want a drink?"

I look at Benson, undecided and waiting for permission. He gives me a nod and she takes that as a yes.

"I saw you two lovebirds sneak off and leave last time we all got together. Not happening again!" she orders. "I'm spending some quality time with your girl this time."

Benson flashes a teasing smile and then runs a hand through his sandy hair. "I'm sure she would love that."

"Give her up for twenty measly minutes, will you?" she teases.

He shyly smiles. Is that a hint of color I find in his cheeks?

I've seen sad Benson. I've seen angry Benson. Confused Benson. Excited Benson. Content Benson. I have never seen bashful Benson, but it sure does make my heart melt.

I blush a little, myself.

She smirks at Benson, seemingly surprised that he's blushing too. "Nick, Greg and Joe are over there." She juts her chin towards her boyfriend and friends.

"Will you be ok?" he whispers in my ear.

I huff at him, offended that he even asks. "Of course. Go do dude things with your dude friends. Melanie will keep me company."

He smiles and places a small, chaste kiss on my lips.

"You guys make me sick," Melanie mumbles half-jokingly. With that, I'm left with Melanie. To be honest, it's not so bad. She's a very pleasant girl and seems to like me.

She clasps my hand and leads me right to the juice bar, where she ceremoniously waves a fifty dollar bill in the air. A tall and handsome African American bartender comes over to us and reveals his pearly whites and turns away.

"You guys have a bartender that looks like that?" I point.

"My dad is a brain surgeon and my mom is a lawyer," she says with a flat voice. "Hell yeah, we have a bar. The hot bartender is a nice perk." She winks.

CHAPTER TWENTY

Then she focuses her attention on the handsome man and says in a breathy voice, "Hello gorgeous. You think me and my friend can have a nice, strong shot?"

"Sure, what would you like?" he asks, shooting her a sly wink as he mixes someone else's drink.

"Two shots of Tequila, please!" she chirps.

I bite my lip. "Tequila?"

"Chicken?"

I shoot her a devious smile and shake my head. I hate Tequila. I made the worst decision of my life on Tequila and ended up in prison for seven years. Tequila is not my friend.

We receive our shots and clink them together, downing the shot. The yellowish liquid burns my throat until my face grimaces. Melanie just laughs at me. She barely made any face at all.

Of course, she's perfect with everything she does. Including drinking fucking Tequila.

"Alright. Two tequila sunrises now, please," she says to him.

"No!" My protest comes out so fast, I even surprise myself.

She smirks. "You'll like this one better. I promise."

"Oh, um… okay." I say, not putting up much of a fight.

She assesses me or a moment before saying, "You don't drink much, do you?"

Before I can respond, the bartender shoves our drinks in front of us. I go to take mine but it's intercepted by Melanie. She grabs my hand and walks me around the corner where we're out of sight.

"Here," She hands me a flask, secretly. "That bartender might be hot, but he never makes the drinks strong enough. This will have you feeling good."

I give her a double take.

This girl is trouble with a capital T. I wonder if Angelina was as cool as her. I would have probably gotten along with her if she was anything like her sister. The thought nauseates me to the core.

Before I can talk myself out of it, I shoot her a wicked grin and down the whole drink in front of her. I feel the stinging liquid burn down my esophagus and my displeased face shows it. Melanie is looking at me like my head has split open and my brain is hanging out.

"Wow. That was impressive," she mutters. "You drank that like a shot. It's a mixed drink."

"Cheers," I say a little too late and clink my drink with hers.

She hands me a piece of gum and drags me back into the crowd of people I will never fit in with. It's only a matter of time before they notice.

CHAPTER TWENTY-ONE

The visit to Angelina's parent's house is not as bad as I stressed. Both Miriam and Jay are incredibly sweet and make me feel welcome. I finally meet him after he comes in from his nightly smoke, reeking of cigars and expensive scotch.

I can tell that they adore and would do anything for Benson. I can also tell that he is the son that they never had.

We eat a huge Portuguese dinner, starting off with Caldo Verde and then a main course comprised of pork loin seasoned with garlic with a side of roasted potatoes, chestnuts and white wine.

After a very fulfilling dinner, we relax on the back porch, everyone talking, drinking, and having a good time. It feels like hours since I've seen Benson, and even though he's around and I know it, I still miss him and want him all to myself.

I'm talking to Melanie and one of her parent's next door neighbors when I feel strong arms envelop me. I look down and see the exact ink-decorated arms that I want to see.

"Mind if I steal this woman?" he asks. "I'd like to introduce her to some people."

They reluctantly let me go and he offers them his most charming smile.

He could probably talk someone into committing murder if he wanted to.

Charles Manson grabs me by the hand and leads me into another hall where it's less crowded. I walk down a spacious hall way, beautifully lit with luminous decorations. As I check out the beautiful architecture and my eyes are going in all different directions, he veers left into a secluded room. It's a smaller room that looks like a spare bedroom, yet it's twice as big as Benson's master bedroom.

I take a look around when I notice that A) there is no one in here and B) there are no windows in the room. I start to wonder where the people he wanted to "introduce" me to are.

Then, I hear the loud click of the door locking. Dangerous blue eyes stare back at me. They almost look angry but that's not what they are and I know it.

Hunger.

Desperate to get me alone.

In one fluid motion, he picks me up behind my knees and lifts me onto the dark oak dresser. Caging me with his arms and pinning me with his hips, he gives me a glare that even Satan would be afraid of.

I'm startled by his roughness but then I catch the sinful grin growing and realize he's far from angry.

"You didn't want me to meet anyone, did you?"

He shakes his head as he nuzzles at the slope of my neck with his nose. "I just wanted to get you alone for a minute."

As if Benson doesn't look gorgeous enough, tonight he's absolutely breath taking. He's encased in a crisp, white shirt that is unbuttoned at the top, with a pair of black, tight jeans that hug his ass just right. No tie on, just a little of his dark chest hair peeking out of his shirt. His muscles are bulging out of his suit and begging to rip the fabric apart. His tattoos are visible at the end of his rolled up sleeves and open collar. I notice a few grays peaking in his whiskers, revealing his true age, but it just makes him all the sexier to me.

Even though his scruff is more grown in than ever, he's made it a point to shave his neck so that I could place my soft mouth on it. At least, that's what I'm thinking.

I'm sure it was all for me.

"So what made you kidnap a helpless girl into a room with no windows?" I murmur against his taut neck, my lips never leaving it.

"Good call. I just noticed that," he says, looking around the room. When his eyes come back to mine, there is a fire in them that can only be read as white hot desire. I can feel his needy hands dance beneath my dress and onto my thighs. The whisper of his fingertips causes me to shudder.

He's playing with his food and he knows it.

CHAPTER TWENTY-ONE

My ability to speak at this point is close to none.

"Are you still mad at me?" His lips are brushing the shell of my ear. He enjoys torturing me a little too much.

"No," I respire, smiling against his smooth skin. It's the truth. I can't stay mad at Benson for very long.

He lowers his full lips to my neck and presses kisses to my quickening pulse. I can feel the blood in my limbs travelling to the center of my body.

Without warning, he lifts me up and wraps my legs around his muscular torso. He throws me on a counter and wastes no time shoving himself between my legs. I lower my head to his and brush my lips against his, but it's not a kiss. It's feather light and teasing.

I crack a smile and he reels me in the rest of the way, not wasting any more time and pressing his lips against mine. It's tender at first, our lips coaxing each other's slowly and cautiously. When our tongues lastly meet, it inclines into animalistic desperation. When I push, he pulls, molding to me like a piece of clay.

I'm the first to part from him, even though it's the last thing I want to do. I push on his chest to get a better look at him. God, he's so gorgeous with disheveled hair and swollen lips.

I go to tell him so, but he places his index finger over my own kiss swelled lips and hushes me.

His eyes are like wild fire, burning into the eyes that are lost in him.

He looks like a hungry lion as he starts dotting my chest with kisses again.

It's not long before he notices I'm thinking too hard. Dropping his hands from my hips, he does his best to make eye contact with me. "What's wrong?"

"It's just… this is Angelina's parent's house. I feel a little weird doing this."

"Doing what?" He stifles a smile.

I tilt my head and give him a "come on" look.

He sighs. "We're behind closed doors. No one can see us. If anyone should feel bad, it's me, but I don't. Not the least, baby. Especially when it's all that I want to do." His eyes become hooded and he lowers his lips to my neck and nuzzles his nose in my hair.

Someone poke me because I think I'm done.

If this has anything to do with his sex addiction right now, I'm surely not making it better by enabling him.

I might as well push the syringe into his veins.

"You're right. I'm sorry." I say, placing a soft kiss on his stubbly chin and letting my lips dwell there. Suddenly, a displeasing thought makes all my raging hormones come to a halt.

"Can I ask you a question?" I ask. I busy myself with my hands so that I don't have to meet his gaze.

He stops my nervous hands by placing them in his. "What is it?" He asks as if he knows it's not an easy question. And he's completely right.

"So um," I pause, hesitantly meeting his gaze. That's a huge mistake because his eyes are so beautiful that I cannot stop staring. It takes me a few moments to think of what I was going to say. "How many women have you, you know, been with?"

I'm so embarrassed to ask such a question, but there is no other question I want the answer to more. He silently laughs and then inhales deeply. I can tell that he is anything but relaxed.

"A lot."

I frown. "A lot isn't a number."

"You never asked me to give you a number," he retorts.

"How many implies a number," I whine. I don't even sound like myself.

I clear my throat, embarrassed as all that is holy.

"If I tell you, you will run for the hills."

"I promise I won't. I'm just curious."

"I know," he whispers and grabs my hand, squeezing it tightly. "Honestly Ginny, giving you a number would be a little hard to do." He searches my eyes and then rakes his long fingers through his hair. "Mainly because I lost count a long time ago."

"You lost count?" I try to keep the surprise out of my voice, but it's definitely there.

I'm trying my best to be understanding and respectful, but I continue to prod, "How about a ball park average?"

My attempt to persuade him is miserably failing. He's laughing at me now, his shoulders quaking silently.

"Well, if I had to give a ballpark," he says, tilting his head in thought. "I'd say…"

"Wait! Let me guess," I interrupt.

He lifts a brow suspiciously and lets me continue.

"Like…. 20 people??"

He gives me a blank stare. I can see the beads of sweat beginning to form on his forehead. "Um, try hundreds. It's in the hundreds by now."

He's the one with busy hands now. He won't even make eye contact with me.

I try not to look too surprised, but the truth is… how the hell does someone have sex with over a hundred women? Was he having sex with a different woman every fucking day? How is that even possible?

I guess I just don't understand it. My eyes flicker up to his as I shift uncomfortably on my feet.

The truth is I'm disgusted.

Revolted.

I feel like I might vomit right on this floor, right now.

He notices I'm uneasy and places his hands on my shoulders. "Please. You said you wouldn't."

"I'm not running," I croak. "I'm… I'm just in shock."

"I know," he whispers. "It's a lot of women. I have no excuses, Ginny. I have an illness that has gotten out of hand many times. I'm doing better now though. You're the only one. I promise you that."

I nod and look at my feet. "I'm trying to understand."

"I know you are, and I love you for it."

My face splits into a grin as he reels me into him, squeezing me tightly as if I may run at any moment.

"Your turn," he whispers, his voice muffled into my neck. I can tell he doesn't want the spotlight on him anymore.

"Well, Jesse was my first... and my only." I turn a little flush, wondering if he finds my inexperience a turn off.

"You've only been with one man?" He seems stunned.

I nod with embarrassment and suddenly feel like I'm burning up.

His grin is playful and it turns out my inexperience is not a concern of his.

"I keep forgetting that I'm much older than you," he murmurs.

"You're not too much older," I say. "You kind of know my situation at this point. I didn't really get to enjoy my early twenties like everyone else did."

"I'm glad no one else has really had you, Ginny. Is that terrible to say?"

"No. I'm glad no one else has had me either."

"Are you mine?"

I nod.

"All mine?"

"Yes. All yours."

He snickers mischievously and wraps his hands around the nape of my neck, squeezing softly. "So, you're not completely repulsed by me, are you?"

"Not completely," I tease. "If it were any other guy I probably would have been."

He doesn't laugh even though it's meant to be taken as a joke. I continue, "I'm not going to sugar coat it for you. It's a lot of women. How do you know that one of them hasn't gotten pregnant? Or that you don't have any illegitimate children out there?"

"Don't be absurd. Annie is my only child."

"How can you be so sure?"

"Well, I guess I can't account to the times before or during Angelina." He breathes and continues, "I was sterilized after Annie was born. I can't have any more children."

"Oh." I nod. I am not necessarily upset but do feel a pang of disappointment. I've never thought about having children, but the thought of having one with this man doesn't seem so bad. To know that I never can makes me feel a little uneasy.

It takes me a minute or two to absorb the news, but once I do, I start to understand where he is coming from. "Well, I guess that was the responsible thing to do."

"Forgive me," he whispers, bowing his head. I've never seen him look so sad or desperate. "I didn't know that someone as lovely as you would be walking into my life." He nuzzles his nose in my hair and softly says, "I only want one woman now. Ginny, since I cannot be your first, please allow me to be your last."

"Of course."

"I'm yours," he says, grabbing my hands and putting one flat against his chest. "Do you feel that? Do you feel what you do to me?"

I do. His heart is beating at a rapid rate, just like mine.

Here I was, rubbing my face into his hand like a cat in heat, and I knew it was wrong. Benson had an awful addiction, one that got the best of him at the worst of times. What was even more awful than that was - I was okay with it, and as of right now, I am condoning it.

I suddenly remove his hands from my face and stiffen my posture. He notices something is wrong and leans back to get a better look. "What is it?"

"Nothing," I look at him impassively.

"Hey," He soothes. "You seem uncomfortable with me now."

I shake my head. "No, it's not that. It's nothing that you did."

"You can't even look at me now," He tilts my chin up to him.

"I just... As much as I want some things, I don't want to make things worse," I say, looking at the wall straight ahead.

Immediately, Benson jerks his head back to look at me. I think I've caught him a little off guard with that comment. "Do things... equal sex?"

I bite my lip and shyly nod.

He forces me to look at him, cupping my face with his big hands. "I'm an adult babe."

"I know."

"You act like you're going to break me."

"I'm afraid I will."

"You won't, I promise."

It's right then and there that I realized Benson had unknowingly broken his first promise to me.

I look him in the eyes, fire igniting deep in my belly. The connection between us is so electric I feel I may explode at any moment. I desperately need his lips on mine.

Just like that, he reads my mind.

With feather light touches, he presses his lips to mine, cautiously slipping his tongue into my mouth. He lightly nibbles at my bottom lip and then soothes it with a generous lick. It doesn't take long for me to give in, shoving my tongue where it doesn't belong and sucking on his mint flavored tongue.

But it's not enough.

Forgotten are the people in the other room. Gone is the thought that I am in someone else's house.

My mind is not my own, and neither are my hands as they reach out to grab him. My body responds to his the only way it knows how. My legs spread wider; my back arches into him as I try to rub my core against his leg.

I need more of him. I wish he could crawl inside of me right now.

He smoothly slides his hand down my abdomen and to the hem of my dress, grabbing the fabric and then lifting it up slowly. He continues kissing and sucking on my tongue like it's his last meal. With nimble fingers, he slips his hand into the side of my panties and penetrates me with a finger.

"Is this what you wanted right now?" he whispers, looking down at me.

I'm a ball embarrassing moans as he slips another finger in. He picks up the pace with his two fingers. What once was a tease is now full on doing me in, but for some reason, my body just won't relax. He feels my stiffness and pushes my shoulders backwards so that I'm leaning against the wall. "You need to relax and let me finger-fuck you because I'm not stopping until you come all over them."

My eyes are wide, two tiny pinholes looking at him in his flush state. It's short lived when he starts to make good on his promise, literally "finger banging" me.

I lose my sense of words. I have no voice, let alone air to breathe. I try to catch my breath but ecstasy quickly takes over, reducing me to nothing but a mewling mess. My hips ride his fingers and the rest of my orgasm as he slows down and peppers kisses across my collarbone. "I think the whole fucking house just heard you," he whispers, doing nothing to hide his shit eating grin.

"This isn't a house," I retort, looking around. "It's a fucking mansion."

He helps me off the counter and brushes the hair out of my eyes.

"I was only being sarcastic. No one can hear you."

"And you know this, how?"

He realizes the predicament he put himself in and gives me a sheepish smile.

Just great.

Angelina and Benson have done it in here, not including him and God knows who else. The unwanted thoughts drive me to envy.

Suddenly, I am lost in my own head again. Not sure if it's the alcohol or my anxiety; I let my contemplations carry me away.

Angelina.
The lies.
The Secrets.
Angelina.
The addictions.
The obsessions.
Angelina.

Without saying another word, I back away from Benson and shake my head. "I have to go."

He tilts his head in concern, not letting go of my fleeting hands, but I still manage to pull them away.

"Don't follow me. Please." Before he can say anything else, I am out of the room faster than the speed of light.

I run through the elegant halls and thank the Gods above none of them are witnessing this mess. As soon as I reach the wet night, I inhale a deep breath of fresh air.

It doesn't solve a damn thing.

I'm hyperventilating now. I'm crying for myself and the life I never had when I should be crying for the life Angelina never had. I am the epitome of selfish.

Maybe if it wasn't so messed up, I wouldn't have to hurt Benson right now. I wouldn't lie. I'd be the perfect girlfriend, in our perfect little world.

Benson will never be able to touch his wife again or cook her meal. Annie will never be able to listen to another bedtime story from her mother, and you can blame me for that. I am their ruin.

Instead of having Angelina, they get me instead. A fucking liar.

I haunch over and place my hands on my knees, trying to catch my breath. I feel like the world is caving in on me, squeezing all of the air out of my chest. I feel like I'm going to die.

A big hand lands on my shoulder, bringing me out of the worst panic attack I ever think I'm having.

I'm not ashamed of my red and blotchy face anymore. I need him to see it. I desperately want him to understand. I'm going to break this man's heart and I don't want to.

You see, he will get over me. But knowing I killed Angelina?

I rise to my full height and square my shoulders. "Benson, I am so sorry."

He shrugs. I can tell he's starting to get agitated. "Sorry for what?"

"Benson, I tried. I really tried," I croak. I don't think I can finish what I'm going to say, but then I hear my scratchy voice spill out of my mouth. "I'm not in love with you anymore."

He's staring me down now as if I'm bluffing. He's waiting for me to reveal that this is all one big joke.

CHAPTER TWENTY-ONE

"You're not in love with me... anymore?" His words come out measured.

I elevate my chin. "That's right."

He stares at me some more, the silence enveloping the humid air. It's so muggy that I'm sweating bullets. Or maybe that's just my nerves. I cannot decipher.

"What type of shit are you pulling?" I can see the flames in his eyes. "So what we did back there was nothing?" he seethes.

"Correct." It comes out so quiet that I can hear my own heart breaking. I gulp and squeeze my hands into balls, preparing for the worst.

What the hell did I just say?

I try to soften the blow a little, "I don't want kids, Benson. I don't want... any."

When he realizes who I am referring to, I hear a hiss of air escape his lips. I am looking at the ground and I plan to never look up.

"I can't believe you just said that," he whispers to himself.

Me either.

I give in and elevate my eyes to his. Propping his hands up on his hips, he asks, "How long?"

"The details, they don't matter..."

"Cut the bullshit!" he roars.

I snap my mouth shut and watch him pace the perfectly manicured lawn.

"Is it your stepbrother?"

"No!" I'm quick to say because that is the actual truth. I don't want him thinking I'm leaving him for someone else. "Definitely not."

"Please don't do this," he whispers with a hint of desperation in his tone. I hate to see him like this. I can tell he's on the brink of tears. ...Or violence.

"You're going through something. The past few days you haven't been yourself. You'll get better. I'll help you. We love each other, Ginny."

"Benson!" I shout. A tear escapes my eye as I give him a stern look. This is going to sting for the both of us. "I'm not in love with you. I never was."
He looks at me with expectation, because let's face it. He knows I'm lying.
I think about getting on my knees and begging for him back at this very moment, but that would be counterproductive.
Without so much as a single word, he turns around and walks back into the big house.
And I watch him go, unable to keep the tears from pouring down my face.

I barge into Jesse's apartment to him playing video games. As soon as he sees my tear stricken face, he drops the controller and walks over to me. He reels me in, holding me tight. "What the hell happened to you?"
"It's over. I ended it with Benson," I cry into his chest.
"Oh baby," he coos, petting my hair.
"I broke his heart, Jesse. I hurt him so badly."
"I know, Gin. But you did the right thing by telling him the truth."
I look at Jesse but don't bother telling him what I really did. What's good for one is good for the other at this point. I'm a liar, and cheater, and a total phony.
I break away from him and start pacing his living room. "I'm leaving town. I can't stay here."
"What? Ginny, that's ridiculous. You don't have to hide anymore. You did your time! You do not have to live in secret anymore!"
"I can't!" I shout hysterically. "I can't stay here, Jesse! I can't be in the same town as Benson! It's either me or him, and his dedication is to his daughter. Who is here?"
I'm hyperventilating again. I don't like this one damn bit.
"Hey calm down." He walks over to me and places his hands on the sides of my arms, rubbing them up and down. "We'll figure this out, okay? My friend Brian can get really

good prices on airline tickets. We can flee for a while. Get out of here. Yes?"

I sniff and nod. Jesse is all I have. He's all I need, really.

"No need to flee the state. A small river or lake will suffice. Just you and me."

I look at him and realize this is probably the best news he's ever heard; me not being with Benson anymore. This is exactly what he wanted. The thought makes me livid even though it's not his fault."

I honestly think about his proposal. Would it be so terrible to get out of here for a few days?

"Where would we go?"

He walks up to me, his eyes lit up. "Anywhere you want."

"You're not using anymore, are you?"

He shakes his head. "Not since the day you were here."

"You stopped cold turkey?"

He nods and looks into my eyes. "It's all because of you, Ginny."

I want to smile but I can't. I keep thinking of how hurt Benson must be right now.

And I'm going on vacation? I'm a fucking monster.

I know there's a conscience in there somewhere because I hurt so deeply that I can't breathe.

We stand in the middle of his living room holding each other like it's the end of the world.

Knock knock!

More like, "Boom boom!"

Jesse lifts his head up and looks at me. I'm sure he's wondering if I know who's knocking.

I definitely know who it is. I give him a look that tells him 'don't freak out' and walk to the door to open it. Before I can even get it open, Benson flies through the door like the Kool-Aid Man and charges towards Jesse.

"Benson!" I shout, jumping in between them just as Benson is about to pounce on him like a hungry lion. I shove him back as hard as I can, even though it feels like I just hit a brick wall.

What can I say that won't make Benson beat the ever loving shit out of Jesse and end up in jail? I wedge him against me and the wall and pull his collar down so that his ear and my mouth are touching. "It was all a fucking lie. I didn't mean any of it!"

Bewilderment meets his eyes as he stands wedged against the wall and me as I fist his shirt. I slowly let go of the material, realizing my hands are raw from squeezing it so tight.

"Everything I said to you was bullshit. Everything. I wish I could say I had to do it, but I didn't have to. I did it to make my life easier. I'm a selfish person, Benson. You don't want anything to do with me."

Benson's jaw drops as he stands frozen, stunned. He doesn't seem angry anymore that I'm here with Jesse, but the territorial look in his eyes tells Jesse not to come any further. "Don't ever tell me what I want or don't want."

He waits for me to answer, but all I can do is bow my head in defeat. I had completely and emotionally given up with dodging these bullets.

"Why would you say those things to me?" he asks, defeat laced into his words.

A deafening silence fills the room as I think of my next lie. This has gone too far.

"Jesus Christ Ginny! He still doesn't know the truth, does he?" Jesse asks, utterly repulsed.

I almost forget that he's behind us, listening to every word.

When I turn around, the look in Jesse's eyes is murderous. He's not as big as Benson, but he could definitely hold his own in a fight. He may be on the slender side, but he has his height on his side.

"Jesse, don't," I plead. "I will tell him. Let me do it, okay?"

Please don't tell him.

"Tell me what?" Benson asks.

"She's playing you like a fiddle, buddy," Jesse spats.

CHAPTER TWENTY-ONE

"Fuck off," Benson growls through gritted teeth.

"Everyone else knows!" Jesse shouts. "I'm surprised he hasn't caught on! But then again, he's blinded by your golden jailbird vagina. Isn't he, Gene-"

"Jesse!" I interrupt.

Benson growls and takes a step forward. "I'll fucking kill you with my bare hands."

Jesse ignores him and looks at me. "You should have told him a long time ago, Gin. You're better than this. I know you are."

I look at Jesse, knowing every word that comes out of his mouth is the truth. I know Benson is expecting me to fight for myself and him, to tell Jesse to fuck off, but I can't. I can't because Jesse is right about everything.

A selfish tear escapes my eye and I make sure to wipe it quickly. Jesse notices this and takes a step back. I don't even have to say anything to him right now. He knows what I need to do.

Our connection is that strong. We don't need words. We never did.

I look at Benson. "Let's go somewhere. We need to talk."

The look in his eyes tells me that he knows this isn't good. That this just may be the second worst day of his life.

CHAPTER TWENTY-TWO

We drive along the lake, the fall foliage starting to make an appearance. Maybe we should talk at the lake. It's bound to be a better idea. I dread the thought of going back to his apartment. I know Benson would never hurt me physically, but I'm still worried about how this is going to go.

My thoughts are confirmed when he stops at a little private beach we've been to once or twice before with Annie. I'm relieved when I see a few families there.

We both get out of the car in silence and nostalgia hits me hard.

Although I don't know her well, I am my mother. We both harbored terrible secrets and ran away from the people we loved. Lying was something we did so often that it just became a part of who we are.

I squeeze my eyes shut, internally screaming at the top of my lungs. My thoughts are so loud that I'm unable to hear our footsteps as we walk against the gravel. I slowly open my eyes to a very apprehensive Benson. The ache in his eyes makes me think of all of the ghastly things that are about to go down. Thinking of Benson's soon to be broken heart feels like acid scorching through my veins. I shudder at the thought.

His brows are worn low, revealing his worry wrinkles and true age. He typically looks so upbeat that when he frowns, it's quite noticeable.

I place my hand over my heart as I audit my shallow breathing. Darting my eyes up to his, I notice his breathing is accelerated too.

"Benson," I whisper. It's all I can really choke out at the moment. I wish that he could read my mind so that I didn't have to talk anymore. The lies, they own me. Completely.

His eyes narrow, reeking of suspicion. He jams his hands in his pockets, something I notice that he does when he's nervous or flustered. "Okay Ginny, it's your stage. Tell me what the hell is going on," he demands.

CHAPTER TWENTY-TWO

Well, there's no going back now. I swallow a lump in my throat and take a tiny step forward.

"I know I said a lot of things," I whisper, looking at my feet. I've never felt so small. "I said a lot of things that were wrong, but I was right about one thing."

He looks straight at me. In fact, he's looking directly through me. "Why don't you let me be the judge of that?"

"When I tell you this, it will be the end of us... but it won't be because I want it that way. It will be because you do."

I can tell he's getting agitated. Although I'm thankful to be in public, I don't want to do this in front of an audience. So I begin to walk and hope that he follows.

"Can we take a walk down the beach?" I ask over my shoulder.

Thankfully, he follows. His apprehension turns to something deeper. Something darker. It's as if he knows something very bad is going to happen. "Okay," he drawls.

I lead the walk down to a little swim hole where there is more privacy. It feels like I'm walking on death row. He follows a step behind me and then we come to a stop, where we are greeted with a bunch of rocks blanketed in green moss, surrounding the most sparkling lake I think I've ever seen. It's breathtaking.

His body is so intensely stiff that it's almost like I'm looking at a statue of a Greek God.

He knows I'm about to turn his world upside down. I guess the one thing I hope out of all of this is that it doesn't hurt him as much as I know it will hurt me.

"I ...don't belong here," I can barely choke out the words without the hot tears streaming down my cheeks. "And I surely don't deserve you."

He tilts his head with a hint of confusion his eyes, all apprehension disappearing.

"Why not?"

I can only hear his barely there words. I lick my dry lips and start to rub my shaking hands together. As usual and right on time, he places his hands over mine and squeezes them. That's when I lift my eyes to his. The concern in his face is unmistakable. "Ginny, you're trembling. Tell me what's wrong this instant."

How can he be so calm when I'm about to destroy his whole world?

"That's the problem. I'm afraid to," I choke out. Taking a long and measured breath, I say, "I just want to say something before I tell you the truth, Benson, I want to tell you that it's fear that's driven me to keep certain things from you. However, don't think for one second that I didn't love you. I loved you so much."

He stares at me but doesn't say a word. All of his attention is on me.

"I'm not who you think I am."

Seven small words; one little sentence. That's all it takes to ruin our lives.

Damn it, his silence is killing me. I wish he'd say something. Maybe a head-nod in acknowledgement would be nice. Anything to let me know he's heard me so far.

But he just stands there with his hands in his pockets, looking at me and waiting.

"I, um," I stutter. My hands rub each other over and over, but I can't feel a thing.

"Spit it out, Ginny," he snaps.

"My last name is not Mitchell," I spit out.

Well, that's a step in the right direction, but still not good enough. He's cocking his head now; looking at me like my hair is neon green.

"My last name is Quinn."

He withdraws his hands and takes a step back.

Shit. My world is finally turning off its axis.

That's when I hear him say something in the faintest voice. Something I would have never expected. It's so quiet that I almost miss it. "I know."

"I'm..."

WAIT.

My jaw almost unhinges and drops onto the floor. I grimace, lifting my head from my feet to his eyes. He doesn't look the least bit surprised.

He knows what? He couldn't possibly.

CHAPTER TWENTY-TWO

He sighs casually and takes a step forward. I immediately take a step back. I'm stunned, and I don't know what to say to him.

"You, you know?" My voice is small. "What do you know?"

He lets out a bitter laugh, looking as casual as ever. Does he think this is funny?

The only red flag that he's just as affected as me is that he won't look me in the eye for long.

"It's nice to finally meet you, Genevieve," he sarcastically says.

Okay. He definitely knows.

I look into his royal blue eyes and I don't see the eyes that adore me anymore. I see eyes that have been through the deepest, depths of hell. Eyes full of hurt and resentment and betrayal.

"You know," I whisper more to myself than him. My heart drops into my stomach. So many questions run through my head. So many questions that I can't think clearly. My emotions begin to get the best of me. Tears pour down my overheated cheeks.

He surprises me when he wipes one of them up with his thumb.

I open my mouth to ask a thousand and one questions but then snap it shut again. I honestly don't want to know if I want to know the answers to my questions.

"I've known quite a while," he softly tells me. He places his thumb in his mouth, sucking off my tear remnants.

Test him, Ginny. Maybe he doesn't know everything.

"What do you know?" I demand.

He chuckles and shakes his head as if I will never learn. "Everything, Genevieve," he says, with my name poison on his tongue. "I know everything."

"Tell me," I insist. "Tell me what you know. Say it."

"I know who you are, okay?" he bellows. His tone makes me nearly jump out of my cheap flats. As his chest barrels up and down, he takes his time with measured breaths.

As if he has recited it a thousand times, he says, "Your name is Genevieve Quinn. You killed my wife."

I stand there, stunned and speechless. Out of the corner of my eye, I see a drop of sweat roll off my forehead and drip down my shirt.

Scratch that. It's not sweat - it's a tear.

I'm crying.

CHAPTER TWENTY-THREE

I'm feeling so many emotions right now, but the one that stands out the most is the one I certainly wasn't expecting. I feel anger. Here I was for months driving myself crazy over a secret I was keeping, and he was doing the exact same thing. He doesn't look the least bit sorry, either.

My chest heaves with too much air, and much too fast. I'm breathing so fast that I'm becoming lightheaded. I begin swaying. Although it is probably just a little, I feel like one of those car dealer canvass balloons in the wind.

Oh my God. I feel like I'm going to die.

"Doesn't feel very good when someone you love lies to you, does it?" he chides.

That catches my attention and pulls me out of my sorrow induced daze.

"I was going to tell you." My voice sounds incredibly weak. My eyes begin to sting with unwanted tears. I quickly brush them away before they make my way down my face. I don't want to cry again.

"When? On my deathbed?" he retorts.

"I was going to tell you right now!" I shout, my voice broken. "Right now, damn it!"

Tears blur my eyes and from what I can see, he's as calm as a clam. He doesn't look like he's ready to reply, so I keep going. "Look, Benson, you don't owe me anything. I know that. I just need to know how long you've known. Please just give me that."

Great. Now I'm begging. Very attractive, Genevieve.

"Let me ask you this… when's the last time you checked in with your parole officer?" he asks evenly.

Oh no. Officer Mitchell. I completely forgot about him and our weekly meetings. Life had been so great lately that I forgot I needed to go. I can't remember the last time I've been to see him. I don't tell him this, though.

I lift my eyes to his but keep quiet. He doesn't look particularly angry or upset, and that makes me worry even more.

"Officer Mitchell, is it?" he asks, a hint of sarcasm laced in his deep voice. "He came looking for you. He asked if Miss Quinn was staying with me. I thought it was your relative or something at first since you said your last name was Mitchell. He told me he was your parole officer and that you missed many meetings with him. When he called you by the name Genevieve, and not Ginny, it really threw me off."

Shit.

"It's funny what the brain can do when it has enough information. It was two hours after he left that I realized that a girl with the same exact name ran over my wife. However, in the papers, she didn't look a thing like you, did she? The pink hair really threw me off."

"I didn't run her over," I say weakly. "She died on impact. She came out of nowhere, Benson. It was an accident, I swear!"

Like it even matters now.

He rolls his eyes. "Whatever it may be, Genevieve." He finger quotes my full name. "I found out who you were a few days ago. Does that answer your question?"

I nod; my face in a permanent grimace.

"Why didn't you say anything sooner?" I prod.

"Why didn't you?" he retorts.

Good call.

"Anyways," he sighs. "I was in shock. I decided not to say anything because I was curious. What's the saying? Curiosity killed the cat?"

"I wanted to know what the woman who took the love of my life away was like."

Ouch.

I flinch at his honest words.

If she was a good person, I'd leave her alone and let her live out the rest of her days. If she was a bad person..." he trails off.

A gasp escapes my trembling lips. "You kept me around for revenge?"

He shrugs. "That's a harsh word, isn't it?"

"Did you even love me at all?" I inquire. My voice is so small I can barely hear it.

His blue eyes drill into mine so hard that I can feel the vibrations.

That's when I feel something else entirely. In the deepest portion of my stomach, a hot ball of lava heats my body and revives my senses, making me feel absolutely everything. "But you, you son of a bitch!"

He looks a little shocked by the turn of events. I go on, "We had sex! You invited me into your home! You let me near your little girl! You... you bastard!" I shove him, hard.

"Was I nothing to you?" I sob. I'm hitting and slapping him with everything I have because I want him to feel the way I feel in this moment. "Was I just some big joke to you?"

"You were everything to me!" he bellows in my face.

With his nose to mine, he gives me a glare that would give a serial killer a run for their money or chopped up bodies. It's intense, and it renders me speechless.

I take a step back and feel my heart burst into smithereens right in front of him. I'd curl up in a ball if it wasn't so muddy on the ground. The thick, grey clouds in the sky really put the finishing touches on this dreary evening.

"I never said I wasn't in love with you."

For the first time tonight, something heavy has lifted in my chest. I can actually breathe for a second.

"Are... are you still?"

I don't think I want to know the answer to that.

"What the hell do you think?" His voice sounds full of defeat.

I give him a nod but still don't feel fully satisfied with the answer.

"Can we fix this? Please, Benson. I love you."

"You killed my wife, Ginny," he says flatly.

"I know. I know there's no excuse. I lied to you for a long time." I can't keep the sadness out of my voice. Tears blur my eyes as I cry out, "It was an accident."

I gulp and begin to brace the inevitable. My fists are squeezed so tightly that I'm surprised there isn't blood dripping from them.

"I know. I know baby," he says, his eyes turning glossy.

Three simple words and my heart starts to piece back together, each stitch in its rightful place again. I inhale deeply, letting his words soak in. He knows it was an accident.

He knows I didn't mean it. More importantly, he knows that I love him.

There's no reason why we can't fix this, other situations are damned. I felt horrible for what happened to Angelina, but she was gone now. Why suffer the rest of our lives for an accident that did not mean to happen?

He opens his mouth to finally say something when my phone goes off. The ring tone vibrates in my pocket as I take it out to look at the screen.

Jesse.

Oh my God, it's Jesse.

I just dropped him like a bad habit.

I accept the call and put it to my ear.

"Guenevere," he slurs.

"That's not my name," I say flatly.

"Eyyyy!" It sounds like he's having a much better time than me, but that makes no sense. I had just left his apartment and he wasn't this happy.

"Jesse..."

"No, it's Benson," he says, his voice dry. "Wouldn't that make this call more exciting for you?"

Benson notices something is wrong and tenses up. I put my index finger up, confident that I can handle the situation alone.

"I just took a lot of heroin," I think he says. "If I can't have you then ... I'll have her."

I clam up, not knowing how to respond to that.

"Yeah, I'm having a hard time talking right now too." He laughs at his own joke.

"Jesse I'll be right there..."

"Genevieve," he says clearly this time. "I just wanted to say something to you before I go to sleep." He pauses, dead silence filling our phones.

"What is it, Jesse?"

CHAPTER TWENTY-THREE

"I hate you. I hate you so much that I never want to see you again."

"Jesse, please, stay right there. Don't fall asleep so help me God," I order and then Jesse ends the call. I look at the screen to make sure.

"Benson, I need a ride back to Jesse's. I think he's in trouble."

He nods, understanding. "Let's go."

As soon as we are in the car, he's turning it on and peeling out of the parking lot. It takes us no time at all to get back on the highway. Benson drives fast and surely, which I appreciate.

"He was talking really weird. I shouldn't have left him alone. I knew he had a problem with heroin. He was only off it for a few weeks. Shit!" I hit the dashboard.

"You can't watch his every move, Ginny."

"I know," I say, my shoulders sagging.

Although I'm grateful for Benson's speeding, I hate that the car ride gives me too much time to think. I bite my fingernails and assume the worse.

Jesse didn't visit me once while I was in prison, let alone phone me. He was not that type of person that smothered. So why was he doing it now?

Jesse was crying for help.

I was going to do everything in my power to help him, even if I couldn't be his lover. He was the only family I had left.

I snatch my phone out of my pocket and dial Jesse's number. So help me God if he shuts his eyes.

"Hey, this is Jesse, leave a message, or don't…"

I let out a huff and press redial.

"What the fuck, Ginny!" he slurs and shouts. He actually sounds bothered to hear from me.

"Jesse, don't you dare fall asleep!" I shout, tears stinging my eyes.

"What the fuck do you care? You don't care about me."

"I do!" I sob. "I do so much! Please, just… wait for me, okay?"

He huffs through the phone and it makes me flinch. I can tell he's about to hang up on me.

"Fucking, please! I'll be there in a few minutes, Jesse."

"You never loved me," he mumbles. If I could picture what he's doing right now, he's on his couch and laying on his back.

"Yes, Jessie!" I cry out. "I do! I still do!"

"Say it, then."

That surprises me to the point of no words. I'm speechless.

"Say it in front of him, and I'll wait for you to get here without falling asleep."

"That's not fair."

"Never said I was fair," he trails off.

"I love you, okay?" I shout. My hands tremble as I squeeze the phone so tightly that I think I may break it.

I can see Benson out of the corner of my eye turning his head towards me. I can't even look him in the eye because I can't imagine how much I just hurt him.

Is it really possible to love two people at once?

Jesse doesn't have a response for once. I wait for him to say something but all I can hear is his heavy breathing, which I'm grateful for.

"I'll be right there, Jesse."

"I'm sorry, Ginny. It might be too late," he whispers and hangs up.

What did he just say? I look at my phone as if it's going to explain what just happened.

I look at a very confused Benson, who isn't paying much attention to the road. "Please, go faster, Benson!"

He furrows his brows in anger and before he can step on the gas pedal, white lights flash in front of my eyes and something makes impact with our car. Benson slams on the break as the car spins out of control.

"Ginny!" I hear Benson scream as his arm goes over my chest to hold me back. Blood is splattered all over the windshield and my hands are shaking uncontrollably.

CHAPTER TWENTY-THREE

All I can hear over the rattled engine is our heavy breathing.

"Benson, what did we just hit?"

"Uh, an animal I think." He seems just as confused as me. Before I can reply, he gets out of the car and goes in front of it to assess the damage. He shakes his head and pulls out a knife. I immediately open the passenger door and dart out to the front of the car. There I see a lifeless doe, a young little thing, bleeding from his mouth. I look down at Benson's right hand where he is cradling one of his knives and start to panic. "What are you doing?"

"It's still alive," he says, pointing to the injured doe. That's when I notice that its chest is rising up and down, very slowly. It is definitely injured beyond return. Benson is probably right when he is thinking to put it out of its misery.

"You can't kill it! You can't…"

"Ginny," he says firmly, grabbing my shoulders and gripping them tightly. "If we leave it right here, it will bleed out and die anyways. Bleeding out could take a while. Do you want it to suffer? Let me take care of this, okay?" He reaches in his right pocket and hands me the keys. "Go to Jesse's. I'm going to take care of this. I'm right behind you, okay?"

Oh God, Jesse!

I shake my head violently in agreement and grab the keys. I don't even know what to think at this point.

So I get into the damaged car and I go.

I pull into the complexes and park right in front of Jesse's apartment. I get out of the car smelling asphalt from the screeching tires.

I can't get out of the car fast enough. Running up to room 180, I peek into the door window and realize it's pitched black in there. I go to turn the handle. It's locked.

I no longer have my key. I check under the welcome mat. Nothing.

As a last resort, I begin banging and kicking on the door as I holler Jesse's name at the top of my lungs. When I notice I'm not having any luck, I think about my next plan.

It's risky, but it's all I have left in me.

I violently pound on the door one last time and get the same response I've been getting.

Absolutely nothing.

The neighbors aren't going to like what I have to do next.

Without thinking about it, I take a few steps back and then launch towards the window, my fist bursting through the sheet of glass. Shards of glass shower me in a painful explosion as I carefully knock out the sharp pieces left around the frame and climb into Jesse's apartment.

"Who's there?" I hear an elder lady shout from an upstairs apartment.

I mean to respond but notice Jesse isn't on the living room couch like I pictured him to be.

I feel the razor-sharp, stabbing pain that stems from my hand and quickly wrap it in a shirt that I find on the ground. It's the only time in history that I'm thankful for Jesse's messy tendencies. The gash is deep and wide, revealing my tendons and bone. It definitely needs stitches, maybe even surgery.

Before I let it freak me out, I snap out of it and look at my surroundings. No Jesse.

I hear someone walk on the shards of glass and turn around immediately. It's Benson, just as he promised, right behind me. He climbs into the window, cautiously, looking flabbergasted. "What the hell, Ginny? You need to go to the hospital, right now."

I know he's just concerned, but I don't have time to explain my actions. I open Jesse's door and he's not in there. He's not in the living room, or his bedroom. He's not in the kitchen, either.

The lights are all off, but the bathroom illuminates the rest of the apartment. I take one more look at the living room and then I shift my gaze to the bright bathroom and that's when I see it.

CHAPTER TWENTY-THREE

A puddle of blood on the floor.

Well, that doesn't look like a heroin overdose.

My heart speeds to an inexorable rate. "No, no, no, no!"

I dash into the crimson stained bathroom, and there he is. Jesse lifeless on the floor in a pool of his own fresh blood.

There's blood on the walls, the shower curtain, and an excessive amount blanketing the ground.

I don't think I've seen this much blood in my entire life. It's absolutely everywhere, and it's stemming from both of his wrists. I look at my hands where a mix of my blood and Jesse's fresh blood mesh together like old friends.

I let out a gut wrenching cry before I fall to my knees and pull him into my arms.

It's ironic how the blood meant to pump his heart to life is now all over my hands.

I did this. I killed him.

"Jesse, no!" I sob. "Wake up, oh God, wake up!" I slap his face hard over and over.

The vibrant color in his face is gone. It's now grey and cold to the touch. I place two shaky fingers on the side of his throat.

His pulse is gone.

His beautiful beating heart spent.

I lie with him on the gruesome floor and hold him as tight as I can.

I brush a few tendrils of his black hair from his pale face and kiss his forehead. I taste copper on my lips and taste even more of it when I go to wipe it off with my hands. There is no avoiding it.

Just when I forget he's here, watching this all happen, Benson squats in front of me with his phone in his hands. "He's gone, baby. It's not him anymore."

I ignore the voice I may or may not hear and kiss his cold, rusted lips. They don't feel like they used to, warm and smooth. Soft and fragile.

There is just no cleaning up this mess. So instead, I bathe myself in it. I'm not letting go of him until I absolutely have to. Plus, I don't think I could stand or walk if I even wanted to.

"Help is on the way, baby. Help is on the way," Benson says, getting off his phone. But it sounds like he is light years away.

I don't look at him. I don't even acknowledge him. I look straight ahead at a bloody handprint on the wall and let the palm lines of Jesse hypnotize me.

I rock him back and forth, holding him tightly, showing affection I never knew I had.

How's the saying go again?

"You don't know what you've got until it's gone."

Guilt consumes me deeply, forcing me to cry it out before the cops and paramedics burst through the doors. I close my eyes and hear Benson talk to them, explaining what happened.

I don't move. I rock Jesse back and forth like I'm putting an infant to sleep.

They ask me questions but I can't find it in my heart to respond. I don't even look in their direction.

I continue to cradle my lifeless Jesse in my arms as the paramedics search for a pulse.

I don't know when they take him away from me. I don't know what Benson's feeling at the moment. All I know is that everything slowly fades to black, and suddenly I feel a sweet release.

CHAPTER TWENTY-FOUR

My head is pounding excruciatingly and my lids are crusted shut. They're not open yet, but that doesn't mean my other senses aren't working. I can smell something very distinct and pungent. It's the smell of bandages and antiseptic.

I'm in a hospital.

I can also feel. That seems more heightened than any of my other senses. The throbbing pain that stems from my hand is more pronounced than ever and reminds me that this isn't a nightmare after all.

When I do unhinge my eyes, the sting of pain in my lids does not go unnoticed. At first, my vision is a fuzzy mess, but at least I can see that I'm in a white and sterile room. As my eyes start to adjust to the light, shapes and colors become clearer.

I'm definitely in a hospital.

At first, I'm not sure if it's my eyes still regulating or if the drugs I've been forced are playing tricks on me, but I notice a dark shadow looming out of the corner of my eye.

Either I'm already dead or someone else is in the room with me.

It doesn't take me long to realize it's Benson and he's slumped over in the chair next to me. I study him for a second, appreciating his beauty. His long crescent eyelashes rest on high cheekbones, causing him to appear way younger than he is. He looks so peaceful that I almost don't want to wake him.

I clear my throat trying to get his attention but end up choking on my own saliva which causes a burning sensation in the back of my throat.

It doesn't take long for the entire room to start spinning on me.

Nausea.

His long eyelashes flutter in response but don't open.

I sit up abruptly and realize that one of my wrists have been restrained by a pair of metal handcuffs.

I'm handcuffed. Why the hell am I handcuffed?

I look at them confusion and yank on them, knowing damn well that they're not going to break.

Benson startles awake from the clatter and erects his posture. He looks a little beaten down with dark circles under his eyes, but he's still as gorgeous as ever.

We look into each other's eyes for a brief second when he offers me a tight smile. It's everything that I need right at this moment. For the first time in months, I feel like everything is going to be okay.

Before I can return the smile, another wave of nausea washes over me. I try to place my hand over my mouth, but forget that my dominant hand is suspended. With my other hand, I search for something to vomit in. "No, no, no,"

I gag uncontrollably, holding my free hand over my mouth and hoping I don't projectile vomit all over Benson's face. He looks alarmed, but when I give him a look of warning, he immediately runs to the cabinets to fetch a bucket.

Before the kidney-shaped cup is pushed into my hands, I dry heave. He plays the part and rubs my back like a good boyfriend, but I don't have time to thank him. I throw up the foulest smelling bile from the pit of my hollow stomach. One would think I'm being subjected to a torture device.

It certainly does feel like torture. Or you know... *karma*.

I let out a gut-wrenching cry and then feel his fingertips brush across my flush neck. He scoops all of my hair in one hand and lightly pushes it out of my face. I look up at him mortified as he dips his shoulders in concern.

I can't believe that he is even helping me. It isn't the most pleasant scenery. I give him an apologetic stare and wipe my mouth. "Am I dreaming?"

"No."

"Am I dead?"

He gives me a "don't be stupid" stare, then dryly says, "Yeah. Welcome to hell."

A sense of humor, that's good news...

CHAPTER TWENTY-FOUR

"Um, about... yesterday... or, earlier today? What day is it?" I ask, confused. It could be next month for all I know.

When he doesn't say anything in return, I continue. "I'm pretty sure you don't want anything to do with me ever again."

He considers it a moment before answering. "You've only been out for a couple of hours. I've had a little time to think about it. When I first found out from Officer Mitchell, I was definitely feeling that way. I feel a lot better now," he sighs. "Because you know what I've realized?"

I wait for him to continue.

He lowers his head. "We're a lot alike, Ginny. More than you'll ever know. And even though letting you go would be the right thing to do...for everyone involved, I can't find it in my heart to."

I absorb what he's saying as I focus on a loose thread fraying from the cheap hospital blanket.

"There's this pull you have on me, and I don't think you're letting go anytime soon."

I clench my fists and hang my head. "Not if I can help it."

His breath quickens as I watch his throat bob up and down. Before I can say anything else to him, he looks away from me and out the hospital window. "I just have to think of my daughter, too."

"I know," I choke. Stinging tears begin to flood my eyes. I welcome the pain like an old friend.

We sit in silence for a few minutes as we let everything in the past twenty four hours marinate in the air between us.

"You were arrested again," he ventures.

I look at my shackles and jiggle them. "Oh, is that why these are on?"

For a second, I think he's going to smile, but instead, he exhales and sits back down. He won't even look me in the eye, not that I can blame him. I've lied to him about everything.

"So I got arrested and I'm in a hospital." I lift my chin and blink once. "Did I break a law or something?"

He shrugs. "I know just as much as you."

Well, that's not what you want to hear.

Then, I start thinking the worst. Am I detained having anything to do with yesterday?

Do they think that I killed Jesse? Did I assault a paramedic?

I don't remember a Goddamn thing.

I sit back on the stretcher when a chill invades my body. Wrapping my arms around myself, I pull my knees up and hurdle into a ball. "Why am I in the hospital, then?"

He chews on his bottom lip and remains silent. It's almost as if he's waiting for me to remember something.

And it comes like a freight train.

The phone call. My fist breaking through a sheet of glass. Jesse with a needle sticking out of his arm and his wrists and the blood splattered all over. There was so much blood.

He's waiting for me to remember the worst day of my life.

My body sags with exhaustion as I whisper to myself, "Jesse…"

"I'm sorry, Ginny," he says, empathetically.

At this point, even taking a deep breath doesn't feel like I'm getting enough oxygen. Now is not the time to hyperventilate, or maybe it is. I'm in a hospital, after all.

"Apparently the artery he hit severed pretty badly. The years of using heroin didn't help, but they don't think it was what killed him. It was his wrists. There was no saving him, Ginny. He was dead on arrival. The paramedics were more concerned about you. You were paler than a ghost. You lost too much blood," he says softly.

I ignore what he says and play last night over and over again in my head. I didn't get there fast enough. The accident and the doe slowed us down. Jesse probably thought I wasn't coming.

Jesse bled out. Alone.

"Jesse is dead because of me." I choke.

He places his hand on my thigh and squeezes. "He did this to himself, Ginny. This isn't your fault."

"How can you say that?" I cry out, causing him to flinch. "He warned me. He practically told me he was going to do it!"

He squints. "What are you talking about?"

"He said he hated me so much that he never wanted to see me again," I whisper.

"Listen, Jesse was sick. You can't blame yourself for what he did. That's like blaming the weather man for rain. It was inevitable, whether you made it in time or not. If not today then another day."

"Then why do I feel this way? Why do I feel responsible?"

Benson bitterly laughs to himself and then speaks in an octave lower. "You didn't do this to him. He did this to you. He let you down. He's no longer here to deal with the consequences. No, that's all on you."

I flinch.

"Let me ask you this. Would you have been happier with him?"

I consider it for a moment. "I love you."

His eyes flash with something I can't quite pinpoint but he doesn't reject the comment, which I'm grateful for. He scoots his chair closer to my bed and holds my restrained hand. On a sigh, he says, "Listen, I'm not trying to call you a victim. I'm saying it would have happened with or without you. He went seven years without you, Ginny. Heroin probably played a huge part as to why he wasn't in his right mind, and you had nothing to do with that. Hell, you tried to stop him. I know none of us are innocent, hell, I have my own demons… but you cannot beat yourself up over this. You just can't."

I squeeze his hand, truly appreciating his words. A tear escapes my eye and I hate that fucking tear. I hate it so much.

"We're both imperfect, but we're perfect for each other. That I'm sure of."

We're both imperfect, but we're perfect for each other.

We stare at each other for a minute before the door swings open.

A heavy set nurse walks in with a stethoscope hanging around her neck and a fresh smile on her face. "Hello there, sunshine."

"Hi," I croak, pressing my hand to my throat. It feels like I've swallowed a cactus.

"How you feeling after a little sleep?" she asks, waddling around the side Benson isn't on and hooking me up to a machine. "I'm just going to take some quick vitals."

She wraps a rough nylon strap around my upper arm and begins to pump with her other hand. The band slowly squeezes my arm to the point of pain.

I know better than to talk while getting my blood pressure taken, but I ask anyways.

"Why was I arrested?"

She tilts her head to one side and gives me a mischievous smile. "You've been quite the culprit lately." She takes the nylon off once she gets a reading and then places the cold stethoscope to my chest. She looks at me as if I should already know the answer.

Come on, throw me a bone.

"Parole violation," she offers.

"Officer Mitchell…" I sigh. "I haven't seen him in weeks. He must be angry with me."

"Yes and no," she drawls. "He's only doing his job, you know."

I nod, knowingly.

"But there is good news, baby," she coos, stroking my flush cheek.

Without warning, she tilts my chin towards Benson so that I'm looking directly at him. "This one is a keeper. You treat him good, okay?"

I nod again.

She smiles at me and then slowly backs up towards the door, opening it a smidge. "Alright officers, come on in," she calls from behind.

Shit! I'm going to be taken away right in front of Benson. How humiliating.

Just as I'm ready to hear my Miranda rights, one of the officers approaches the empty side of my bed and

CHAPTER TWENTY-FOUR

unlocks my cuffs, freeing my wrists. "Someone paid your bail, Miss Quinn. You'll be getting a letter in the mail for your court hearing. Try to stay out of trouble, will ya?"

My eyes go round as I witness the sight in front of me. Before I can even respond to the officer freeing my hands, both of them are out the door.

I think I'm in shock.

The nurse clears her throat, causing me to snap out of my reverie.

"I am going to go have a chat with the doctor real quick to see if you're up for discharge. I'll be right back."

As soon as she shuts the door, my eyes begin to glisten with gratitude. He notices this and springs out of his chair. He sits on the edge of the stretcher and smiles with his eyes.

"You bailed me out?"

"Yes," he admits.

"Why?"

Maybe I shouldn't ask, but it's all I can think of. Why would he want to save me?

A line appears between his brows, drawing them together. "Would you rather I didn't?"

"I just, I can't believe you'd do that after everything I've done to you."

He places his hand over mine. "I'd do anything for you."

I gulp. "I don't deserve you."

"I could say the same," he whispers. "That I don't deserve you."

I smile and then our moment is over with as soon as the nurse walks back in.

"Now Benson, if you could just step out for a minute, I need to talk to Miss. Quinn privately before she leaves. You don't mind standing out in the hallway, do you dear?"

"Not at all," he responds.

"He can stay." I look at Benson, who looks surprised by my response.

Benson slowly sits back down. "Are you sure?"

I nod confidently. No more secrets.

The nurse shrugs and then closes the door with the three of us in the room. Benson looks a bit uncomfortable to be present, but I can't afford to keep anymore secrets from him.

The nurse's smile slowly fades into a straight line. I don't know her well but from the looks of it, she seems concerned. She glances at her chart and turns the page, reading the material on it. "Now dear, we must discuss some of your test results."

I look at her with mystification. "Test... results?"

She sighs. "We went ahead and ran some tests, because of that nasty cut that you have on your hand. We just wanted to make sure that everything was okay."

"Is something wrong?"

"No honey. Nothing is wrong with you." She smiles. "Let me finish."

I flash an embarrassing smile and let her continue.

"When you came in with the ambulance, you were screaming in pain. Your blood pressure was high and you were losing a lot of blood" she says, talking to both Benson and I. "So we were going to give you some medications... to lower your BP and to ease your pain."

I nod, desperately wanting her to get to the point.

"But, in order to give Narcotics, we need to make sure you're not pregnant. We had no way to get your consent because you were comatose. So we went ahead and did extreme measures just to be safe."

My heart drops into the pit of my stomach.

I can see Benson's body shift uncomfortably out of the corner of my eye, but I'm too afraid to look him in the eye.

I can hear my breathing accelerate. I can feel my temperature rise. I can see that my skin is starting to flush. I can taste my own saliva, which warns me that I'm about to vomit. I can smell ... something.

Oh god.

I can smell everything. Every. Little. Detail.

"You're pregnant, dear."

CHAPTER TWENTY-FOUR

I spare a glance at Benson and he's glaring back, looking like a deer in headlights. However, if you really look into his eyes, you can detect something darker. It's almost as if he expected this.

The few times Benson and I had been sexually active were recent, not to mention he is infertile.

It was safe to say that this wasn't Benson's baby. It was the man's who just died in my arms

I give her a look that asks 'how is this possible?', but I know better than to ask that question. I know just how possible it is. All it takes is one time and science.

The nurse's smile begins to fade when she notices that this is a problem for Benson and me, rather than a celebration

I could start explaining, apologizing, beg him to give me yet another chance. I could cry and act like I don't know how this happened. That I don't remember it. I could deflect the blame like a true narcissist.

That would just be another lie.

I hang my head low and choose silence. After a few long seconds that feel like a lifetime, I raise my head and lock eyes with him.

"Congratulations." Benson finally chimes in, as he stands to his feet. Adjusting his sleeves with great precision, he doesn't even spare me a glance before he leaves the room.

"I'll wait for you in the car," I vaguely hear him say.

If my life wasn't already over, it definitely was now.

CHAPTER TWENTY-FIVE

The drive home is so thick with tension that I think Benson's car is going to spontaneously combust. After a few minutes of driving in pin dropping silence, I take a fleeting look in his direction. I wish I didn't, because what I see concerns me.

His lips are set into a thin line and his nostrils are flared. His movements are fast and jerky as he takes turns and switches lanes. His knuckles are white and bulging as he squeezes the steering wheel for dear life. I don't think I've ever seen him this angry.

I lost Jesse. Now, I was going to lose Benson. The two people I have ever loved. Simultaneously.

And to think, I did this to him; to them.

I watch the man in front of me. This big, bitter and broken man who can't even find it in his heart to look at me anymore. I was killing him, and I might as well have severed Jesse's arteries myself.

All because I couldn't be honest with either of them.

I didn't know what was going to happen, but I knew one thing. I was a murderer, and now I had to deal with the consequences.

I look out the window and watch the green landscape pass by in a beautiful blur. I didn't even know where he was taking me. I wasn't even entirely sure if we were going back to his place, or if he was going to dump me in a river somewhere.

My bet was the latter.

When we approach his house, I'm a little surprised. I check him as he shuts off the engine and glares straight ahead, as if the whole neighborhood is set on fire.

I look at him and desperately try to gain some absolution, but he doesn't return the look. He doesn't give me that satisfaction.

I can't blame him.

I bounce in my seat like a popcorn kernel when I hear the car door slam. He gets out of the car abruptly, giving me two choices. I can either follow him inside, or give him some space.

Nope.

We walk inside in silence as he darts right past me and heads for the nearest wall. Resting his forehead and fists against the wall, it's almost as if he needs it or else he's going to collapse. His breaths are heavy and ragged as I watch his broad shoulders rise up and down. His broad back faces me. It taunts me.

You'll never have this again

He doesn't want me to see his reaction; that much is obvious. Burrowing his face in his hands, he pinches the top of his nose and exhales.

I step forward, but instantly take two steps back. I'm not going to be able to console him, not this time. I really should have just left him alone. I should have gave him time and waited in the car, but as usual, I'm a selfish bitch. A glutton for punishment.

I stand in the doorway and wait for the right opportunity to step in.

It all happens in a swift blur, his fists brutally smashing into the wall and the dry wall shattering to the ground like a hail storm. If I didn't know any better, I would have thought it was an explosion. A jolt surges through me and my heart rate instantaneously rises.

It's not until the panic completely takes over that I think about bolting out the door.

That's when I hear it. Inaudible sobs racking his big body against the wall, helplessly. The scene is enough to bring me to my knees, but I can't hear a sound coming from him.

Nothing could have prepared me for this moment.

I want to hold him. I want to tell him that I don't want anyone else but him. I want to tell him that I am so in love with him that it physically hurts and that I made a horrible mistake by sleeping with Jesse.

But that just wouldn't be the truth.

The truth is that I love two men with all my heart and soul. One was dead because of me, and the other one was on his way out.

All I can do in this moment is watch him grieve the loss of our love.

He makes a gut-wrenching noise that is unmistakably heart shattering. His sobs become louder as his body quivers become heavier. I never knew sounds that small could come from such a big man.

I can't take it anymore. I have to do something.

I slowly approach him from behind and carefully envelope my arms around him. To my surprise, he doesn't stop me; however, his body stiffens to my touch. His muscles are tense and twitching under my arms, as if they can't wait to break out of his skin.

I rub my face on the back of his shirt, ridding my own tears. I don't deserve to cry. I don't deserve him. I'm aware of this yet I still hold him tightly, not wanting to let go. Knowing that eventually my time was up.

He erects his posture; his expression changing from distressed to unhinged anger. His face is red and swollen. His eyes are bloodshot; his lips raw.

The sadist pervert in me wants to soothe them with a lick, but I know better than that.

I quickly cross my arms over my abdomen, holding myself tightly.

He begins to pace, slow but measured steps back and forth across his living room floor. I stand there while I let him compose himself.

When I'm almost positive he's calmed down, I approach him like I would a rabid animal.

Before I can even reach him, I'm roughly grabbed by my upper arms and swiftly pinned against the wall.

Stuck against the wall like a dead bug, I look at him with a fear I've never felt before. His eyes blaze into mine with fury, and a little remorse. He may be a little surprised with what he's done, but he doesn't apologize or let go of his grip on my collar. He tightens it.

His eyes are darker than I've ever seen them. If I didn't know him well, I'd say I'm well on my way into a body bag.

His eyes dart down to my chest, watching it rise and fall from exertion.

"Benson," I pant.

"Shut up!" he barks.

That went well.

"Benson, please. We have to talk about this."

"Is it Jesse's?" His eyes dart up to mine, his voice thick with emotion.

When I don't answer, he squeezes his grip around my arms and pushes me into his wall of a chest. His grips are beginning to become painful. I tilt my head, hoping that he isn't actually going to make me say it. I give him a pleading look and try to escape his hold by wiggling out of it, but he doesn't budge. His eyes are like wildfire, and they're coming to burn down my entire being.

"Did you fuck Jesse?" He jerks my arm roughly, spit flying into my face. To an outsider, this would definitely come across as domestically abusive, and maybe it is, but all I can think in this moment is that I deserve this.

He jerks my arm again to get my attention and I groan, hoping he will loosen his steel like grip on me. What could I even say that I haven't already? What was the point when all I've ever done was lie to him?

"Benson, I,"

He cuts me off by pulling himself nose to nose with me and roaring, "Are you trying to kill me?"

Shock is the only thing rolling through me, like thunder. I've never been so aware of anything in my life. Benson has gone off the rails and there's no stopping him this time.

He grips the sides of my arms and jerks me when I don't respond.

"How could you do this to me?" he seethes, his hot and forceful breath winding my hair.

I don't know. I didn't mean to. I never meant to hurt you.

I feel completely defenseless. All I can do is let the loud sobs escape my quivering lips. Hot, unwelcome tears begin streaming down my face. I check him to see if there are any remorse in those indigo eyes, but they are completely blank.

I quickly shake my head from side to side, in denial. I shoot him a desperate look through my tears and hope he will find it in his heart to calm down. But he doesn't calm down. If anything, his eyes become more dangerous. I didn't know this man at all. This wasn't Benson. This was the man he constantly warned me about.

He stops shouting, but doesn't loosen his death grip on me. Instead, he leans into me as if he's given up. He rests his chin on my shoulder, smothering his face into my neck and continues to sob.

What have I done?

I lean against the wall, carrying most of his weight on me as I let him cry. In fact, I whimper with him, my breaths heavy and uneven.

He slowly lifts his gaze, which would be unreadable if it wasn't so wet and swollen with grief.

"I was going to marry you," he whispers. "But you can't help yourself, can you? You had to fucking lie to me about everything… about Jesse," he pauses as if the rest is too painful, and then he screams at the top of his lungs, "About killing my fucking wife!"

Desperately wanting him to get this out of his system, I stare at a tile on the ground and let him shout it out. However, he doesn't like that one bit. When I don't respond to him, he slams his bloody fists into the wall again, this time missing my head by an inch.

I scream when they make impact with the wall and squeeze my eyes shut. I can only hear the drywall sprinkle to the ground on top of my own sobs. Not exactly the most pleasant sound in the world.

"Is that how you show people you love them, Ginny? By fucking and lying your way through life?" he seethes.

Tears well up in my eyes and I nod. "I'm fucked up! Okay?" He takes a step back, taken aback with my answer. "I didn't know how to tell you. It was never supposed to happen!" I don't recognize my own voice through my pathetic cries.

"You fucked that druggie! God, did you ever love me?" He seizes me up, looking at me with disgust. As if I am the dirt on the bottom of someone's shoe.

"Benson, I do love you. I made a mistake the night we got in a fight," I cry. I wanted him to know. I needed him to know. "You were with Janet at the time!"

"We both know I wasn't with her that night. I passed out after you left."

"Benson, I made a mistake,"

"Oh, a mistake?" he mocks, his eyes brooding.

"Yes!"

"That's a hoot," he retorts. "Misspelling a word. Forgetting to set your alarm. Those are mistakes! What you did was not a fucking mistake."

I go to touch him again, but he slaps my hands off of him. "Don't touch me," he grits out.

"Benson, come on," I choke over my own sobs, finally letting the tears freely fall. I have no shame. I am not above begging. "Let's talk about this, please."

"No more talking." He bumps chest to chest with me. "I'm sick of talking."

"I love you, that wasn't a lie."

He stares at me, and I almost think he is going to soften up. But before I can even blink, his face is back to stone. His face is dipped in agony. He won't take his eyes off mine.

"Show me, then," he glares at me, his tone authoritative.

I shake my head with so much confusion that it has my head spinning.

"Show me how much you love me," he says again. He roughly gropes me up against the wall, and the sadistic side of me loves it. However, all I can think of in this moment is that Benson isn't in his right state of mind. He's a mad man set out for revenge, a sex addict desperately wanting to feed his inner monster.

I shake my head. "You don't want to do this."

I try evading his forceful gropes by pushing and slapping his arms away, but he is relentless.

His facial features relax, but his eyes say it all. There's a darkness in them I've never seen before. With a mocking tone, he asks, "What, you don't love me now that you've seen me at my worst?" He takes his index finger and lightly drags it down the most sensitive part of my neck.

This was a side of Benson that I was always curious to see. This was the side that he warned me about. Although I knew this, I was still turned on to the point of no return. The heat of his close proximity certainly didn't help, or the way his expert hands knew just how to touch me.

As he closes the small gap between us, I can't help but to lose my breath. I squeeze my legs shut and hope that the ache will magically go away.

"Of course I love you," I pant. My voice is barely a whisper, and the heat between us is so hot that I swear I'm going to melt into a puddle at his feet.

"Show me," he demands, his voice a low seductive growl. He rips my sweat shirt right off my back in one fast motion. I whimper from its loss.

To my surprise, I am entirely too horny to get mad about my new hoodie I just bought.

With a one track mind, my hands immediately go to unbuckle his belt, my motivated eyes never leaving his. His eyes flash with heat as he admires the way I'm not resisting his commands anymore, but submitting to them.

He finally releases his death grip on my arms to allow me to remove his pants. With eager hands, I pull down his waist band as his eyes ravish me. Watching his impressive erection jut out, I take time to appreciate what's right in front of me. Well-endowed just didn't do him justice.

It seems we're finally on the same page, for once. With removing our clothes.

His aroma invades my senses as he lifts me off my feet and wraps my legs around his torso. Violently ramming

CHAPTER TWENTY-FIVE

me into the wall, he briefly leans back to see if I'm okay and then forcefully crashes his mouth onto mine. His tongue assaults my mouth with a force so intrusive its borderline desperate. He explores my body with his rough hands like he's found a brand new land. "Say it," he whispers

Say what?

Yanking my hair by the ponytail, he pulls my head back so that I'm meeting his blazing eyes.

"You being scared. It turns you on."

"You think so?" He forces me to look right at him by grabbing my hips and holding me in place. "I know it," he whispers.

Before I can think of a rebuttal, he leans in and bites my bottom lip hard. I yelp, my hand immediately going to my swollen lip.

I see a ghost of a mischievous smile spread across his face, confirming what I've already known all along. He's more twisted than I could ever be.

"Although you don't deserve it because you're a little fucking liar, I'm still going to eat you out until you're screaming my name so loud that someone thinks you're being murdered," he growls.

What did he just say?

Slowly, he reaches for the bottom of my tank top and peels it off me. I obey and lift my arms to speed up the process. He yanks my bra down roughly and manhandles my breasts while kissing my neck. I can feel my nipples erect under his forceful touch and then they're gone.

Wait, why did you stop? Touch me there again please!

Before I can ask him any of those questions, he hikes me up into his arms and carries me upstairs. Without a word, he tosses me onto the bed and unzips my jeans, peeling them off slowly, his determined eyes never leaving mine. Not missing one spot, he traces small kisses along my lower belly to the edge of my panties. I squirm under his warm lips and expressive hands. He steadies my hips and gives me a warning glare as if I'm moving too much. Continuing his assault on me, he kisses directly over the fabric of where I need him the most.

"Oh my God," I moan. "Please don't stop. Don't you dare stop!"

He slips his hand in my underwear and his middle finger slides into me effortlessly. "My God. You're ready to come already, aren't you?"

I ignore him as I ride his hand, trying to rid the ache that overwhelms me to no return. He pulls his hand away dramatically and brings it to his lips, licking off my glistening juices. "Fucking hell, Ginny. I knew you'd taste this good."

I almost lose it when he licks the remaining juices off his bottom lip.

Crawling slowly and predator like, he covers my body with his. When we're nose to nose, he whispers so low that I barely hear him. "I'm going to fuck you now. However I want it. You're not to touch me, do you understand?"

I nod and brace my hands on his shoulders. He catches my wrists and pins them above my head. "Are you deaf? I said no touching," he warns.

Before I can react, he rams into me so hard that I let out an exhale I didn't even know I was holding. Burrowing his face into my neck, he bites my feverish skin and soothes it with the lap of his soft tongue. Grazing my nipples with his fingertips, he stares at me with a reckless look, waiting for my next action. I thrust my hips forward, desperately wanting the friction. I need it. He rewards me with a fast and hard thrust, watching me as I fall apart in his arms.

"Please Benson. Go faster. This is torture."

"Good," he grunts, violently stretching me again.

"Oh!" I whimper.

It is then he begins to slam into me a rhythmic motion, giving me what I want. What I so urgently need.

"Had to lie to me and be a dirty little slut." He pants, his voice heavy with emotion.

I'll take how to ruin a moment for 500, Alex.

I place my hands on his biceps and try removing him from me, but he doesn't have any of it. Pushing down all of his weight onto me, he slowly pulls out of me and presses his lips to my ear. "You want me to stop?"

"No!" I cry out.

Wait, what?

He starts harder and faster, making me cry out in agonizing pleasure.

"You never could make up your mind, could you? Me, Jesse, then me, then him... now me again. Say it. Say you're a lying, filthy whore. I want to hear you say it," he growls and thrusts even faster.

I was so angry, but too turned on to stop.

I sink my long fingernails into his solid back and dig them down his moist, taut skin. The nails make linear traces of blood and welts all down his back.

He grunts and releases inside me, filling me with his anger, his desperation, his addiction.

Benson has finally fed his inner monster.

I am going to come completely undone at any second now. He must know, because he comes to a complete stop and ejects himself out of me slowly. He lazily lowers his lips to my ear and whispers, "You're not coming until you give me what I want."

I lift my head up. "I thought you just..."

He shakes his head. "No, that's what I needed. Now give me what I want, Ginny. I want to hear you say it," he growls.

I look at him with confusion. What does he want me to say?

He backs up even more when I don't answer him.

"I'm a fucking liar!" I shout, yearning for the ache in my hot, sensitive flesh to be released.

"What else?" He enters two fingers inside me gradually, rocking in and out of me. His wicked eyes are all I see. He's enjoying this a little too much.

"I... I don't know!" I shout and he slowly begins to eject his fingers, shaking his head in disappointment.

"I'm a lying whore!"

He lets out a dark chuckle and keeps going, his thumb brushing my sensitive numb.

"Please, let me come," I moan. I'm shamelessly begging, now.

Keeping his eyes on me, he lowers himself onto my hips and hisses. "Open your legs all the way, you know, like you did for Jesse."

I comply and he still looks displeased. Flicking his eyes up to mine and slapping the inside of my thigh, he barks, "More!"

My eyes are closed, but I can feel his fingertips kneading my thighs. I can feel his hot breath right where I need him the most. Opening my legs the rest of the way, I feel a wet warmth assault my core, swirling it like an ice cream cone. Everything below my waist is wound up so tightly, the pressure almost too much to handle.

He takes his time swirling his tongue over my sensitive nub, in a circular motion, relentlessly. I let out a long, agonizing moan that I didn't know I was holding.

Squirming like a worm, I spare a glance down at him and my suspicions are confirmed. With a manic smile on his face, he seems to be enjoying this torture way too much.

With hooded eyes and a persistent tongue, he holds my hips in place and keeps working in a figure eight motion right where I need him to.

The white, hot flash of ecstasy comes in a wave so powerful that I can barely hear my own cries. All my senses are dulled, except for the one that currently counts.

I feel everything. In every fiber of my being.

After riding out the colorful current of stimulation, my body pulsates into a satisfied coma.

He pulls out, taking the condom off and walking to his bathroom. He takes an unusually long time, but I give him the space he needs right now.

When he comes back, he lays on his back next to me, his eyes focused on the ceiling.

Our heavy breathing is all that can be heard. The air is stifling with regrets and broken promises.

Did we just hate fuck?

After a while, he rolls over on his side and faces me, and I swear that I see a flicker of remorse in his eyes. "That's

CHAPTER TWENTY-FIVE

what it's like to be with me at my worst, Ginny. That's what you'd be in for if you stayed."

I roll over to my side so that I'm face to face with him. "What do you mean if I stayed? Of course I'm staying."

He averts his gaze, unable to look me in the eye.

That's when I realize things are about to change. He's always been the one to assure me that this relationship was strong enough to survive anything.

I nudge him. "I'm staying, right?"

He exhales, looking me in the eye. "No. You're not."

Instead of saying anything or fighting him on it, I begin to wonder if I misheard him. Benson and I have been through the ringer. Surely, he wasn't giving up now.

Tears well in his eyes, sorrow finally making its appearance. "I'm sorry Ginny, but you have to leave. You have to leave and not come back."

I furrow my brows, hoping that I will wake up from this nightmare at any moment now.

"Can you do that for me?" he whispers.

It's then that I see the desperation in his eyes. He really wants me to leave. I've officially pushed this broken man away.

I shake my head. "You don't mean that."

He sits up, his back facing me. He doesn't like my answer at all. I see his shoulders rise and fall.

"Get your things and get out," he says calmly. However, he is everything but calm. I notice his hands are shaking.

I get up off of the bed and walk around so that we are face to face. Squatting down to him so that were eye level, I plead with him. "Please don't do this, Benson."

He looks down at his feet and then his hot breath is in my face. "Get the hell out!" He shouts at the top of his lungs. He springs up to his feet and walks away from me. "Now! Right the fuck now!"

I spring to my feet and head to the door when I hear him shout, "Leave. I don't want you anywhere near my child. I don't want you anywhere near me... ever again."

I stop in my tracks and turn around at the door. My eyes swell up with thick tears. "I'd never do anything to hurt Annie. I love that little girl."

His face is unreadable. We have an intense stare off that feels like hours, when in reality it's only a few seconds. "You almost killed her seven years ago."

A tear falls down my face and onto the ground. For a second, I don't know how to respond. How do I even respond to that? I almost feel like I can't.

"You're right." I say out loud, even though I'm talking to myself.

Benson absorbs my answer silently and lays back down on his bed as if he's given up on life.

Not long after that, I gather my things while Benson silently sobs under his pillow.

Then I leave, and he doesn't stop me.

There is only one place left to go. He isn't exactly happy with me at the moment, and it's possibly the last place I'd want to go.

I'd almost rather be back in prison.

CHAPTER TWENTY-SIX

...TWO WEEKS LATER

"I did something I probably wasn't supposed to do."

I look up from my sugary cereal and into the eyes of Officer Mitchell, who is eating a much healthier breakfast than me. He wears a guilty look, as if he just told me the truth about Santa Claus.

Officer Mitchell, what are you hiding?

It was either his house or my father's house, so the choice was cake. He had made some calls to get me into a women's shelter a few hours away. After one too many attempts; this time I was really going to go.

"Do I even want to hear this?" I ask, bracing myself.

Taking a deep breath, he says, "I looked up your mother."

I immediately look back to my cereal and take a bite. "No."

"I know, I know. Trust me," he explains. "The woman left you. Makes your father look like parent of the year."

I snort, the milk almost spewing out of my nostrils.

"But she's changed. She is remarried."

I give him a boring glare.

"You have a baby sister. She's 17 years old."

I let out a bitter laugh. "She didn't waste any time, did she?"

"If you are unable to build a relationship with your mother, then maybe you'd like to try with your sister."

Dropping my spoon, I look at Officer Mitchell, giving him a 'are you done yet' look.

"Listen, I am not asking you to meet her, Genevieve. I'm not asking you to reunite with her. I just simply wanted to let you know that when you go to this woman's shelter, four hours away, with no one you know... your mom and sister live a half hour away from there. I contacted her, but I didn't tell her where you'll live."

"Why would you even reach out?"

He shrugs. "You need someone out there."

"I have someone?" I point to my belly. I know damn well that's not a good enough answer.

He laughs. *The asshole laughs.*

"No," he retorts. "You have someone you will need to take care of. That you will need to be the perfect model citizen for. That's not the same thing. You need someone who will be there for you. You need a support system, Genevieve."

"Oh, so my mother who was never there for me is the right choice? Or my sister who hasn't even hit puberty? Can't wait to tell her that her big sister was arrested for manslaughter and got knocked up by her step brother. That'll be a hoot!" I take another bite of my cereal.

Officer Mitchell's lip curls into a smile. "Like I said, you don't have to talk to her. I just want to let you know that she lives a half hour away from where you're staying. That's all."

"Thanks for that," I sarcastically reply.

Honestly, I knew he meant it out of the goodness of his heart, but it's something I didn't want to hear. I didn't want to see my mother who left me when I was a kid. I didn't need her. I've gotten this far without her. Not to mention all of the pain and resentment I held against her wasn't going to magically disappear.

The women's home would have to do. The night before, we talked about the place I would soon be living. He told me the success stories of some of the girls he had brought there. One of them was a television producer in Los Angeles. Another was an environmental lawyer. He gave me the hope that I didn't know I had. He made me realize that at the ripe age of twenty five, I should be building an empire, not a worse reputation.

"What do you love more than anything, Genevieve?" he asked me last night.

"Art. I love art."

His eyes light up with an idea. "How about being an art teacher?"

I grimaced. Teaching was the last thing I wanted to do.

"What do you want to do with art?"

CHAPTER TWENTY-SIX

"I want people to know my work. I want them to look at one of my paintings and feel what I feel when I'm painting them."

He taps his index finger with his chin, deep in thought. Then his eyes meet mine, a knowing smirk on his face. "How about opening your own studio? Ever think of that?"

That's exactly what I thought of. I nod. "Yeah."

"Anything is possible with a business degree, Genevieve."

So that's what we've been doing the past couple weeks. We were calling the local college where I will be staying and signing me up for business and art classes. I even have a few job interviews lined up.

I rub my belly and look out the window. I'm obviously not showing yet, but I can feel them there. I have my first appointment in a couple weeks to see if everything is alright. My baby. *Jesse's baby.*

Getting my luggage ready, I look up when I hear Officer Mitchell approach the living room.

"You ready to go?"

I nod and lift my overly packed luggage.

He pushes my hand out of the way and grabs it. "Let me get that."

I give him a 'come on' look. "I can carry bags, you know."

"I know," he says in a higher pitch than usual. He grabs the bag and walks out the door first.

I roll my eyes and follow him to the car. We go to leave but I pause at the passenger door.

I'm going to be on my own again without anyone. I'll be in a home with troubled people just like me. Oh, and I was doing it all pregnant. Was this even a good idea?

Officer Mitchell notices that I'm fretting and drops the bags. Walking over to me, he grabs me by the shoulders and gives me a soft shake. "You need this. You need the support and so do all these women. You're going to make a beautiful life out there. You're going to make friends. There's nothing for you here."

Great, he reads minds.

"I have you."

He smiles, almost blushes. "I will always be here for you, you know that."

I smile and choke back some tears. "You're right. I need to get out of here. At least for a while."

He nods and opens the car door for me. "And who knows, maybe you will actually like it. Build a life there with your child."

"Maybe," I whisper. I look down at my belly and swear I feel something. Even though it's way too early, I still hang onto hope that it's my child telling me everything is going to be ok.

It's the weirdest thing. I don't feel so alone, anymore.

We rush into the station and find my bus, which is already waiting for everyone to board. The gas of the big vehicle assaults my senses.

With college season starting, the station is infested with 18-year-olds.

He drops my bags and asks, "Hey, you need any money?"

"No, no. I don't need money. I've been saving up. At least I did something right," I joke. "Thank you though."

He nods, running a shaky hand through his grey hair. He actually looks nervous, as if he's sending his own kid off to college. It kind of feels that way. It definitely would look that way from a bystander's point of view.

"You call me if you ever do need money, okay? If you need anything at all."

"I will," I assure him.

He nods sharply. "Okay."

We exchange a long and awkward hug with a lot of back patting. Grabbing my suitcase, I walk to the bus and stop at the steps. I turn around once more.

He waves and I almost lose it. This man has shown me so much generosity. My eyes begin to swell with tears as I climb the rest of the steps and take a seat towards the back of the bus. I scoot in towards the window and look back out to see if he's still there.

CHAPTER TWENTY-SIX

Lovers are saying goodbye, families are sending their kids off to school, business men and women are travelling to their next destination. The wind picks up, giving the air a chilly breeze that only late summer can provide.

People rush their goodbyes as more board the bus.

I take a look out at the thinning crowd and that's when I see him. In the back, he's leaning up against a post. As if he didn't mean to be found.

He came for me. I'm not exactly sure who told him, but I have an idea. Looking at Officer Mitchell one more time, I smile wide.

He smiles back, knowingly.

I let my eyes drift back to Benson. He stands in the middle of a crowd with his hands in his pockets. Well-blended in, but then again, he's all I see.

Our eyes lock and I almost think about getting back off the bus.

I lift my hand cautiously and press it to the window. With a tender look in his eyes, he returns the gesture, raising his hand and giving me a soft wave.

He came to say goodbye.

I feel a warm tear make its way down my cheek and quickly wipe it. I don't want this moment to end. I want to tell him I love him. I want to tell him I'm sorry. Before I can communicate anything, the bus jerks forward into drive and I feel my heart crack into smithereens.

As fast as he came, he was gone.

I missed him already. I think about begging the bus driver to turn around, but then I look down at my stomach and remember that I'm not alone anymore.

The bus continues down the bumpy New York roads that haven't been fixed, and all I can do is think of the kind of life that I want to provide for my baby.

It wasn't here.

It wasn't where I lost my freedom and sense of dignity. It wasn't where I built a life of lies and memories I'd rather not remember.

It's just you and me now, little one.

CHAPTER TWENTY-SIX

"Happiness can be found in the darkest of times, if one only remembers to turn on the light." - Albus Dumbledore.

"More teenagers and young adults die from suicide than from cancer, heart disease, AIDS, birth defects, stroke, pneumonia, influenza, and chronic lung disease, COMBINED." - (Jasonfoundation.com)

No matter what is happening to you or what problems you are struggling with, hurting yourself isn't the answer. You are not alone. Call the National Suicide Hotline. 1-800-273-8255

Made in the USA
Middletown, DE
31 August 2023